Number 7, Rue Jacob

Critical Praise for *Disturbing the Dark*
by Wendy Hornsby

"Captivating... Descriptions of the charming and historic Normandy region, including details of delicious home-cooked meals, provide welcome relief from the accounts of past and present crimes."
—*Publishers Weekly*

"Fans of Maggie MacGowen will find plenty to chew on in the latest installment in the series. It's got everything: buried secrets, an old house, a cobweb-filled cavern, even a treasure map. *Vive Maggie!*"
—Kenneth Wishnia

"The story flows effortlessly and moves quickly. The setting has us in its clutches—very realistic. A definite vacation in France, if you don't mind bones and a body..."
—*Mysterious Women*

"*Disturbing the Dark* is very much a character-driven story about people with whom you become involved and care. It's a story of the sins of the past, and the ambitions of the present, and causes you to stop and consider both."
—LJ Roberts

"The small, rural village setting makes for a perfect backdrop to Maggie's investigation, giving the story a kind of Agatha Christie feel to it. This change of venue coupled with a solidly developed murder mystery plot make *Disturbing the Dark* a most enjoyable entry in this series."
—*Mysterious Reviews*

Mysteries by Wendy Hornsby

Number 7, Rue Jacob

A Maggie MacGowen Mystery

Wendy Hornsby

~

Perseverance Press / John Daniel & Company
Palo Alto / McKinleyville California
2018

Copyright © 2018 by Wendy Hornsby
All rights reserved
Printed in the United States of America

A Perseverance Press Book
Published by John Daniel & Company
A division of Daniel & Daniel, Publishers, Inc.
Post Office Box 2790
McKinleyville, California 95519
www.danielpublishing.com/perseverance

Distributed by SCB Distributors (800) 729-6423

Book design by Eric Larson, Studio E Books, Santa Barbara, www.studio-e-books.com

Cover photo by Malirka/iStock

10 9 8 7 6 5 4 3 2 1

LIBRARY OF CONGRESS CATALOGING-IN-PUBLICATION DATA
Names: Hornsby, Wendy, author.
Title: Number 7, Rue Jacob / by Wendy Hornsby.
Other titles: Number seven, Rue Jacob
Description: McKinleyville, California : John Daniel & Company, 2018. | Series: A Maggie MacGowen mystery
Identifiers: LCCN 2017054698 | ISBN 9781564745996 (softcover : acid-free paper)
Subjects: LCSH: MacGowen, Maggie (Fictitious character)—Fiction. | Women motion picture producers and directors—Fiction. | GSAFD: Mystery fiction.
Classification: LCC PS3558.O689 N86 2018 | DDC 813/.54—dc23
LC record available at https://lccn.loc.gov/2017054698

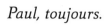
Paul, toujours.

CAST OF CHARACTERS

Maggie MacGowen
    Casey, her daughter
    Elizabeth Duchamps, the mother who raised her; Mom
    Max Duchamps, her paternal uncle, lawyer, and agent
    Élodie Martin (Grand-mère), her grandmother
      Élodie's offspring:
      Gérard Martin, Maggie's uncle
      Isabelle Desmoulins, her biological mother (deceased)
        Freddy Desmoulins, Maggie's half brother
        Lena, his ex-wife*
          their sons: Philippe and Robert
Guido Patrini, Maggie's film partner

Jean-Paul Bernard, Maggie's fiancé
    Marian, his late wife
    Dominic, their son
    Karine Lepage, his sister
    Dr. Émile Lepage, Karine's husband
        their daughters: Suzanne and Victoria
    Victoria Bernard, Jean-Paul's mother

* See *The Paramour's Daughter*

Number 7, Rue Jacob

1

I RANG THE BELL at number 7, rue Jacob a third time. From somewhere behind the imposing iron gates fronting the narrow Left Bank street, I could hear a buzz, but no one responded. A passing car splashed icy mud on my jeans. I swore, I shivered and rang the bell again. For once, I didn't care that I was in Paris. I hadn't been to bed for two days and I hadn't had a bath for far too long. My phone was dead. When a second car sprayed me with road muck I pushed the buzzer and held it. Finally, a voice crackled over the speaker set into the wall beside me: *"Oui?"*

A noisy service van passed behind me so I leaned in closer to the speaker to be heard. "Madame Gonsalves? I'm Isabelle Martin's daughter, Maggie MacGowen. My brother told you I was coming."

"Freddy? No. He told me nothing." But, slowly, the tall gates began to part. As they opened, I peered through the growing gap, curious as I got my first glimpse at the intimate world hidden behind those barriers. A massive house rose like a great stone bastion around three sides of a well-swept cobblestoned courtyard. What kept the structure from being foreboding on that dark, drizzly morning was that the façade of each of the three wings was architecturally distinct from the others, so that the overall impression was a bit fanciful. A Baroque wing with a mansard roofline and a sandstone country château bookended a tall Gothic *éminence grise*. Clearly, the house had been erected in phases, likely over a long span of time, and probably by a succession of owners. The number of marked parking spaces along the sides of the courtyard meant that the whole had been subdivided into flats. But the location in the sixth *arrondissement* of Paris meant that the price of even a studio apartment here would be breathtaking. Beyond my means, anyway. I could not quite accept the fact that, through inheritance from someone who was a stranger to me, my mother, Isabelle, I owned a piece of it.

After a deep breath, I grabbed the handles of my two suitcases, the heavier of them full of camera gear, and started through the gates. A round, flame-haired woman wearing a calico apron over her woolen skirt came out through a side door and stood in my path; the racket of a television game show leaked out the door behind her. As she walked toward me, she folded her cardigan across her full bosom and eyed me warily, as if I might be selling vacuum cleaners or kitchen gadgets out of my big black cases.

"Madame Gonsalves?" I asked again, making sure she was the concierge my grandmother told me watched over the complex.

The woman's response was a shrug that conveyed, Who else? I waited for her to challenge my presence, but she took the handle of the camera case from me and said, "You're finally here, Maggie MacGowen."

I said, "So, you were expecting me?"

"Expecting you sometime, yes, of course. But today? Right now? *Non.*"

Mme Gonsalves wasn't very young or very fit and needed both hands to push and tug the big wheeled bag across the courtyard. I offered to take it from her, thinking about my cameras bouncing along the cobblestoned pavement, but she waved me off, keeping up a steady stream of chatter in Spanish- or Portuguese-accented French that I struggled to understand. "That brother of yours, what can we do? Freddy should have called me so I could turn on the heat and get the cleaners in. Head in the clouds, that one. A good boy, yes? But—" A shrug to let me know that my half brother was a hopeless cause. "And those boys of his and their friends. *Oh-là!* So much noise. Can they walk without kicking a football?"

Freddy, as I knew him, was hardly a man with his head in the clouds, and I thought his two sons were well behaved. For teenagers. Frankly, I didn't give a damn about the woman's issues with them now that I was through the gates and making progress across the courtyard toward my goal, namely a hot bath and a bed and some quiet after nearly three days stuck in airports or jammed into packed airplanes.

Mme Gonsalves took out a heavy ring of keys and opened a freshly painted blue door in the central of the three wings, the Gothic confection. I followed her up one flight of stone stairs and through the only door leading off the landing. For a moment, I stood in the dimly lit vestibule of my late mother's apartment, almost afraid to venture into the darker rooms beyond. I was told that when I was very young I lived in a Paris apartment with her. But certainly not in this one. When I was little more than a baby, I understand, I was jettisoned out a window. I bounced on an awning and fell to the street below, where strangers rescued me. That story didn't jibe with this place where the tall windows opened onto a terrace over the courtyard and not onto a street. Wherever the event happened, it determined the course of the rest of my life. Shortly thereafter my father took me away from Isabelle, who had once been his paramour, and carried me off to California where he lived with his wife, the only mother I ever knew or knew about until recently. Other than random images that flash during nightmares, I have no recollection of Isabelle or the brief time we had together. Now she's dead, and I will never know her.

About a year and a half ago, I met Isabelle's family for the first time. They welcomed me: my half brother, Freddy; my ninety-three-year-old grandmother; an uncle, Gérard; and many, many cousins. But I still felt that I hovered at their periphery, unsure about who might resent an interloper, me, who had equal inheritance rights to an estate that could be substantial. Was Freddy maybe sending a message to me by neglecting to warn the concierge that I was coming? No, that wouldn't be like Freddy. More likely there was so much happening in his life that notifying the woman had simply slipped past him.

Mme Gonsalves flipped on a light in the main salon and uttered, *"Oh-là!"* as my camera bag met the floor with a worrisome *thunk*.

Beyond the lovely, well-tended courtyard, behind the freshly painted front door and the broad stone staircase, the beautifully appointed apartment looked like a fraternity house the morning after a kegger. Mounds of used bath towels—now stiff and dry—wads of soiled athletic socks, food wrappers, dirty dishes, beer cans, empty wine bottles, and random heaps of cast-off clothing and sports equipment had moldered into a rancid, testosterone-rich stench. I knew that after Isabelle died, and after Freddy's marriage fell dramatically apart, my half brother and his two teenage sons lived a bachelor existence in Isabelle's apartment. They had decamped last spring to the family farm estate in Normandy, where Freddy had a large building project underway. But surely Freddy would have cleared up this mess long before now. Madame Gonsalves pulled a telephone out of her pocket and launched into a fierce-sounding conversation with whoever answered; was it Freddy? While she gave orders to the poor soul on the receiving end, I went around opening windows to bring in some fresh, though chilly, February air.

"Madame, non, non, non!" Phone in hand, the concierge closed the windows again. "Do you think you are still in California, Madame MacGowen? No, it is too cold today for open windows. I have turned on the heat, but it will do no good if you insist on heating all of Paris."

"Is there a washing machine?" I asked, thoroughly chastened. She pointed: "Kitchen."

I pulled my dirty clothes out of the smaller suitcase, leaving the bag nearly empty, and headed for the kitchen. A modern full-sized washer and dryer were maybe the prettiest things I had seen all day. With the concierge still arguing on the phone in the salon, I dumped out the clothes and started sorting. Shorts and tank tops from the Laos leg of my trip, long johns and thick socks from the Ukraine bit, all were tumbled out onto the floor and sorted into piles by color.

For the previous four months, I had traipsed across Europe and Asia with a film crew, shooting sites that still harbored unexploded ordnance left over from various wars. I make investigative films for a living, most recently under contract with one of the big American television networks. During the summer and into fall, before the bomb project came along, my film crew and I had happily followed my grandmother around the family's farm in Normandy, capturing beautiful footage of the place, its people, their quirks, commerce, and traditions. I was as in love with the footage we had captured as I was with its subject. Until one morning, when, as we filmed, remains of a company of World War II German soldiers were unearthed from one of Grand-mère's carrot fields. Naturally, there ensued conversation about local farmers and builders who, in the course of their work, accidentally but regularly detonate explosives left over from World War II. It was an interesting but minor passage in the film, or so I thought. When I took the raw footage back to Los Angeles, where I live and work, the project, and my life, took an abrupt right turn.

I learned early on as a filmmaker that the meanings of words in Hollywood contracts can be frangible, dependent on the whim of the folks in charge. My production unit had a new project head, an extravagantly tattooed youth who was ambitious to make a name for himself. That meant originating his own projects, not fostering through the projects of his predecessor. One morning, as the rough cut of my film spooled before him, he kept saying, "Pretty, pretty, like to visit there" without great enthusiasm. But when he came to the footage of the discovery of the remains of a German Wehrmacht company among Grand-mère's carrots, he sat up sharply and hit PAUSE. Turns out the young genius had just been to the dentist—root canal, worst day of his life—where he read a magazine article about an old man in eastern Germany who lived in a camp trailer next to a bomb crater where his ancestral home had stood for centuries. Satellite imaging of the area, done during

the course of who-knows-what sort of civic improvement project, revealed the path of a previously unknown, or long-forgotten,
unexploded bomb that had burrowed deep below the man's home
during World War II. To save the old guy's village, the government
detonated the bomb, destroying the house and leaving him the
bereft owner of a hole in the ground. The article went on to discuss
the global issue of unexploded ordnance in former war zones.

After watching film of the skull emerge from Grand-mère's car-
rots three more times, my new boss said, "You have good stuff here,
Maggie. Real pretty. But hell, let's go find those bombs for Spring
Sweeps. You can do this family hearts-and-flowers shit later."

Two weeks after that one-sided conversation, on October first,
my film crew and I were on our way to Flanders to film the Iron
Harvest, as the annual retrieval of World War I and World War II
combat leftovers from the farmland of Western Europe is called;
roughly a hundred tons of live and spent shells are unearthed
from Flanders fields every year. Lugging our gear, we traipsed from
those muddy fields to unexploded bomb sites under densely popu-
lated Berlin, into Ukraine, and finally off to look for unexploded
ordnance left by the covert American raids over Laos during the
Vietnam War. It had been an adventure, a dirty and exhausting
one. Now, four months later, the last of the raw footage was wing-
ing toward Los Angeles in the custody of my film partner, Guido
Patrini, and I was taking a little time off in Paris. On Monday morning, five days from now, I had an appointment with a producer at a
French television network to discuss their offer to pick up the Normandy film project the American network had, essentially, dumped.
But the first item on my agenda was to spend precious time with
my fiancé, Jean-Paul Bernard. Though Jean-Paul expected me to
arrive sometime during that week, he did not know, yet, that I was
on the ground and at Isabelle's apartment. As soon as I charged
my phone, I would tell him.

With the first wash load started, I put my dead phone on its
charger and plugged it in. When there was enough restored power
to turn the thing on, I punched in Jean-Paul's number. My hand
shook a little as I waited for him to pick up. I hadn't seen him since

Christmas, but until five days ago, we spoke daily, no matter where in the world either of us was. Now, for five days my calls to him had gone directly to message. And for the first time he had not returned them. Had he lost his phone? Fallen under a bus? Decided to climb Everest? Whatever, wherever, I left yet another message, telling him I was, at last, in Paris.

There was a twenty-four-hour accumulation of messages in my own voice mailbox. First, I called Mom, my real mom, the woman who raised me. She had left several messages during the time I was without a phone, each more insistent than the last. It was eight A.M. Thursday in Paris, so it was ten P.M. Wednesday in Los Angeles, where she lives. Though it was late, I doubted she was asleep, probably waiting for me to call or worrying about why I wasn't. Everything was fine, Mom told me when she picked up, but she reminded me that she worried whenever I was gallivanting off somewhere and she couldn't reach me. Not that she called me every day, but that didn't mean she wasn't always thinking of me, or worried about me, especially when I was off digging up explosives. After a few minutes of ordinary "How's your day?" conversation, she was reassured that I was still mostly intact. I wished her a good night and promised to call again in the morning. Her morning. My daughter, a college junior, was in her dorm room studying. Or so she said. We filled in some blanks since our last conversation, I promised to deposit money into her account, and she went back to her books. As soon as she clicked off, I made an electronic transfer of funds into her account. Guido, my filmmaking partner, should be in the air somewhere over the Pacific, headed home to begin editing the footage we had captured during our odyssey across former war zones, so I wouldn't be able to speak with him until he landed. I left a message telling Guido that I had a meeting Monday with the French television people. Last, I left a message for Freddy, telling him that after two days of cancelled or delayed flights out of Asia, I was finally at Isabelle's. I said nothing about the state of the apartment.

Breakfast on the plane, served before dawn local time, had been a rubbery disk concocted from some egglike substance, canned peaches, and a stale sweet roll. I was hungry. The refrigerator under Isabelle's kitchen counter was smaller than the one in my daughter's dorm room, not untypical in Europe. Inside I found two bottles of Perrier, a beer, and a desiccated chunk of some stinky cheese: about what I expected. I took out a Perrier, found an opener, and wandered with it back into the main salon. I found Madame Gonsalves gathering my nephews' dirty socks and bath towels. She leaned a hockey stick against the wall and looked up at me.

"Cleaners are coming," she said.

"When will they be here?"

One shoulder rose slightly. "Thirty minutes? Forty?"

"Good. Thanks. If you'll excuse me, I need a bath."

I saw her to the door and shot the deadbolt.

Already the room was warm enough that I could take off my coat. In my stocking feet, I walked around, exploring Isabelle's private little world. High ceilings and large rooms with tall windows gave the impression that the apartment was larger than it actually was. Besides the small but functional kitchen, there was a spacious main salon with a dining table at one end, a small side room that Isabelle apparently used as an office, two large bedrooms, and a single but huge marble-lined bathroom. The décor was an interesting mélange of stark modern pieces and good-quality but comfortably worn and ordinary furniture that somehow lived together in interesting harmony. The only jarring note I found was my face among the array of framed family photographs displayed on a long table behind the sofa. I had not known Isabelle, did not recognize her the one time I saw her before she died. However, though I wasn't aware of it, from time to time as I grew up on the far western edge of a different continent, she would fly over to lurk around me, sneaking the photos that she put on display here in her home; illicit souvenirs of the daughter she had relinquished. Knowing the issues her visits had created, in deference to Mom, I opened a drawer and swept the photos of me out of sight.

Isabelle was a stranger to me. I admit to having a guilty, maybe morbid, curiosity about her because, like it or not, she was my mother. Over the year and a half since I learned that she existed I had pieced together bits and scraps of information about her, but she was still a mystery to me. I lingered in her office, looking for hints, any little clue about what she thought, what she loved, who she was. The room seemed to have been spared the clutter that took over the rest of the apartment during its bachelor era. Books in three languages—French, English, German—lined the walls. Most of the titles had something to do with harnessing energy, nuclear power, physics, computers, climate change, or agriculture. I didn't see a single novel on the shelves. My late father, a physicist, who had once been Isabelle's mentor—and lover— never had much interest in fiction, either, though poetry was a passion.

A fine layer of dust coated the orderly desktop. I tried to imagine Isabelle sitting there. When she worked at the computer, she would have faced the door with the monitor at the center of the desk in front of her. To the left of the computer, there were a telephone, a clean pad of paper, and a cup full of pens and pencils. There was nothing else on the desk except a small, elegant leather-bound book. I could see that it was old, and looked much handled. Perhaps a beloved volume of poetry? The leather cover had worn away at the corners, revealing wood underneath. When I lifted the cover, I half expected to find an inscription written by my father on the fly leaf. Instead, I found another puzzle.

Clearly, this little volume was a treasure; no wonder Isabelle kept it close. The script was very elaborately hand-scribed on vellum or parchment, with richly, brightly illuminated capitals twined with flowers and scrolls and birds. Over the years oil from people's hands had turned the edges of the leaves brown. I couldn't read the text, but I recognized the first capital, a richly illuminated *pi*, the Greek equivalent of the Latinate letter *P*, and saw that the text was indeed structured like poetry. A Book of Psalms, in Greek, was my best guess.

Isabelle, I was told, was a committed atheist. If this were a little volume of the Psalms, was it anything more to her than poetry? An object of beauty? Maybe she had taken up the study of Greek. Until

I saw that gem of a book, I had little interest in anything I might inherit from Isabelle's estate. I closed the wonderful book and gently placed it inside the top right-hand desk drawer to keep it safe.

I grabbed my toiletries kit and padded off to the bathroom. Half an hour later, I was clean again, wearing a mostly clean collection of clothes, some of them mine, some I'd borrowed from my teenage nephews' bureau drawers. Someone's trainers, tossed into a bathroom corner, were dry and fit me well enough that I appropriated them. I was in the kitchen switching my wash when the cleaners arrived. Two young women, their heads shrouded by hijabs, came in, arms loaded with the tools of their trade. The older one accepted the hand I offered and gave it a quick shake.

"Thank you for coming, Madame," I said.

"Fitting you in is most inconvenient," she offered as a curt greeting, narrowing her eyes to let me know that she was not at all happy to be there. "We will do what we can, but we haven't time to complete a thorough cleaning. *Oui?*"

"*D'accord.*" Sure, whatever. That issue settled, they went straight to work on the mess as if they were familiar with the house and its sloppy inhabitants. I did my best to stay out of their way.

The telephone on Isabelle's desk rang as I was walking past with a stack of freshly laundered clothes. I glanced in at the phone, but kept walking. This wasn't my house or my phone, and anyone who knew I was there would call me on my mobile phone, so I thought I should let it go to message. But the younger of the two cleaning women looked from the jangling phone to me and back with an expression of great puzzlement and reproach as if to say, "Answer it already." So, I picked it up.

"Maggie?" Jean-Paul. How did he know where I was and how did he get Isabelle's number when even I didn't know what it was?

All I could think to say was, "Where are you?"

"Have you pencil and paper?"

I pulled the pad on the desk closer and took a pencil out of the cup. "Yes."

"I need you to go out and find an Internet café, any Internet café. Pay with cash and access this email." He gave me an electronic address and a PIN to access it. "There is a message for you in the draft message box. Follow the instructions. Will you do this?"

"Of course. But why? What's going on?"

"I'll explain when I see you. Now, please write this down." He recited a string of numbers. "Turn your mobile phone to airplane mode, then turn it off, and leave it in the apartment when you go. Same with your laptop."

"You're being very mysterious, Jean-Paul."

"I'm sorry, *mon coeur*, but yes. Can you trust me? Will you do this?"

"Up to certain obvious limits, of course. I mean, if you're giving me nuclear launch codes, my love, then sorry, no deal."

He laughed. And then he coughed.

I said, "I need you to tell me you're okay."

"I'm fine." He answered, too quickly, with no little joke about how I might make him feel better when we were together. "Maggie, I miss you. I love you. If there were anyone else I could ask, I would. I hope you can trust me."

If anyone other than Jean-Paul had given me those instructions, I would have laughed and hung up. "When will I see you?"

"Tonight, *chérie*. Will you go find an Internet café now?"

"Sure." I heard a vacuum cleaner start up in one of the bedrooms. "I'm on my way. I'll call you when I get back."

"I'm sorry, but no, you can't call me. Do you know what a burner phone is?"

"A throwaway," I said.

"Exactly. This phone is a burner. When we say good-bye I'll toss it. I'll see you tonight and explain everything." There was a click and the line went dead.

I have never known exactly what Jean-Paul does. He always says he's a boring businessman, but I have never bought that. When I met him, he was the French consul general appointed to Los Angeles, a position that seemed to have more to do with promoting French trade and helping French citizens who wandered into problems in the U.S. than with the sort of spycraft he seemed to have access to. If I ever needed information on just about anything, from counterfeit masterpieces to stolen military weapons, the more arcane the better, Jean-Paul could make a phone call to the appropriate friend and find it. Always without explaining just who he had called or how they were connected except to say that they were at school together. More recently, since his recall home to France from Los Angeles, he worked with a trade group, something about representing European Union exports to the global marketplace. But he was always a little vague about the details.

As Jean-Paul gave me his instructions, I suspected that he was staying off the electronic information grid because he had been hacked, or was being cautious to prevent being hacked. But why? Whatever was going on with him certainly smelled intriguingly cloak-and-dagger. While I hoped I just might be on the verge of finding out something more about Monsieur Jean-Paul Bernard, I was also worried about his safety. Global wars have been fought over trade routes and the protection of monopolies on products and commodities. But there are also quieter, undeclared wars among commercial competitors. The scary thing is, those private commercial wars are not bound by the rules of the Geneva Convention.

My own coat was damp and mud-spattered. I rummaged among the coats and jackets hanging from the hall tree in the vestibule, found one that would do nicely, a handsome flannel-lined waxed canvas with a Barbour label that, from its size, was probably Freddy's; he was a tall, broad-shouldered man. I slid my wallet and the keys Mme Gonsalves left for me into a pocket, and told the cleaners that I would be back soon.

The jacket was far too big for me, but it was dry and it was warm, and it covered me to the knees. I pulled up the collar and walked briskly up to boulevard Saint-Germain and then headed in the general direction of the Sorbonne, thinking that I was likely to find an Internet café in an area where students congregate. The first place I spotted was a few doors down from the Odéon Métro station, a bright new door on the ground floor of an ancient building. Inside, the room was redolent of coffee, tobacco, pot, and unwashed youth. But it was warm. I gave the attendant a few euros from my meager stash, assuming he wouldn't be interested in the Laotian *kip* I hadn't yet exchanged, chose a terminal in a far corner, as far from a cluster of young men playing a noisy video game as I could get, sat down and opened the email account Jean-Paul had given me.

The draft message he left me was very strange. First he asked me not to use credit or ATM cards, and again told me to keep my telephone and laptop in airplane mode and turned off, and to leave them in the apartment. The next part was cryptic: "Always aim for the moon, and remember how far it is to China." Hoping for explanation, I clicked on the URL imbedded in the message and up popped the home page for an airline. Mystified, I studied the page. In the top corner, there was a box for an itinerary number. I punched in the string of numbers Jean-Paul had given me over the phone and found a boarding pass for a flight that left that afternoon at two o'clock from Orly Airport, Paris, headed for Marco Polo Airport, Venice. The boarding pass was issued in my name.

2

VENICE? I LOOKED at my watch: the plane was scheduled to leave in five hours, at two P.M. I printed the boarding pass, folded it into my pocket, and erased my session history before logging out of the computer. Not using credit cards was one thing, but I had business to take care of and there were people who would worry if they didn't hear from me. I spotted a couple of pay phones against a side wall of the café. At the service counter, I bought a *café au lait* and a prepaid calling card, using cash, so that I could tell my grandmother that I had arrived. Otherwise, she would summon Interpol to track me down.

"Ah!" Grand-mère said, clearly surprised when she heard my voice. "It's you, my dear. I didn't recognize the number. Where are you now?"

"Paris," I said.

"With Jean-Paul?" she said with a satisfied little sigh in her voice. My grandmother is in love with the idea that I am in love with her old friend's handsome son.

"Not yet. I'll see him tonight. My phone died, Grand-mère, so while the cleaners are working at Isabelle's apartment I ducked into a café to let you know I'm here."

"The cleaners are there now? Why are the cleaners there now? Freddy gave very clear instructions to Madame Gonsalves to have the place cleaned last Monday. I heard him repeat the date twice. Such inefficiency! Why they keep that woman is a mystery to me. Useless. She is simply useless."

"Maybe she's losing her hearing and didn't quite understand the message," I offered, thinking about the volume of her television. "I'm leaving some of my things at the apartment, but I won't be staying. At least, not for a while."

"Of course." She was happy again. "You're going to Jean-Paul."

"Yes. We're getting away for a few days. I'll let you know when I'm back."

"When you get back, I know you'll bring Jean-Paul for a visit, won't you? It isn't such a long drive from Paris to Normandy. Or you can take the train to Caen and I'll have Freddy pick you up. I've decided that since he's here building his cottages I'll just stay for the winter. Besides, my big old house in Paris costs too much to heat."

"I imagine it does," I said, though I doubted her big old stone farmhouse in Normandy was any more economical to heat than her townhouse in Paris. I suspected that having Freddy nearby was at the heart of her decision. "I'll speak with Jean-Paul about a visit. See you then."

"*À bientôt, ma chère* Maggie. My best to your Jean-Paul."

The next call was to my Uncle Max in Los Angeles. Max is both my lawyer and my agent, and my primary fusspot among several contenders. I called his message-only number to let him know that I was fine, that the meeting with French television was set for Monday morning, and that I would be in touch in a few days. I assured him that my film production partner, Guido, was on his way back to L.A. to get started on post-production of the unexploded bomb film. No worries. Honestly, no worries. And by the way, my phone died so don't try to call me.

As far as I knew I hadn't lied to him. But then, I didn't know enough about what was going on to lie about much of anything.

My next issue was money. I rarely carry very much cash. At

the airport, I had exchanged the rest of my Ukrainian *hryvnia* for euros, but after paying for the taxi in from de Gaulle that morning, and then for the computer time and a phone card, I was broke. Jean-Paul asked me not to use credit cards or an ATM, but that was not actually a problem because I had another source for cash.

Freddy and I were co-heirs of our mother, Isabelle's, complex estate. A year and a half after her death, the estate was still generally tied up by various arcane French inheritance laws and procedures. However, there was one account, a tontine, separate from the estate, that had been set up jointly by my late father and Isabelle naming me, their natural child, as their equal owner as a strategy to circumvent all sorts of tax and inheritance laws. As the sole survivor of the tontine, the funds now belonged to me alone. Out of everything I was to inherit from Isabelle, whom I had not known, her share of the tontine was the only asset I felt entitled to because it came to me far more from my father's efforts than it did from hers.

Dad had worked on an energy-related process for many years before Isabelle came along. Ordinarily, a graduate student, as she was then, who spent a single year assisting on a research project, would expect to receive no more than a mention somewhere in any paper he might publish, as well as the possibility of presenting the research with him at a professional conference or two. And nothing more. However, Dad split the significant earnings from patents on the process with Isabelle as a way to support me, their love child. Neither of them is around to ask, but I suspect he continued with the arrangement after he took me from her as a way of paying her off.

As soon as I learned about the tontine, I made sure that Mom received a regular allowance from Dad's share of that account, small compensation for her husband's infidelity and for all the years of putting up with me, the product of Dad's infidelity. But, so far, I had only made personal withdrawals from Isabelle's share to cover incidental expenses when I was in Europe; a little play money, as it were. After Jean-Paul's cautions about using cards or making electronic withdrawals, I decided that it was time to tap into what had become a substantial pot. In person.

~

MONSIEUR Revere, the banker who oversees the tontine account, seemed genuinely happy to see me. But he always does when I reassure him that I intend to leave the account right where it is, in his care. On that cold February morning, he was casually elegant in the way that French men can't help being, wearing a navy sweater vest under a beautifully tailored charcoal suit. With graceful, easy charm, he ushered me into his office. Before I had settled into the deep brocade chair in front of his polished desk, hot tea and tiny pastries were brought in and set in front of me by an assistant. This, I had learned, was protocol; refreshments and pleasantries first, business second.

I was hungry, very hungry. But I restrained myself and only took two little pastries, savoring them; has anything ever been as delicious as something, anything, fresh from a French bakery?

"Your family is well?" he asked.

"I haven't seen them since Christmas," I said. "But, yes, everyone seems to be fine. And your wife?"

His eyes sparkled when he said, "My dear wife is very well, indeed. Our daughter tells us we're to become grandparents during summer."

"Congratulations. How wonderful for you all," I said. "I'm sorry for the circumstance, but I enjoyed meeting your wife last spring. She will be a wonderful grandmother."

"I'll pass that sentiment to her." The sparkle was gone from his eyes when, after a sip of tea, he asked, "And your brother, Frédéric, how is he faring?"

"Freddy's coping, I think. Staying busy with his boys and his building project."

"I hope he doesn't bear ill-will toward me. If there had been any way I could have gotten out of testifying about your accounts at his wife's trial, I certainly would have welcomed it."

"He understands, Monsieur Revere. You did no more than audit the books. His wife committed the crime."

"A sad business, embezzlement," he said with a sigh. "Very sad."
"Indeed."

"So, Madame," he said, pouring me a second cup of tea, a signal that it was time to get to my reason for coming. "A little withdrawal, I understand. How much would you like?"

I took a third tiny pastry and nibbled off a corner while I thought about that innocuous question. How much cash would I need when I got to Venice, and what would I need it for? Maybe hotels? Another airline ticket? Food? Ransom? I had a vivid imagination, but no facts.

"Not so little this time," I said. His eyebrows rose. "Ten thousand, please. In cash."

"Euros, not dollars?"

"Yes, euros. Is that a problem?"

"No. Of course, the funds are available. But, Madame, that is a great deal of cash to carry around. Perhaps you would prefer it in the form of a counter check?"

"No, cash please." I set the empty teacup on the desk and leaned forward to look him in the eye. "Monsieur Revere, do you have any idea how much a Paris couturier-original gown might cost, even if it has been worn once?"

"Ah, yes, I see." He relaxed visibly, smiling, a man who knows women well. "A private sale. What denominations would you prefer?"

"One hundreds, I think. Anything larger can be cumbersome to use. And I'd like one thousand of it in small bills, please."

"As you wish. Please excuse me for just a moment. More tea?"

"No thank you," I said. For the next ten minutes, I looked everywhere in that handsome office except at the four perfect little pastries still on the plate in front of me. I needed food, real food, and not a belly full of sugary, buttery treats, no matter how delectable they were. When M. Revere returned, he resumed his seat and counted out ten thousand euros in front of me on the desk. When I nodded, he zipped the cash into an elegant green leather pouch and presented it to me.

"Enjoy your gown, Madame," he said with a little flourish. "And welcome back to Paris."

Welcome back, indeed. I hadn't actually lied to him, either, and it truly was genteel of him to have concern for my safety. But before I felt better about telling him about a beautiful dress I would never buy, I had to remind myself that it was none of his business what I wanted my money for. I shook his hand, thanked him very much, wished him well, and walked out into the bank lobby. I stopped long enough to transfer the thousand in small bills into my own wallet. As I walked back toward the apartment on rue Jacob, I kept a hand in the coat pocket that held the cash-stuffed leather pouch, lest it fall out or get lifted by sticky fingers, and entertained myself imagining the grand party I was not wearing that couturier dress to, one I would expect to enter on the arm of Jean-Paul. Along the way, I stopped at a bakery for a take-out sandwich—French ham and cheese in a length of baguette with tomato and fresh basil— and at a greengrocer for a few apples. The next stop was a small neighborhood electronics shop.

"I need a prepaid telephone, please," I told the much-tattooed young clerk behind the counter; I wanted a burner phone of my own. I would do as Jean-Paul asked and leave my phone in Paris, but I'd be damned if I would disconnect myself entirely. During the two days that I spent shuffling through airports, rescheduling missed connections and cancelled flights without a phone, I became keenly aware how much I depended on the damn things to tend to essential business, to stay connected with those I care about, to find my way around, and even to know what the weather is going to be. I caught the clerk's attention and said, "Make that three."

"Three?" A terrorist or a drug runner can look like anyone, and it seemed that the clerk was trying to decide whether I was someone to worry about. Who needs three prepaid, therefore unregistered, untraceable telephones?

With a broad American smile, the sort that makes the more restrained French think we might be half wits, I said, "Have you any idea how exorbitant the telephone bill might be for a parent on vacation in Europe with three teenagers who send endless texts and photos and posts to their friends in the States without any regard for the cost of transmitting data? The national debt would pale in comparison."

Of course, he said, he understood. What model would I like? He showed me several. I wanted to be able to remove the battery so I needed phones that did not have a solid case. When I suggested that I would likely need to change SIM cards as we moved about the world, he raised his eyebrows, but showed me a model with a snap-off back. The battery was just below the SIM card slot. I said, Yes, please, three of those. How much time will we load onto the phones? We talked it over like old friends and he suggested that we start with two hours each and when they were used up the kids could spend their own money to reload them, *n'est-ce pas?* I answered, *"Oui, d'accord,"* and the deal was done.

On the counter, there was a display promoting prepaid credit cards. Sometimes cash is useless, such as when you need to make flight or hotel arrangements over the phone or the Internet. While the clerk was distracted, activating my phones, out of his line of sight I unzipped the green leather bank pouch, counted out thirty bills, and tucked them into my wallet. When the clerk came back I pointed to the display and said, "And three of those, please."

He needed a moment to think about that before he asked, "For what amounts?"

I smiled. "A thousand euros each should do it."

"Your children are very fortunate to have such a generous parent," he said as he pulled three cards from a locked drawer. With a smile, he added, "Maybe you'd like to adopt me?"

I laughed. "I have my hands full as it is. But if I decide to trade one in, I'll call you first."

Transactions complete, the affable clerk tucked my purchases into a plastic bag and shook my hand. "Enjoy your travels, Madame."

I wished him farewell, took the handle of the bag, and turned for the door just as a man came in from outside, letting in a gust of icy air. The shop was very narrow and the man, a very large man enveloped in a very large coat pulled up over his chin, seemed to fill up most of the available space. He wore a knit watch cap pulled down so low over his brows that all I could see of his face between collar and cap were pale, almost colorless gray eyes and a cold-reddened nose. He trained those pale eyes on me long enough to make me uncomfortable. Nodding toward the door, which he blocked with his bulk, I said, "Excuse me."

Instead of moving out of the way, as I expected, he pulled off his cap and grinned at me. "We've met, have we not?"

I took a good look at him. He was tall and very blond. Not beauty-salon blond, but the real thing; nearly translucent hair, eyebrows, lashes. Because I make films that have my name and face all over them, and that are regularly broadcast on an American television network, it isn't unusual for people to recognize me. Or to think they recognize me. Offscreen, walking around, I do not wear TV makeup or have my hair styled and lacquered in place, so when people recognize me it is more common that they think that we went to school together or shop at the same supermarket than to realize that I have a face they saw on the television in their living room. Also, because of what I do for a living, I meet a lot of people. Many I remember, more I do not. When I saw this man's pale eyes and white hair, I knew that I had never seen him before. My first thought was that he was looking for female company and had pegged me for a fellow tourist. Even if all he wanted was a little chitchat, I wasn't interested. I said, with what I hoped was a modestly polite smile, "No, sorry. I don't believe we've met."

"Yes, I'm sure of it," he persisted, holding his cap against his chest. I could not place his accent. Not quite British. Dutch or Scandinavian with a British education? Eastern European? "Perhaps over a coffee we could discover where we knew each other."

"Thank you for the offer, but I'm afraid I haven't time." I gestured toward the door. "If I may."

"Ah! Sorry, yes." After some complicated choreography, he shifted a bit to one side and held the door open for me. As I ducked under his outstretched arm, which put me uncomfortably close to his body, he said, "It's cold, *ja?*"

I answered, *"Oui,"* though he had spoken to me in English, the first person to do so all day. During the last year and a half, I had become quite proficient with French. So, what was there about me that clued him, I wondered, as I went out into the cold?

When I turned onto rue Jacob, I saw the two cleaning women walking away from number seven, and felt relieved. With them gone, I would have a quiet place to relax, to eat without getting jostled, perhaps to get a brief nap, and to figure out what to pack for a jaunt to Venice when I had no idea what I might need.

Mme Gonsalves intercepted me as I came through the gates. "Madame MacGowen, a delivery arrived for you."

She handed me a white paper bag imprinted with a green cross, a pharmacy bag. I thanked her and took it without asking any of the questions running through my mind, and refrained from opening it right there where she could see the contents, though I suspected that if she were curious she could have opened the bag when it arrived. Instead I crossed the courtyard and went straight up to Isabelle's apartment, clutching the bag against my chest. I didn't know what was going on, but seeing the green cross on the bag was not reassuring. As soon as I had locked the front door behind me, I hung my purchases on a hall tree hook and opened the white bag.

Two prescription vials with large white tablets, a box of sterile gauze pads, a roll of surgical tape and a tube of antibiotic ointment. I examined the labels on the bottles. I know enough about drugs to recognize what they were: an antibiotic and a generic for hydrocodone-acetaminophen, a painkiller. My name was on both prescriptions, but someone else was sick and in pain, and because the prescribing physician was Jean-Paul's brother-in-law, Émile Lepage, I was afraid they were intended for Jean-Paul.

Fear can make you stupid. And so can fatigue. I sat down and made myself breathe, to think. Jean-Paul had sounded all right on the phone. He coughed once, and that meant absolutely nothing. He kept the conversation brief and on message, the arrangements he made for me had taken some care and attention, so at least he was coherent when we spoke. For the next three and a half hours, until my plane departed for Venice, I needed to keep that in mind and not to imagine seventeen dire scenarios. The best way to do that was to get busy.

First, I plugged in the burner phones so that they would be fully charged when I needed them. Next was the issue of what to bring. In the armoire of the bedroom Freddy's sons shared, I found a good, somewhat worn backpack. Into it went a couple of changes of my freshly laundered underwear, some silk long johns, a black turtleneck, black wool slacks, a string of pearls because one never knows, a red Pashmina, two T-shirts, a black V-neck sweater, and the usual toiletries kit. When the phones were charged, I pulled the batteries out. I found three zip-top sandwich bags in a kitchen drawer and put a phone, a charger, and a battery into each one. I changed into fresh jeans—my own—and put one of the cell phones into my pocket. The other two went into the backpack with the pharmacy bag. I zipped up the backpack and set it beside the front door, ready to go.

My two big suitcases were still in the vestibule where I had left them. To get them out of sight, I lugged them into the boys' room and shoved them into the armoire. Before I closed the door, it occurred to me that by using only disposable phones, I could be functionally without a camera, and I'm never without a camera. From the larger bag, the camera bag, I selected a palm-sized high-definition video cam that also took good still shots, and packed it along with an extra battery pack and two photo storage cards into a fitted case that went into the backpack.

My own coat was still damp, so I decided to hang on to Freddy's coat. It was waterproof, warm, and had deep pockets for phone, money, and passport. When the coat pockets were packed and buttoned shut, I cleaned the boots I had arrived in and pulled them on. I was ready to go, and there were still three hours until departure. With nothing else to do, I decided that I might as well head for the airport and wait there. Ordinarily, I would pull out my phone and call for a taxi. Instead, I decided to walk up to boul' Saint-Germain where there was sure to be a cab stand.

I made a quick circuit of the apartment, making certain that windows were locked. The cleaners wouldn't win medals for their work, but they had effectively removed the *eau de* gym socks from the place and made order out of the worst of the mess, and it would do until I returned. Whenever that might be.

The telephone in the office rang. I ran in to get it, expecting to hear Jean-Paul's voice.

"Maggie? Émile Lepage here." Jean-Paul's physician brother-in-law.

"Émile?" Cold white panic rose from somewhere deep inside me. *"Ça va?"*

"Me? Fine, thank you. Happy I caught you. I'm just turning onto rue Jacob. Will you please open the gates and let me drive in out of the cold? It's beginning to sleet."

"Sure" was the best I could think to say; how many people knew I was there? After I hung up I went to the panel next to the front door and pushed the button marked PORTE to open the gates, and hurried down the stairs to wait for Émile. The big iron gates were already parting by the time I opened the front door. As Émile drove through, he spotted me and aimed his Citroën for the open space closest to the blue door. The car had barely come to a complete stop before he was out. With his coat pulled up over his head, a black medical bag hugged close to his chest, he made a dash toward me.

"Getting colder," he said once he was inside. "We'll have a good snow tonight."

He handed me his bag so that he could shed his sleet-speckled coat, which he then draped over the stair rail. We exchanged *les trois bises*, kisses to both cheeks and the third that is saved for familiars. When I extended his bag toward him, to return it, he took my wrist, pressed his fingers on my pulse and looked at his watch.

"Your pulse is racing," he said, releasing my wrist.

"I'm sure it is," I said, gathering up his coat as I led him up the stairs and into the apartment. "First, you send over prescriptions for pain and infection, and dressings for a wound I don't have. And then you show up. Émile, what is going on?"

His shoulders and palms rose, the French gesture package

meaning, Who the hell knows? "I was afraid it was for you, Maggie. That's why I'm here. Our Jean-Paul telephoned, telling me only that the medications had been prescribed by a physician abroad and that I should send instructions to a pharmacy here and have them delivered to you straight away. I did as he requested, Lord knows why, but I told him that I would need to see you to make sure that you're all right. He was adamant when he told me not to come. Of course, he had to tell me where to have the pharmacy deliver, n'est-ce pas? Et voilà." Another shrug, just one shoulder, finished his sentence: and here he was.

I glanced toward the telephone on the table. "He gave you this number so you could call me?"

"He did not." With a little laugh, he pointed toward the ceiling. "For that I went to a higher power. I called my mother-in-law, who called her good friend your grandmother, who was only too happy to share that bit of information so that we could invite you to our home for dinner. So, Maggie, now that I see that you are fine, I am worried about Jean-Paul. Where is he? I want to see him for myself."

"So do I. Will you drive me to Orly?"

He eyed me as he thought through that question. "You are going to him?"

I nodded. "If I tell you where, dear Émile, you might tell your wife, who would tell her mother, who would immediately call my grandmother, so—"

What I said apparently made perfect sense to him. He reached into his suit-coat pocket and brought out a card with his contact numbers and handed it to me. "Of course, I will take you to the airport. In exchange, you must promise me that you will call me if anything—anything—is wrong. D'accord?"

"D'accord," I agreed. "Ready?"

We put on our coats, I slung the backpack over my shoulder, but before we got out the door, Émile spotted the bags with my uneaten lunch and fruit hanging from a hook on the hall tree, where I had left them, forgotten in my rush to see what the pharmacy had sent over.

"When did you last eat, Maggie?" When I took too long to answer, he grabbed the bags and handed them to me. "You look very pale and quite drawn. For strength, you will eat this while you wait for your plane. And when you arrive at your destination, you will get some rest. Doctor's orders."

At Orly, Émile dropped me at the curb outside the departure lounge, kissed my cheeks, and then merged back into traffic headed toward central Paris. With no luggage to check and a boarding pass in hand, I went straight to the security area, suffered the usual humiliations, put myself back together, and made sure that I was still in possession of my essentials. On the way to the departure gate assigned to my flight, I acquired a paperback book, a bag of trail mix, a bottle of water, and a cup of coffee. I found a seat near the gate, ate my sandwich, opened my book, and settled in for the wait until my flight was called.

Mid-February, the beginning of two weeks of *Carnevale* in Venice. The plane was packed with boisterous people who had started celebrating early. *Carnevale di Venezia* is more subdued than the semi-controlled riots you might find in Rio or New Orleans. To begin, it's generally cold in Venice at that time of year, so there aren't legions of nearly naked people parading in the streets. There are public events, of course, and plenty of alcohol, but most of the real partying is private, fancy-dress, indoors, and very expensive. Did I say, plenty of alcohol?

Boarding seemed to take forever as people jostled for overhead bin space. My fellow passengers had not packed lightly for the festivities, perhaps bringing elaborate costumes with them. The plane had unassigned seating and I lucked into a window spot, stuffed the backpack under the seat in front, and hunkered in for the duration. I was distractedly watching baggage handlers on the tarmac below my window when the woman in the aisle seat reached across the empty seat between us and gave me a gentle nudge. She flicked her chin toward a man approaching down the aisle. The very blond man from the electronics store that morning was waving a hand, trying to get my attention over the heads of people shuffling forward down the aisle in front of him.

"This time you can't deny that we've met before," he said with a broad grin when I looked up and saw him. "In the shops today, yes?"

"Oh, sure," I said without enthusiasm.

"What a coincidence." A woman in front of him turned to deliver a scowl at him; he was quite loud. "Going to Venice for *Carnevale*? Let's hope the weather clears up."

I was saved from further conversation when a young man with the requisite little hipster beard and close-cropped hair dumped a duffel onto the middle seat beside me and made a fuss trying to stow an oversized bag into the already full bin above us. I leaned toward the window to stay out of his way and opened my book. By the time my neighbor settled in, the blonde had been impelled along toward the back of the plane by the tide of passengers behind him.

The book I bought was written by a favorite author. But I reread a passage I had already read at least twice, and closed it. My mind was elsewhere. Jean-Paul had given me all sorts of instructions, and a ticket to Venice, but he hadn't given me a contact number or said that he would be at the airport to meet me. If he wasn't there, where the hell was I supposed to find him?

The flight was over almost before it began, ninety minutes between takeoff and landing. Eager to deplane, I was stuck behind the slow shuffle of people collecting their gear before I could shoulder my backpack and stream out with the mob. I looked over feathered hats and long-nosed *Carnevale* masks for Jean-Paul as we approached baggage claim and the exits beyond. Air travel within the European Union is very like travel within the United States. Passengers get "sterilized" before they board their planes, so no one bothers with them when they disembark at their destination. No customs to go through, only a passport check.

"Quick flight, yes?" My fair-haired buddy elbowed his way through the crowd to walk beside me. "I think water taxi is the fastest way in. Shall we share the ride?"

"Thank you, but no," I said. "I'm being met."

At least, I hoped I was. Instead of finding Jean-Paul, though, I spotted a wiry little man among the water taxi pilots holding a card with M DUCHAMPS printed in thick black letters. Margot Duchamps is the name on my birth certificate, the American version, and Marguerite on the original French, a tidbit that Jean-Paul, but not many strangers, would know. I caught the taxi man's eye, pointed at myself and walked toward him.

"M. Duchamps? Not a monsieur, eh!" he said, gesturing for me to follow him to the baggage conveyer. "Your luggage?"

"I don't have bags to claim."

"Then we go."

"Where do we go?" I asked, falling into step close beside him.

With a shrug, he said, "Ca'Giuliano," as if everyone would know that we were going to Giuliano's house. But who was Giuliano?

We walked out of the airport, past rows of bright posters and costumed vendors hawking tickets for expensive *Carnevale* events, and into a cold, foggy afternoon. An icy wind blowing straight down the Adriatic from the Alps hit me in the face as I followed the man I assumed had been sent by Jean-Paul—would anyone else know I was arriving?—down a long lagoon-side walkway toward the ranks of water taxis parked along the quay. I was handed into a beautiful teak craft and offered a seat in the low, open-front cabin behind the pilot wheel, out of the wind if not out of the chill. I had many questions, but my driver wasn't a chatty sort. How far? Not far. Who arranged for you to pick me up? My dispatcher.

I gave up and stayed inside the relative shelter of the cabin, watching our progress through the side windows. The boat sat low in the water as we crossed the white-capped lagoon, moving with traffic along the inbound lane of the dredged boat channel. On either side of the channel the water was so shallow that we could look wading birds right in the eye as we passed them, a strange sensation. The birds paid no attention to us.

Suddenly, like Camelot rising from the mist, the domes and towers of Venice began to appear along the gray horizon. As always, it was magic. Soon, on our left, the many-domed Basilica di Santa Maria della Salute loomed out of the fog and we turned, heading into the Grand Canal. Along both sides, colorful *Carnevale* crowds paraded into and out of shops and cafés, around kiosks and pavilions set up on open piazzas and on the steps of magnificent churches that were offering musical performances. Gondoliers ferrying tourists glided into and out of side canals, calling, *"Oi!"* to warn of their approach. It was all a grand circus and the more I saw of it the edgier I became. I needed to find Jean-Paul. Now.

After we passed the modern white shell of the Guggenheim Museum, I leaned out of the cabin and asked again, "How far?"

"Not far."

A few minutes later, as we approached Accademia Bridge, the driver cut his engine. Silently, we glided under the bridge and then, immediately and skillfully, he maneuvered the boat into a short and narrow inlet between massive palazzos on the left and a small grassy park on the right. Beyond the strip of grass there was an open piazza filled with revelers visiting commercially sponsored covered pavilions. Improbably for this automobile-free city, a new-model Fiat was being craned off a barge and onto a platform in front of one of the pavilions. My driver threw out a line and on his first try snagged an iron cleat bolted into the stone seawall, pulled us in and tied up the boat. He hopped out and offered his hand to me. I was hardly back on *terra firma* before he began releasing his line.

"Where am I going?" I asked, baffled, feeling a bit forlorn, as I looked at the collection of buildings rising around me.

The driver was already backing out toward the canal. He tipped his head toward the tall palazzo built tight against the canal, and called out, "Ca'Giuliano," and was gone.

A small tile plaque affixed high on the front corner of the massive peach-colored house reassured me that this was, indeed, Ca'Giuliano. I looked along the side wall, saw no door, but started walking, hoping to find a way in. About thirty feet down I came to a filigreed gate that led to a dark and narrow walkway between two tall houses. Ahead, on the left side of the walkway, there was an arched opening. I pushed through the gate and ventured in. Behind me, I could hear rock music coming from the piazza, but everything immediately around me seemed eerily quiet, except for the echo of my own footsteps on the stone walkway. Twice I looked around to see if someone else was there. But I was alone.

Through the arch there was an elevator, secured by a digicode lock. And no intercom, no tenant directory. I sighed: Now what?

Jean-Paul's email message said, "Always aim for the moon, and remember how far it is to China." When people spend a lot of time together, they develop their own private little codes, a sort of language of their own. When Christopher Columbus set out from Spain in 1492, he believed that China was less than 3000 miles due west from Europe. He was wrong, and because of that error he collided with America and changed the world in unexpected ways—some good, some horrific—and destroyed his own life. When either Jean-Paul or I have a big decision to make, the other will pose the question, "Have you measured the distance?" Meaning, have you considered all the possibilities?

I punched in 1492, the year of Columbus's monumental blunder, and the elevator doors slid open. Inside there were four buttons to choose from. Because the fourth floor was as close to the moon as I was likely to get at that moment, I hit number four. At the top, the elevator opened into a small, frigid atrium. I stepped out and knocked on the only door. I waited. And knocked again. When no one came, I was ready to turn and leave. To do what? Go to every door in the building to see if Jean-Paul might be there, or go on a treasure hunt for yet more inscrutable clues? Instead, I tried the handle. The door swung open.

Not knowing what to expect, I worked up a lame excuse in case I hadn't cleverly figured out Jean-Paul's coded instructions after all and was instead intruding on strangers: Stupid tourist, lost, wrong address, hand over all your cash and no one gets hurt. But no one seemed to be there at all.

The apartment was silent except for the muffled racket from the piazza below. I looked around: The space had once been the attic of a very large house. Open-beamed ceilings sloped down on two sides from a high central peak. A kitchen was on my right in the near end of the long central space, a plank dining table sat in the middle, and a well-appointed *stanza*—living room—at the far end looked out onto the Grand Canal through tall casement windows. Built into the eaves on both sides were, I suspected, bedrooms and bathrooms. The door on my left was ajar. Hanging onto the straps of my backpack in case I needed to flee, I pushed the door open enough to peer through.

Closed shades left the room, a bedroom, nearly dark. A crack of light from the partly open door of the en suite bathroom threw a silver line across the end of an unmade bed and a tangle of soiled clothing heaped onto a chair. Someone in the next room turned on water. As quietly as I could, almost afraid to breathe, I began to back out, ready to run for the front door. But then I heard a cough and knew who was on the other side of the bathroom door. I knocked once before pushing it open.

Startled, Jean-Paul spun around from adjusting bathtub taps. The love of my life stood there wearing nothing except a three-day beard and a dirty sling that immobilized his left arm against his chest. Intricate black stitchery closed twin gashes on his handsome face, one above his left eye, the other on the cheekbone below. His body was so covered with bruises and abrasions that he looked as if he had been tied to the bumper of a pickup and dragged along a country road. Something very bad had happened to him, but here he was, mostly intact. Mostly. And smiling his sweet, self-effacing upside-down French smile, as if he needed to apologize for the sorry state of the corpus he presented to me. I fought back tears as relief, shock, over-active imagination worked through what might have been. He responded to my look of horror by reaching for me with his free arm.

"It isn't as bad as it appears, *ma chère*," he said as I hesitated before moving into his embrace, afraid I would cause pain. "It only hurts when I laugh."

"Says you." I laid a hand along his injured cheek when we kissed. "You have a fever."

He nodded, a single backward bob of his head, acknowledging an unfortunate truth. "I present to you a pathetic wreck. A stinky one, too. I had intended to get myself cleaned up before you arrived, but I'm afraid I fell asleep, and— What time is it?"

"About three-thirty." He leaned on my shoulder getting into the tub. The edge of the sling gaped a bit as he bent forward, giving me a view of a large, oozing dressing over his left chest and shoulder. "What the hell happened to you, Jean-Paul?"

"It's a long story," he said with a deep sigh as he sank into the warm water.

"I have nothing but time." I found a bar of soap, a face cloth, and a towel in a linen cupboard at the end of the vanity. While he washed himself, I shrugged off my coat and knelt beside the tub to get a better look at his injuries. There was no cast or splint on the arm immobilized by the sling. "Broken shoulder?"

"Fractured clavicle."

"And what's under the dressing?"

"A gash."

"A gash?" I repeated. "A little swordplay, and you lost?"

"If it were, at least I might have had a chance to fight back." He looked up at me. "Maggie, I was hit by shrapnel."

"Dear God." I fell back on my haunches. "Where were you?"

With a little laugh, he settled further down into the water. "Apparently, in the wrong place, yes?"

"Apparently." I unzipped my backpack and took out the pharmacy bag. "Émile sent you a care package. Let me get you a glass, and then you damn well better tell me the whole story. From the beginning."

The kitchen was well stocked with dishes and equipment, but there was nothing in it to eat except some condiments at the back of the refrigerator. I filled a glass at the sink and took it back to the bathroom.

"How long have you been here?" I asked as I tapped a pill out of each of the vials and handed them to him.

"Since early this morning." He shrugged, and the movement made him wince. "Around four."

"When did you eat last?"

"Yesterday." He swallowed both pills with a single gulp of water. "Sardines out of a can, which is ironic."

"Why ironic?"

"I was brought here on a fishing boat."

"That explains why that filthy sling smells like dead fish. You might as well soak it because we'll have to change it, if I can figure out how it's constructed. Interesting engineering. And that's very nice embroidery work on your face. Who put you back together?"

"A Belgian plastic surgeon and a Japanese orthopedist."

"I'm guessing they weren't on the fishing boat with you."

"*Non.*" Quickly, he dunked his head under water and came up slicking his streaming hair away from his forehead. In his lightly accented, genteel English, he said, "Just me, the fish, and two smelly Greeks. Good men, both of them. They got me here safely and only asked for most of my money and my watch in exchange. No, the doctors who patched me up were on staff at a *Médicins Sans Frontières* hospital in a refugee camp on an island off the coast of Greece. You know the MSF?"

"Doctors Without Borders," I said. Years ago, I worked on a documentary about the MSF. To me, the doctors, nurses, and technicians who volunteered with the international organization were true heroes. With no compensation and no fanfare, and sometimes at great personal risk, they go into the most benighted, besieged places in the world, set up state-of-the-art medical facilities, and do battle with whatever plagues present themselves, sometimes as bombs fall around them. Miracle workers, often. Everything they have in their medical arsenal comes from donations. And as no good deed ever quite goes unpunished, what they offer—modern medicine—and who they are—outsiders—aren't always without controversy. Like the rich uncle who swoops in at Christmas bringing gifts to his poor relatives, their presence can breed resentment among the local powers that be. Sometimes to the peril of both doctor and patient.

"Were you in Greece with the MSF?" Prodding him to continue as I picked at the tape holding the shoulder dressing in place, trying to figure out how to get it off without ripping out strips of his dark chest hair.

"We did visit the MSF hospital, yes." He leaned forward so I could soap his back, what I could see of it. The sling was encased in a second sling that tied around his torso to both support the arm and keep the shoulder stable. "Do you remember Eduardo Suarez?"

"A polo player friend?"

He nodded. "He's also one of the top research chemists in Spain. A Eurozone consortium on refugees sent Eduardo and me into one of the larger refugee camps—a miserable hellhole—as observers. The hospital was the one bright spot in the place, and even it is woefully understaffed and undersupplied relative to the need for medical care there. We spent two days speaking with people, taking photos, recording what we saw, making notes for a report to the consortium."

"Someone in the camp attacked you?"

"*Non.*" As he leaned back again, he took my soapy hand, pressed it against his hard belly and held it there. His voice was full of emotion, sometimes anger, sometimes pain. His grip on my hand tightened as he spoke. "Eduardo and I had just driven out of the camp. We wanted to catch the afternoon flight out of the little regional airport near the fishing village where we had been staying. We were talking about our report, or maybe the topic was women's legs, but we heard a buzzing, saw something in the sky coming toward us from over a little rise; we were no more than three hundred meters from the camp gates. The object was right on us before we understood it was a drone; not very big, the ordinary sort you can buy in an electronics store. For a moment, it hovered over the road ahead of us, and then *ka-boom!*"

"*Ka-boom?*"

"*Exactement.* The drone dropped a payload on the road directly in front of us. It doesn't take much explosive to wipe out a crappy little rental car and leave a crater in the road."

"Jesus, Mary, and Joseph, Jean-Paul."

"*Oui.*" Again, a slight shrug, as if resigned to the vagaries of life.

"Was the bomb intended as an attack on the refugee camp or the MSF hospital? By terrorists? Anti-immigration wackos?"

"Reasonable targets for those, yes?" He waited for me to agree.

"But, sorry, no, I'm afraid that the target was none other than Jean-Paul Bernard."

"You?" I sat straight up.

"I know, eh?" That sweet little smile again, meant to reassure me. "I have come to conclude that this was a very personal event. The question is, who would want to kill me? I mean, I think I'm a fairly lovable guy, *d'accord?*"

"*Oui, d'accord.* I think you're entirely lovable. Not very huggable at the moment, but lovable. So, who have you pissed off?"

"I hope you can help me figure that out." He trained his big brown eyes on me, and yawned. "The pain med is kicking in."

"Good."

I helped him out of the tub and gingerly wrapped him in the towel. He rested his head against me as I dried his wet hair. For a moment, we were quiet. If one can have nightmares while awake, I was having a doozy as I imagined possibilities for things that could have, but did not, happen to Jean-Paul. Hadn't happened yet, maybe.

We shared a lovely, reassuring kiss. We were together again, and for the moment, we were safe.

I found a clean white sheet in the cupboard and then rummaged through vanity drawers until I found a pair of nail scissors before following him into the bedroom. He sat patiently on the edge of the unmade bed, supporting his left elbow with his right hand, while, first, I deconstructed the soiled sling, and then as I snipped away the hair stuck to the surgical tape holding the gauze dressing to his wound. By the time I finished removing the tape, the top of his chest looked like it had been mowed by a tiny drunk. He took a deep breath and the old dressing fell onto his lap. When I saw the mincemeat underneath, I started to cry.

"It isn't as bad as it looks," he said, reaching for my hand.

"Says you. What monster did this to you?"

He laughed. "That is the question, yes?"

"Damn them, Jean-Paul." I took out some of my angst on the sheet, tearing it into wide strips to make two new slings, one for now and one in case we needed it later. "Let me guess: the MSF doctors told you to avoid doing anything that would put stress on the wound. To just go to bed until the bone and the flesh had some time to heal, right?"

He bobbed his head, meaning, grudgingly, yes. "But I could hardly stay at the MSF facility and take up one of their scarce beds, could I?"

"Some people could." I wiped my eyes on the corner of his damp towel. "You've pulled out a few of the stitches and it looks like the wound is infected. Why didn't they at least start you on antibiotics?"

"They offered, of course, but Maggie—"

"I know. Scarce supplies."

"I thought I would be in Athens the next morning, where I could get the prescribed drugs. But things don't always happen as planned, yes?"

"Too true." As gently as I could, I spread antibiotic ointment around the wound. "When I go out for food, I'll try to find some butterfly bandages to close the edges until we can get you to a doctor. One with plenty of beds and drugs, I hope. In the meantime, I'll lay new gauze over it and hope you lie still until I get back from the market."

I spread out the original, sodden, sling on the floor and studied it for a minute, trying to figure out its structure. Then I did my best to fold lengths of the clean sheet to match what I saw. The trickiest part would be putting the new sling on Jean-Paul without disturbing the clavicle or touching the wound over it. For a moment, I considered giving him a second pain pill to knock him out for a while, because I knew any movement of the shoulder and the infected sutures would hurt. While I mulled over-dosing him, I assembled the new sling. It would be neither as intricate as the original, nor as pretty, but I thought it would do its job of keeping his shoulder immobilized until we could find a doctor.

"Your Japanese orthopedist must have studied origami," I said as I eased the fabric under his bent elbow and laid it over his right shoulder, avoiding the wound on his left. "I can't recreate what he did, but I think I understand what he was trying to do."

As a distraction while I struggled with the sling, he said, "We have hardly spoken since you landed in Vientiane. Did all go well in Laos?"

"Ah, Laos," I said, leaning around him to tie the two ends behind his neck. "I don't know where to begin. Laos was amazing. Warm. Beautiful. Deadly. I hate to admit this, but the twerp at network who put a cork in my Normandy project and sent me off to chase down unexploded bombs was right. Finding dead German soldiers in Grand-mère's carrot field and the conversation about unexploded ordnance from World War Two was probably the most interesting part of the Normandy footage for viewers. Going into Flanders, Germany, Ukraine, expanded that theme, and we shot great stuff. But Laos, my God, Jean-Paul, it's the scope of the problem there that blew me away."

"Pun intended?"

"*Ka-boom* is certainly the topic of the day, isn't it?" The sling supporting his elbow was in place. I set to work on the second part, immobilizing the left arm with a second binding that wrapped around his torso. "When the U.S. pulled out of Vietnam, we left behind something like eighty million tons of unexploded shit in Laos. That's a little more than eleven pounds of *ka-boom* per capita. And it's everywhere."

"*Merde*," he said, smiling his usual ironic smile. "And here I am whimpering over the effects of a single insignificant little bomb."

"Oh, go ahead and whimper," I said as I tied the last of the fabric ends. "How does this feel?"

"Good," he said. "Solid."

When he had convinced me that the construction was, indeed, quite comfortable and that I hadn't cut off circulation to his left hand, he asked for the clothes he'd left in a heap on a chair. I could smell them before I touched them; a holey fisherman's sweater, a pair of well-worn denim dungarees, and flimsy rope-soled canvas shoes.

"Where did you get those things?" The clothes stayed on the chair while I helped him lie down. I pulled the duvet over him and tucked it in; he was shivering. I retrieved the apples and the bag of trail mix I had acquired in Paris and gave them to him.

"My kind fishermen gave me those handsome clothes," he said, patting the bed beside him. I kicked off my boots and lay down with him, exhausted. "My own clothes were shredded, of course. I left the hospital wearing scrubs. I planned to pick up something to wear and a new telephone—mine was destroyed—at the local shops when I was driven into the village. But—" He hesitated too long.

"Something happened, yes?"

He nodded, munching trail mix. "Long version or short version?"

"Long version, please." I scrunched a pillow under my head and settled in to listen.

"Because of his injuries, Eduardo had to stay behind at the MSF hospital, some concern about broken ribs puncturing a lung. But after I was patched up I managed to catch a ride into the village along with a young volunteer nurse from Sweden. Her service time was up, and she was on her way home. The local airport is very small, only two commercial flights a day, one in early morning and one late in the afternoon. Before we left the camp, I booked a room in the village hotel, and planned to leave in the morning. The nurse, Ingrid, was scheduled to leave on the afternoon flight, but because of all the fussing over me at the hospital, and the bomb crater on the access road, Ingrid missed her flight. She had no choice but to stay over. But the village inn was full by the time we arrived. What else could I do, but give her my room?"

"Please tell me you didn't sleep on a bench somewhere."

"*Non.*" He crumpled the empty trail mix bag and tossed it onto the bedside table with surprising force; a great black pall seemed to have dropped over him, an unbidden sadness. Before continuing, he was quiet for a moment, rubbing the injured shoulder as if to comfort it. I wondered whether I'd worn him out. Probably, I had. All I could do was be there close beside him until he was ready to go on with his story. After a deep breath, he turned to give me a game little smile and the we're-in-the-hands-of-fate shrug with his one good shoulder.

"Our driver, a young local," he said, "knew a fisherman's family that had a spare room they rented out. We three, the driver, Ingrid and I, ate dinner together in the hotel restaurant. I handed her my room key, we all said good night, and the driver and I went to the fisherman's house. In the morning, we stopped by the hotel to pick her up to go to the airport. When she didn't answer her phone, we asked the desk to have a maid check on her. I thought she might have overslept or was in the shower. But—"

His voice caught and he needed another moment before he could go on. In a quavering voice, he said, "In the night, her throat was cut."

"She was murdered?"

"*Oui.*"

I met his eyes. "You think it was meant to be you?"

"My first thought was that we should never have left her in the hotel alone; the village is a bit rough. But she was not assaulted, nothing was taken. There were no signs of struggle. Apparently, sometime in the night, while she slept, someone slipped in, slit her throat, and was gone. It made no sense. But then, my shoulder began to throb and I remembered Eduardo sitting at the edge of the road, bleeding, trying to breathe, and it occurred to me that the room was registered in my name, paid for with my credit card. We told no one in the hotel that Ingrid would be staying in the room instead of me; we thought she would be safer that way. In truth, by the time we finished dinner there was no one around to tell. The reception desk was dark, the hall was empty. No one else knew she was there. So, unless that isolated village harbored a madman, Ingrid was not the intended victim."

"What did you do?"

"First I checked on Eduardo; he was okay. So, was I alone the target?" He cocked his head and looked me in the eye. "What does your Big Bird tell you to do when you're trying to find something?"

I had to think. "Walk backward through your memory."

"That's exactly what I did. If I was the target, how were my attackers finding me with such precision? The drone hit was spot-on, but the hotel was a miss. So, what was different?"

He waited for me to mull that through. I went back over his

story, and found a little detail. "Your phone was destroyed. They tracked you using the GPS locator function in your telephone until the phone was destroyed. Even then, they could find you by hacking into your credit cards to see where you used them."

He reached out and pulled me tight against him and planted a noisy kiss on my forehead. "How do I love thee, Maggie? Let me count the ways..."

"That explains why you want to stay off the grid. So, what's the next move?"

"You fight fire with fire, yes?" He raised his palm with an apple on top of it, as if holding up the obvious answer, and smiled his upside-down smile. "So, I thought, I'll fight a hacker with a hacker. I went to the best I know, a little sixteen-year-old misfit who lives here in Venice, over on Giudecca. And, my love, I'll need you to rendezvous with him at exactly forty-two minutes past five o'clock tonight."

"You're a fun date, Jean-Paul." I kissed his cheek. "I never know what's going to happen when I'm with you. But I always know it will be interesting."

He laughed. "I can say the same about you."

"You can't just disappear, though. Not after what happened to you and Eduardo. People must be worried about you."

"I told everyone who counts that I was sneaking away with you for a week or two, and threatened dire consequences to anyone who dared interrupt us."

"So, why am I here, except to offer succor?"

"I hope that's reason enough. As you can see, I need your help. I was also worried that whoever is doing this would make a target of you, to get to me. And I couldn't bear that risk. So, I knew I had to make you invisible, and get you out of Paris as soon as I could. But I didn't know when you would arrive. You were expected two days before you turned up."

"Bad weather, delayed flights, cancelled flights; I had only been at Isabelle's about an hour or so when you called."

He nodded, clearly no surprise there. "I asked Madame Gonsalves to call me as soon as you showed up."

My first thought was that the old bat did know I was coming, after all. But my next thought had a strange and gritty edge that made me sit straight up. I wanted to hear him repeat something he'd said. "You had Madame Gonsalves call you?"

The question seemed to puzzle him. "Yes."

"The concierge at Isabelle's building?" I watched his face.

"Yes. She saw you at the gate and rang me immediately; there is a security camera."

"She left me standing out in the street, in the cold, while the two of you chatted?"

He smiled sweetly as he bit into the apple. "She told me you were getting impatient; I could hear the street buzzer through the phone."

"You know her that well?"

With a dismissive shrug, he said, *"Bien sûr."*

"Of course? What do you mean, of course? How the hell do you know the concierge at Isabelle's apartment so well? No, *why* would you know her?"

"I hired her."

"You did? Why you?"

"Your Uncle Gérard asked me to find someone who could keep an eye on Isabelle."

"But why would Uncle Gérard have anything to do with hiring their concierge?"

"Their?"

"The building's owners."

For a moment, he looked at me with pure confusion written on his face, at a loss for an answer to a question he either could not parse or the answer to which was so obvious that the only mystery for him was that it wasn't obvious to me. And then, a light seemed to flicker on behind those deep brown eyes. He pushed himself up against the headboard and took my hand.

"Maggie, have you read the terms of your mother's Isabelle's—will?"

"Read it?" I said. "Hardly. It's complex and it's written in French legalese. I wouldn't understand all of it even if it were written in English. I turned the pages while my *notaire* explained it to me. Does that count?"

"Did your *notaire* explain to you about number seven, rue Jacob?"

I settled back down, leaning on my elbow, watching his face while I thought about the question. No glimmer of light flickered on for me. I shrugged and said, "She told me that I have inherited an interest in Isabelle's apartment on rue Jacob."

"Apartment? Is that the word she used?"

I thought for a moment. "No. She said residence."

"Aha." He picked up my hand and kissed it. "I think I see now where the canyon in this conversation opened up. When the coast is clear and we are back in Paris, we will find you a *notaire* who speaks better English. But for now, let me explain rue Jacob."

He let out a long breath while he decided where to begin. "So, *ma chère* Maggie, you know that from time to time Isabelle battled personal demons."

"She was bipolar."

He nodded. "When she was in balance, she was remarkable. A force, yes?"

"So I hear."

"You know she was a scientist with many accomplishments. But you may not be aware that she was also a very astute business-woman. When she first saw number seven, rue Jacob, the place was a disaster. Part of the roof had caved in, there was water damage, the leaky plumbing was a century old, or more, the electricity—impossible!—floors had collapsed, and there had never been central heat. But Isabelle saw its potential when anyone else would have seen a tear-down, and she was determined to acquire it."

"Who owned the place?"

"That was the first issue for Isabelle to conquer," he said. "Both the Vatican and the local diocese claimed it, but a defunct order of nuns still held the title. To complicate the issue, the neighbor-hood, afraid some big chain store, like the Gap or Benetton up on the boulevard, would move in, had the property designated as a historic treasure to protect it."

"It was a convent?"

"It was. The Little Sisters of Saint Jérôme Émilian ran a school and orphanage there for centuries. But times change. By the 1970s the order was impoverished, reduced to just a few very old women. The Vatican closed the order and sent the survivors to a retirement facility in Switzerland. The place remained empty for decades, deteriorating, until Isabelle decided she wanted it. She moved, you could say, heaven and earth, and somehow she managed to strike a deal that both the Vatican and the diocese accepted, and that appeased the neighbors at the same time."

"What about the nuns?"

"Long gone," he said. "Silenced by the grave."

I scrolled mentally through the bits and pieces I had gleaned about Isabelle over the last year and a half. A project of that scope just did not seem economically feasible for a civil servant like Isabelle to undertake, even with the earnings from the tontine. I said, "To buy and restore that property would cost a fortune. Where the hell would Isabelle come up with that much capital?"

"Restore?" He chuckled. "It was a complete rebuild, from basements to attics. And yes, it cost a fortune. Three fortunes to be exact. Isabelle came up with considerable capital, but she still needed financing, and she needed someone with building experience. So, she invited her brother, Gérard, to join her as a partner."

"Makes sense. Uncle Gérard is a developer. He has worked on far larger projects than that one."

"He certainly brought the expertise, but he was, as usual, embarrassed for cash. He made up for his deficit by borrowing, let's say, much of the building material and some of the work crews from a large project he was directing in southern England."

Good old Uncle Gérard. "He stole the building materials?"

"You say *tomayto*, he says *tomahto*, but yes, we discovered later that some of the material was delivered without invoices. And someone else paid the salaries of some of the workers. Your uncle gave a whole new dimension to international partnership on this one." He set aside his apple core. "Britain will find that Brexit hinders many little larcenies, *n'est-ce pas?*"

I looked at him askance, seeing a whole new dimension to the man. I found his complete lack of moral outrage to be oddly sexy.

But then, after a couple of months apart I found even the bit of towel lint caught in his three-day beard to be sexy.

"Don't you worry about my Uncle Gérard. He'll find a way to work around the barriers and be just fine, whatever the future holds," I said, knowing only too well what my uncle was capable of. "I'm afraid to ask, but you said the project took three fortunes. Who was the third? Their pigeon? Their cash cow?"

"*Moi.*" He grinned, kissing me full on the lips.

"I should have known," I said, getting to my feet. "And that explains how you came to hire Madame Gonsalves. Is the woman part of your vast information network?"

"Not mine," he said. "But someone's. Your concierge is an old Basque separatist. Probably still good in the trenches."

"Something to keep in mind." I found a pad and a pencil on the nightstand. "Tell me your sizes and I'll get you some clothes while I'm out."

"Um." He paused, blushed. "*Mon coeur,* maybe we should just wash that wretched pile in the chair. It's my turn, I'm afraid, to be embarrassed for cash. At the moment, I have very little and I don't know how long my scarce resources need to stretch."

"*Ne t'inquiètes pas,*" I said, Don't worry, as I retrieved my coat from the bathroom. I pulled out the green bank pouch, unzipped it, and handed it to Jean-Paul. With a look of wonder on his battered face, he thumbed the sheaf of bills inside.

"What did you do, rob a bank?"

"No. I just walked through the front door and said, Please."

"How much is this?"

"I withdrew ten thousand. Then I bought a few prepaid phones and some credit cards. There should be something around sixty-eight hundred in there."

Laughing, he took my hand and kissed the palm. "*Ma chère,* you never cease to surprise me. I certainly picked the right sidekick to go into hiding with."

"Glad you think so. Anyway, we won't have to hitch a ride out of here on a fishing boat," I said. "The condition you're in, that's a good thing. But, Jean-Paul, why, exactly, are we hiding? Can't you just go to the authorities and ask for protection? Or summon one of your well-connected friends?"

"Not until I know who's behind all this. And why." Suddenly, he looked up at me. "Who knows you are here?"

"In Venice? No one except you, me, passport control, and the airline," I said. "My grandmother and Émile know I was leaving Paris to meet you—Émile drove me to Orly—but they don't know where I was headed."

He laughed softly. "Émile and my sister will have something interesting to talk about over dinner tonight, yes?"

"I'm sure." A thought occurred to me as I was pulling my boots back on, getting ready to go out to the shops and on to a rendez-vous with a misfit youth. "Jean-Paul, if you're short of cash, and you weren't using your ATM or credit cards, how did you pay for my flight?"

"I used a burner phone to call the one person, other than you, that I know will keep a secret and never betray me." He leaned closer and whispered, "My mother."

"Your mother? Keep a secret? How long until she tells her dear friend, my grandmother, who will tell my brother, Freddy, and my daughter, and so on, and so on, and so on?"

He shook his head. "*Jamais*. Never. Not when I told her it was important. I needed her to help me find you in Paris, and she did; she called your grandmother for information. She made your travel arrangements using a prepaid telephone and prepaid credit card in case she was being monitored. There will be questions to answer later, many questions. But until then, she says nothing."

"Not even a word to Émile and your sister?" I was still dubious. I've seen how quickly the intra-family information network can broadcast bits of news.

"Not a single word from Maman to anyone. But I can't say the same for my fishermen friends, or anyone at the airline or the taxi company that brought you here."

"Did your mother also rent this Venetian nest for us?"

With an enigmatic little smile, he said, "No. The apartment belongs to my friend, Gille."

"Someone else you trust, then?"

"Not very much, no. But Gille doesn't know we're here."

I was appalled. "Aren't you afraid he might walk in?"

"Not at all. Gille hates *Carnevale*. This is the last place he would show up."

"Lordy." I looked around the well-appointed apartment and thought, with a few pangs, about how I had ripped up the owner's thousand-thread-count sheet and wondered what the etiquette was for replacing ruined linens. And with a flashback at the state of Isabelle's apartment when I walked in, I cringed at the thought of leaving soiled towels and bedding behind for Gille to walk into.

"What time is it?" he asked.

I looked at my watch. "A little after four. Tell me about this rendezvous I'm to make at forty-two minutes after five."

"Get to the Rialto Bridge a few minutes before the meeting time. Stop to admire the display of red handbags at the front of the third shop from the San Marco end, as you face the lagoon. If you find one you want to buy, so much the better. While you are looking among the red bags, someone will tap you on the shoulder three times. Don't turn around, don't try to see who it is. Wait a decent interval, and then continue across the bridge as if you are any tourist."

"You're kidding, right?"

"No. I am serious. Dead serious."

3

NOT KNOWING HOW long we would be in Venice, at the Accademia vaporetto stop I bought two unlimited use Tourist Travel Cards from a machine, good for seven days' travel on the Venetian water bus system. The cards were still in my hand when the vaporetto headed toward Rialto pulled up to the boarding float. I merged into the surging human mass getting aboard and nabbed a spot at the outside rail. It was bitter out; the first of the promised snow flurries danced on the water as we headed up the Grand Canal. We passed two oncoming vaporetti packed with passengers and riding low, headed toward the Piazza San Marco where there was to be a parade of some sort and fireworks that evening. As I debarked at the Rialto stop, I made a mental note to walk home later to avoid the jammed buses headed back toward Accademia on their way toward San Marco.

Feeling paranoid, as I made my way toward the modern Coin department store in the Cannaregio district, I watched my rear, taking a zig-zag course through the narrow Venetian walkways that coursed between ancient buildings. Now and then, I stopped at shop windows to see if anyone was following me. People walked past in a steady stream without seeming to take notice of me.

Every time I stopped, I took out my little video camera and shot a few frames as if I were any other tourist, except that my target was always the faces of people around me, and not the iconic architecture or beautiful doors or the odd cat grooming itself in a window. The sun had already disappeared below the rooftops, and shadows were long when I opened the front door of the brightly lit department store. When I passed a rack of women's coats on sale on the ground floor, it occurred to me that Freddy's coat would suit Jean-Paul better than it did me. It was way too big for me, and would be a bit big for Jean-Paul, too; my brother is a tall, broad-shouldered man. But the size would accommodate Jean-Paul's sling. After I shopped for him, I planned to go back downstairs and look at the coats on the sale rack.

Upstairs, in the third-floor men's department, I began pulling out clothes that looked like the sorts of things Jean-Paul might wear, and that were warm and practical, and handing them to the sales clerk who had appointed herself my assistant. Two pairs of jeans, a couple of button-front flannel shirts a size too large, a heavy cardigan, underwear, long johns, socks, and a pair of all-weather leather shoes with a lug sole. After I paid for his things, I started back down the stairs toward women's coats on the ground floor. And that's when I spotted my tail.

The tall blond man I had run into earlier was lingering near the bottom of the stairs, in the women's shoe department, pretending, I thought, to be interested in some really ugly green pumps with a four-inch heel. Freddy's big coat was hanging over my arm. I slipped my camera out of a pocket and, using the coat as a shield, snapped a few surreptitious frames of the man. His head was down, but with the zoom function I got a good shot of his face reflected in the mirror placed on the floor where women could check out the shoes they were trying on. Just as he looked up, I stepped off the stairs and onto the mezzanine, ladies' lingerie. Randomly, I pulled a handful of bras off a rack and asked to be shown to a fitting room, a place the blond man could not follow. And where I could have a little time to figure out a strategy for escape. The black-clad maven of lingerie who hovered at my elbow looked from the bras dangling from my hand to my chest, scowled, took them from me and quickly selected half a dozen others before leading me to a fitting room.

Not since I was thirteen, being fitted for my very first bra, had a sales clerk joined me in the fitting room. Until now. As she unhooked the first of the bras, and with no safe way to exit coming to mind, I stripped to the waist. I put my arms through the straps she held for me. After she fastened the back, she cupped my breasts in her hands, gave them a little jiggle, made an adjustment in the straps, then stood back for me to look in the mirror. The bra was wonderful, the best-fitting, most comfortable little wisp of a garment I had ever worn. We tried two others, but agreed that the first was the best.

"*Quanti ne desideri?*" she asked, scrolling up her fingers one at a time. How many did I want? I hadn't planned to buy any, but the bra was wonderful. And I felt I should reward her efforts, or pay a sort of rent for this place of refuge. I held up two fingers. But she shook her head and announced, firmly, "*Quattro.*"

When I nodded that four bras was just fine, she handed me my old bra and shirt and opened the fitting room door. Instead of going right out, though, she peeked through, motioned to a clerk who was passing by with a customer, and whispered something to her. The other clerk walked out through the opening to the sales floor and came right back. She gave a nod and my lady closed the door again.

"*Signora,*" she whispered, her back against the door. "There is a man; tall, white hair—You know him?"

"He's a pest," I said. "He was on my flight and now he follows me everywhere. Is he lurking out there?"

She nodded as she pointed down, which I took to mean he was down on the ground floor still. "You don't want to see him, *sí?*"

"*Sí.*"

She touched the end of her nose. "I knew this. That's why you ran in here, to stay away from him."

When I nodded, she *tsk*'ed, and with great disdain, said, "These guys, Euro trash. They come at *Carnevale* to drink and pick up girls.

They see a pretty girl, and, like lions, they stalk her. Make like big *scooch*, eh? They don't go away, don't hear No. They have their way, eat her alive. And then what? They fly away home. Maybe have a wife and kids somewhere. *Bastardi*."

She folded the chosen bra. "Wait here. You need something more from store, I'll get."

"It isn't from your department, but I do need a coat."

She glanced at Freddy's coat hanging from a hook, gave my body another assessment, pulled a phone out of her pocket and made a quick call. Within a few minutes, there was a tap on the door and a second clerk handed in half a dozen coats. The two women studied me, had a brief conversation, and agreed on two of the coats for me to try on. The second one fit beautifully, covered my ass, had a zip-out blanket lining, deep pockets, and cost the earth, even marked down twenty-five percent.

"I'll take it," I said. "I'll wear it now."

The second clerk, with a nod, took small scissors from her pocket and snipped the tags. I handed over one of the prepaid credit cards and, as instructed by my helpers, sat down on the little chair in the corner of the fitting room while my purchases were rung up. When my bra lady came back, she carried a shopping bag large enough to hold my new bras as well as Freddy's coat. Like a conspirator, which I suppose she was, instead of sending me back out into the open store, she bustled me along the short hallway outside the fitting rooms, through a door into a stock room, down a freight elevator and, when the coat clerk, who was waiting outside, gave a signal that the coast was clear, showed me out through a service door that opened onto a quiet back passageway. It was dark out there, and spooky, but I could see all the way to the end where it intersected with a second narrow walkway that ran along a side canal.

"*Grazie*," I said, offering her my hand. "*Grazie mille*."

"*Prego*," she answered, leaning in to kiss my cheek. "Women, we stick together."

Then she closed the door and I was alone. In the dark.

Staying to the back side of the district, using less-traveled

walkways in a residential area, away from the tourists, I wended
my way toward the Rialto Bridge and my 5:42 rendezvous. It was
only a ten-minute walk, and I had a little more than twenty minutes
to make it. When I came upon a small neighborhood beauty supply
shop, I went in and picked up a few basic toiletries for Jean-Paul:
toothbrush, comb, razor, the shaving gel he used. Laden with purchases, at 5:36 I was studying a display of red leather handbags
in front of the third shop from the San Marco end of the Rialto
Bridge.

While I waited for someone to give my shoulder three taps, I
was bumped and jostled by the great swirling tide of tourist shop-
pers, but I held my spot, pretending to be one of them, looking for
souvenirs. The red bags were beautiful, so the task wasn't difficult.
I found one that I particularly liked. It was small and flat, just
big enough to hold a phone, some cash, and the wallet with my
passport. The bag had a long sturdy strap that I could wear across
my body and under my coat, a safer place to keep valuables than
a pocket. The price was quite reasonable, all things considered,
so I held it up to the proprietor, who had been keeping a close
eye on me from behind the counter of his narrow store. He came
forward, smiling, showed me the price tag. I nodded, handed him
cash, and he took the bag to his counter to ring up and wrap.
While this transaction was in process, I felt three quick taps on
my shoulder and knew my mission was complete. The clerk, with a
little bow, presented me with my new bag, said, *"Grazie, signora."*
I responded, *"Prego,"* tucked the package he gave me among my
purchases, and sauntered on, though I wanted to run all the way
back to the apartment where Jean-Paul waited.

Throngs of people headed toward San Marco, filling the walkways. To avoid them, I crossed the bridge to the opposite side of
the Grand Canal and turned toward Accademia, walking fast. From
nowhere, someone grabbed my elbow, hard, pulling me back. I
spun around, spat "Fucking *scooch*," not knowing exactly what the
word meant but liking the sound of it. My knee was up, ready to
jam into the groin of the tall blond freak.

"Maggie, Maggie, honey pie. Hold on. It's just me. Handsome, almost-sober Roddy. Hell, I chased you all the way across that damn bridge."

"Roddy Combes." I was so taken aback to see my old friend from the land of television that I nearly fell over backward until I got both feet firmly planted again. "What the hell are you doing here?"

"Chatting," he said. "Because that's what I get paid to do, right? Paid a great deal, in fact. The network sent me over to chat up some of the glossier celebs who are in town for the frivolities."

"You're taping your show here, in Venice?"

"Some bits, anyway," he said. "I go from the pre-Lenten non-sense of *Carnevale* here in Venice to the sex and drunken revelry of *Fasching* in Munich over the weekend. I finish up in London on Tuesday at the Great Spitalfields Pancake Race. If, that is, I'm not too fekkin blootered after Munich to get there."

"Do celebs join the pancake race?" I asked, heart still racing.

"If I promise to aim a camera at them they will do just about anything." He laughed his famous, great, deep *haw-haw*. A long time ago, when Roddy and I were both newcomers to television, we had worked together at a network affiliate in Texas. I was anchoring the weekend news broadcast, and he was the weatherman. He got the job, as he would be the first to admit, not because he knew anything at all about meteorology, but because he had a charming Scots brogue and that great big laugh; viewers loved him. Over time, his accent and his quirky dry wit elevated him from making even bad weather sound like fun, to hosting one of the late-night talk shows. Chat shows, he called them. He got paid millions to yuck it up with celebrities four nights a week.

"But you," he said. "What are you doing here? Last I heard, you were in Asia trying not to step on land mines."

"Who told you that?" The question sounded sharper to my ear than I had intended, but under the weird circumstance I was in, every creak and leaf fall sounded suspicious. It isn't paranoia when people actually are trying to get you, is it?

He said, "I ran into your skinny producer at some network holiday gaff. Does that woman ever eat?"

"Food scares her," I said, dialing back my over-active alarm system. He was just good old Roddy, for chrissake, not some sort of murderous spook. Still, he didn't need to know anything more than he already did by just bumping into me at the end of the Rialto Bridge: his stock in trade, after all, was talk. "But, yeah, I'm on my way home from Laos. Bad weather, redirected flights, fate, and here I am."

"That explains why you look like hell, my dear Maggie. When was the last time your magnificent carcass found a bed?"

"Days," I said.

He nodded toward my big shopping bags. "And to make it yet more fun, I'm guessing that the arfing airlines lost your bags yet again."

"Pisser, huh?" I wasn't about to explain my situation to him. "Good to see you, Roddy. But I am tired. And a bed awaits."

"Oh ho," he said with a leer. "Could that devastatingly handsome French diplomat, the one you showed up with half-naked in all the tabs, be waiting in the same bed?"

"If he were, no one would get any sleep, would they? Sorry to say, I'm solo tonight."

"Listen, girlie-o." He fumbled in a pocket, pulled out a pen and a business card with the network logo, and started writing on the back. "A few of the bright, overpaid movie young'uns are dropping by tonight after the Mozart fest to chat for the cameras. Go take a nice nap, comb your hair, put on a face and some of those new duds, and join us. I'll give you a glass of something strong, park you on a sofa next to some irresistible film stud, turn the camera on you and do a YOU'LL NEVER GUESS WHO I RAN INTO ON HER WAY BACK FROM THE MINEFIELDS piece. It'll make a nice promo bit for whatever the hell you're working on. Drop by any time after about ten. Actually, come anytime. Just flash this card to my security guy and he'll show you aboard and ply you with drink."

"Aboard?" I asked. "Aboard what?"

"We're in Venice, right? Surrounded by water. What else could I do but get the network to hire a great fekkin yacht for me?"

"Sounds good, Roddy, but another time, friend. I'm too tired to deal with camera lights and witty repartee."

"If you change your mind." He handed me the card. "I'm

moored at Marina Sant'Elena. Directions are here. The tub is a quick walk from the Sant'Elena SX vaporetto stop."

"Thanks, Roddy." I slipped the card into my jeans pocket. We exchanged cheek kisses and a quick embrace. As I turned to leave, he called my name.

"Are you sure you're all right, lass?"

"Right as rain, whatever that means."

"Currently, cold, wet, dreary," he said, nodding toward the leaden skies.

"That's about right," I said, turned again and walked away.

The day had indeed been cold, wet, and dreary. After the sun went down, the wind came up and the temperature plummeted. My new coat was warm, but it didn't cover my knees. I pulled up the collar and pulled the sleeves down over my fists and cursed myself for not buying gloves. My feet ached with cold. I longed to get back to the warm apartment. Without hope of finding space on a crowded vaporetto, I stuck with Plan A and walked to Accademia; it wasn't very far. I crossed the bridge, but though I felt thoroughly miserable, instead of going straight up to Jean-Paul, I continued on to the neighborhood market on Campo Santo Stefano where I gathered food for dinner. When at last I unlocked the front door, the apartment was quiet and dark, the only light coming in through the big canal-side windows in front. Without turning on lights, in case someone below was watching for them, I shot the deadbolt on the front door, stowed the groceries in the refrigerator, and took the bag of toiletries into the bedroom, leaving the rest of the shopping on the dining table.

Clearly, I had been followed, or somehow tracked, when I left the apartment earlier. Probably, I thought, the blondie had followed me in from the airport to find out where I was headed. He might have seen the water taxi pull away from the inlet where I was dropped, but because I'd had a head start and no one pulled in behind us, I strongly doubted that a tail would have seen which house I entered. Blondie could lurk on the piazza below and watch for me to emerge, but he still wouldn't know which apartment I was in. Unless I snapped on the lights as soon as I got home and gave us away.

In the bedroom, Jean-Paul snored softly. I peeled off my boots and jeans, climbed under the duvet beside him, and quickly fell asleep. Fireworks, probably from San Marco, woke me from a deep, dark place. Still groggy, I snuggled into Jean-Paul. While I slept, he had wrapped his free arm around me and pulled me close. I didn't want to disturb him, so I just lay there, staying quiet. There was another BOOM! And a flash of red light.

"*Non!*" he screamed and sat straight up in a panic. His eyes were open, but he was seeing something far away as he pleaded: "*Je vous en prie!*"

"Jean-Paul." I wrapped an arm around him and brushed his hair off his forehead. He wasn't as warm as he'd been when I arrived, but he still had a fever. "Shh. We're okay. It's just fireworks."

He let out a deep breath and sagged back against the pillows. "Sorry. Bad dream."

"You cried out."

"Ah," was all he said.

"Hungry?"

"Very."

I checked my watch. It was almost eleven; I had been asleep for nearly five hours. Reluctantly, I dragged myself to my feet and went to the bathroom to wash my face. Jean-Paul followed. He leaned against the door jamb, and watched me.

"You made the rendezvous?" he asked.

"Yes. I guess." I filled a glass and gave him his next dose of meds. "Someone tapped my shoulder three times. What was supposed to happen?"

"Did you check your right coat pocket?"

"No." I dried my hands and face and retrieved my coat from the bedroom doorknob. In the right-hand pocket there was a USB memory drive that I had not put there. I held it up to Jean-Paul, who stood nearby. "This?"

"That." He kissed me as he took it off my palm. "Congratulations."

"What is it?"

"I told you I hired a hacker," he said, following me back into the bathroom. "I asked him to check all of my accounts to see what has been hacked, and then to search backward to find out who is doing it. That little drive should have his work product to date. As soon as we can, we'll find an Internet café, plug in the drive and see what he discovered."

"Your hacker can't have come cheap," I said, getting out the razor and shaving gel and guiding him to sit on the edge of the tub so that I could shave the left side of his chest before taping the dressing back over the shrapnel wound. "How did you pay him?"

"I used a credit card. My hacker told me he wanted a fresh transaction to start his search."

"Do you trust this little criminal?"

"I need to trust him." When I finished patching him up, he took the razor from me to shave off his three-day beard. "For now."

"Why does that not fill me with confidence?" He was still naked, shivering. I picked up the nail scissors I'd left on the counter and headed out. "I'll get your clothes."

I turned on the light over the stove, dumped out the shopping bags on the dining table, and started snipping tags. When Jean-Paul came in from the bedroom, freshly shaved, he dressed quickly, needing only a little help with buttons. He smoothed his shirt front, tucked in the empty sleeve, smiled, and said, "Thank you."

"*Prego.* How does everything fit?"

He pulled out the jeans waistband to show me they were big. "I think I must have lost some weight after three days on canned sardines. A few days of Italian pasta and I'll gain it back. What did you find to eat?"

"Pasta."

I make no claim to being anything more than an adequate cook, if that. Everything I bought came in a package, needing only a little heating and assembling before it was ready to serve. We had fat sausage-filled ravioli, bottled sauce, some shredded Parmesan, and mixed salad greens poured out of a plastic bag into a bowl and tossed with the vinegar and olive oil that our erstwhile host, Gille, had left in a cupboard.

After his first few bites, Jean-Paul looked up. "So, no trouble?"

"Maybe."

He put his fork down. "Maybe?"

I took the camera out of my coat pocket and found the shots I had taken of the tall blond man. "This guy was in the shops in Paris this morning, and on my flight to Venice, too. He tried to start conversations both times. When he turned up in Coin tonight while I was shopping, I got some help from the staff to duck out the back to avoid him. Do you recognize him?"

"No." He manipulated the image and handed the camera back to me. In the center of the screen now there was a second man, one I hadn't noticed, standing a little distance away from the blonde, near the store's front door, watching the crowd outside pass by the big windows. Or was he watching the store behind him reflected in the tall windows? There was nothing that made him stand out. He was compact, medium height, medium build, medium brown hair that was not neither long nor short. Average, ordinary, an invisible man in a crowd. Jean-Paul tapped the image. "Him I recognize. Sabri Qosja. From Kosovo A different sort of explosive left over from a war."

"How do you know him?"

"After the Kosovar conflict—this was fifteen, sixteen years ago—Qosja and his father, and some hundreds of others, were brought before a panel of the World Court in The Hague to testify about war crimes they had witnessed or were accused of committing. I sat on the panel and asked a question from time to time."

"You remember him out of some hundreds?"

"Yes, and a few others," Jean-Paul said. "Qosja's story was a common one. When the war started, he was very young, very naïve, ripe for adventure of a certain sort. He joined a separatist faction with his father, and they went off together to fight. During the conflict, opposition forces took over their village, destroyed their home, their farm, slaughtered the mother and younger children. When the two surviving Qosjas learned what had happened, they went on a mission of revenge. Rape, torture: unbelievable cruelty. They weren't alone in that. Our concern was that their personal war of revenge would escalate into full-scale war all over again. The reason I remember Sabri Qosja is that his father wrote out a confession, taking all blame for what happened and exonerated his son. Then he hanged himself."

"Jesus, Mary, and Joseph," I muttered. "What happened to Qosja, the son?"

"Nothing." Jean-Paul shrugged. "No legal punishment, anyway. I can't speak for the state of his soul. I do know that when it was over, he had nothing to go back for. No home, no family, no education to speak of, other than what he learned on the battlefield. The only skill he had to fall back on was the craft of warfare. After the peace, he went rogue, became a hired gun, a mercenary. The element that makes Qosja and men like him dangerous is, they have no ideology, no code beyond loyalty to whoever is paying them at any moment."

"And perhaps nothing left to lose?"

"Perhaps that," he said.

"Do you think he's trying to get you out of revenge?"

"After so many years?" He raised a palm, showing skepticism. "If he wanted revenge he could have taken me out at any time. No, I think someone sent him."

"So, the question is, who hired him?"

"That," he said. "And why."

"Time to find out. I saw an Internet café on Campo Santo Stefano that's probably open most of the night," I said. "After we eat, I'll go try to find out what your hacker gave you."

"And if Qosja and friend are outside, waiting?"

"We can't hide here forever, Jean-Paul."

He glanced at the front door, which I had bolted and chained when I came in. But he said nothing. I thought he looked frightened. The previous spring, we survived a harrowing ordeal. Together. I learned then that in a predicament I could always count on Jean-Paul to be, first, level-headed, and next, decisive. It wasn't like him to be at a loss for what to do, or to hesitate to engage when a threat lay at his doorstep. It certainly wasn't like him to run.

I took his hand. "What happened in Greece shook you to the core, didn't it?"

He nodded. "I wanted to keep the young woman, Ingrid, safe.

But she would have been better off anywhere that night than in a hotel room registered in my name."

"You can't hold yourself responsible for what others did to her, Jean-Paul. Or did to you and Eduardo."

He met my eyes. "I thought I was protecting you by getting you out of Paris. But here we are."

"Exactly. Here we are. Now what?"

For a few moments, he stared off into the middle distance, saying nothing. I began to worry that more than his body had been injured in the explosion. But then his focus came back to me and he smiled, that sweetly wicked smile that meant that all his circuits had come back on board. He said, "When you want to know where the enemy is, sometimes you have to run out of the forest to draw his fire."

"We're going to make a run for it."

"We need to get back to Paris," he said. "We have more resources there. I want to know what my hacker discovered, but first we need to get out of Venice."

"Shall I call a water taxi?"

He dismissed that idea immediately. "We'd be too vulnerable alone. There's safety in a crowd. The city always puts on late trains for *Carnevale*. Let's try to catch the overnight to Milan or Florence. If we aren't followed, we can catch a morning flight to Paris."

I sighed as I forked another ravioli; they were very good and I was very hungry. The apartment was warm and comfortable. I had hoped that we could hole up there for a while longer, to give Jean-Paul some time to heal, and for both of us to rest. Knowing who was waiting out there for us, however, made any thoughts of resting disappear.

"First things first," I said, catching his eye. "Eat your dinner. Who knows when we'll eat again. Even the condemned are entitled to a last meal."

4

WE WEDGED OUR WAY onto a crowded vaporetto at the Accademia stop, headed toward the train station. I pushed in first, trying to protect Jean-Paul's injured left side as he got on behind me, but it was useless. The crowd pressed in all around us, surging and swaying as the water bus moved along the black, storm-tossed water of the Grand Canal. He never complained, but by the time we reached the train station, his face was ghostly pale. We were disgorged with the mass onto the wet pavement, again with me leading the way. Rain had given way to heavy sleet and there were treacherous patches of ice underfoot. A woman in front of us slipped and somehow managed to kick both of us in the shins as she fell on her ass. I think she was drunk. I think a lot of the people around us were drunk. It felt to me as if we had landed into a noisy nightmare we couldn't wake from.

While Jean-Paul stood with his back to mine, scanning the crowd, on the lookout for the blonde or Sabri Qosja, I queued up at a ticket machine and used one of the prepaid cards to buy two first-class seats on the train to Padua, only because the train was already in the station and was due to leave in five minutes. Otherwise, we would have to wait nearly an hour to catch the connecting trains to either Milan or Florence. I thought that when we got to Padua, a short trip, we could figure out what to do next. Tickets in hand, I gripped the empty left sleeve of Jean-Paul's coat in my right hand and used the backpack over my left shoulder as a sort of battering ram, muttering, *"Scusi, scusi,"* when anyone glared, to open a path among the crowd of aimlessly milling people on the platform so that we could board our train before it left the station.

After a collision with someone who came in from the side, I heard someone behind me sniff, "And I thought the Canadians were supposed to be ever so polite."

Jean-Paul laughed, so I knew that he would be all right; I had been afraid he was on the verge of passing out. A conductor handed us into a first-class carriage just before he called out, *"Signori, tutti in carrozza!"* We sank into the nearest available seats and sighed in relief. We were in, the all-aboard had been called, and we were about to leave Venice. Intact. And that's when I spotted them.

The blonde and Qosja arrived by water taxi. They stood on the station platform for a moment, their eyes glued to their telephone screens like half the people we saw. Without looking up, Qosja's index finger homed in on us as if it were the arrow of a compass and we were magnetic north. The blonde was searching at windows as they walked along outside our train, coming closer. I nudged Jean-Paul. He opened his eyes and looked up just as the two men hopped into the car ahead of ours. The train had already begun to huff, the whistle blew, and I felt the wheels under us rumble to life. I grabbed the backpack and we bailed out of our seats, staying low as we raced for the rear door. We were four steps from our goal when the conductor climbed in and pulled up his stool.

I called out, *"Scusi, scusi,"* and pointed at Jean-Paul, who indeed did not look well. When I caught the conductor's eye, I did my best to pantomime vomiting. The conductor, who would be the guy who had to clean up any mess if that sort of event actually did happen, understood well enough that, with a horrified look on his face, he handed us down onto the platform just as the train began to chug forward. We both faltered a step, off balance. This time, Jean-Paul grabbed me by the coat sleeve and pulled me into the middle of a clutch of well-lubricated youth who had watched our clumsy exit with great and noisy amusement. We ducked in among them, hunching low, using them as a shield against the eyes of anyone looking out from inside the train.

"Shh," Jean-Paul said to them, touching his lips. "Her husband is on that train."

A boy whose head was shaved except for a long green hank that fell over his eyes, aimed a grubby finger at the stitchery on Jean-Paul's face. "He do that to you, mate?"

With a nod, Jean-Paul said, "Bastard."

The kids, about an equal number of boys and girls, older teens, Brits from the sound of them, thought this was terrific fun and closed in around us, making a great show of nonchalance— nothing happening here, nothing to see—that would never win them any acting prizes, but did shelter us. I was able to peek out through gaps between shoulders, bags, and arms as the train gained momentum. Through the windows, we watched Qosja and the blond enter the rear of the car we had vacated, Qosja still with his eyes focused on his telephone screen, or whatever device he held. Before the inter-carriage door closed behind him, his head popped up. He looked around, confused. After another glance at the device he pivoted and pointed right at us as he shouted something at the blonde. But it was too late for them to get off the moving train. The last I saw of them as the train passed by was Blondie's face pressed up against a window, mouth set in a grim and angry line as he searched the platform, looking for us.

"Is that him?" one of the tattooed and pierced girls asked me. "That white-haired old wanker?"

"Yes. That's the beast. Thank you for your help."

"*Prego,*" she said with a self-conscious giggle. Then, with a wise-ass grin, she announced, "You see, as I was just saying, the whole world has gone to shit. If the mummies and daddies are fooling around, what's left?"

Jean-Paul and I both laughed as we straightened up and brushed ourselves off. These kids were just about the same ages as my daughter, Casey, and his son, Dominic. Would our beloved off-spring have done the same for a couple of over-forty delinquents? I wondered.

"The old wanker has a tracker app on ya'," a tall, skinny sprig offered. "He put 'un on your mobile like my dad did on me. Always knew where to find me, my dad did."

I looked at Jean-Paul and he nodded. The kid was right. We were being electronically tracked. But how? Our pursuers couldn't be using our never-used, anonymous, batteryless telephones to locate us. So, how were we giving off signals?

Just then, a vaporetto pulled up to the stop outside the station and out poured another throng of chilled, party-weary humanity.

Jean-Paul slipped his hand around my elbow. "Come along, my delectable little Canadian. Time to leave."

"It's cold out here," I said to the group, nodding toward a café on the far side of the platform that was still open. "Before your train comes, may we treat you all to a hot drink? Maybe a snack?"

There was general agreement that that was a good idea. I folded some euros into the hand of the kid whose dad had put a tracker app on his phone and said, "This should cover the tab."

They walked us as far as the vaporetto stop, and after a round of farewells, they headed off toward the café amid a welter of chatter.

The only other people on the vaporetto when it pulled away from the train station was a young couple necking on the rear seat, and the pilot. We sat near the front, ready to make a fast exit if we needed to.

Jean-Paul cradled his left elbow, and I knew his shoulder ached. He was scarily wan. When I laid my hand along his cheek, he turned to me and asked, "How are they tracking us?"

I had no idea. As the vaporetto carried us away from the train station, we went over everything in our possession. Without their batteries, the phones didn't send out locator signals. I had disabled the picture-sharing capability on my camera before I left Paris. So, what was left? We emptied the backpack, making two piles on the seat between us: the freshly laundered clothes I brought with me, the things I bought for him that afternoon, the paperback book I

picked up at Orly, the red handbag from the shop on the Rialto
Bridge. One by one, we examined every item, and then gave the
backpack I had found at the bottom of an armoire in Isabelle's
apartment a very thorough going-over before putting anything
back inside. Even the leather bank pouch was turned inside out
and prodded.

So far, we had found nothing among our meager possessions
that, even by the greatest stretch of the imagination, could be
transmitting our location to someone. That did not change the
fact that, somehow, we were doing exactly that. As I put the red
handbag back into the backpack, I thought about how easy it had
been for Jean-Paul's hacker to slip the little memory drive into
my coat pocket. All day, I had been surrounded by people, been
pushed and crowded, bumped into, stumbled around, squeezed
in beside. Anyone could have slipped a tracking device on me at
any time.

Except, it had to have happened before I left Paris.

The first time I saw the tall blond man was in Paris. He came
into the shop where I bought the telephones. It was a small shop,
but even so, there was room for him to step aside when I wanted to leave. Instead, he crowded the door so that I had to brush
against him and walk under his arm to get out. At the time, I simply
thought he was creepy, and I was happy to get out of there. Later,
when he showed up on the same flight, I thought it was just bad
luck.

I wrapped my Pashmina around Jean-Paul's neck and said,
"Give me your coat."

Without question, without hesitation, he did. I spread the
heavy coat over our laps and as I examined it, I tried to remember
everything I could about the brief moment of physical contact
between me and the blonde in the electronics shop. He'd held the
door open with one upraised arm, but where was the other hand?
I remembered the blast of cold wind coming through the open
shop door, and regretted that I hadn't brought a scarf. Just as I
walked past him, I flipped up the collar of Freddy's coat to cover
my ears.

So, cuddled next to Jean-Paul on a hard vaporetto seat, I flipped up the collar of Freddy's coat. And found it. The coat had a hood that folded into a slit under the base of the collar. A slender piece of molded black plastic, no more than a quarter of an inch wide and twice that in length, was attached to the fabric inside the hood slit by a pair of fine, sharp wire prongs. I pulled it out and handed it to Jean-Paul.

"*Merde*," he said, shivering, as he looked at the pernicious little device. "How easy it is, yes?"

"Very." I helped him back on with the coat. "You were right. They went after me as a way to get to you. I'm guessing that they put a watch on Isabelle's apartment until I showed up. And then just followed me right to your doorstep. Jean-Paul, I put you in danger by coming."

"Maggie, *mon coeur*, how long do you imagine they would have been happy following you around the shops of Paris before forcing your hand?"

"Maybe sent a loaded drone over rue Jacob to get me?" I tucked the ends of the Pashmina into his coat, smoothing it over his chest before buttoning him up. "We're here now. What might have happened doesn't matter now, does it?"

"*Non.*" He tossed the tracker into the canal and watched the ripple it left after disappearing below the surface of the dark water. "*Adieu, mes amis, adieu.* But, what next for Maggie MacGowen and Jean-Paul Bernard? We can't go back to Gille's apartment. Any ideas?"

"Just one," I said. "I ran into an old friend today, Roddy Combes. Do you know who he is?"

He nodded. "He has a talk show on American TV. He's here, in Venice?"

"Yes." I pulled Roddy's card out of my jeans pocket and handed it to him. "He's throwing a party tonight on a yacht moored at Marina Sant'Elena. If we go to him, maybe he'll give us a bed for the night. Or a warm corner to curl up in. He's bound to have a computer we can use."

"Do you trust him?"

"I do. As much as I trust anyone right now."

Jean-Paul seemed skeptical. "It's late. Will he be up?"

"He told me his party would start after ten, so he must be up still. Right now, I think our options are potluck at Roddy's, or necking on the vaporetto all night."

"The latter would be lovely if these seats weren't so damn hard. Save my spot, I'll be right back."

He went forward to speak with the vaporetto pilot. There was a lot of gesturing and pointing and discussion. I pulled up my collar and settled down into my coat, hands in pockets, and watched beautiful Venice—La Serenissima, the most serene—glide by. At last, all was quiet. The pavilions had gone dark for the night, their raucous music silenced. Random lights from palazzo windows and verandas of small hotels tossed glitter across the caps of the rippled water. I have always loved the heady pleasures of Venice. But even though we had found the tracking device and disposed of it, menace seemed to lurk down every dark walkway or side canal. I shivered, and it wasn't entirely because of the cold.

Jean-Paul and the pilot shook hands and parted. As he settled back down beside me, he said, "We'll change at San Marco; the vaporetto to the marina will be right along."

Happily, the crowds at San Marco were nearly gone, and those few people who were left weren't headed toward the yacht harbor. We took seats a few rows from the front and huddled together against the cold.

"So," I said. "We're partners."

He kissed the top of my head. "Through thick and through thin, yes?"

"I meant business partners; rue Jacob."

"Oh." A strange, pensive look crossed his face while he seemed to think that through. When he turned to me, there was a deep furrow between his brows. "I suppose, yes. I hadn't thought of it that way, but yes, you and I now share ownership of number seven."

"Along with Uncle Gérard and Freddy."

"We really must get you a more informative *notaire, chérie*." He wrapped his good arm around me and pulled me closer. "Isabelle and I bought out Gérard's share a long time ago."

"That must have cost a bundle," I said; just how wealthy was Isabelle? And Jean-Paul? I had never asked.

"It would have been prohibitive if we had to come up with cash," he said. "But the situation was more one of Gérard paying us back by signing over his share of the building than us paying out anything to him."

"He borrowed money from you?"

Jean-Paul shook his head. "Not as simple as that, no. Number seven is a very old building, yes? Three buildings, in fact, tenuously connected by the cellars. There were some fixtures—a stone fireplace surround, about a hectare of hand-carved oak paneling, a few pieces of very old artwork, some books; that sort of thing—that Gérard removed during construction and sold. Without consulting Isabelle or me."

"He pocketed the cash?"

With a little shrug, and a surprisingly fond smile, he said, "*Gérard, toujours Gérard, oui?*"

"A lot of money?"

He nodded, still smiling softly. It was a puzzle to me that Jean-Paul and Gérard were still good friends. But they were.

"So," he said, "Gérard has been out of the picture almost from the beginning; it was Isabelle who found him out. The next little item your *notaire* should have been clear about telling you is that Freddy has no inheritance rights of any degree to rue Jacob."

"How is that possible?" I asked, taken aback. "I thought all of Isabelle's estate was to be divided equally between Freddy and me. Everything share-and-share-alike."

He looked at me askance. "Everything?"

"Oh," was all I could manage as several little cogs slipped into place. Everything in Isabelle's estate was to be divided equally between Freddy and me, except for the tontine she set up with my father to make certain that any income from Dad's patents and any earnings from investment of income from those patents, would pass directly to me, their natural child, and to me alone. Feeling a bit ill, I remembered Freddy once saying he wanted to tap his share of the equity in Isabelle's Paris apartment—*résidence*—to help fund the building project in Normandy he was working on. I asked Jean-Paul, "Did Isabelle use royalties from her patents to invest in rue Jacob?"

He shrugged. "I don't know where her money came from; I never asked. I only know that I share title in rue Jacob with a tontine that was originally owned jointly by Isabelle, someone named Alfred Duchamps, and their daughter, Marguerite Duchamps. I only learned that Maggie MacGowen, a face familiar to me from American television, was in fact Marguerite, the sole survivor of the tontine, when your Uncle Gérard asked me to arrange the transport of Isabelle's ashes home to France from Los Angeles. I admit I was intrigued by that, but until now I hadn't really thought about the implications of sharing the property with you. Should we shake hands or something to seal this partnership?"

"I could think of doing something more interesting than shaking hands," I said. "But, in the meantime, do you know if Freddy knows he has no claim on rue Jacob?"

"*Bien sûr.*" Of course. "Now he does, anyway. When Isabelle's will went into probate, Freddy petitioned to separate his expected share of her ownership at rue Jacob from yours and mine so that he could use it as collateral for a loan. I would have turned down his petition even if you had co-signed it because such a loan could put the entire property at risk if he defaulted. But before I could respond, the *notaire* informed Freddy that he has no legal claim whatsoever to any part of number seven, rue Jacob."

"What a blow that had to be, with all the other crap he's had to deal with. Was he angry when he found out?"

"I asked Gérard to explain the facts to him. Your uncle had already turned down Freddy's attempt to get a loan against his expected inherited share of your grandmother's Paris townhouse, and for the same reason: A default would jeopardize Gérard's share, and yours. Your uncle told me Freddy seemed to be more embarrassed than angry."

"When was this?"

"Sometime last spring. April, May? After his wife's trial, at any rate."

"I was with Freddy in Normandy most of the summer, and he never brought it up. But his wife—his ex-wife by then—had just been convicted and I know he had other things on his mind. And maybe after he heard from the *notaire*, he thought there was nothing to discuss."

"Or, was who inherited what from Isabelle a topic he was afraid to bring up?" He playfully nudged my shoulder with his. "Remind me, please, who was it his wife embezzled from?"

"Me."

Jean-Paul took my arm and began to rise. "Here's where we get out, partner."

Standing in the boarding float, waiting for our ride, I looked around, searching for a tail. But there was no one in sight. No one at all.

"I think we shook them," I said.

"For now."

We were the last passengers on the last vaporetto run to Sant'Elena for the night. The marina was at land's end, the last stop on the line. It was very late and very bitter out: Roddy could hardly turn us away. Could he?

The long johns under my jeans helped to break the biting wind blowing in from the open water of the Adriatic as we walked along the marina causeway looking for Roddy's berth. But it was still nasty and cold. I grew up in California so I just do not get along well with this phenomenon called winter. I longed to get inside somewhere warm, and happily would have crashed any of the parties we could see through the windows of moored yachts that we passed along the way. At the far end of the marina, tied stern-to-bow with a craft befitting a Greek shipping magnate, we found Roddy's rented sea-going palace. A smartly uniformed behemoth came out to meet us as we started up the gangway.

"I'm a friend of Roddy," I said, showing the big man the card Roddy gave me that afternoon. Without saying anything, but never taking his eyes off us, he pressed a buzzer on a device in his hand. Immediately, a speaker somewhere crackled to life and Roddy's voice boomed through the night: "Permission to board granted, Maggie MacGowen."

As we walked up the gangway, I looked for the security camera that had showed us to Roddy and found several. Jean-Paul saw them, too. He slid his hand through the crook of my elbow, leaned in close, and said, "Smile."

A steward appeared from nowhere to usher us into the main salon. We walked through big double doors and right into the hot glare of a bank of television lights and cameras. When Jean-Paul balked, I put my lips to his ear and whispered, "It's okay, it isn't a live feed. We won't be anywhere near here when this airs, if it airs. And it could be useful later."

He seemed skeptical, but he didn't run and he didn't duck.

Under the lights, I could just make out some details of the opulently appointed salon. Lots of polished brass, teak, and white leather upholstery draped with maybe a dozen of the current crop of Hollywood's beautiful people. As a group, they looked too perfect to be real: perfect hair, perfect television makeup, perfect clothes on perfect bodies, all apparently perfectly happy to be where they were, that is, within range of an active camera lens. The steward was helping Jean-Paul and me off with our coats when Roddy, fully pumped up into his jolly on-camera—host mode, thrust a microphone toward us and launched into his patter. I thought he'd been tippling.

"Hey, look who has just blown in off the minefields of Laos. My old friend filmmaker Maggie MacGowen and her handsome French diplomat boyfriend. Welcome, welcome, you two. Ever so happy to see you."

"You haven't seen us," I said, snagging a glass of wine off a passing tray. "We aren't here. Haven't been seen for days. Just, *pfft*, vanished, both of us."

Roddy leaned toward the camera and winked. "I wonder where they could be."

When he stepped back, he wrapped an arm around Jean-Paul

and, with the microphone held close to his lips, he whispered: "Any clues as to when you two might return?"

"None at all," Jean-Paul whispered back into the mic. "We're quite happy being nowhere."

Standing that close to Jean-Paul, drunk or not, dear old Roddy couldn't miss the lines of fine black stitches and the sleeve without an arm. He backed up and said, "Dear God, man, did you step on one of Maggie's landmines?"

I caught Roddy's eye and made the CUT gesture with my hand. For just a moment, he hesitated. But then he looked straight into the camera and made the same gesture. The film lights went out, a grip came over and claimed the microphone, and, as if on cue, everyone in the room seemed to melt back into reality. As a group, without the camera to make them shimmer, Roddy's guests looked a bit dispirited. Bored. The sudden shift was surreal.

"Maggie," Roddy said. "What the hell?"

"Can we have a private word?"

Without excusing himself, and without anyone seeming to pay much attention, Roddy led us out of the salon and down a short flight of stairs and into a small sitting room that had been set up as an office. He dropped into a big leather chair and said, "So tell old Uncle Rod what's going on."

"We're in a bit of a pickle, Roddy, and we need some help."

"A bit of a pickle, Maggie? Or serious trouble?"

"Trouble enough." I took out my camera and showed him the shots I had taken of our two shadows. "These men have been tracking us. The blond guy followed me from Paris this morning. The other one, Sabri Qosja, is a known hired gun. We have no idea what they want, though we have a hunch that whatever it is, we won't like it. For now, we think we've shaken them off our tail."

He nodded toward Jean-Paul. "Did these blokes do that to you?"

"*Oui.* They or their friends."

"With fists?"

"No. Plastic explosives."

"You're lucky to be alive, man." Roddy leaned forward, sweetly concerned, and very serious. "What do you need from me?"

"Tonight," I said, "the use of your computer and a safe bed. We'll do our best to disappear in the morning."

He took the camera from my hand. "I'll print up some copies of your shots and have my security lads keep a watch out. Shall I send your photos to network research, see what they can pull up?"

I looked at Jean-Paul. He thought for a moment before he said, "*Pourquoi pas?* That's a better resource than anything I have access to at the moment."

"By the way." Roddy extended his hand to Jean-Paul. "We haven't actually met. Roddy Combes here, general horse's arse, but a well-practiced one."

Jean-Paul smiled as he took the offered hand. "Jean-Paul Bernard here, a sorry wreck of a man."

"Good to know you. Now: computer is on the desk behind you. I'll have a steward show you to a stateroom when you're ready. Have you eaten?"

"We have," I said. "Thanks, Roddy. Sorry to interrupt your party."

"If I were an honest man, I'd tell you that I wasn't having the least bit of fun. And neither are they. Maggie, I'm getting too old to chat up this generation of celebrity kids. Bugger all if they absolutely don't get half my jokes; no common frame of reference is the thing. And I refuse to even try to understand the crap they pass off as music. Rap? What the hell is rap, anyway? Lord, they bore me. And I know that the only thing about me that they find to be the least bit interesting is their fekkin faces in front of my fekkin cameras."

I extended my half-consumed glass of wine. "You need this more than I do."

He threw back his head and laughed his great big *haw-haw* laugh. "There's plenty more where that came from; you keep it. Anything else I can do for you two?"

"One thing," I said. "Please hold that bit you shot with us upstairs. Pretty soon, someone is going to notice that Jean-Paul and

I have fallen off the face of the earth, and there will be questions. If that happens, will you consider broadcasting the piece?"

"What do I say about it?"

"I don't know. Jean-Paul?"

"I think we dropped by on our way to sail the South Pacific. Tahiti bound. Maggie, have we eloped?"

"Honeymooning in the South Pacific? Sure. Great idea."

"I'll hold the tape," Roddy said. "But you have to promise me the scoop on this story when all is over and done with. And if you do manage to elope, I get the story first. Deal?"

"Sure," I said. "But, Roddy, I'm not much of a celebrity. I doubt anyone but our mothers will pay much attention. Or care."

"I can make it as big a story as I want to," he said with a resigned sigh. He studied the carpet at his feet for a moment before he looked up and caught my eye. "Was Laos wonderful?"

"It was. Very wonderful."

"That's a trip I should make."

"You couldn't get there on this bathtub, you know. It's a land-locked country."

"My tenure on this bathtub, as you call it, expires on the mor-row. No, I was thinking more along the lines of trekking out with a camera crew."

"Are you after my job, Roddy?"

"I am certainly bored with my own." With effort, he pushed himself out of his chair and moved toward the door. "Whistle if you want anything. I need to go summon water taxis to carry my guests away. It's bedtime for this old fart."

I heard his heavy steps on the stairs leading up to the main salon.

Jean-Paul went to the computer on the desk and plugged in the USB memory drive his hacker had dropped into my pocket on the Rialto Bridge. While he pored over the report, I curled up in a deep leather chair, sipped the wonderful wine, tried to stay awake, and enjoyed the first truly peaceful moment I'd felt for a very long time. After a few minutes, I set my feet on the floor, yawned, stretched, and asked, "What are you finding out?"

"Exactly what I suspected. We were both hacked: credit cards, ATM use, emails, social media sites. And there was a tracker app placed on our phones. Your trail went cold in Paris this morning, and mine went cold in Greece on Sunday."

"Who's doing this to us?"

"My little juvenile delinquent says our hacker is a kid he knows in Taiwan."

"He knows him?"

"Knows his work, anyway. These hackers are usually really young guys. For them, hacking is a sport, something like a real-world version of online video gaming. They set up challenges for each other, and when they score, like taggers they sign their work. Then they brag online to each other. Skillful, yes. Wise, no."

"I thought my mobile phone was secure," I said.

Jean-Paul shook his head. "When the American intelligence agencies couldn't get into the mobile phone of a dead terrorist and the manufacturer wouldn't help, who did they turn to?"

"Some kid," I said, dismayed. "I can't believe, though, that this little asshole in Taiwan would send a loaded drone after you, or slit a woman's throat, or follow me across Europe. So, who hired him?"

"Don't know that yet. Our own little Venetian asshole, whose online moniker is AnoNino, put a RAT, a Remote Access Trojan, on the computer of the hacker in Taiwan, who calls himself crouchingdragon. Before the crouching dragon discovered the RAT on his system and removed it, AnoNino was able to find a recent series of electronic cash transfers to a credit card the boy apparently has access to; the kid is too young to have his own bank account. The routing numbers trace back to a bank in London."

"Can AnoNino attach a name to the transfers?"

"He's working on it." Jean-Paul pulled the memory drive out of the computer's USB port and set it on the desk. "He found the bank, but hacking into a bank's database to find the name on an account might be beyond him. Good little spook that he is, though, he managed to trace the tracker app backward, so now we have a phone number."

"Do you want to call the number?"

"Not yet. As soon as we do, they'll just toss the phone, if they haven't already. The good news is, the only interest seems to rest on you and me."

"That's good news?"

He shrugged, meaning yes. "They aren't hacking or tracking our children, *chérie*. Or anyone in our families. Guido: no trail. No one is following Eduardo Suarez, or anyone else in the EU consortium that sent the two of us to Greece. Knowing that is important to me. If whatever this is, is only about me, or about you, maybe it will be easier to figure out."

"If we live long enough."

He laughed softly. "If that, yes."

"So, if no one is monitoring friends and family, it should be okay to make some calls, right?"

His little shrug said, *Bien sûr.* "That might change once Qosja and company discover they've lost track of us, but yes, do it while you can. I'd like a word with a friend who has better access to bank information than AnoNino. Maybe he'll be able to find something useful for us."

"You trust him?" I asked.

"As much as anyone." He opened the backpack, gave me one of the phones, took another for himself, and fished a credit card out of the bank pouch. As I dialed Mom's phone, he was thumbing keys on his phone with impressive agility for a man with one hand.

It was after one in Venice, so it was late afternoon in Los Angeles. Mom answered on the second ring.

"Maggie? Whose phone are you calling from? Where are you? Your grandmother called from Normandy hoping I knew where to contact you. Everyone seemed to be calling her, looking for you. Then Guido called. Promise me someone didn't knock you over the head and leave you for dead in a dark Paris alley."

"I'm fine. I'm with Jean Paul, and he's fine, too. How are you?"

"Me? Worried sick. I know something is going on, Maggie."

"What if we're just lounging in some fleshpot, sun on our bellies, rum drinks with little umbrellas in our hands?"

"What if you're not. Don't schmooze me, young lady."

I laughed. "The last person who called me young lady was a shoe salesman who tried to give me an ankle massage."

"Age is relative, my love. Now, where the hell are you?"

"Truthfully, I'm on a yacht in the Adriatic with Jean-Paul. I'm only telling you this so that you don't call out a search party. Do let folks know we're fine. But please don't broadcast where we are: not Casey, or Grand-mère, or Gracie Nussbaum, or the six o'clock news team. If anyone asks, please just say that you heard from us, and everything is just peachy. We've both been working crazy schedules so we're taking a well-earned break, staying under the radar, just resting up."

"How much of that is true?"

"Enough of it so you won't have to go to confession if you repeat it."

"You know very well that I haven't been to confession for over twenty years."

"Mom?"

"Yes, dear. Your secret is safe with me."

"I love you," I said.

"A good damn thing you do. Kisses to you both." And she hung up.

Jean-Paul had finished with whatever he was doing on his phone and was eavesdropping on the end of my call; he adores Mom, and it's mutual. "How is Elizabeth?"

"Mom is just fine," I said. "Learn anything?"

"My friend is working on the bank routing number. And I have an update from AnoNino," he said. "Monsieur crouchingdragon has sent out a challenge to his network of hacker friends. The first to spot the two of us and identify our location will get some sort of prize."

"Spot us how?"

"That is the game, yes? They are invited to be creative."

"What are we going to do about it?

"We're going to wait until we hear back from our little criminal. That means we have to keep this phone turned on so he can get in touch with us. He'll let us know if someone puts a RAT on the line."

"There must be something more we can do."

He sagged back into his chair. "My head is swimming. Right now, all I want to do is take another pain pill and go to bed. Tomorrow will start early, I'm afraid."

Bed sounded like a good idea. We gathered our things and headed for the door. Immediately, a steward appeared. With a little flourish and bow, he said, "Your stateroom is just along here."

I slung the backpack over my shoulder and waited for Jean-Paul. We had only gone a few steps down the passageway when someone called my name. A soft female voice. We all turned. A young woman wearing full on-camera makeup, shiny form-fitting pants, and a shoulder-baring silk blouse, stuffed her mobile phone under her waistband as she rose from the top of the stairs leading up into the main salon; clearly she had been waiting for me to appear. On very tall heels, she took a tentative step toward me.

"Maggie," she said. "Do you remember me?"

I did, sort of. I had to look past the clothes and makeup before I recognized her, though her name eluded me. She had been an intern on a project Guido and I worked on together maybe a year and a half earlier. Guido had recruited her from among his acolytes at the UCLA film school. Like all the student interns Guido brought into our projects over the years, she was bright, talented, beautiful, young, female, and ambitious. For many of his recruits, and certainly for this one, Guido was a potential rung on their ladder to film greatness, and they were, too often, notches in his belt. What set this young woman apart was that she hadn't stayed with us for very long. Without giving notice, she dumped Guido and our project for something shinier. Now, as she walked toward me, for all the painted-on veneer labeling her as an entertainment-world insider, a member of the film cognoscenti, or wannabe of same, she reminded me of a street urchin; all hope abandoned.

But what was her name? A place name, I thought, running through some possibilities—Dakota, Nevada, Atchison, Topeka, or Santa Fe?—before it came to me. "Sierra?"

She smiled, relieved, it seemed, that I did remember. "It's been a while," she said, venturing further down the stairs.

I handed the backpack to the steward, told Jean-Paul to go ahead, and promised that I would join him very soon. He kissed my cheek and with a skeptical backward glance followed the steward to a stateroom a few doors along the passageway.

Sierra's first question: "How's Guido?"

"Last time I saw him, he was fine."

"He was with you in Laos?"

"He was."

There was an uncomfortable pause while she decided on the next thing to say and while I tried to figure out her angle. Finally, she said, "He must hate me."

"I wouldn't know." And I wouldn't. I was so thoroughly fed up with Guido's often messy sexual pursuits that he knew better than to bring them up around me. He was my age, forty-three, and his conquests were rarely less than twenty years younger.

"I'm sorry I just walked out on you the way I did. It was wrong of me. Immature. I hope I didn't leave you in the lurch."

"We managed to muddle through. The program aired last May."

She acknowledged the truth of that with a sad bob of her head before forcing up a smile. "I saw it. It was wonderful. I was hoping for a screen credit. Guess I didn't stay around long enough to earn one, huh?"

I stifled a yawn. "It's late. Was there something?"

"Sorry to keep you," she said. "I just wanted to say hi."

"Good luck to you, Sierra." I turned and walked toward the stateroom where Jean-Paul was waiting.

"Maggie," she said. I looked at her over my shoulder. "Give my best to Guido."

"Will do." I turned again and walked away, feeling like a hard-hearted bitch. She was just a kid, trying to make amends. Maybe she had learned something useful after leaving us, as she said, in the lurch. And maybe not.

I was snuggled up in a very luxurious bed, dreaming about something I can't remember, when I became aware of the thrumming of the yacht's huge engines. I rose enough to look out the porthole next to the bed and saw that we were moving. My first thought was to wake Jean-Paul, but he looked so peaceful that I disentangled myself from him as quietly as I could, pulled on my jeans and a sweater, and slipped out of the stateroom into the passageway outside. I had gone only a few steps before the steward appeared.

"Signora," he said, gesturing for me to precede him. "Signore Combes wishes to see you on the bridge."

The bridge looked like the control center at NASA Houston. The man I assumed was the captain by the amount of gold braid on his uniform, stood with his first mate in front of a multi-tiered flashing, blipping digital console, absorbed by the complexities involved in powering up and piloting the vessel they commanded. Roddy and his musclebound security man were to one side, in front of a bank of security camera monitors.

"Gentlemen, Signora MacGowen," my escort announced when we walked in.

The captain and the first officer glanced away from their posts just long enough to tip their caps to me before turning back.

"Jay-zuss, Maggie," Roddy said, waving me over. "I was about to blow a whistle to rouse you. You must sleep the sleep of the dead."

"Not yet," I said, hesitating near the door. "We're moving."

"Yes," Roddy said with feigned enthusiasm. "How does breakfast in Ravenna sound?"

"I thought you were headed for Munich next."

"I'm sure I can find my way to Munich from Ravenna. Maggie, luv, come have a look."

Roddy and the security man made room for me between them. There were six screens flashing images from security cameras that were strategically placed around the entire perimeter of the yacht. The cameras followed Sabri Qosja, this time sans telephone, piloting a quiet, ten-foot wave-eater motorboat along the yacht's starboard side. At mid-ship, he pulled in close enough to stick something to the hull before he motored into the darkness of the marina beyond camera range.

"Is this live?" I asked.

Roddy shook his head. "Fifteen minutes ago. That's the fella, Qosja, is it?

"It is."

He tipped his chin toward the security man. "By the time Horst here got a skiff into the water to give chase, he was gone."

"What did Qosja put on the hull?"

The security man, Horst, picked up a gray rectangular box about the size of a deck of cards. An antenna stuck out of the top, next to a flashing red light.

"Is it ticking?" I asked.

"Yup," Roddy said. "Horst has seen this sort of device before. It's a radio-activated detonator. Someone can send a signal by phone or by radio from as far as a hundred miles away. Maybe more. The call comes in, activates the detonator, detonator sets off the attached explosive, and *boom*."

"You're just going to let it tick?" I was ready to go grab Jean-Paul and bolt.

"*Ja,*" Horst said. "If we block the signal before we get out to sea, he'll just come back and try again. Or try something else. But I disarmed the detonator. See?"

He turned the box on end and flicked a little button. "Fail-safe switch. The device can still receive, but it won't go off. This model is used in construction, not warfare. Cheap. Easy to come by."

"It isn't very big. How much damage—" was as far as I got before Horst handed me a plastic-wrapped block of stuff, about the same shape and weight as a pound of butter, but that looked and felt like modeling clay. I smelled it before handing it back. "Is this gelignite, or something like it? Plastic explosive?"

Horst nodded. "Enough to blow a damn big hole in the hull."

"But it's harmless, right?"

"Without a detonator, yes," Roddy said. "Horst wants to know how this Qosja fella knew you were on the boat."

"I told you earlier, someone was tracking us. But we found the locator thingy and tossed it into the canal. We thought we were in the clear."

"Maybe there's a second transponder," Horst said. "Or many. Mind if I take a look?"

"Please do," I said, gesturing toward the door.

We were walking down the stairs, me, Horst, Roddy, in that order, when the door to one of the staterooms opened and Sierra, bed hair, barefoot, clothes clearly put on in haste, stepped into the passageway.

"The boat's moving," she said, clearly not happy about the obvious. She had a phone in her hand, her thumbs moving furiously. "Where the hell are we going?"

I reached out and snatched the phone out of her hands. She was typing a Tweet: "WTF, yacht's moving. Where are we—"

I handed the phone to Roddy.

"A better question," Roddy said after seeing the Tweet, "is who the hell are you and how the hell did you get onto my boat?"

"I'm a guest," she answered, not the least chagrined. "Give me my phone."

"Guest of whom?" he demanded, passing the phone to Horst.

"Mitch," she said. "Mitch invited me. My phone, please. Now."

Roddy pushed through the ajar stateroom door behind her and shouted in his great big voice, "Mitch, you perv, front and center."

There was a rustling inside the darkened stateroom before a very rumpled Mitch appeared wearing only boxer shorts. I knew him. Mitchell O'Meara was a line producer at the television network that employed both Roddy and me. I had worked with him several times, and now and then ran into him at the studio or on film shoots. His wife, Ellen, worked in the editing bay. Nice lady.

Mitch stood leaning on the door jamb, sleepy, probably either still a little drunk or already suffering from a hangover. He rubbed his eyes, yawned, sniffled, scratched before seeming to come to. When he looked up, finally, he spotted me.

"Hey, Maggie. What's up? Saw you come in earlier, but you disappeared before I had a chance to say hi. It's been a while. Heard you were out of the country working on something."

"Hey yourself, Mitch," I said. "How's Ellen?"

He quailed, said, "She's good."

"Mitchell, tell this guy to give me back my phone."

"What?" he said, eyes all squinty.

Horst paid no attention to Sierra as he scrolled through her Tweets. He stopped at one, tapped my shoulder and showed me. "OMG my former boss Maggie MacGowen is here now. Love this yacht. #veniceCarnevale #roddycombes #santelena #mmacginvestigates." A grainy photo followed of Jean-Paul and me as we took off our coats when we arrived. He scrolled to another: "Big chat with former boss Maggie MacGowen on the yacht. Hope to work with her again. She's sleeping over, too. Yayy!"

I said, "Lordy. Should have known. How many people who were here last night sent out photos or messages like these?"

Roddy held up his hands. "They were instructed to keep a lid on that shit, but it's the price we pay, Maggie, when we put ourselves out there."

"Well, now we know how Qosja found us," I said. "Damn. Damn. Damn."

"I want off this boat," Sierra demanded, nearly in tears. "And I want my fucking phone."

"Sierra, honey," I said. "You're just not doing yourself any favors right now."

Horst, still scrolling through her messages, barely glanced up. "You'll get off when we dock tomorrow."

"Mitchell!" she gasped through sobs. "Do something."

After a deep sigh, Mitch turned to Roddy. "Hey, man."

"Pally, do you remember that crisp white paper you signed? The one about not shifting proprietary shite onto social media without permission? Or the one about not having overnight guests without clearing them first with Horst?"

"Sorry, man. Sorry. It's not really overnight yet, though, is it? I mean, the sun isn't up. And whatever the deal is with the chick's phone, man, I didn't know what she was doing. I was asleep."

"The chick?" Sierra screeched, grabbing for him. "You piece of crap. The chick?"

Roddy looked weary. "Horst?"

With a sigh, Horst took Sierra by the elbow, whispered something into her ear that quieted her protests, and walked her back up the stairs and out of sight.

"Where's he taking her?" I asked.

Roddy held up his palms. "Dunno. He'll either make her walk the plank or tuck her up in sick bay."

"Rod?" Mitch said.

"Go to bed, Mitch. Tomorrow will be a very long day for all of us. Be warned that I will devise some onerous penance for you to perform."

Mitch nodded and turned to go back into his stateroom, but paused, seemed to listen for a moment before slowly looking around at Roddy. "Is the boat moving?"

"Nah. You're just drunk. Go on, pally, go sleep it off."

"Thank you, Roddy," I said, stretching up to kiss his cheek. "Sorry to have landed all this on you."

"Hell, Maggie, no apology necessary. Nothing as interesting has happened since— Since I don't know when."

"I wonder what's next."

"Horst thinks that sometime tomorrow there may be a report of an explosion of unknown origin aboard a yacht sailing the Adriatic. It would be unfortunate, but entirely possible, that two of my guests will be lost at sea."

5

"GUIDO, I NEED A FAVOR."

After a pause, Guido managed to say, "Maggie? Why did you track me down through the studio switchboard? You know my number. And why the hell are you in Italy? I thought you were going to Paris."

"Enough with the third degree. And how do you know I'm in Italy?" I sat on the edge of one of the big chairs in Roddy's office, afraid that if I sat back and got comfortable I'd fall asleep.

"Max called, looking for you. He has a Google alert on both of us, you know, so he gets a ding every time your name or mine pops up on social media in case there's a fire he needs to put out. Always looking out for us, your Uncle Max. Anyway, someone tweeted some stuff about you at a party in Italy. Max called me when he couldn't get in touch with you."

"The tweeter was your old buddy, Sierra."

The name opened a quiet gap in the conversation for a few beats. "No shit? Her? What's she doing in Italy? Who cares. What are *you* doing in Italy? And what's with all this weird phone stuff, huh?"

"Guido." It was late. Or early, depending on one's point of view.

And I was cranky. I sounded cranky. Snappish, actually. Not a good way to begin asking for help. "Sorry. I'll fill in the blanks later, okay? How close are you with your Italian cousins? I need a car."

"No, not okay. Tell me what's going on, Mags. Why do you need a car?"

"To get the hell out of Italy."

Again he paused, probably working things through. "Are you in some kind of trouble, partner?"

"Yes. That's why I need help finding a car."

"You can't just rent one?"

"No. So, back to the beginning: how close are you with your Italian cousins?"

"I stay in touch with the ones who owe me money," he said. "You want me to ask one to steal you a car?"

"I hadn't thought of that. I was hoping for a loaner."

"A loaner," he repeated, sounding doubtful. "There are a few things I need to explain to you about men and their cars and why they don't lend them to strangers who are in trouble. So, why don't you tell me what's up and I'll see what I can do."

I told him, in brief, about the situation. At least, the little I actually knew about what the situation was. Bombs he understood. And cyber-stalking by known mercenaries. I told him that we would dock in Ravenna at about eight o'clock in the morning, Italian time, and that I would need wheels.

"See how easy that was, Mags? I'll make some calls and get back to you."

"Let me give you a phone number to use."

"What happened to your phone?"

"Guido, this is a burner."

"A burner? A throwaway?"

"Yes. After I hear back from you, I'm throwing it into the Adriatic."

"No, really, where's your phone?"

"Guido—"

"Okay, okay," he said, and wrote down the number I gave him. I started to say good-bye, but he headed off onto a new topic. "Hey,

I got the message you left about the meeting with the French TV people on Monday. Are you going to make it? Do you need me to come over and take the meeting?"

"I hate to ask you to get right back on an airplane, but would you? Even if I do manage to get there, you should sit in on the discussion. The decision about working with them, or not, isn't mine alone to make."

"I'll book the first flight I can get. You going to put me up in Paris?"

"Yes, of course. It's number seven, rue Jacob, on the Left Bank. The concierge, Madame Gonsalves, will be expecting you."

After we said good-bye, I curled up in that big cushy chair for a nap because I didn't want the phone to wake Jean-Paul when Guido called back.

By seven in the morning, I was showered and dressed and feeling almost rested when Jean-Paul took me by the hand and we left our stateroom to follow the smell of coffee coming from somewhere upstairs. Jean-Paul's color was better and his fever seemed to be gone, hopeful signs. When he awoke at dawn that morning and discovered that we were at sea, I told him about Sierra's posts and the potentially explosive reappearance of Qosja shortly afterward. And about my conversation with Guido.

"Somehow," he said with a little smile that morning as we walked up the stairs to the main salon, "it seems appropriate that we will meet Guido's cousin—"

"Luigi Cadelago."

"Luigi Cadelago, in the Ravenna cemetery."

"I think it's all about the location and not the function of the site," I said, kissing his freshly shaved cheek.

"How will we recognize this cousin?"

I had to laugh. "He'll be driving a refrigerated fish delivery van."

He shook his head. "I can't seem to get away from fish, can I?"

We found Roddy at a table set for breakfast in a dining room off the main salon. I took the chair the steward held out for me on Roddy's right. Jean-Paul took the seat on his left.

"Top o' the mornin'," Roddy said, pouring coffee into our cups as the steward set plates of prosciutto, fruit, and herbed eggs in front of us. "You two look surprisingly fresh."

"It's a beautiful morning," I said. "Just what I ordered."

Roddy laughed. "Good, because the captain promises more of same for the coming week, with a possibility of snow flurries by late this afternoon."

The day was, as expected, cold and gray. Though the sea around us was full of chop, the ride in that pleasure palace was as smooth as a sail across a quiet lake, as if the Adriatic didn't dare ruffle the comforts of the tender souls who would travel on such a sumptuous vessel.

Roddy rested his elbows on the table and asked, with a sigh, "Was it warm in Laos?"

"It was perfect." I savored the lovely food on my plate. "Warm, dry, green."

"I've been thinking about our conversation last night," he said, holding my eyes.

"The one about you taking over my job?"

He chuckled. Just a hesitant little chuckle. "Not yet, anyway. No, but how about taking me along when you go back to Laos?"

"What makes you think I'm going back?"

"The look on your face when you talk about it," he said. "Business unfinished, I think. Tell me I'm wrong."

"You aren't wrong," I said. "I would love to go back and spend more time. We barely touched the surface during the three weeks we were there. If I did go back, I would want to include Cambodia and Vietnam as well. But first I'd have to sell the idea to our august employer. Or find another backer."

"Rumor has it that you might be ready to jump the mother ship for a different television home," he said. "One in France, of all things."

The comment took me aback; no one should know that except me, Guido, Uncle Max and the French TV folks I was meeting with on Monday. If I got back to Paris in time, that is. I turned to Jean-Paul, but he shook his head. He hadn't said anything. I asked, "Says who?"

"I read it in the trades," Roddy said, reaching for the jam pot.

I needed to call Uncle Max, who was my agent, among other things. It would be like Max to plant a story of that sort in the entertainment news—the trades—just when I was about to come up for contract renewal. Especially if the story was true. And it was.

"We'll see," I said. "We'll see."

"I've been thinking about branching out into something new myself." Roddy leaned forward, more earnest than I had ever seen him. "Perhaps investing some of the obscene salary I'm burdened with in a worthwhile film project of some sort. I was thinking that, if you're available, we might work together over the summer hiatus."

"Summer is monsoon season in Laos," Jean-Paul offered, accepting a coffee refill. "But if you want a worthwhile topic, I would be quite happy to set you up with Doctors without Borders in any number of sites around the world. Or perhaps you would be interested in refugee camps."

And so the conversation went, until we approached land. A steward came into the room and leaned close to Roddy. In a very soft voice, he said, "Captain asked me to tell you, *signore*, that we will drop anchor in twenty minutes. The motor launch will be waiting to take guests ashore whenever they are ready."

"Ravenna?" I said, looking out the window, trying to see some identifiable landmarks. But we were too far away from shore. I felt apprehension gurgle up through the middle of the lovely breakfast. The yacht had felt like a cocoon, a lush and well-fortified shell against people who meant us harm. We couldn't stay, but I hated to go, not knowing who might be out there. Waiting.

Roddy asked, "You're being met?"

"So we are told," Jean-Paul said, rising and offering his hand to Roddy. "Thank you, Roddy. In our current situation, we can only repay your kindness with profound gratitude. But we hope that very soon we will have the opportunity to reciprocate properly. Without the fireworks, of course. And no mercenaries on the guest list."

"Oh, my Maggie girl," Roddy said, rising to pull Jean-Paul

by the proffered hand into an embrace that made the poor dear wince in pain. "What an amazing catch you've made, luv. Such charm."

He released Jean-Paul and gave me a similar squeeze, adding several noisy cheek smooches. "You two turned a pathetically mundane romp into an adventure. It is I who should thank you. However," he said, releasing me from his grip. "You might repay any perceived debt by giving serious consideration to what was said here. I hope we are able to do a deal, if not this summer, then soon."

Jean-Paul's smile told me that he liked the idea of trekking off with Roddy and a film crew. It was something to think about, certainly.

Mitch, freshly scrubbed and crisply dressed but shaky from hangover, chose that moment to wander into the dining room. Using both hands, he managed to pour himself a cup of coffee without spilling very much. He didn't speak until he'd downed half of it. "Where the hell are we?"

"On the briny," Roddy said.

"I can see that, Roddy." Clearly, Mitch was unhappy. "We're pointed south. Last time I looked, Munich was due west from Venice. Over land."

"That is my understanding."

"Where are we? I have us all booked on a flight from Marco Polo Airport at two o'clock this afternoon so that we can get to Munich in time to set up to shoot in Marienplatz tonight."

Roddy turned to me. "Is this Friday?"

"Unless I've lost a day, it is."

"So, then it must be time to decamp for the nonsense in Munich." He aimed a finger at Mitch. "Better get on the horn, my dear producer, and rebook the mob on a flight leaving from Ravenna right away. Our tenure on this old scow expires at noon. I'd ask for an extension but I have a visceral sense that the owners and crew will be happy to see our backsides. They're just a bit nervy about the attempt last night to blow a hole in the hull."

Mitch leaned over to look out a window. "There's a hole in the hull?"

Roddy just shrugged; life is full of little mysteries, he seemed to be saying. I stretched up and gave his cheek a last kiss. "Thank you, for everything."

"Prego," he said with a little bow.

I turned to leave Roddy to deal with his producer, but came right back. Leaning in close, I asked him, "What about the girl?"

"She's having breakfast in bed and will be back in Venice in time for tea," he said, squeezing my hand. "None the wiser about where she's been. In the meantime, Horst has her mobile under lock and key."

Bundled up against the cold, Jean-Paul and I were handed into a sleek shore launch tied up off the yacht's stern, and sent on our way across the last stretch of open water toward the Port of Ravenna. We sat mid-ship, between the first mate at the helm and Horst in the stern, the latter scanning the horizon through binoculars as we sped toward land.

We passed the yacht harbor and the shipping container facility, and entered a long, narrow waterway, the Canale Candiano, that coursed between a commercial fishing pier on one side and wide, empty white sand beaches on the other. A tall iron fence marked the end of the beach and the beginning of the city's ancient cemetery. The closer we came to our meeting point, the more Horst seemed to vibrate with intensity, training his glasses on every tall commercial fishing cabin, shuttered beach concession stand, and moss-covered stone monument that we passed. Watching for a sniper's rifle to appear? Or a security camera, which, all things considered, could be as dangerous. I felt exposed, trapped in the open boat with nowhere to hide, and nowhere to run.

Jean-Paul gripped my hand. "No shadow, yes?"

"Not yet. Here we are, out of the forest and we haven't drawn fire."

"As you said, not yet."

Hardly reassuring, but as we proceeded I began to relax. We could see all the way to the open sea behind us, and no one was following. Unless it was Guido who hired Qosja, an unlikely prospect, there was no way for the people who had pursued us to know ahead of time where we were meeting cousin Luigi. But once we left the shelter of Roddy's rented yacht, we were in the open, and vulnerable.

I learned early on working in television that the safest place to be is in a state of anonymity. I have always been uncomfortable when strangers recognize me somewhere out in the world beyond the television screen. I have been stalked before, and accosted or followed by strangers, so this isn't an unearned queasiness. But, I was thinking as we passed along the cemetery's iron fence, the investigative films I make for American television are rarely seen outside the U.S. and Canada. In Europe, away from places where American tourists gather, I could be—I most likely was—anonymous. Bundled in my coat, collar up over my ears, all that a camera could capture would be the form of a woman of a certain size. It was a comfortable feeling. For insurance, I pulled up Jean-Paul's collar as well.

The first mate cut the motor and drifted in close to a small pier just outside the cemetery's main entrance. When he jumped out to tie up the launch, Horst came forward to stand tight against our backs, and stayed close as we were handed out, first Jean-Paul, and then me. We thanked them both and shook hands all around. I shouldered the backpack and we turned away from the water and our protectors. The road in front of us, via Cimitero, was empty. Not a soul in sight.

"He is meeting us here?" Jean-Paul asked me.

"That's my understanding," I said, checking my watch; we were a few minutes late. "The dock near the front gate of the cemetery, Guido said."

Gesturing toward the road, he said, "Shall we?"

I turned and waved as we started down the road, a last thank you and good-bye, but saw that Horst and the first mate were waiting on the dock for our ride to show up. If he didn't come, what then? I could see the outskirts of Ravenna in the distance, less than a mile away. When I heard the blast of a train whistle, I knew that there was a Plan B nearby. But after we had walked no more than twenty yards, a small blue tradesman's van with PESCE CADELAGO and a jumping fish painted on the side panel careened around a curve in the road and sped toward us. We stayed at the side of the road, on a little berm, and waited. So did Horst and the first mate.

The van passed us, made a U-turn, ready to head out again, and came to a stop beside us. The driver, a wiry youth whose family resemblance to my old friend Guido was remarkable, from the chiseled features to the set of his shoulders, hopped out and trotted around the van to open the passenger door.

"Io sono Luigi." He offered his hand to me. "Maggie?"

"Sí, ciao," I said, using a tenth of the Italian words I know.

"S'okay," he said. "I got pretty good English."

"This is Jean-Paul," I said.

"Luigi Cadelago," Luigi said, giving Jean-Paul's hand a virile pumping. "Sorry I'm late. Delivery, you know? So, where we go?"

"What's your schedule?" Jean-Paul asked, ushering me into the van. There was a single, not very wide bench seat to accommodate the three of us. Very cozy, but at least the cab did not smell of fish.

"After Ravenna, next is Bologna," Luigi said, holding the door for Jean-Paul to climb in beside me. "Then a stop here, there, some other places. Last is Parma. Every day the same. Deliver the fish, pick up the meat and cheese, drop it off in Ravenna, go home, sleep, meet the fishing boats tomorrow morning, start all over."

He ran around and climbed in behind the wheel and started the engine. *The Barber of Seville* blasted from quad speakers. Shouting over the music he said, "Except today, deliver fish, pick up friends of Guido. So, where you go?"

"Bologna first," I said, gesturing toward the volume knob and smiling at him.

"Sure, sure." He turned down the sound. "Then where?"

"And then maybe on to Parma. I've always wanted to see Parma. Have you, Jean-Paul?"

"Of course, yes." He looked at me and shrugged. Why not? "Unless we are charmed and decide to stay on in Bologna."

Bologna, the first stop, was a fast hour's drive away. Luigi wended his way through the narrow streets of the ancient market area—the Quadrilatero, he told us—and parked half-on, half-off the sidewalk. I could smell the market even before he opened the van door. Curious, happy to stretch our legs, we got out and kibitzed with him while he prepared his delivery. A cloud of cold vapor washed over us when he opened the van's double back doors. First Luigi checked a computer-generated order form atop a clipboard, climbed inside and pushed half a dozen cartons toward the doors. He pulled a barcode scanner off his belt and flashed it over a line of code on the order form and then the line of code on the end of each carton. Satisfied, he loaded the scanned cartons onto a hand truck, told us he would be five minutes, and set off at a jog into the narrow alleyways of the market.

I smelled bread, and meat, garlic and earthy spices. I turned to Jean-Paul. "Who knows what's ahead. Think we should lay in some emergency provisions?"

With a nod, he took my hand and we followed Luigi, but at a somewhat slower pace. To save time, we divided our list and dashed into the shops nearest the entrance, regretting that we didn't have longer to explore the medieval marketplace. When we met again, Jean-Paul had collected a chunk of mortadella and a wedge of Parmigiano, a bottle of still water and a bottle of Prosecco. I held open the net bag I had acquired and he added his purchases to the carrots, figs, apples, and bread still warm from the oven that I found in the shops. As an afterthought, we ducked into a cutlery shop and bought a paring knife with a five-inch blade. Luigi was just locking the back of his van when we rejoined him.

Luigi set our bag behind the seat. Immediately, the smells of fresh bread and garlicky mortadella filled the cab.

"Makes me hungry," Luigi said with a grin as he maneuvered through the narrow streets of the city center and out onto the toll road toward Parma.

"Would you like something to eat?" I asked.

"No, no," he said with a glance at the dashboard clock; it was just nine-thirty. "You keep for later. We get to Reggio nell'Emilia, we get a little *caffè corretto*, maybe nice little snack to keep our strength up until lunchtime."

Luigi wanted to talk about television. His cousin, Guido,

was a big shot in the family because he worked in Hollywood. I
didn't have the heart to tell Luigi that our studio was out in the
far-from-glamorous San Fernando Valley, and anyway Luigi, clearly
happy to have people to talk to during his time on the road, didn't
leave an opening in his conversational stream for us to add much
more than a nod or two-syllable response. He told us that Guido
made sure that his family saw every bit of film he worked on. Luigi's
grandmother, who was Guido's aunt, would invite all the neighbors
in to watch whatever Guido sent over. They thought that Guido
was handsome enough to be a movie star, and maybe were a little
disappointed that he wasn't, but they were still very proud of his
job. And of course, then, they knew who I was because my name
and my face show up on many of the films Guido has worked on
over the last fifteen years.

"Soon as I saw you, I knew it was you, Maggie MacGowen,"
Luigi said, dodging a big rig that was straining up a steep grade. "I
see you all the time on the TV. You look pretty good. My grandma
thinks you should let Guido talk sometimes. You know, let her see
his face."

"Something to think about," I said. Guido, I knew, didn't want
to be on camera. He was very happy doing what he does so well.
But that was a topic my film partner could discuss with his family,
not I.

We came out of gently rolling foothills, barren in winter, onto
a broad, flat plain. Luigi exited the toll road at Modena and made a
round of fast deliveries at several small restaurants while we waited
in the van. The last stop before returning to the toll road was at the
Lamborghini factory.

"They eat good at Lamborghini," he said, climbing back into
the driver's seat when he was finished. "Better than across the river
at Ferrari."

We were on a secondary road headed toward the town of
Reggio nell'Emilia when the phone in Jean-Paul's pocket dinged.
There was a text from AnoNino. As soon as Jean-Paul opened it, a
cascade of texts followed.

"*Merde alors,*" he muttered.

"What?"

"I asked AnoNino to sign up for crouchingdragon's challenge to hackers so that he could monitor everything that came in." He held the phone so I could see the images people had sent in hope of winning the prize for locating us. One after the other, shots of men and women that resembled us in some way, sometimes couples, sometimes singles, had been posted, with location. Many of the images were grainy, apparently taken by security cameras, others were quite sharp, perhaps snapped by telephones. Most were shots of strangers. But some were of us.

There was a sequence of shots following our progress up the Canale Candiano in the yacht's motor launch that morning. Boats carry transponders. Clearly, someone had hacked the system and tracked Roddy's yacht to Ravenna harbor, and then hacked into security cameras attached to the cabins along the fishing pier. Each shot came from a different angle, had different quality, but they were all clear enough to be recognizable; Jean-Paul, me, Horst, and the first mate, all in profile, motoring up the canal. The very last entry in the sequence was a video, just a few frames, shot at such a long distance that we were visible as little more than dark gray blobs moving along the water until we debarked the launch at the cemetery. Taken with the whole, that last piece made it clear enough where we were at ten minutes after eight that morning.

"Clever little buggers," I said. "There are a lot of mistaken sightings, but your friend Sabri Qosja will pick us out of the mass right away."

"I'm sure he will." Jean-Paul's phone dinged again. This time the image AnoNino sent showed us, very clearly, standing beside Luigi's van at the Bologna marketplace twenty minutes earlier. I glanced at Luigi. As far as I knew, all he had agreed to do was give a ride to his cousin's friends. I doubted he knew anything about the dogged mercenary on our tail.

"How far is Reggio nell'Emilia?" I asked Luigi.

"Pretty close. You can wait maybe fifteen, twenty minutes? I make a delivery to nice little hotel. We take a break there, get a *caffè*, go to toilet."

"Sounds good," I said. A coffee did sound good. A toilet wasn't a bad idea, either. At the next town, I hoped, we could say good-bye to Luigi before he was dragged even further into our mess. But maybe, I thought with rising dread, it was already too late.

The road we traveled was straight, the terrain flat, traffic light. I kept checking the side mirrors for a tail, but saw nothing that seemed out of the ordinary. I caught Jean-Paul doing the same. We were so focused on the road that we both startled when an incoming message dinged the phone in his pocket.

"Game's changed," he said after he read the message. "The prize has been upped for the first person who can not only spot us, but stop us."

"Stop us how? And do what with us?"

"There are no rules about how and what."

"Crazy guy," Luigi said, eyes on his side mirror. He steered to the right, edging toward the narrow gravel shoulder, put his arm out his window and waved for someone behind us to pass. "What's he trying to do? Fuck my bumper?"

"What is it?" Jean-Paul asked, looking around.

"*Proprio uno stronzo.*" Luigi laid on his horn. "What you say, big asshole? Guy on a motorcycle. Pass me, *idiota*, pass."

Like a sudden gust of wind, the motorcycle came up on our left. The helmeted driver seemed to pause when he was abreast of Luigi's window. He took a good look inside, made eye contact with me, then raced on.

"*Basta,*" Luigi said with a big sigh. "Crazy man, eh?"

"Luigi," I said to get his attention as the motorcycle sped out of sight. "What did Guido tell you about us when he asked you to give us a ride?"

"Tell me? Not much. He says you have some kind of trouble and you need some help. What can I say? I owe Guido too much. Here I am."

"The trouble is, someone is stalking us."

Both of Luigi's hands were on the wheel, but he directed a thumb toward Jean-Paul. "I didn't want to ask before about your face. Not nice, you know? But this guy, he the one did that to you?"

"Probably a friend of his, but yes."

"Not that guy on the motorcycle?"

Jean-Paul shook his head. "Different guy, but same problem, I think. Look, there's a reward offered on the Internet for anyone who can stop Maggie and me. I am afraid, my friend, that the idiot on the motorcycle wants to collect the reward. He may be back."

"I'm sorry," I said, touching Luigi's arm. "You didn't bargain for this. Please, drop us off at the next place we come to."

He looked out the windscreen, scanning the vista. There was nothing around us except broad, empty fields covered with frost. "No," he said, bringing his focus back to us. "No. I promised Guido. That's sacred, *sí*?"

"It's sacred when you know what you're promising to do," I said. "But you didn't know."

"We can talk later." His eyes were on the road ahead. "Like you said, the guy's coming back."

He was. Coming toward us, fast.

"Hand me the Prosecco," Jean-Paul said as he rolled down his window. I reached back and dug it out of our shopping bag, having a general idea what he intended to do with it. As he took it from me, he caught Luigi's eye. "Can you give me an angle?"

"*Sí*. Get ready."

The bike accelerated as it switched into our lane, approaching us head on. Luigi did exactly what the biker would expect him to do. He veered into the oncoming traffic lane to avoid a collision, but he waited to do it until the bike was no more than twenty feet away. Just as the bike's front wheel crossed the plane of the van's front bumper, approaching on the passenger side, Luigi pulled hard to the left. At that moment, Jean-Paul, eye-to-eye with the motorcycle's driver, flipped the heavy Prosecco bottle out the window. It exploded against the pavement inches from the bike's front wheel, showering bike and driver in a spray of amber glass and foaming liquid. The bike spun out as Luigi corrected course and sped forward.

I watched the motorcycle lay over, dumping the driver in an

ass-over-teakettle roll as it skidded along the pavement, spewing bits of glass and metal along the road as it went.

"Did he get up?" Luigi asked, looking concerned.

Jean-Paul, watching the side mirror, said, "He's sitting. He'll be all right, but his bike won't. Good driving, *mon ami*. Good driving."

"Good team." Luigi held out his palm for Jean-Paul to slap. "When I see him, I think we have a highway pirate."

"Does that happen often?"

"Not so much," he said. "There's nothing to steal except fish. Drivers don't carry cash. Everything's electronic, you know? I scan the fish going out of the truck, the buyer scans it coming in to say delivery is complete, and boom, his bank pays mine. Safer that way, yes?"

With a sinking feeling, I asked, "Your buyers can track delivery?"

"*Sí*, sure. Go on the Web any time, find out where I am, what time I get there."

Jean-Paul muttered, "*Merde*. I'm a fool."

"We've accomplished what we set out to do," I said, patting his knee. "You said that when you want to know where the enemy is, sometimes you have to run out of the forest to draw his fire. We're out of the forest, my dear, and we drew fire. Now that we have some idea where to aim, I think it's time for us to fire back. What prize is crouchingdragon's employer offering to stop us?"

He frowned as he sent the question to AnoNino. The answer came back immediately: a five-hundred-euro electronic gift card. And bragging rights.

I took my camera out of my pocket and scrolled to the photos I had taken of Blondie and Qosja in the department store in Venice. Using the camera on Jean-Paul's phone, I took a screen shot of each one.

"Send these photos to AnoNino and ask him to launch a challenge to his hacker buddies. Find the current location of either of these men, last seen in Venice early this morning, and win a thousand-euro gift card. The winner is the person who sends in the most recent location, with time-and-date-stamped photos as proof."

"Why not?" he answered, his thumb already busily tapping the phone's keys.

"Some kind of game?" Luigi asked, a furrow between his brows.

"A deadly game," I answered. "The problem right now is this: It looks like someone saw me and Jean-Paul with your van in Bologna and hacked into your business's tracking system to find us. Even if you drop us off somewhere, they may still be tracking your van and come after you. Is there any way to disable the system?"

"Disable it?" Luigi wagged his head from side to side as he thought. After a moment, he said, "Only one way. I call in, say the truck is broken and I got a tow to Reggio nell'Emilia. Mamma—Mamma runs the office—posts to customers that the equipment is down, deliveries will be delayed. The truck still sends a signal so Mamma always knows where to find me, but we park the truck and we leave it for one day, maybe two. No good tracking a truck going nowhere, yes?"

"What about your deliveries?" I asked.

"Everybody gets their fish today, don't worry. I got a friend drives the same route; we meet for *caffè corretto* in Reggio every day. He'll get me and my load to Parma and get me home tonight. Won't be the first time one of our delivery trucks broke down on the road."

I turned to Jean-Paul to see what he thought. He shrugged his good shoulder, which I interpreted to mean, Why not?

"Could work," I said. "Unless someone pops up between here and Reggio. You need to park the van right away."

"Okay." Luigi seemed doubtful. He thought for a moment, and then he pulled out his phone and sent a text. "I know a good place, not far. We can get a nice *caffè* while we wait for my friend and be back on the road quick. No worries."

"Luigi, Jean-Paul and I need to bug out, now."

Luigi looked at the open farmland all around us and shook his head. "I can't leave you alone. What if another guy comes?"

"We'll be okay. I've seen a couple of bus stops along here. Jean-Paul?"

When he nodded I looked back at Luigi. "Will you drop us at the next bus stop?"

"Where do you go?" Luigi asked, brows again furrowed.

"Depends on where the bus is headed," Jean-Paul answered. "As long as it's away from Reggio."

As soon as he saw the next bus sign in the distance, Luigi took his foot off the accelerator. I knew he didn't like our plan and was playing for time, trying to come up with a good argument. But he did pull over and stop. He grabbed our shopping bag from behind the seat and got out with us.

"I owe you, Luigi," I said, kissing his cheek.

"You owe me nothing." He gripped my shoulders and kissed both cheeks. "All in the family, eh?"

Jean-Paul offered his hand. "Thank you, my friend. I hope we meet again. But be careful, please."

"For a guy with one arm, you throw damn good," Luigi said, taking Jean-Paul's hand in both of his. "You should get another bottle of Prosecco. For protection."

We saw an old green bus lumbering up the road.

"You sure?" Luigi asked, watching it approach.

"Luigi, I'm not sure about anything right now." I reached for the shopping bag dangling from his shoulder. "But this is the best we can come up with for now. When you get home tonight, promise you'll call Guido and tell him you're safe. He'll get the message to me."

"Sure, sure. You, too, tell Guido." He patted his chest over his heart. "All day, I worry."

There was another round of cheek-kisses and handshakes, and then the bus stopped and the driver opened the doors. The sign on the front announced PER S. FAUSTINO. Without being asked, Luigi got up onto the bus's first step to speak with the driver, a round little man with a huge white mustache. After an animated discussion with much gesturing and arm-waving, Luigi climbed back down and gallantly took my elbow to help me up.

"He's going north," he said over my shoulder to Jean-Paul. "It's the local, lots of stops. But in San Faustino you can catch the express bus to Milano, or if you want, get the bus south to Firenze. Is that okay?"

Jean-Paul said, "Very okay. *Grazie.*"

From the bottom step, I turned and gave Luigi a little wave, worried about what might happen to him on the road ahead. His last words were, "Make my grandmother happy. Put Guido on the TV."

"I'll try," I said. Jean-Paul gave his shoulder a last pat and we climbed aboard.

The bus was old and barely heated, and the upholstery was cracked, but it was clean, and most importantly, did not have a security camera trained on the passengers. Only about a quarter of the seats were occupied. There were a few older men, a trio wearing blue work clothes, and a pair of youths, but most of the passengers were women, some with small children. As we made our way to seats, just about everyone looked up and watched us, because that's what people do when there's something or someone new to look at. Once we sat down, they lost interest in us and went back to their conversations or naps or telephones, and ignored us. I caught Jean-Paul checking on people with telephones, as I was, to make sure no one aimed a camera at us.

When Jean-Paul sighed, I turned to him and put my hand against his cheek. He felt warm, but not feverish. I pulled the water out of the shopping bag and his meds out of the backpack and handed them to him. I asked, "How do you feel?"

"Quite well." He swallowed his pills and handed me the water. "A lot better than yesterday. And you?"

"Other than a sense of impending doom, I'm fine." I took a long drink; being stalked is thirsty business. "Do we have a plan?"

"I believe we are safer in Paris than we are out here, in the open," he said, glancing up when the driver announced the next stop, the train depot in Rubiera. "We can get a flight out of Milan, if you agree."

"I will feel better when we're behind Isabelle's iron gates, so yes, I agree."

At the Rubiera depot, the bus shuddered to a stop and two

old men hobbled down the aisle toward the exit. The driver got out first to give the men a hand down the three steps to the pavement. There was a moment of conversation before the two walked on toward the depot platform and the driver reclaimed his seat. For a fleeting moment, I considered taking the train. It would be faster than the bus, certainly faster than this local line. But then I flashed on the thought of being trapped inside a speeding train with Blondie and Sabri Qosja closing in on us. Jean-Paul grabbed my hand and looked at me, concern etched on his face; had I called out?

"*Ça va?*" he asked.

"Yes." I covered his hand with mine. "I'm okay."

"Yes?"

"Yes." I leaned against his shoulder and took a couple of deep breaths. We were okay. For the moment, at least.

Four women carrying shopping bags got on at the depot. The driver greeted them like old friends, closed the doors, waited for them to take their seats, and drove on. The next stop was on the street between an outlet mall and an industrial park. The three men who wore work clothes got out, as did a clutch of women. When they were on the pavement, about half a dozen people, men and women, got on, all of them carrying shopping bags. I checked my watch. It was almost eleven, time for traditional working Italians to shop for food to prepare at home for lunch.

The old bus tipped and swayed as the driver navigated a roundabout and backtracked onto the two-lane road to San Faustino. Outside the windows, there wasn't very much to see. A leaden sky with the green tinge of impending snow hovered low over naked fields. Here and there, industrial parks built out of cream-colored cinder blocks broke the monotony of gray sky and brown earth. We stopped at a large gym where mothers carrying swim bags herded little ones out of the bus, chatting together without pause while they tended to the occasional kiddy tumble or fuss. The two youths who were on the bus when we boarded got off at a large farm equipment showroom; their hands were stained dark with motor oil. The last stop was at a crossroads where there was a row of shops: a greengrocer, a bakery, a butcher, a tobacconist, a wine shop, and a trattoria that sent the rich aroma of strong coffee into the icy morning air. We waited for the other passengers to go ahead of us. As Jean-Paul and I buttoned our coats and gathered our bags, the driver pointed at us then gestured toward a sign on our side of the nearby intersection.

"*Per Milano,*" he said. And then turning to point toward the far side of the intersection, he said, "*Per Firenze.*"

"*Grazie,*" Jean-Paul said, waiting for me to precede him out.

"*Ciao,*" the driver answered with the traditional backward finger wave as we started down the bus steps. Quickly, we moved away to let the waiting passengers, all of them with laden shopping bags, climb aboard.

"Coffee," I said as I took Jean-Paul by the arm and steered him toward the trattoria. We joined a row of locals standing at the tin counter. He ordered two *caffè corretti* and two pastries. The proprietor piled the pastries onto a single plate, which he skidded down the counter toward us. Two coffees in tiny cups quickly followed.

"*Cin-cin,*" Jean-Paul said before he downed his coffee in a gulp.

When I lifted my cup to take the first swig, I knew there was more than coffee in my little cup. "What's in here?"

"Grappa," he said, knuckling his cheek under the line of stitches. "That's what makes your coffee 'correct.' Drink it fast. It'll warm you."

I don't know whether it warmed me or numbed me to the cold, but the potent alcohol added to the strong coffee certainly took the edge off that very stressful morning. We shared the pastries—they were delicious—gathered our things and went back outside. We found a sheltered alcove at the end of the row of shops and waited there, out of view of passing traffic, until we saw the Milan bus approach. This bus was big, new, and shiny. We waited for most of the passengers queued at the stop to board before we came out from the alcove and joined them. Tickets were purchased with a credit card at a machine behind the driver's seat. As the two of us talked together about which buttons to push and where the printed tickets would come out, the driver turned and said, "*Per Milano?*"

"*Sí,*" Jean-Paul said, pulling the tickets from the slot when they appeared. "*Milano.*"

The driver waved impatiently for us to move out of the way of the couple that waited behind us. As newcomers, we competed for seats already taken by shopping bags, wheeled suitcases, coats, and a couple of boxes with tractor parts. With a few hand gestures, we negotiated with a woman to move her shopping bags to her side of the aisle so we could have two seats together. The seat backs were high, letting us cocoon ourselves from the other passengers, except for the woman across the aisle, who closed her eyes and began to snore softly as soon as the bus pulled away from the stop.

We were now on an express bus, speeding along the Autostrada del Sole, a sleek toll road, with no more stops until Milan. After we crossed the Po River, the landscape changed from flat plains to gentle foothills. In the distance, I could see snowcapped Alps rising above a gathering storm moving in from the east. That morning, Roddy's yacht captain had told us that a Siberian Express was expected to descend on Europe overnight, meaning heavy snow and ice. I hoped we could get a flight out before the storm hit. I'd dealt with more than my share of cancelled flights already that week. Though for the moment we were snug and warm, and together, it wouldn't last long. The trip to Milan would only take an hour and a half. And then what?

"Lunch in Milan," Jean-Paul said, looking up from his telephone.

"And then home for dinner."

"You can say home and mean Paris?"

"If you're there," I said, turning to him. "As the owners of number seven, rue Jacob, do we get our pick of any of the apartments?"

He laughed softly. "We can choose from any that become available, of course. But there are no vacancies just now, except for Isabelle's own apartment which, by the way, she owned outright. If you can't be comfortable in her place, be prepared for a good wait for another. Our tenants tend to stay for a very long time. Indeed, many stay until the mortuary van comes for them."

I was trying to imagine myself living in Isabelle's apartment—my apartment now—when Jean-Paul lifted my chin and kissed me.

"Is there a reason you wouldn't be happy in her apartment?" he asked.

"Too early to say. I was hardly there before I left again." I asked, "Would you be comfortable at Isabelle's with me? Or would you prefer to stay at your own place?"

He studied me for a moment in the quiet way he has. I knew his wheels were turning, but what I couldn't read was which question he was thinking over, if either. We had not lived together, and though we had decided to marry, we had yet to get to the when, where, or what-next steps to make that happen. Those issues probably would not have arisen if he were still assigned to work in Los Angeles, my home base, or if the French television network and I had finalized an agreement and I were to work in Paris, his bailiwick, or if we both hadn't been traveling, separately, nearly constantly ever since my grandmother popped the Champagne corks in celebration of our impending union. There were a lot of decisions to make.

"I wonder," he said at last, "which ghost you would be more comfortable living with, your mother's, or my wife, Marian's?"

"Interesting question," I said. "Does Marian haunt your house?"

"She does not haunt me, any more than your late husband haunts you. But I put the question to you. So?"

"I have never been to your house, so I can't answer."

"We haven't had the occasion, or made the occasion to go there. My fault, I suppose. I wasn't sure how you would feel," he said, still watching me closely. "Except for removing Marian's intimate things, I left the house very much as it was when she died, in part for our son's comfort, and for the rest because I accepted the Los Angeles consulship so soon afterward. In the months since I've been back I've been too busy to notice that it might be time to call in the painter or to buy new sheets. But we could do that, you and I, if you wish. The other issue, of course, is that the house is in the suburbs. The commute by train is no problem, but when

the transit union goes on strike, and they do regularly, the drive
into Paris is a nightmare."

"With a little paint and new sheets, I think I could exorcise
Isabelle from her apartment, as well. But it isn't very big. You would
have the office, but my work takes up a lot of room. I suppose I
could rent space somewhere."

"You wouldn't need to," he said. "There is plenty of room in the
cellars at rue Jacob for you to set up a comfortable work space."

"Cellars? Plural? What's down there?"

He shrugged. "Utilities. We installed central heating, plumbing, and new electrical service when we did the renovation. And
all the conduits and machinery and so on are down there. There is
a storage area for tenants and a maintenance shop. The rest, just
empty space. Except for the library, of course."

"What library, of course?"

"Ah, yes. No one explained to you about the library, did they?"

"Nope."

"Remind me, as soon as we're back in Paris, to find you a new
notaire," he said, knuckling his cheek again.

"Do the stitches itch?"

"I'll be very happy when they're out."

"When are they supposed to come out?"

"Yesterday."

"We'll have Émile take care of it in Paris tonight. If we get to
Paris tonight," I said. "Now go back to, What library?"

"Yes, well, that's another complication left to us by the Little
Sisters of Saint Émilian when we acquired number seven."

"The library belonged to the convent?"

"Yes." He looked at me askance. "That property has a very interesting history. A very long history."

"Until we get to Milan, we have nothing but time. I'm all ears."

"Well, then, where to begin?" While he thought, he kept worrying the areas around his sutures. When he looked over at me,
I expected to hear, "Once upon a time." Instead, he said, "*Chérie*,
you've been stitched up once or twice, yes?"

"Sure."

"You've watched the doctor take out the sutures?"

I nodded. "I've taken out my own a couple of times."

"Good. Then you know what to do. Did you bring the little scissors from Gille's apartment?"

"You want me to take out your stitches?"

He took my hand and kissed it. "I beg you, please. Put me out of my misery."

"Here?" I glanced at the woman across the aisle; she still had her eyes closed. "Now?"

"*Bien sûr.* Why not?"

Why not, indeed. I pulled up the backpack and fished out the pharmacy bag from Paris where I had stowed our little medical kit: tape, sterile wipes, antiseptic ointment, scissors. We pulled up the armrest between us so he could lie across my lap. He looked very comfortable; with his knees bent and his feet on his seat and his head on my thighs, he might as well have been napping at a picnic.

I did the best I could with sterile wipes to carefully clean the area around the wounds and the sharp little scissors. When I was ready to snip the sutures, I asked him to cover his eyes with his hand in case the bus hit a bump. If I was going to stab him, better to hit the back of his hand than his eyes.

"All set," I said. "Now, tell me about the library. The long version."

~

WHILE he cleared his throat, and began, I started with the suture on his cheek that was the furthest from his eye. Carefully, I pulled up the surgeon's beautiful little knot, slipped the pointed end of the scissors into the gap, and snipped. Using my fingers like tweezers, a couple of tugs pulled the first bit of stitching free. He didn't even wince. Then I went on to the next one. And the next.

Jean-Paul was a natural storyteller, but it didn't matter very much what he was saying at first; it was enough just to hear his voice, to have him close beside me. But as the story about number seven, rue Jacob unfolded, I found myself drawn in, intrigued, focused as much on the story as on the storyteller.

Jean-Paul did not know who the original owners of number

seven were, but some centuries ago the property was bequeathed to the Little Sisters of Saint Jérôme Émilian, who converted the existing palatial home into a convent and school for abandoned girls. Saint Jérôme Émilian, he told me, as I pulled out yet another stitch, is the patron saint of abandoned children. Though the nuns at Saint Émilian took in children, there was no basket left at the gate to receive babies dropped off in the night; foundlings were not welcome. The nuns' charges might be orphans whose wealthy families died during one plague or another, or who had been given the boot by a stepparent. But most of the girls were the illegitimate offspring of wealthy men, children who were, like me, the paramour's daughter. No matter who she was, a girl would not be admitted through the high iron gates on rue Jacob unless she came with a generous financial gift to the convent and an endowment sufficient to support her for the rest of her life.

I wanted to believe that the fathers loved their daughters, as mine had loved me, and were providing for them in the best way possible at the time. Few men in any era could take their lovers' offspring home to the missus, as mine had done, and expect the children to be welcomed. There are more possibilities for extracurricular children now, and fewer stigma, but it wasn't so very long ago that the father of a bastard girl would likely not be able to find her either an appropriate husband or an honorable way to support herself. For wealthy fathers, handing a girl over to the virgins of the church to raise, with the expectation that she would one day take religious orders and disappear from society, was a common enough solution. Think of poor Héloïse after her dalliance with Peter Abélard.

Jean-Paul told me that the convent school at number seven, rue Jacob trained their wards to be teachers and nurses, and, according to Isabelle's research, ran a very busy scriptorium where nuns and novitiates, hunched over their desks, painstakingly copied and recopied scripture, church-approved history, official decrees of the state, music, and whatever else was put in front of them.

"It was a very well-respected scriptorium," Jean-Paul said. "Isabelle discovered that Saint Jérôme Émilian often worked in concert with the scriptorium nearby at Saint-Germain-de-Prés, when it was still a monastery, producing manuscripts for the libraries of kings and cardinals. Magnificent illuminated documents. And, they assembled a library for their own use."

"That explains the little volume of Psalms I saw on Isabelle's desk."

"A volume of Psalms?" He took his hand away from his eyes and sat up a little. "When did you see it?"

"Yesterday. That's the only time I've been in her apartment."

"Describe the book."

I shrugged, holding out my palm. "It's no bigger than my hand. Leather-bound, handwritten on parchment, with illuminated capitals. In Greek. It's beautiful."

"You saw it on her desk?"

"Yes. Is that a problem?"

"I know Isabelle didn't leave it there, so I wonder who took it from the library. Only the two of us have keys."

"How do you know she didn't put it there?"

"I was in the apartment after Isabelle was killed in Los Angeles," he said. "Your Uncle Gérard asked me to be with Freddy when the police came to interview him about her death. I can assure you that there was no volume of Psalms on her desk then. Afterward, I went down to the library to make sure all was in order, as I do from time to time, and found it intact, door bolted."

"Lie back down, I'm almost finished. And explain to me why you're upset about the book being on her desk."

"Oh-là, it is so complicated, that problem." He lay back and covered his eyes again. After a deep sigh, he said, "I told you there was a dispute over who held title to rue Jacob, the nuns, the diocese, or the Vatican, when Isabelle wanted to buy it. Ownership of the library is an even bigger war, and one that has not yet been resolved. Maggie, when the diocese and the Vatican sold the property to us, they did not know the library existed. Anyone who could have told them had long ago ascended to heaven. At least, that's where I assume nuns go. It's possible that the last few nuns didn't know it was there, either.

"During the renovation, our workmen took down a heavy oak door in a far corner of the basement, and *voilà*, a great discovery. Everything was a jumble, of course. Overloaded shelves had collapsed in one area, for the rest—a general disorganization. Stacks of handcrafted books piled on tables and chairs. Adding to the clutter were crates of state documents and church texts that apparently were entrusted to the convent during the French and later Russian revolutions. Perhaps at a time when the churches were shut down and worship was suppressed, the convent was off limits to the French revolutionaries because it was an orphanage for little girls. I wonder how many of those revolutionaries had parked an illicit child with the nuns. In the meantime, the king lost his head and the church lost its luster, and no one ever came to reclaim the books and charters and decrees and official records that had been left with the nuns. The Russian documents? A mystery.

"Isabelle turned to the Sorbonne for help to make order out of the mess. As soon as they walked in, the scholars realized what was there and advised us that the collection belonged in a museum. Isabelle, Gérard, and I agreed. We signed the library over to the rare books section at the Louvre, with the caveat that they would make it available to researchers."

"Jean-Paul, hold still, please."

"It was an exciting discovery, yes? And, ouch!"

"Sorry," I said. "That little stitch up in your hairline was a bugger to get out. Go on."

"The Louvre, naturally, sent out a press release. The papers covered it, there was a photograph. Not a good one, but clear enough about the state of things. Right away, the Louvre took away the French state papers. But, of course, the Vatican claimed the convent library, and so did the diocese. Almost from the beginning, the Louvre, the Vatican, and the diocese have been in a three-way suit for possession. At the moment, the issue sits exactly where it has been for the last eighteen or nineteen years. At impasse."

"In the meantime," I said, "the library sits in the cellar."

"Exactly. Except that the church has demanded that the library remain sealed until there is a resolution."

"Why? I'd think they would welcome scholars. They must want to know what's there."

"You would, Isabelle and I did. But the issue for the church is that some of the volumes are very old and may have errors, meaning that they may contradict more recent rulings on dogma. He who controls the media controls the message, yes?"

"You said you and Isabelle invited in scholars right away. Doesn't the church object?"

"Of course," he said, peeking at me through his fingers. "But what can they do? The library is on private property. They tried to get an injunction to have the room sealed, but our lawyers countered that there are holdings in the collection that Rome has no claim to and therefore, Rome has no authority to block access to the entire library. A judge wagged his finger and warned Isabelle to keep the works in contention locked up, and Isabelle, being Isabelle, smiled at him and did exactly as she pleased."

"She allowed researchers in," I said.

"Serious scholars, yes."

"You said that the French state papers are long gone. So, what's there that Rome can't claim?"

"The Russians. The Louvre thinks that tsarist expats saved precious church documents from the bonfire, and brought them to Paris with them."

"And left them with the nuns at rue Jacob," I said. "Is it possible that some Russian aristocrat had entrusted a mistress's daughter with the nuns, and knew where to turn?"

"Maybe so," he said.

"Sounds like Isabelle was as good at figuring out a work-around as her brother, Gérard."

"Oh, yes. The one court order Isabelle was scrupulous about obeying, was that all of the work of scholars has to be done *in situ*. Nothing leaves the library, except that from time to time we allow museum staff to remove volumes for restoration. Fortunately, the cellar has always been cool and dry, so the collection is surprisingly well preserved, considering the age of some of the documents. But time, bookworms, woodworms, and rot have done their work.

When a volume goes out for repair, it goes out and comes back with an escort."

"Maybe the little book of Psalms went out for repair and somehow was left on Isabelle's desk. Maybe they couldn't find the keys that day," I said, leaning my face close to his, looking for the best way to snip one of the finer sutures. "Where are the keys?"

"I keep mine in a safe. But I don't know where Isabelle's are."

"Maybe Freddy knows," I said.

"Freddy," he said. "Perhaps the puzzle is solved. Freddy is fascinated by the library. When was he at her apartment last?"

"I don't know. I'll ask him." The last stitch came free cleanly and went into the little spiky pile of sutures I had deposited on the window ledge. I used another antiseptic wipe on the wounds to clean them and then spread a thin layer of antibiotic ointment over the area. When I was finished, I leaned forward and kissed his lips. "All done."

Tentatively, he touched the wounds. "How does it look?"

"Good. Healing well. How does it feel?"

"Better, a hundred times better." He sat up and returned the kiss. "Thank you."

"*Prego*. But if it's all the same to you, I'd rather you didn't need me to do that particular favor ever again."

"I'll try my best."

"Please do."

His phone signaled there was an incoming text. While his thumb was busy, I pulled out a phone, put in a battery, and called Freddy.

"Maggie," Freddy said with surprising enthusiasm. "I am so happy—so relieved—that you've called. I've been trying to reach you since yesterday morning. I am so very profoundly embarrassed that Maman's apartment was a disaster when you walked in. I had no idea it was in such a bad state because I had scheduled the cleaners to come in after the holidays. When I knew you were coming, I left a message for them to tidy up before you arrived. So, when Grand-mère told me the cleaners had not come and that crap was scattered around, I thought there might have been a break-in, though it would take a team of commandoes to get past Madame Gonsalves. I finally reached the cleaners and they told me that over the holidays there was a kerfuffle between them and my son, or one of his friends. So, they refused to go in. When I asked Philippe to explain, he promised he would make amends with the cleaners; they've been with Maman for years, very reliable. Phillippe promised me he would apologize to the ladies and arrange everything. But—"

"The holidays: is that when you were in Isabelle's apartment last?" I asked when I could finally get a word in.

"Yes. I should have asked you first. But I knew you and Jean-Paul were in California with family, and our visit to Paris was a last-minute decision. I took my boys skiing right after Christmas. A couple of Philippe's English boarding-school friends came along, nice enough youngsters, I thought. Neither of them had been to France before, let alone Paris, so we agreed to stay on for a couple of days before they had to go back to school, to show them some of the sights. Going to Maman's when we were in Paris was the natural thing for us, so I didn't think twice about it. In future, I shall call you first."

"I hope you had a good time," I said.

"We did. We were to leave on New Year's Eve in the afternoon," he said, sounding defensive. "Robert needed to get home to finish a school project. But Philippe and his friends didn't need to be back across the Channel for school for another week. They asked if they could stay on for one more day to see the big Paris New Year's celebrations. They're eighteen, away at school already, responsible for themselves. With Madame Gonsalves on watch, I knew they couldn't wander too far astray, so I allowed it. Apparently, however, they stayed more than one night, and did something to offend not only the cleaners but the downstairs neighbor when they were there. I hope that when Philippe gets home for the spring holiday he will have a better explanation ready than the one he's given me. But, I do ask for your forgiveness."

"There's nothing to forgive, Freddy."

"I know I should have asked permission to use the apartment."

"I think we're even. My coat was wet, so I borrowed yours without asking."

There was a pause. "What coat?"

"Green, waxed canvas with a Barbour label."

"Ah, the coat. One of the boys left it. He has been very anxious to get it back."

"There we are, then. I was happier to have a warm, dry coat than I've ever been to have a tidy house. Tell Philippe's friend we're even."

He laughed a bit too hard and I realized just how worried he'd been about my reaction to the mess at Isabelle's apartment. After all, we don't know each other very well, my half brother and I. Sometimes I find myself walking on eggshells around my newly discovered French family, so it made sense that they would still be cautious around me.

"Freddy," I said. "The reason I called was, I wonder if you know where Isabelle kept the keys to the library."

There was a pause before he said, "Library? The library in the cellar?"

"That one."

"I don't know where they are. Maman has a strongbox in her office. They might be there. Or maybe Madame Gonsalves keeps them. Or knows where they are. Probably she does because someone has to let in the readers from the university when they come."

"I'll ask her."

"Other than the readers, no one goes down there. But you're probably curious to see it."

"I am."

"Are you in the apartment now?"

"We're in transit. With luck, if the weather holds we may be back by tonight."

"Safe travels. See you at Easter, if not before."

Jean-Paul had already finished his texts when I turned off the phone. I asked, "Learn anything?"

"No word on the big blonde, but Sabri Qosja was spotted by

one of our reward-seekers in Lyon twenty minutes ago, waiting for a train."

"Headed for Paris?"

He shrugged. "If that's where he's going, and he catches the midday TGV, he'll be there to greet us."

"Comforting thought."

"As soon as we know when we'll arrive, I'll alert Madame Gonsalves to watch for us."

"You told her Guido is coming?"

"I did, this morning." He slipped his phone into his pocket. "There was another message, a very interesting one. I told you that I sent the bank routing number AnoNino discovered when he hacked crouchingdragon to a friend of mine, yes?"

"You did."

"My friend traced it to an account owned by a company called InterCentro, which appears to be a holding company for some Russian business interests."

"Have you done something to offend the Russians? Or have I?"

"Both of us, probably. It isn't difficult to offend the Russians," he said. "As much as I would like to catch the first plane we can to Paris, we need to hear what else my friend has found. We're joining him for lunch in Milan."

"When?"

He turned my wrist to look at my watch. "In forty-five minutes."

At the exit for the Milan Linate Airport, the driver left the Autostrada and announced we would arrive in *cinque minuti*, which with even my very limited Italian meant we had only five more minutes in the shelter of the bus.

"Where are we meeting this friend of yours?"

"In the financial district. If the coast is clear, we can get out here and catch a taxi."

"And if the coast isn't clear?"

"Then we hope no one is waiting at the next stop."

Someone was waiting. Three of them, in fact. Boys that looked to be in the fourteen- to sixteen-year-old range lurked along the passenger drop-off curb outside the big doors of the departure lounge. They all had phones in their hands, watching people. A taxi pulled up and a man and a woman who fit our general description got out. I watched one of the boys snap their photo as the couple waited for the driver to fetch their bags from his trunk and set them on the sidewalk. On his signal, a second boy moved in closer to be in position to follow the couple into the terminal. The two boys hovered, seemed to wait for something. The kid who took the photo suddenly brightened and with an air of happy expectation, checked his screen. His face and posture showed disappointment as he waved off his friend. To us, it was clear what caused them to be disappointed: they got word that the couple from the taxi was not us. Jean-Paul had watched this little drama along with me.

"On to Plan B," I said as we turned our backs to the window. About half the passengers were out of their seats, wrestling with their stuff, filling the aisle as they prepared to exit. Ducking to avoid a backpack when a man turned to speak with someone behind him, I asked, "Why aren't those kids in school?"

"Schools close for lunch. Everyone goes home to eat with the family."

"I suppose that when I was their age, I would have skipped lunch to earn five hundred bucks. Even divided three ways, that's a lot of money for a young kid."

"It would pay for a lot of video games."

The aisle cleared, the driver closed the door and announced the next stop. Central train station, Milan, in twenty minutes.

I said, "At the train station, if all we see are kids like those, I think we should cover our faces and make a dash for the cab stand. They're not likely to catch a cab and follow us. But if the blonde turns up, what do we do?"

"Get a cab, and go. We're meeting Luca at a private club; the blonde won't get past the door."

"A private club?" I said, looking down at the pullover sweater and jeans I had worn for the last two days. "A posh private club?"

"Probably. Luca is a posh sort of guy."

I pulled up our backpack and fished around until I found my black sweater and slacks. And my string of pearls. This I have learned: If I stand up straight, square my shoulders, tilt my chin up just a little, and wear pearls, I will never feel underdressed.

The woman across the aisle was awake after all the hubbub in the aisle earlier, watching what I was doing because there wasn't much else to see. I smiled at her, peeled off my sweater and the T-shirt under it and laid them across John-Paul's lap. As I slipped my arms into the sleeves of the black sweater, she pointed at my new damn-near-perfect, and very expensive, bra and gave me a nod of approval. I nodded back, and slipped the sweater over my head. Boots and jeans came off, slacks went on. The waistband felt loose; I must have lost some weight during the four-month international trek looking for unexploded bombs.

I unwrapped the new red purse I bought at the shop in the Rialto Bridge, and packed it: wallet with passport, the green bank pouch stuffed with cash, a fresh telephone and its fully charged battery. I brushed my hair, slung the purse over my head and put an arm through the strap to wear it across my body, and last, looped the string of pearls around my wrist a few times. I was ready for all comers.

Jean-Paul watched all this with great amusement. As I folded my old things and put them away, he said, "Very nice. How do I look?"

"You look wonderful. You're wearing a button-down shirt and a very good cardigan. You could be a visiting scientist."

"Not quite." He took my hairbrush and ran it through his hair. "Now I'm ready."

I kissed him. "And you're wearing a very expensive coat that belongs to a stranger."

"Freddy isn't a stranger," he said.

"That isn't Freddy's coat. He thinks maybe one of his son's friends left it at the apartment over the holidays."

All he said was, "Hmm."

We didn't spot anyone lurking when we got off the bus at the massive train depot in central Milan. That did not mean that no one was there, or that someone hadn't hacked into the security cameras around the depot, or anywhere else along the way. It only meant that we didn't need to run between the bus and the cab stand. But we did hurry. Clearly, a train had just arrived. We could see a swarm of passengers surging toward us through the wide doors of the art deco depot. Luck and speed were with us, and we snagged the first cab in the queue at the cab stand. Jean-Paul gave the driver the address, and we pulled away from the curb. That's when I saw him.

The big blonde bailed out of a cab that pulled up at the far end of the queue, and started off at a run toward the depot. I nudged Jean-Paul, but he was already watching. Just as our cab wedged its way into the traffic lane, the blonde checked his phone, snapped into a one-eighty turn, until he faced our way. He didn't look directly at us as if he had a tracker on us again, but only at the stream of cabs leaving the depot and the long line of people waiting for them. Before I lost sight of him, he had tried to jump to the front of the line but was forcefully rebuffed. Last I saw, he was on his ass, shaking his head as if dazed. I snapped his picture, because why not?

I looked at Jean-Paul, he smiled and said, "*Merde*. At least, now we know where he is."

When I thought about it, in the context of the crazy video game that we seemed to be trapped in, it made a sort of sense that the blonde would show up at Milan's central transportation hub. We knew we were seen on the road to Parma, but we did not arrive there. If our pursuers assumed we were headed toward Paris, as we assumed they did, once we left the road to Parma where would we go, and how would we get there? If instead of catching the bus, we had hijacked or hitchhiked a ride, most likely, we would head northwest to Milan to find transportation. So it didn't take very much imagination for the blonde to show up when and where he did. The only blip in that bit of rationalization was the message he received that made him turn our way just as our taxi pulled away. Out of an abundance of caution, I took the paring knife we bought in Bologna, still wrapped in brown paper, out from under the cheese in the shopping bag and slipped it into my handbag.

A thought occurred to me when I saw the bank pouch in there. I asked, "Who pays for lunch?"

"I'm sure it will be on Luca's club account. I doubt you'll even see prices on the menu, if you're given a menu at all."

"My, my, sugar pie, the circles you travel in," I said as we drove out of central Milan toward the financial district. I unzipped the bank pouch and pulled out a wad of cash. "You may need some of this before we get to Paris."

He hesitated, but he accepted the money. Without counting the bills, he folded them and slipped them into his right front pants pocket.

The city center was an architectural salad, from Gothic through Baroque and art deco to modern cheap-and-practical. But the financial district was an apparition out of a sci-fi movie. Tall crystalline structures shaped in cylinders, or undulating waves, or clusters of stand-alone arcs, and a tall, narrow, jagged shard, seemed to have risen out of some architect's wild acid trip. Every high-rise façade was glass, and from the direction we were approaching every façade had nothing to reflect except its high-rise neighbors and the bleak winter sky above.

"Is this the Emerald City?" I asked. Jean-Paul shrugged, unfamiliar perhaps with the reference. I said, *"The Wizard of Oz.* Dorothy, Toto, Kansas?"

"Ah." He smiled as he looked up at the buildings out his window. "Green, yes, for money. Though even American money isn't actually green, is it?"

"I suppose not." We could converse easily enough in either French or English, and though we understood the words the other used, sometimes we still needed a translator.

The driver pulled over at a designated taxi stop along a stone-paved circular plaza, and we got out. Four very tall semicircular buildings ringed the plaza. Through gaps between the segments I could see the Alps to the north, the old city to the south, and glass neighbors east and west. While I waited for Jean-Paul to pay the driver, I was thinking what a nightmare it would be to try to find my way home after dark, especially after a few drinks,

if I lived in one of those identical towers. Standing in the middle
of the plaza in the middle of the night, with no visible sun to cast
shadows, what would be one's frame of reference? It occurred to
me as I looked for landmarks that what I was actually doing was
scouting an escape route.

Jean-Paul took my arm as the cab pulled back onto the street,
and we started walking. It was cold, but it felt good to be outside
in fresh air, and moving.

"Do you know where we're going?" I asked.

"*Bien sûr.*" Of course, he would. "Two blocks that way. At the
top of the building that looks like the London Gherkin."

We walked past sleek glass façades and sleek Italian people,
through a massive, shiny glass door, into a futuristic lobby that
rose through the center of all forty-one stories of blue-tinged glass
above. Jean-Paul gave our names and the name of our host to
a man in a Pucci-esque uniform standing watch behind a high
counter. The man snapped his fingers and a woman in a similar
uniform escorted us to the cylindrical glass express elevator that
rose through the center of the lobby, pushed the only button on the
panel, and wished us a good day. When the doors opened again, a
young man wearing a perfect black suit greeted us.

"Signore Ponti has arrived and is waiting in the Gehry dining
room. May I take your coats?"

I checked my pockets before handing mine over, and Jean-Paul
did the same. The backpack and still-fragrant shopping bag dangled
from my hand.

"Do you wish to check your bags with your coats?"

I had to think for a moment about relinquishing the backpack.
In the end, I kept it, gave him the bag with the stinky mortadella
and cheese, half bottle of water and a loaf of bread that must have
been smashed flat by now. As I did, I said, "Handle gently, please,
this is very special. Very special, indeed."

That seemed perfectly reasonable to him. He handed our things
to a young woman who appeared as if from nowhere before he
ushered us past the club's main dining room, down a marble-lined
hallway to a door marked GEHRY. With a little bow, he opened the

door and gestured for us to go through. Shoulders back, chin up, pearls gleaming on my wrist, new red bag diagonally across my torso, tatty old backpack hanging from my hand, I took Jean-Paul's arm and entered.

The room was small. I had the feeling it had been furnished especially for our luncheon trio. A round table set for three sat dead center, a sideboard with serving pieces was against the far wall, and, in a corner, there was a seating area with three upholstered chairs and a little table for coffee or cocktails, or feet if one dared. *Posh* doesn't quite describe the quiet opulence of the room or the man who broke off his conversation with a black-suited waiter to greet us. Our host, Luca Ponti, was a compact man of about Jean-Paul's age, fifty, whose posture suggested that there were lifts inside his handcrafted shoes. Small in stature, maybe, but big in charm and presence.

"Bernard, my dear friend, how happy I am to see you." Grinning broadly, he opened his arms to Jean Paul, saw the empty sleeve, acknowledged that there was an injury with a sympathetic nod, and adjusted his approach so that he only lightly touched the left shoulder when he enveloped Jean-Paul in an embrace. Cheeks were kissed, and then he turned his full wattage on me. "And you are Maggie."

Introductions were taken care of and we were seated. At a signal, the waiter served us cold, bubbly Prosecco in tall crystal flutes and Persian melon wrapped in prosciutto. I noticed that the melon was not cut into the usual long wedges, but was in bite-size pieces to accommodate Jean-Paul, who could not ply knife and fork with only one hand. I wondered, then, how much Luca already knew about what had happened to his friend.

While we ate, the two men caught up on personal news: Jean-Paul's son, Dominic, was in the first year of his *baccalauréate* course, preparing to enter university; Luca's daughter was about to make him a grandfather for the first time; my daughter, Casey, was in her third year at UCLA, studying physiology and biology. All our mothers were, by God's grace, quite healthy, thank you. The melon plates were taken away and the pasta course arrived: perfectly al dente bucatini tossed with roasted root vegetables, garlic, and olive oil, and finished with micro-thin shavings of black truffle. A second wine, an amber-colored fifteen-year-old white from Friuli, was poured into new glasses and exclaimed over as conversation segued to shared histories.

Though they spoke often, the two men had not seen each other for over three years, not since before Jean-Paul left for his consular appointment in Los Angeles. The last time they were together, Luca said after some thought, was at the memorial service for Jean-Paul's wife, Marian, whose sudden death from an aneurysm was still incomprehensible. "So young, so lovely, so full of life."

Luca knew that I, as well, was widowed before I met Jean-Paul. He covered my hand with his, looked at me with moist brown eyes, and said, "Now, I am afraid, it is my turn to mourn."

Jean-Paul froze with a forkful of pasta halfway to his mouth. "Carla? My friend, what happened?"

Luca shrugged, made a little moue. "She ran away with a Swedish photo-journalist named Analiese."

There was a pause, a stillness so profound it seemed as if the earth had stalled on its axis. And then they both burst out laughing. I looked from one to the other, at a loss.

"Well, who could blame her?" Jean-Paul said, wiping his eyes.

"It is sad, yes? But who wouldn't prefer a tall, beautiful globe-trotting Swede to an aging, balding businessman with lifts in his shoes?"

"I wondered why you were walking so strangely," Jean-Paul said. "Have lifts helped at all?"

"Not yet, but I'm hopeful. Dating was trying enough when I was young and had all my hair, but now? I dread getting out there again. Tell me, how did you two meet?"

"My grandmother arranged it," I said.

"Do you think she would help me find someone?"

"You're pretty cute," I said. "She just might keep you for herself. But, before I let you anywhere near my dear grand-mère, tell me why you two find it so funny that your wife left you."

"It isn't the first time she's left me," Luca said. "It's the first time this year, but then this is only February."

"Do you expect her to come back?" I asked.

"She always does," he said. "The last time she left—a young guy she met at the gym—I moved her things out of my bedroom. This time, I moved them into a little apartment in the Brera district. I finally came to realize that when I come home in the evening, if I need drama, I can turn on the television. And, if I tire of it, I can shut it off again."

I asked, "How did you and Jean-Paul meet?"

"University," Luca said after a glance at his friend. "A graduate course in international affairs. I was very disappointed during the first seminar to discover the topic was trade and not, you see, affairs."

"Some idiot tossed us into the same room in a student hovel in New Haven," Jean-Paul said. "Two years we spent together in that hole. I learned to tolerate Luca, and actually found him to be almost likable. Loveable, even. Except he snores like a dying diesel engine."

"It's true," Luca said. "It's so bad I even wake myself."

"What sort of work do you do?" I asked, setting my pasta fork across my plate so the waiter could remove it.

"The hardest work I do," he said, quickly glancing at the waiter as he relinquished his plate, "is avoiding work. But I am paid by a commission that endeavors to protect European trade. My project at the moment is counterfeits. Take for example your very handsome handbag. At first glance, it could pass for Prada's Esplanade model. But on second glance, I could see that, though it was made in an Italian factory, perhaps even the same factory Prada uses, which would be no surprise, the bag is not in fact a Prada. I was happy to see that it did not pretend to be. Your bag has no counterfeit Prada logo or the signature zipper lock. It is instead a *pastiche*, an homage, perhaps, but it isn't a Prada. And it's legal because it doesn't pretend to be other than it is, a very attractive red handbag."

"What would you do if it were a counterfeit?" I asked.

"Confiscate your bag, of course. Grill you about where you found it, go after the vendor, find his source, shut them all down. Or shut them out at the ports."

He and Jean-Paul went on to talk about the problem of keeping cheap knockoffs of very expensive European designer goods from pouring out of Asia to buyers around the globe. When he was consul general of Los Angeles, I knew that Jean-Paul had worked with American customs to keep counterfeits of French luxury goods out of the marketplace. The conversation was interesting, but I knew we were not there to talk shop over lunch with an old friend. Though the waiter was nearly invisible, it quickly became clear to me that we would not speak of anything of substance until the meal was over, and we were alone. To all appearances, Jean-Paul and I were out-of-town visitors, sharing a meal with a friend. And nothing more.

When the waiter left the room to fetch the next course, Luca waited for the door latch to click before leaning in close to speak to Jean-Paul. He kept his voice low. "I did as you as you asked and spoke with Eduardo Suarez. He explained to me what happened."

"Where is he now?"

"At home in Madrid, resting. He asked me to assure you that he's all right. But, are you?"

Jean-Paul nodded, just a forward jut of the chin as the service door began to open again.

A beautiful whole steamed sole was wheeled in on a cart. The fish was boned beside the table and served with white asparagus finished with olive oil and grated Asiago cheese. The discussion turned to the weather, and general hopes that the coming storm would be the last before spring. The fish plates were removed and, at last, icy cold Limoncello, dark chocolate gelato, a bowl of hot-house strawberries, and black coffee were served. Luca thanked the waiter, who bowed and left the room. When he was gone, the real conversation began.

"Jean-Paul, I sent your identification of Sabri Qosja to my contact at Interpol." Luca cleared the table in front of him to make space for the laptop he pulled out of a case on the floor beside his chair. "They were quite interested to learn that he's back in Europe. The last information they had was that he was brought up on charges for kidnapping and assault in Argentina a year ago. Authorities in Argentina told my contact that Qosja fled the country before trial and somehow the charges went away."

"The charges went away?" I said. "Was someone bought off?"

"Probably," Luca said with a sad little smile that meant to me that such an activity was not only common, but to be expected. "Using the bank routing number your little Venetian hacker found, we were able to find a London account, as I told you, that belongs to a company called InterCentro. There was no direct financial link between InterCentro and Qosja. However, we found a payment from InterCentro to a somewhat spurious private security agency that recruits trained combat veterans. Mercenaries, if you will."

Luca tapped a few computer keys and the home page for a company called ProtX4 popped up. The graphics were bright, the services offered provocative: Need to recover assets or locate missing personnel? Need an armed courier, escort, or bodyguard? Need firearms training for you or your staff? ProtX4 has the right man for the job. There was a disclaimer at the bottom of the home page that local laws were always strictly obeyed, but the print was quite small.

"In the U.S. you can go to Guns R Us and fill your trunk with weaponry," I said. "But this is Europe. You can't carry weapons here, but is it legal to hire armed protection?"

"There are circumstances, yes," Luca said. "The web site is very careful to offer nothing that is strictly illegal, though what actually occurs is another matter. I'm certain, for example, that sending in an armed drone is beyond the law. But that happened, yes?"

"Were you able to link Qosja to ProtX4?" Jean-Paul asked as he scrolled through the web site's tabs.

"We did. In truth, Interpol did the work. They have been following a fairly regular stream of electronic deposits from ProtX4 into the accounts of various less-than-savory sorts that they keep tabs on. Qosja is among those they watch. Because ProtX4 contracts its workers by the job, it is sometimes possible to link an individual with a particular event by the dates of payment. Their contractors receive an advance fee before the job, and a final payment when, and if, the job is completed. When I contacted Interpol, they already knew that just a week ago ProtX4 made an electronic transfer to Qosja's account in the Cayman Islands. Interpol's forensics agents then tracked backward to see who had paid ProtX4 at nearly the same time, and among those they collided with was InterCentro."

"Provocative," I said. "But is that proof?"

"Alone, no. Our agents found that just two minutes after funds were sent to Qosja, ProtX4 made an identical deposit into a numbered account in Macau. The Macau account is owned by this man."

Luca tapped a computer key and the big blonde's face filled the monitor. The photo was several years old, but there was no mistaking him for anyone else.

"Meet Johann Bord," Luca said. "Though I believe you have already met, yes? Is this not the man in the photo you sent me?"

"Glory be," I said. "You're a wonder, Luca."

"Don't credit me," he said with a smile. "All the work was done by Interpol's investigators and forensic accounting people. Because Interpol keeps tabs on ProtX4, they are very happy to help. It was their face-recognition software of your photo that gave us Bord's name. Once they had a name, they could pull his dossier from their files."

"Who is Bord?" Jean-Paul asked.

"Like Qosja, he's a man without a country. He was raised in Apartheid-era South Africa; the family were Afrikaans, farmers, old Dutch Boers. After Apartheid, their plantation was burned out, a bit of payback, one supposes, and they emigrated to Zimbabwe. When Bord came of age, he joined the army there, then spent a few years with the national police. For the last twelve years, he's worked as a freelance investigator, promising he can find anyone, anywhere in the world. Kidnapping seems to be his forte, but rumor is that he's out of favor; one too many screw-ups. The recent payment from ProtX4 was the first since he was deported from Singapore last spring. And that my dear friends, is all I know."

"Deported, why?" Jean-Paul asked.

"Carrying a weapon."

"He's here, in Milan," I said, pulling out my little camera and scrolling to the photo I took of Bord on his ass at the train station. "He missed us by minutes."

"Interesting." Luca took out his phone, snapped a screen shot of my picture, tapped out a message, and sent it somewhere.

"You amaze me, my friend," Jean-Paul said, patting Luca's shoulder. "But can you tell us who or what is InterCentro?"

"I wish I had more to tell you, but you only dropped this on me last night. So far, I've found very little except a list of their board of directors." Luca leaned down and pulled a single sheet of paper from his case and handed it to Jean-Paul. I got up to read over his shoulder. There were five Russian sounding names on the page. Not one of them was familiar to me. I looked at Jean-Paul, but he shook his head. Nothing to him, either.

"Who are they?" I asked.

"Russian oligarchs, would be my guess. Two are in Brussels, another in New York, one in Shanghai, the last in London. The company is registered with the EU as an organization that promotes Russian arts and culture globally. I'm sure it's a front for something nefarious."

"I'm impressed, Luca, that you got this far," I said. "Thank you, I think. I don't know of a single reason for these folks to have any interest in me. But I can't speak for Jean Paul because I honestly do not know exactly what it is he does, though he certainly has connections to a great network of very interesting, sometimes spookily interesting, friends."

Luca laughed. "Jean-Paul, you haven't told Maggie what you do?"

"Of course I have," my Prince Charming said with all innocence. "I am a quite boring businessman, and that's all I am."

"What is that business, though?" I asked.

Luca leaned in close to me and took my hand. "If he told you—"

"I know," I said. "He'd have to kill me."

"So let me tell you," Luca said, sitting back again. "Jean-Paul is the ultimate consultant. He is brought in by companies and public agencies to solve problems. He goes in, he looks around, listens to people, puts his thumb on the problem, delivers a report, and then he goes home for dinner. Unless someone sends in a loaded drone."

I looked at Jean-Paul. "That's it?"

He shrugged, smiled. "I think you would say that's it in a nutshell."

"Sometimes, do people take offense?"

"*Bien sûr.* Usually the ones who are at the center of the problem I'm there to help resolve." He stood up and stretched. "But no Russians I can think of. Certainly no one on that list."

"Luca," I said, glancing at my watch. "Do you need to get back to your office?"

"Not for a while. In Italy, my dear, lunch takes as long as it takes."

"May I borrow your computer, and a pen?"

With a little bow, he moved the laptop in front of me and took a pen out of his case. Using the list he gave us, I started Googling and making notes next to the names on the list. In January, one of the two men in Brussels, and his wife, attended a gala celebrating a Tchaikovsky series performed by the Moscow Symphony Orchestra. The man in Shanghai was present last week at the opening of an exhibition of the tsars' Fabergé eggs at an art museum. The exhibit would run through Easter. On Tuesday, the man in London was scheduled to present a lecture in Canterbury about holy ikons of the Russian Orthodox church. He was also on the board of the Parent Sport Council at a school in a London suburb; his son captained the rugby team. And so on. Everything I saw seemed innocent and, with the exception of rugby, it was all arts-and-culture related. If so, I asked Jean-Paul and Luca, why did their company, InterCentro, hire people to drop a bomb on

Jean-Paul, try to blow a hole in a yacht while we slept, and follow us around? No one had an answer.

"What now?" I asked Jean-Paul.

"Home, I hope." He sat down beside me in front of the computer, opened a travel information site, and looked for flights between Milan and Paris. He found several with open seats that were scheduled to leave later that afternoon. He made notes on the back of Luca's list of names, folded the sheet, and tucked it into my not-a-Prada handbag. He saw the wrapped knife I had put there after we saw the blonde at the airport. We made eye contact, but he said nothing. Before he zipped the bag closed, he took out his next dose of antibiotic and swallowed it with cold coffee. "We'll wait to buy the tickets at the airport, *d'accord?*"

"Yes," I said. I did agree. We didn't want to give the gamers who were tracking us any more lead time than was necessary. I erased our search history and gave the computer back to Luca. "Thank you."

We rose; it was time to go. There was a little back-and-forth between the two men about which airport to use, and the best way to get there, before Luca called for a car to take us to Malpensa, the largest of the three regional airports. Luca kissed my cheeks and told me how lovely it was to meet me, at last. But when he turned to Jean-Paul, he clamped a hand over his good shoulder and held on.

"We have been friends a very long time, have we not? Like brothers," he said, searching Jean-Paul's face. When Jean-Paul agreed that they had, Luca began to scold him. "So why did you wait so long to come to me? Eduardo told me you went into hiding after the drone incident. That was five days ago. You know I would have come for you. I would have sent tanks in for you if necessary. But did you call? No. Have I done something that makes you distrust me?"

"Luca." Jean-Paul pulled him into a one-armed embrace; Jean-Paul was a full head taller. "You have to understand. I was afraid. I saw our friend Eduardo blown into the air and covered in blood; I had to breathe life back into him. That same night, a young woman who was sleeping in the hotel bed where I should have been was brutally, coldly, murdered. No one outside of the commission that sent us knew where Eduardo and I were going; it was an inspection tour. So, had a friend, a colleague, done this terrible thing to us? When I found out that I had been hacked and was being followed, I was afraid. I was afraid for myself, and I was afraid for everyone I know. I felt I was poison. Even though I know now that they have targeted only me and Maggie, I still feel like poison. So, Luca, my dear Luca, how could I risk contacting you until I knew it was safe to do so? What if your grandchild never got to know you because I asked you for help?"

Luca pulled back, but didn't let go. With a wicked little smile, he kissed Jean-Paul's cheeks, looked ceilingward, and said, "Dear Lord, if the baby is a boy, please don't let him go bald because of me."

"I hope he has your pure heart," Jean-Paul said, grinning. "But you might save those lifts for him."

"I'm praying for a girl."

Jean-Paul laid his hand along Luca's face. "All forgiven?"

"Almost." Luca took a step back, pulled a handkerchief out of his pocket, and blew his nose. His telephone buzzed. "The car is here. I'll ride shotgun to make sure you get to the airport."

Outside the room, we were helped on with our coats and handed the shopping bag. I exchanged shrugs with Jean-Paul. We had dragged the bag and its contents around for hours. He smiled. "Let's hang on to it. Might be our dinner tonight," he said.

"Unless a genie filled the refrigerator at rue Jacob, I'm afraid it might."

He slipped his hand around my elbow and we followed Luca back down the elevator to the lobby. As we walked across that expanse of polished marble, we could see a black Alfa Romeo Stelvio waiting at the curb with its back hatch and passenger-side doors open. Before we went out the front door, both Jean-Paul and I hesitated, taking time to check the area around the car; I saw no one. Luca went straight ahead, gesturing for the driver to shut the hatch—we had no luggage—as he stepped out onto the sidewalk. Seeing nothing to worry about, we scurried behind him, headed for the car's open back door.

There was a blur to my right and the blonde, Johann Bord, seemed to fly at us. I don't know which of us he was aiming for, but Jean-Paul stepped in front of me to intercept him, and took the blow. Time seemed to speed up and slow down at once as I saw Jean-Paul fall, hard, onto his injured side, but he had managed to deflect Bord, to knock him off balance. Something metallic clattered to the pavement as the big man flailed the air, trying to right himself. He stooped and scrabbled around trying to retrieve whatever it was. I grabbed my handbag's zipper pull, gave it a yank, found the knife, and plunged it, still wrapped, into the underside of Bord's forearm, driving the blade in through muscle and tendon until it hit bone. The brown paper wrapping around the knife blossomed bright red.

"What do you want?" I demanded, seething, as I withdrew the blade. He gripped his arm and fell to his knees. The wrist hung loose, a marionette with its strings cut. I held the knife back, ready to plunge it into his flesh again if he got up. "Tell me what you want with us."

"Stay away," he said, grimacing and pale. "Just go away and stay away."

Luca had Jean-Paul by the waist, got him to his feet, and impelled him head first into the car before two security men hurrying toward us across the lobby could make it out the door. With a signal from Luca, the driver was in his seat behind the wheel with the motor running. Luca took the knife from my hand and gave me a firm push toward the car. I piled in and he slammed the door behind me. I rolled down the window. "But, Luca—"

"Go," he said. "I've got this. Just go."

"We can't leave Luca," I said as the driver maneuvered into traffic.

"*Sí, signora,*" the driver said, but kept going.

Jean-Paul was still on the floor between the seats, where he landed, gray with pain, struggling to keep himself upright when the driver made the first turn to put distance between us and the scene developing on the sidewalk. The last glimpse I had of Luca, he was talking to the security men. And the big blonde looked like a pile of cast-off clothes someone had dumped on the sidewalk.

There was a stunned silence in the car, though my heart pounded so hard I couldn't hear the *thrum* of the car's engine. I got down on the floor beside Jean-Paul, out of sight. With shaking hands, I helped him off with his coat, afraid of what I would find when I unbuttoned the cardigan and the shirt underneath and peeled them away from his injured shoulder. Some of the gashes made when flying shrapnel hit his upper chest were deep, needing both internal and external stitching to hold the edges of the torn flesh together. Some of the sutures had pulled free and now bled. I took gauze and sterile wipes and antibiotic ointment out of the backpack.

Making busyness a distraction from thinking about what just happened, what might have happened, I tore open a wipe and cleaned Bord's blood from my hand, rubbing hard to still the shaking.

Jean-Paul took my hand and kissed the palm. "Don't worry about Luca, *ma chère*. By now, he has contacted Interpol. They will come in to advise the local police about Bord's history, and the situation will be managed. Trust me, he is better off without us there."

"Luca does more than track counterfeit handbags, doesn't he?"

"Yes. When he said he would have sent in tanks to help me, he wasn't necessarily exaggerating."

"And you?" I asked. "Do you do more than help people resolve problems?"

"Not much more, no. But some of those problems might need Luca's ability to call out tanks to resolve."

"I thought that was probably the case." I put pressure over his wound until the bleeding stopped. Then I cleaned the area, replaced the dressing, and adjusted the sling. After his shirt was buttoned again, I handed him the water bottle and a pain pill; he hadn't taken one since the night before. He hadn't needed one. Now he would.

He put the cap back on the water bottle and caught my hand when I reached for it. His color was coming back.

"How do you feel?" I asked.

"Fortunate," he said. "And vulnerable."

"How did he find us?"

"Hacked taxi dispatch? Who knows?" He settled back against the seat. "When we get to Paris, I want to lie low until I have two useful arms again."

"You're plenty useful as you are, but I like the idea of staying out of sight for a while, as long as you're there." I straightened his collar. "You took quite a blow, but you stopped him. He had something in his hand. Did you see what it was?"

"I didn't see anything until he was on top of us. Where did he come from?"

"Behind a planter, I think. Whatever he had, you made him drop it."

"Maybe Luca found it. We'll ask him about it later."

"Poor Luca. What a mess we left him."

"Luca is in his element. He'll be fine. But you: you went after Bord like a ninja. Where did you learn to do that?"

"Nowhere." I shook my head. "Credit pure adrenaline. There was no time to think, I just acted. Lucky the knife was in the handbag, otherwise I'd have swung the shopping bag and beaned him with a very nice chunk of mortadella."

He chuckled. "Another reason to hang on to that bag."

By then, we had left Milan and were on the Autostrada dei Laghi, speeding toward the airport. We scooted up onto the seat and fastened the seat belts. Jean-Paul leaned his head back and closed his eyes as the pain pill began to work. I pulled out a phone and the card that his brother-in-law, Émile, had given me in Paris, and called the mobile number. Émile took the call, but didn't speak; he wouldn't have recognized the number I was calling from.

"Émile, it's Maggie."

"Where are you?"

"On our way to Paris. I'll let you know when we get in. Can you come by the apartment on rue Jacob tonight?"

"We? Jean-Paul is with you?"

"He is."

"How sick is he?"

"You can ask him yourself. But when you come, bring a suture kit and a proper sling for a broken clavicle, please."

Jean-Paul opened his eyes as soon as he heard me say Émile. I handed him the phone. A few bruises, a little patching up, nothing to worry about, he told his brother-in-law. Yes, please reassure Maman everything is fine. Yes, Sunday lunch would be lovely. Yes, we'll call with flight information as soon as we have it. He said good-bye, closed the connection, and handed the phone back to me.

"Émile will pick us up when we arrive."

At Malpensa Airport, the driver parked in a red zone, and the police patrolling traffic said nothing to him. He escorted us to the ticket counter, probably as instructed by Luca, tipped his hat, and said good-bye. We bought tickets for a flight leaving for Charles de Gaulle Airport in an hour. The agent asked for our passports. She looked at mine and handed it right back. But she gave Jean-Paul's careful scrutiny. I expected her to say that the Italian police were coming for us, so we should wait. But what concerned her was the condition of his booklet. The passport had been in Jean-Paul's jacket pocket when the drone blast hit him. The cover was scuffed and singed, and there were brown, bloody fingerprints on one corner. She looked from the document to the empty sleeve of his coat, raised her eyebrows, and asked if he needed special accommodation. He smiled, thanked her, and said that early boarding would be appreciated, telling her she was *très gentille*—very kind—for asking. She blushed.

Friday afternoon in the dead of winter wasn't a bad time to get through the security checkpoint in Milan, especially if one carried nothing except a string bag with cheese and garlicky sausage, and a few clothes stuffed into a backpack. We shuffled through security without any issues and made our way to a VIP departure lounge with forty minutes to spare before takeoff. Jean-Paul got us through the lounge door with an electronic key card. The only other people in the private lounge were a family of four—mom, dad, two young teens—from England, and two businessmen who spoke quietly together in Arabic. As people do, all of them looked up when we came in, then lost interest and went back to whatever they had been doing. The lounge attendant brought us tea, as requested, and we settled in to wait for our flight to be called.

The English parents seemed to be a bit frazzled, and their youngsters, a boy of maybe fifteen and a girl a year or two younger, were restless. From their conversation, I gleaned that their scheduled flight to Heathrow that morning had been cancelled because of weather, and it would be several more hours before they could catch a flight out. The girl announced that she was *bored*, but her older brother seemed mesmerized by whatever he was fiddling with on his phone. I rested my head against Jean-Paul's intact shoulder and closed my eyes, feeling suddenly exhausted; a post-adrenaline let-down, probably.

"Mummy!" I was startled upright by the boy's voice. "Look quick. It's them, you see? It's them."

"Don't point, Trevor," the mother admonished.

"Sorry. But do you see?"

There was a moment of quiet before the mother said, "Yes, you may be right, darling. But no need to make a fuss."

The father said, "What is it?"

"That silly contest Trevor got caught up in this morning," the mother said. "You know the one, spot these people and win a prize. Trevor has been prowling the airport half the day looking for them."

Jean-Paul rose, went over to the boy, and took the phone out of his hand. I followed and looked over his shoulder. There we were, captured in a series of photos taken throughout the day. The most recent was about three hours old, snapped as we dashed for a cab at the Milan railway station. I had every intention of getting out of Italy without another photo of us going out into the ether, so I looked from the mother to the father.

"How appalling," I said. "Who would do something this despicable to us? What a horrible invasion of our privacy."

The father held out his hand and Jean-Paul gave him the son's phone. He scrolled through the photos. "Explain this, Trevor?"

Trevor seemed to shrink a bit. In a shaky voice, he said, "It's just a game, sir. Kids all over Italy have been playing it today."

"A game?" The mother wanted to know, taking a turn to look at the kid's phone. "How can it be a game if this lady and gentleman aren't engaged in the play? Explain to me exactly what you are to do."

"If you find these—" He held an open hand toward us, an alternative to pointing, while he searched for a way to explain to his parents what he was up to. "These targets. If you find these targets before they get to Paris, take a photo, submit it, and then detain them for a bit, you can win the prize. It's a big one, Mummy, five hundred euros."

"Detain us how?" I asked.

"They only said to be creative."

"Creative?" Jean-Paul asked. "What would that entail? Interfere with us? Kidnap us?"

"I guess. I suppose. I don't know."

"Trevor," the mother said. "How very dreadful. What did you plan to do if you found them?"

"He's just a boy, Sherry," the father offered, obviously hoping to sweep this all away.

"Whose game is it?" Jean-Paul asked, nailing the kid in the eye.

The kid just shrugged and thrust his hands into his pockets, looking thoroughly abashed. "I don't know."

"You must know if you hope to claim the prize," I said.

When the kid only hung his head and did not answer, the mother snapped him to attention with a single, sharp "Trevor."

Trevor took the phone from his father, pulled up a new tab, and gave it to me to see. AnoNino had already told us that the offer was made through the hacker in Taiwan, but this was the first time we had seen the actual posting. The bit about keeping us from reaching Paris was a new and interesting nugget.

Jean-Paul had his own phone out. When the other end was picked up, he explained where we were and what was happening. Then he read off the information on the kid's screen that gave information for logging onto the so-called contest and submitting photos. He said *yes* and *no* a couple of times, and then he asked, "What happened after we left?" He listened for a moment, then asked, "Did Interpol intervene?" Another pause to listen. "Who took him into custody? Maggie said he dropped something."

Trevor and his parents stood with similar wide-eyed stares as they listened to Jean-Paul's end of the conversation; the sister wasn't bored anymore. When he put the phone away, I asked, "Luca?"

"Under control. Bord is in hospital, and in custody. He was carrying an injection pen. It was sent for analysis, but Luca suspects he was ready to hit us, or one of us, with a dose of some sort of sedative." When he handed the boy's phone to the father, he said, "This isn't a game your son has been playing. Some very dangerous people have devised this contest as a means to stalk my wife and me. You can see for yourself by looking at me what they are capable of. They are determined to hurt my dear wife as well. I hope, sir, that you think of your family's safety and well-being and put an end to Trevor's participation. If you asked me for advice, and you haven't, I would tell you to destroy that telephone before they can use the information Trevor has already given them to track him and make a target of your family as well."

The father said, "Interpol?"

"Indeed, yes."

Trevor looked horrified at the suggestion of destroying his phone. He held out his hand for it. "Sir?"

Dad dropped the instrument onto the floor and crushed it under his heel.

"Wise decision," Jean-Paul said.

We were no safer in that tony private lounge than we would be out among the hoi polloi. I gathered up our bags and we left, quickly, before the attendant could announce that our flight to Paris was boarding. Again, the fewer people who knew where we were going, the better off we were.

Pre-boarding for our flight was underway when we reached our gate. I told Jean-Paul to lean on me and look pathetic when I told the gate agent that we needed extra assistance to board. She looked at the raw scars on his face and the empty sleeve, scanned our boarding passes, and waved us aboard. The flight was uneventful. And short. Alitalia got us into the air and back on the ground again in an efficient hour and a half. The flight was less than half-full, so deplaning in Paris was quick and painless, as well.

My ear began to adjust from hearing Italian, which I do not understand, to French, which I mostly do, as we walked through the airport toward baggage claim and the exits beyond. Out at the curb, Émile and his wife, Jean-Paul's sister, Karine, were waiting for us.

I had met Karine the previous summer when I was in Normandy working on a film project. She is a painter, an art teacher, and though elegant in the way French women are, she was also just a bit Bohemian: the bright scarf with long, unruly ends; dark hair wound into a loose chignon anchored with a much-used paintbrush; a splotch of cadmium yellow on the elbow of her beautiful black leather coat. While her husband, Émile, a doctor, a man of science, was constant and steady, Karine had a passion for passions. They seemed to make the perfect couple.

Les bises were exchanged on the sidewalk, and after the cheek kissing and much *tsk*-ing and *oh-là-là*-ing and rapid-fire questions about what had happened to Jean-Paul, we were released from their tender clutches to get into the backseat of the family car, a vintage Range Rover SUV with a tangle of easels piled in the back deck.

"Be careful where you sit," Émile cautioned as he handed me into the backseat. "There might be daubs of wet paint. There usually are."

Jean-Paul's phone dinged as we merged onto the freeway into Paris. He read the text, then handed me the phone. The note was from AnoNino. The first part was, the contest to find us and keep us from getting to Paris was over, with no winner. The second part of the message, however, took away any relief we might have felt about the end of surveillance: Sabri Qosja was spotted in Paris, at the Gare de Lyon, ten minutes ago. If he caught a taxi at the train station and headed for rue Jacob, he could be there waiting when we arrived. Fighting rising dread, I handed the phone back to Jean-Paul. He sent a text to someone, and then he placed a call to Madame Gonsalves. He told the concierge to expect us soon, and warned her to be on the lookout for Qosja. He listened to her for a while, thanked her very much, and put away the phone.

"Everything okay?" I asked.

He nodded. "She knew there was nothing to eat in the apartment, so she stocked the kitchen. Just a few essential things, she said. Expect a feast."

"Nice of her."

Karine leaned around to speak to us. "Madame Gonsalves has a crush on Jean-Paul, so keep an eye on him."

"I can't blame her," I said. Then I asked, "You know her?"

"Oh, yes. I am fascinated by the library your mother rescued during the renovations," she said. "As soon as I heard about it, I knew I had to sketch it, just as it was found, before they organized everything. The original room was a beautiful mess. I spent about a week down there with my pad and charcoal. So, yes, I know Madame Gonsalves."

"I would love to see the sketches," I said.

"Any time; they're up on my web page. I still go down from time to time to study the work of the scriptorium nuns; the calligraphy and illumination are exquisite. Of course, the library looks nothing like it was originally, not since the librarians and historians got their hands on it. The collection has been tidied up, catalogued, and shelved on factory-made shelves in a climate-controlled room. Very orderly. The documents are magnificent—some of them, anyway—but something about the original state of the collection, the dusty patina the whole of it acquired with age and neglect, has been lost."

"You aren't suggesting that we should have left the library as we found it," Jean-Paul said.

"No," Karine said with a sigh. "But still."

Jean-Paul reached up and patted the arm she rested on her seat back. It was a gentle, fond gesture. She smiled back at him.

"You're going to look like a gangster, Jeep, with those scars."

"I'm aiming for swashbuckler," he said. "Maybe I'll grow a big beard."

Émile laughed. "Maggie, do you approve? Should he grow a beard?"

"It's his face, his whiskers, his decision. But it's my choice whether to kiss it or not, right?"

"*Bien sûr,*" he said with a chuckle.

"Something to consider," Jean-Paul said, scuffing my cheek with the five-o'clock shadow on his chin.

It was early evening in Paris, after the worst of rush hour. When we came off the peripheral road, the City of Light was ablaze. A gentle snow fell. I held Jean-Paul's hand and, with the sense of wonder I always feel in Paris, I watched as landmark after landmark rolled past the windows. Skillfully, Émile negotiated his way around the Arc de Triomphe's insane roundabout and somehow emerged, intact, out the opposite side. I was impressed, and told him so. He shrugged; it was something he did twice a day, going to and coming from work. We crossed the Seine on the Pont d' Alma, caught a glimpse of the Eiffel Tower awash in a shower of glittery snow, down rue de l'Université until it became rue Jacob, and then a long circle around the block because rue Jacob is a one-way street. We saw no one on the sidewalk, and no one followed us, but not seeing Qosja was little comfort. If Bord had followed me from Isabelle's apartment on Thursday, Qosja knew where to find it on Friday.

As we approached number seven, I pulled out the apartment keys Madame Gonsalves had given me and pressed the button on the attached fob to open the big iron gates. I sensed that Jean-Paul was as anxious as I was for them part quickly to let us in, and then to close quickly once we were safely through. Madame Gonsalves came out of her apartment next to the gate as soon as we drove in, and followed us across the courtyard carrying a large shoe box.

"*Zut alors,*" she uttered when she saw Jean-Paul. "And how is the other man?"

"In hospital," he said. "But Maggie gets the credit for that."

"Maggie does?" Karine said, eyes wide.

Jean-Paul squeezed my bicep. "*Bien sûr.* Comes by it naturally. Did I ever tell you about the time her grandmother slashed a Nazi's throat?"

"You did." She seemed dubious.

"Don't make Maggie cross when she's holding a knife, sister dear."

"Lordy," I said, unlocking the front door and leading the parade inside.

The apartment was spotless. Not a dirty towel or athletic sock in sight. As soon as we were inside, Émile, carrying his medical bag, took Jean-Paul by the arm and walked him down the hall to the bathroom to tend to his wounds. Karine went into the kitchen to find the bottle of wine Madame Gonsalves told us she had left on the counter next to the refrigerator. While the others were busy, the concierge emptied the box she brought in onto the table behind the sofa and began going through the contents with me.

"These are the utility bills," she told me. "Isabelle put them on automatic payment, and that was fine with Freddy when he and his boys lived here. But I thought you would want to see them and decide for yourself."

There were also a few Christmas cards from people who, clearly, hadn't updated their mailing lists since Isabelle's death; a professional journal with a notice that it was time to renew the subscription; some belated condolence notes addressed to Isabelle's family; and a sheaf of maybe two dozen letters, most of them on university letterhead. Requests by scholars to access the library, Madame Gonsalves told me, snapping the rubber band that bound them together. No new permissions had been granted for well over a year because Jean-Paul had been in Los Angeles until recently and Isabelle was— Madame Gonsalves crossed herself instead of uttering the word *dead*. However, she told me, out of fairness, Jean-Paul had asked her to continue unlocking the library door for scholars who had work in progress when the event she would not name occurred.

"You have access to the library keys, then?" I asked.

"How else would they get in?" she said, leading me into Isabelle's office. She opened the top desk drawer and took out an old tin box that had once held throat lozenges. She shook it, heard nothing, flipped the lid, dropped it onto the desktop when she saw it was empty and, with some urgency, began shuffling through the top drawer. Out came paperclips, rubber bands, pens, random notepads, and a stapler. Finally, after reaching to the very back, she found a set of keys on a brass ring. She handed me the keys, and went back to examine the old tin box, opening and closing the lid several times, hearing it click shut, with a look of consternation on her face. "The keys must have fallen out."

"Thank you," I said. "I had no idea where to look for them."

She opened and closed the box again, shrugged, and set it back inside the drawer.

I took out the little volume I had found on Isabelle's desk earlier and showed it to her. Her eyes grew wide.

"How did that get here?" she said, scolding. "Madame was very strict, nothing leaves the library."

"It was on the desk when I arrived."

She started to shake her head, but when a thought occurred to her, she said, "You better ask Freddy."

Karine was coming in from the kitchen with a bottle of wine and glasses on a tray when we walked back into the main salon. She poured a glass, a deep garnet red, and handed it to me. "I think we all need this."

Madame Gonsalves declined the proffered wine, told me she was happy we were back, but she had a program coming on television in a few minutes. Before she went, I showed her the photos of Sabri Qosja and Johann Bord, and asked if she had ever seen them.

"This one," she said, touching Bord's nose. "He came by a week ago—Wednesday, Thursday?—asking if there were any vacancies. I told him no, but he didn't like the answer. He said he knew someone had died and that her apartment was still empty and he wanted to see it. I told him it wasn't available. He wanted to know who he could call about it. I told him he was talking to her. Finally, he left."

"Where did this take place?" I asked.

She waved over her shoulder. "He was outside, on the street, talking to me on the intercom. I don't think he knew I was watching him on the security camera. He'd scrunch up his face and flip me the finger when he didn't like what I said. Even if there was a vacant apartment, I wouldn't let him have it. That guy, *un joyeux trou du cul.*"

I didn't understand the words, but I got their meaning well enough.

"There's soup on the stove," Karine said. "Did you make it, Madame?"

The concierge shrugged, dismissing her gesture, a very kind and generous gesture, as if it were of no importance, only what one does every day. She turned to me. "Monsieur Bernard, will he be all right?"

"I'm sure he will," I said. "Some scars, but he'll heal."

"I worried, you know, when the delivery came from the pharmacy yesterday. You looked fine, so I knew it was for him. Tell him I'm glad he's okay."

"Thank you. I know a nice bowl of your soup will make him feel a lot better."

The modest shrug again, but color rose in her face and she smiled. She got as far as the door, tapped her head as if she'd just remembered something, pulled a scrap of paper out of her apron pocket and handed it to me.

"This little pest came by twice," she said. "He was here at the New Year with Freddy's boy, Philippe. *Mon dieu*, the racket those boys made. Poor Monsieur Griffith in the apartment below. He complained twice about all the running up and down on the stairs at all hours. Playing some game, the boys told him. After they offended the cleaners, I told them I was going to call Freddy if they didn't stop."

"Did they quiet down?"

She shrugged. "They left. Anyway, this one came by twice. He told me he left his coat behind and he needed it. Could he go back in and get it? I told him he could ask you when you got here, but I didn't let anybody in without your permission, or unless Freddy was with him. I thought he might cry."

"When was this?"

"Two weeks ago? Maybe three. That was the first time. Second time was last week sometime. Early in the week, I think. He said he had a note from Freddy so it was okay to let him in. I told him to slip the note under the gate. I took a look at it and I knew that Freddy didn't write it. I told the kid I would call Freddy to check, and he said never mind. I haven't seen him since."

The note made me smile. There was a time I regularly forged my parents' signatures on notes that looked very much like this one, usually when I wanted to ditch school. I never got away with it. The nuns, my keepers in high school, had my parents' signatures on file.

If there were any doubt, they would call Mom and Dad to verify that I was a wannabe truant. The kid's note read like something I might have written when I was maybe sixteen: "I give permission for Val Barkoff to enter the apartment to get his coat, the one he forgot. Signed Freddy Daymoulan." He misspelled Desmoulins. I set the note aside to show Jean-Paul. Had Freddy or Madame Gonsalves mentioned young Barkoff's name? Through the fog of a long day, it rang a distant bell. I understood why he would be upset when he couldn't get his expensive coat back. I wondered whether Madame Gonsalves might have been more accommodating if she had come to like the boy. I was happy that she had not.

"Everything all right?" Karine asked. She was in an easy chair with her stocking feet up on an ottoman, wineglass held between both hands, looking very comfortable.

"At the moment, yes." I took the stack of library requests and my wine and sat down opposite her. After a lovely sip or two, I set the glass on a side table and opened the first letter. "You called Jean-Paul 'Jeep.' A family nickname?"

"When I was tiny I couldn't say Jean-Paul, so he became Jeep, and Jeep he still is. For me, anyway. I love my big brother very much. Is anyone going to tell me how he got hurt?"

"It's a long story. I'll let him tell you." Out of curiosity, I scanned the letters as we talked, now and then passing an interesting one to Karine. They were exactly what I expected, earnest requests for access to certain texts or topics from graduate students or university faculty, though some were from independent scholars, with brief descriptions of research projects and the reasons those projects needed access to the convent library. Most had enclosed a *curriculum vitae*, a summary of their academic accomplishments, and some graduate students added letters from senior faculty advisors. They came from across Europe, the U.S., and Canada. Several were second or third requests; no one had looked at the requests since Isabelle died, a year and a half ago.

Madame Gonsalves had stacked the letters chronologically, with the most recent on the bottom. It was the last two letters in the pile that got my attention, both with the same letterhead, one sent early in January, the other on the first of February, three weeks ago. As soon as I saw the return address, I sat up straight and tore into the envelopes. I snapped open the folded pages inside, found a routine-looking access request and a follow-up. But it was the signature that got me to my feet.

"Excuse me," I said. "I need to speak with Jean-Paul."

On my way to the bathroom, I snatched up the note from Val Barkoff and the little book of Psalms from Isabelle's office, and tried to keep from running down the hall. Karine followed close behind. I'm afraid I was so focused on getting to Jean-Paul that I ignored her stream of questions.

"Almost finished here," Émile said, looking up from the brace he was buckling around Jean-Paul's torso. The shirt Jean-Paul had taken off lay in a heap on the floor with my homemade sling tossed on top of it. "The patient needed a bit of repair, just a few new sutures, but he's healing well. As soon as he gets a shirt on, I want to take him over to the clinic to get a nice picture of that bone, just to make sure."

"Oh, Émile," Karine said. "They've been through enough for one day. Can't it wait until tomorrow?"

"No," he said, smiling sweetly as he made a last adjustment to the brace. "If Jean-Paul refractured the bone during the fall this afternoon, we need to reset it, now."

"What fall?" she wanted to know.

"Jean-Paul," I said, handing him the kid's forged note. "Philippe's friend, the one who left the coat, pushed this under the gate."

"Okay," he said, handing back the note after reading it. "He can't spell Desmoulins and he wants his coat. So?"

"Maggie, Jean-Paul will need a clean shirt," Émile said. "The old one has a bit of gore."

"There's one in the backpack," I said as I handed Jean-Paul the two letters, and gave him the kid's note again.

"*Merde,*" he muttered, looking between the signature on the letters and the name on the note. The return address on the letters was InterCentro, the Russian company that paid the agency that hired Bord and Qosja. The signatory, the man who wanted permission to study the library's collection, was Boris Barkov, an expert, he said, on Russian Orthodox iconography and literature. The spelling of the surname was a little different from the boy's, but the pronunciation would be too similar for this to be a coincidence.

According to the list Luca gave us, Boris Barkov sat on the InterCentro board of directors. When we Googled him earlier, we had learned that he was to deliver a lecture next week on holy ikons and manuscripts of Russian Orthodox churches. And that he sat on a parents' advisory council for a rugby club at a boarding school in England.

"Philippe goes to a boarding school in England, doesn't he?" Jean-Paul asked.

"Yes, but I don't know which. I'll have to ask Freddy." I handed him the volume of Psalms. "The script is very ornate, and it's difficult to read. When I first saw it, I thought it was Greek, because the illuminated capital is *pi*, the Greek equivalent of the Latinate *P*. But I was wrong. It isn't Greek, Jean-Paul. The text is written in the Cyrillic alphabet of Russia."

"*Merde,*" he said again. "It's probably one of the books that showed up here during the Russian Revolution."

"What the hell is going on?" Karine demanded to know.

"We're going to the clinic," Émile said. "Karine, if you don't mind, I understand your brother has a clean shirt in the backpack in the vestibule. Please get it for him, because we are going right now."

6

"*THAT WAS A FIRST* for me," I said, fluffing my pillow before lying back on it.

"What was?" Jean-Paul draped a leg over mine.

"Sex with a one-armed man."

"Oh yes? Something you might consider again?"

"I might." I kissed the side of his face. "I very well might."

He laughed and pulled me against him. "What else is on the agenda for the day?"

"A shower, coffee, whatever Madame Gonsalves left in the kitchen for us to eat, and then down to the library. I am dying of curiosity."

"I pray you aren't dying of anything," he said, disentangling himself from me and the sheets. "Don't forget, someone is coming to install a security system this morning."

I groaned, got to my feet, and found something clean to wear in the suitcase I had left open on the floor of Isabelle's room the night before. "How does your shoulder feel this morning?"

"Better, much better."

"I am very happy you didn't re-break the bone when you hurled yourself into Bord."

"I'll be happy when this damn brace comes off," he said, sitting on the edge of the bed. "Back to the agenda: I would very much like to go by my house today. I need to get some clothes and pick up a laptop. But I also want you to look around the place and decide if it feels haunted or if it's just too hideous for you to ever consider as a place to live."

"I doubt it's hideous," I said, turning around to look at him. "Why did you say that?"

"One day, soon I hope, we need to decide on a place, or places, to land together. I assume we will always have two homes, but what will they be? Will you keep your house in California or find a *pied-à-terre*? We'll be there often, of course, but how often will depend on where either of us is working. The same for France. Do we keep my house, this apartment, or do we start over and find something of our own? So much to consider. I have only one requirement, and that is, whatever we decide, we will end up in the same place most of the time."

Jobs, families on two continents, friends, finances, houses full of stuff: so much to sort out. My head was spinning a bit, so I sat down on the bed beside him. He put his arm around me and none of that seemed to matter anymore. I looked up at his handsome, scarred face, and changed the subject. "How long will the workman be here?"

A little shrug: "Not very long. Once he has the cameras installed outside, all he has to do inside is connect the wires to a control panel he'll put on the wall near the front door."

"Where will the cameras be?"

"He'll tie you into the existing street camera, and put up new cameras over this building's outer door and your apartment door. You'll be able to monitor all three from inside. The street-cam works through a Wi-Fi connection, but the cameras on this building will be hard-wired and connected to nothing except your control panel."

"No one can hack them."

"Exactly. You can come and go without putting on TV makeup because you won't be on camera."

"Good." I took a deep breath. "Shower, food, camera guy, your house, library—in that order. Does that sound all right?"

"Perfect. I'll take you to lunch at my favorite local."

"It's a date." I gave him a last kiss and headed for the bathroom.

We just sat down to eat when the security camera installer arrived. As Jean-Paul had said, it didn't take very long to drill a hole to connect a wall panel to the cameras the man had already installed outside. He was showing me how to toggle between cameras when our first test of the system knocked on my door. A tall, distinguished, angry-looking man stood on my doormat. With Jean-Paul and the installer as backup, I risked opening the door.

The man standing there seemed about to launch into a verbal fusillade, but stopped abruptly when he actually looked down and saw me. Scowling, he said, "Who—?"

"I believe that's my question to you. Who are you?"

"I happen to live in the apartment downstairs. The formerly very quiet apartment downstairs. Whoever you are, I want you to know that I have no intention of putting up with any more racket from you people. I got my fill over the holidays, thank you very much. And now you're at it again. I came in from the bakery to a cacophony of machinery shaking the very walls."

I put out my hand. "You must be Barry Griffith, my new neighbor. Lovely to meet you. I am Maggie MacGowen, Isabelle's daughter. This is my fiancé and your other landlord, Jean-Paul Bernard, and this is the workman who has installed new security cameras over the doors. I am profoundly sorry about the noise; we should have warned you. He's just finished. Won't you come in for some coffee? There are croissants, as well, but I'm afraid they're yesterday's."

He took in a deep breath, thought for a moment, and then he smiled. "I am delighted that at last we meet, Madame MacGowen. And Bernard, my apology, sir. I didn't see you there."

Jean-Paul bobbed his head, accepting the apology. "Monsieur Griffith."

Griffith held up a net shopping bag that smelled deliciously of fresh bread. "Thank you, yes, I would love coffee. It's damn cold out and I am numb to the core. Keep yesterday's croissants, I bear fresh brioche, still warm from the oven."

I found cups and plates, spoons and knives in the sorts of places where they are usually stowed in a kitchen, and butter, jam and milk in the refrigerator, thanks to Madame Gonsalves. The men helped carry things out to the big dining table in the salon. I was becoming adept with the French coffee press, the *cafetière*, and showed off a bit with the plunger before pouring the coffee. Barry Griffith, a francophone Canadian from Montreal, turned out to be interesting, smart, and very funny. I had some questions for him about building etiquette, trash days, recycling, and things I needed to know to get along with our neighbors.

Each wing of the *résidence* functioned as a separate building. Jean-Paul told us that this was a matter of safety and efficiency, to prevent people, water, and fire from wandering where they shouldn't. The only area accessible from all three wings was the basement, because utilities and storage were below. However, residents only had keys to the basement door that led into their own central hallway, and not for the doors up to the other two wings.

Mention of the basement brought up the issue of Philippe and his noisy friends over the holidays. According to Griffith, the boys had engaged in some sort of electronic tag or war game that they played in the basement and up and down the stairs that led past his doorway up to Isabelle's, and even the two floors above. Griffith, on the ground floor, heard them below him, in the basement, at all hours of the day and night, slamming heavy doors, yelling, running, and generally making an unholy noise. He said that Philippe, who had always been such a nice youngster, seemed powerless to stop his friends, even though he could be heard pleading with them to quiet down. The last straw was on their last day there, when they could be heard arguing. Doors banged, feet pounded down the stairs, and then silence, blessed silence, reigned once more. Until the installer showed up with his drill that morning. Again, I apologized for not warning him.

When Jean-Paul went out to speak with the workman, I moved the conversation with Griffith to the topic of the library. He told me that Isabelle had invited him down several times. Turns out, he taught history at the Sorbonne, and though his area of expertise was twentieth-century Asia, he thoroughly appreciated the collection and cherished those invitations.

"Knowing what's below my feet, I feel sometimes as if I'm living above a secret pirate cache, a treasure worth more than its weight in gold."

"How much do you think it's worth?" I asked.

He drew back, appalled. "You aren't considering selling, are you?"

"Of course not," I said. "But treasure inspires lust in the hearts of some men. After the gauntlet we've had to run during the last few days, I am wondering if maybe there isn't a pirate with a shovel out there, just waiting to dig up this particular treasure."

"A gauntlet, you say?"

"I don't know how else to describe it," I said, pouring him the last of the coffee. "But what do you think the collection downstairs might be worth on the open market?"

He shook his head. "There are all sorts of documents down there, some are priceless, some are little more than interesting relics. Value can only be set by the marketplace. If I were a wealthy man, and I am not, I would certainly make a bid on some of the ornate government records deposited here during the Russian Revolution, if only to save them from some oligarch buying them to frame and hang over his sofa."

"Why did you say oligarch?" I asked.

"Did I?" He furrowed his brow and thought for a moment. "I suppose that came to me because some weeks ago, when I had a few colleagues in for drinks, a friend in medieval studies told me that a Russian man came into the department asking for information on how to gain access to the rue Jacob library. She knew he wasn't an academic because he wore a custom-made suit and was followed by a complement of burly bodyguards. But she was intrigued enough by the story that she shared it with me, knowing that when she was in my apartment she was standing nearly on top of the library."

"Did she get a name?"

"It wasn't she who spoke with the man, but I'll ask," Griffith said. "Is it important?"

"Possibly." I put the lid on the jam pot and covered the butter. "Mr. Griffith, do you know what happened to the convent that was here?"

He shrugged, a very French shrug. "Changing mores, probably. You know Saint Jérôme Émilian was originally a haven for bastard daughters? With better birth control, more opportunities for women no matter their origins, the extraordinary cost of keeping an official mistress; over time the convent lost its *raison d'être*. The stream of young *illegitimae* and the endowments attached to them dried up. From what Isabelle told me, by the end of the Second World War, the convent was only surviving on fumes and the random sale of furnishings."

Jean-Paul closed the door behind the workman and asked Griffith and me to come and check out the new system. We fooled around with it, toggling between cameras, seeing cars spray slush as they passed by on rue Jacob. A cat ventured out onto the snow-covered courtyard. No one stood in the hallway outside Isabelle's apartment.

"Could I be connected to this?" Griffith asked. Jean-Paul handed him the workman's card and told him he would need to install a separate system, but it could be done.

"Maggie," Jean-Paul said after a last look at the weather on the street outside the gates. "If we're to get to Vaucresson for lunch, we should go soon."

"Ah, Vaucresson. Such a lovely area," Griffith said, clearly in no hurry to leave, though he did get back to his feet. "There's a wonderful public garden. But of course, how silly of me; it must be covered in snow."

Jean-Paul opened the door, we thanked Griffith for the brioche and the conversation, told him we would love to come down for drinks sometime very soon, good to meet you, nice to see you, and good-bye.

Griffith was nearly out the door, when he turned. "I haven't seen a car in your space. How are you getting to Vaucresson?"

"Train," Jean-Paul said.

"The weather is filthy. Let me drive you to the station. Don't say no; I'm heading off to Amboise for lunch with friends, so I can drop you on the way."

We were very happy to accept the offer. After we bundled up, we checked the street again on the new monitor to make sure that anyone we didn't want to see wasn't lurking outside the gate, and went downstairs to wait for Griffith.

Jean-Paul told me earlier that his home was an easy commute, as long as the trains were running. On that snowy Saturday morning, we sped west through the outer neighborhoods of Paris, to the white-shrouded suburbs. One village or town looked very much like the others: shops, houses, open space, followed by houses, shops, open space; like a string of beads along the rail line. Through a curtain of snow, I saw some men on a golf course, well bundled up, hitting bright orange balls across a pure white green.

"Dedicated golfers," I said.

"Idiots," he answered, with a fond smile.

The Vaucresson station looked like any suburban commuter station; we might as well have been in Connecticut. I don't know what I expected, but I was a bit disappointed that it was so ordinary. Jean-Paul took my arm and we walked along the platform to the parking lot, where his black Mercedes waited, with motor running.

"How did you arrange that?" I asked when I saw it.

"I called Ari and asked him to meet us."

"Ari?"

"My factotum," he said. "He is caretaker, gardener, house cleaner, repairman, horse groom, and sometimes driver."

"Where did you find such a person?"

"In a refugee camp. Ari was a medical doctor in Syria before the civil war. Lost everything. He's a good man. But I have to warn you, he suffers from Post-Traumatic Stress Disorder, so avoid making loud noises or sudden moves around him."

Ari, a tall, slender man with close-cropped hair and a

perpetual-looking five-o'clock shadow, climbed out to open the
car's back door for us. The two men greeted each other with an
embrace and *les bises*. I was introduced, and offered a perfunctory,
rather shy, handshake; he did not meet my eyes.

We drove through streets lined with naked trees. The houses
I could see were large, usually set back from the road, shielded
behind landscaping. Did I say big? Ari turned into a long graveled drive that ended at a stark, ultra-modern confection. Except
for garage doors and narrow window slits, the two outer walls I
could see were featureless slabs of sandstone that was disconcert-
ingly very nearly the same color as my winter-white flesh. I had
the feeling that if I stood nude against those walls I might disappear altogether, except that my curves and bumps might give me
away against that flat surface. And in that weather, I'd turn blue
and freeze my naked ass off, so this wasn't something I actually
contemplated doing.

Ari pushed a button, a garage door opened, and we drove into
a comforting clutter of garden tools, a collection of bikes and ski
gear, broken lamps, and drippy paint cans. After the stark exterior,
the house's warm interior was a surprise: rustic wooden floors, stair
rails, and beams; comfortable-looking, practical furnishings. Essentially, the house was a giant triangle. Garages, offices, utility room,
kitchen, and upstairs bedrooms were built along the right-angled
back wall. The rest of the house was a single, vast open space with
soaring ceilings. The hypotenuse of the triangle was a long glass
wall, two stories tall, that opened out onto a large terraced garden
with a swimming pool and a small guest house, where, Jean-Paul
told me, Ari lived.

"Not what you expected?" Jean-Paul asked, wrapping his good
arm around my waist as I stood at the edge of the space between
the kitchen and the massive salon, taking it all in. The interior, if
not cozy, was accessible, friendly, stunning. That much I expected.
The scope of the wealth that made these casual comforts possible
was the surprise.

"I didn't know what to expect," I said. "Except maybe stables."

He pointed across the garden. "Go through that gate. The
stables are at the riding club next door."

Looking up at the beamed ceiling, I said, "We've never talked about money."

"What's to say?" he said, nuzzling his chin against my temple as he followed my gaze upward.

"Quite a lot, I expect."

He shrugged, making light of what could be a very touchy subject. "We'll need to sit down with a pencil before we take the next step, of course. But after I show you mine and you show me yours, what's left to discuss? The tax and exchange issues involved in moving money back and forth between France and America can be difficult and costly. I believe that the ideal situation would be to use any American income and assets as much as possible when we are there, and French income and assets when we are here. What do you think?"

"In a perfect world, that would work. Especially if we had similar incomes. But we don't. When we do get married, my widow's pension from Mike goes away. If I don't sign a new contract with the network, or if I decide to work in France, my American income will nearly disappear. If we need to depend on residuals from my old films and earnings from my meager investments to live there, we might end up sharing Casey's dorm room."

He laughed. "I hope, then, that she's a better roommate than Luca was. Less smelly, anyway. But I have investments in America, so don't worry, we won't go hungry."

"Jean-Paul, have you ever had to worry about money?"

"Please don't hold it against me, but no. Early on, Marian and I had to keep a strict budget, and both of us had to work, but we never did without the essentials and a few luxuries. My parents went through the great depression and the world war, like yours, and vowed that their children would never be hungry or have holes in their shoes. They worked very hard to make that a reality. I understand their sacrifices, and I understand the toll the struggle took on them. And I fully realize the advantages I have had in life. If I have had any success, I give all credit to Maman and Papa."

"Don't forget," I said. "They also gave you looks, brains, and charm."

He laughed. "Are we talking about you, or about me?"

"Your family story could be mine, if you leave out surviving the Nazi Occupation."

"If you mean your American family, yes." He turned my chin to look up at him. "You still don't think of your grandmother and your brother, and so on, as family, do you?"

"Not yet. I love Grand-mère, and I am fond of my uncle, my cousins, and Freddy, but I don't know them well enough yet to think of them as family."

"In time, maybe." He kissed me. "Shall I give you the tour?"

I was relieved for the change in topic. Both topics, money and blood kin.

We went from room to room. They were all comfortably and practically furnished. Dom's room was what one would expect for a teenager's quarters, posters and books and computers, scuff marks on the walls, sports gear piled in corners. A framed portrait of his late mother sat on a dresser, with a school necktie draped over it. There were a couple of standard guest rooms. And then the master bedroom, the room Jean-Paul had shared with Marian. I felt a flutter in the pit of my stomach when he opened the door. But there were no ghosts. Marian's side of the walk-in closet was empty. There were no half-used pots of face cream on the vanity or shrines to the dead wife on the bedside table. It was just a bedroom. A man's bedroom.

Jean-Paul pulled out a familiar weekend bag and packed it with the efficiency of a frequent traveler while we talked about our horses and what to do with them. Mike and I had rescued two horses that we kept in a corral in the front yard of the house we had shared in the Santa Monica Mountains above Malibu. They were lovable if not beautiful nags, trail horses that we rode for fun. Jean-Paul belonged to a polo club and had kept a string of polo ponies, though he'd hardly had time to ride since I'd known him, and now had only two. What to do with all the beasts? I could not imagine old Red or Rover getting along with the polo crowd, but I thought that Jean-Paul's ponies might be very happy ambling along our rugged mountain trails, assuming we would be in the

U.S. often enough to ride them. That conversation got us nowhere, so we moved on to our offspring.

My Casey was at UCLA, a year from graduation, and then on to graduate or medical school somewhere. Jean-Paul's son was in the first year of a two-year preparatory course before entering one of the *Grandes Ècoles*, the elite French colleges. Since fall, when Jean-Paul's appointment to the consulate in Los Angeles ended and Dom and his father returned to France, Dom had lived with his maternal grandparents nearby in Versailles because Jean-Paul's work required him to travel frequently. That is, our kids were grown, out of the nest. The issue of aging parents was more problematic, with many details to be worked out. Falling in love was the easy part. The issues that attached, not so much.

Jean-Paul took a coat of his own out of his closet and stuffed young Val Barkoff's coat into a duffel. We stopped at his downstairs office for a laptop and a couple of files. He rolled back a Persian rug to reveal a safe built into the floor. He knelt, spun the combination lock, and pulled out some cash, a credit card, and a ring of labeled keys. The cash and the card went into a pocket, and everything else went into a leather messenger bag. On our way to the kitchen, where he retrieved a bottle of Port, he called Ari and told him we were leaving. There was a brief conversation about one of the horses and what to do with some produce in the refrigerator, some words of reassurance that Jean-Paul felt fine, and then he promised that we would be back soon.

"Ari worries," Jean-Paul said as he put his phone into his cardigan pocket.

"Are you his family now?"

"His haven, certainly. Friend, yes, I hope. Family, no. Family sits down to dinner together, and they share the intimacies of life. Ari eats only halal food, so he cooks for himself in the guest house. He never drops in just to chat or watch a movie with me. I think I can best characterize our relationship as symbiotic—we need each other. I have watched him grow stronger with time. One day, he'll be ready to go back out into the world. But for the time being, this arrangement works for both of us."

Mentally, I added one more issue to resolve before we decided where we were going to live. And that was, Ari.

We ate lunch at a bustling bistro among the shops on the village's main street. I was introduced to old friends, nodding acquaintances, and the proprietor who stopped by our table on the pretext of saying hello, but who actually wanted to know how Jean-Paul acquired his injuries. Jean-Paul's simple answer to everyone's questions, subtle and otherwise, was, "Slipped on the ice." Some may have believed him.

After lunch, we followed Jean-Paul's normal Saturday routine and shopped for groceries. His injuries earned him a bag of chocolate-dipped shortbread cookies from the sympathetic baker, an extra piece of cheese—excellent calcium for repairing bones—from the *fromagère*, and *les bises* from the butcher's wife, though I suspected she was happy for the excuse, any excuse, to smooch him; I always was. A visit to the wine shop and the greengrocer finished the rounds. We stowed our purchases in the car, and headed back to Paris with Jean-Paul driving his Mercedes. The day was still frigid, but it had stopped snowing. The highway, the Autoroute de Normandie, was clear and traffic was light all the way into the city. We made the turn onto rue de l'Université twenty-five minutes after we pulled out of the Vaucresson car park.

Rue Jacob is a narrow, one-way street. Jean-Paul circled around the block to approach the apartment from the correct direction. As he turned off rue de Seine onto rue Jacob, we saw the flashing blue and red lights of an emergency vehicle and the usual gawkers gathered on the sidewalk. I craned up from my seat to gawk along with them as Jean-Paul slowed to a stop. There were an ambulance and two police cars, with various uniformed people milling about. Looking past the police cars, I could just see the top of the head of a person sitting in the open back doors of the ambulance, talking with the officials. As soon as I realized who it was, I was out of my seat belt, reaching for the door.

"Madame Gonsalves," I said on my way out of the car. I ran. Jean-Paul was right behind me. In a few strides, he overtook me and got to the concierge before I did. She was conscious, alert, holding a towel to the back of her head while a paramedic examined her bloody knees and a policewoman questioned her. There was a puddle of fresh blood quickly freezing on the sidewalk.

"Monsieur Bernard," she cried out, reaching a hand toward him, hurrying him. He sat beside her and wrapped his arm around her shoulders as he asked questions: what, who, how bad. Still holding the towel to the back of her head, she leaned against him and wept. After a great, heaving sigh, she composed herself, and blew her nose into the handkerchief Jean-Paul offered her.

"What happened?" Jean-Paul looked from her to the hovering policewoman.

"He came up behind me." The concierge pointed at me. "It was him. That man you showed me. He hit me on the head and grabbed my handbag."

The policewoman scowled at me. "Do you know who is she talking about?"

I pulled my camera out of my pocket, opened the shot of Sabri Qosja, and showed it to Madame Gonsalves. "This man?"

She started to nod, but winced and didn't. "Yes, that man."

I handed the camera to the officer. "His name is Sabri Qosja. Interpol is looking for him."

The young woman still scowled, clearly doubting me. Jean-Paul took over, explaining who to call, and why she should. She wrote down the names and numbers he gave her, pulled out a phone and stepped away, still holding my camera. When she gestured for Jean-Paul to come, I took his seat next to the concierge.

"I am so sorry," I said. "Tell me what happened."

She took a breath and let it out again, a long sigh. "That guy, he came up behind me and hit me with something. Then he grabbed the handle of my handbag and cut it. But—" The shadow of a smile crossed her face.

"What?"

"*Le trou du cul* made a mistake." Her smile broke open. "He looks at me and he thinks, Ha! Easy target, just a weak old woman. He thinks that once he knocks me down on the ground, I'm finished, too feeble to fight him. Stupid *con* wasn't expecting it when

I gave him one of these." She made a fist and feigned punching upward with the heel of her hand. "Technique I learned in commando training. If I'd had a better angle, I would have killed him. Surprised the hell out of him, though. Hurt him enough to drop him to his knees. When he was down, moaning like a baby, I followed with a swift straight-on kick to the face. Heel of my shoe smashed bone: I heard the nose go, I felt it flatten. That blood over there on the sidewalk, *chérie*? It isn't mine."

"Jesus," I said. She spat, landed a loogie right in the middle of Qosja's spilled gore. Turning away, I said, "He hurt you."

"Just a bump on the head. Skinned my knees going down." She reached around behind her and retrieved her handbag with the broken strap. "*Grand espèce de voyou!* Couldn't even take a handbag from an old woman."

Again, I didn't know all the words, but the meaning was crystal clear. Somewhere in Paris that afternoon, there was a mercenary, *un grand espèce de voyou*, walking around with a broken nose and probably two black eyes. Poor bastard, not that I had sympathy for him.

"What did he want from me?" she asked with a palm-up shrug. "I have nothing."

"I think he wanted your keys," I said. "He was hired by someone who has been trying to get access to the library in the basement."

She looked at me for a moment, then burst out laughing as she pulled her key ring out of her coat pocket and held it in her fist with keys jutting out between her knuckles like a weapon. "Fool. No woman buries her keys in her handbag where she can't get to them if she needs them."

There was a brief argument between Madame Gonsalves and the paramedics who wanted to take her to the hospital for overnight observation. She had too much work to do, and besides, she didn't want to miss her Saturday night TV programs. Jean-Paul came over, took her hand, told her he wouldn't be able to sleep worrying about her if she went home without seeing a doctor first. Besides, he promised, she would be able to watch television from her hospital bed. When she was ready to come home, he told her, we would come for her in the car. With that promise, she let the paramedics strap her onto a gurney. With a last wave, she was on her way.

As we watched the ambulance leave, I turned to Jean-Paul. "Where did she go to commando school?"

He shrugged. "Somewhere in the Pays Basque, probably. Up in the mountains. I told you she was an old Basque separatist, yes?"

"You did." He took my arm and we walked back to the car, still parked in the middle of the street, blocking traffic. "How many refugees have you taken in over the years, Jean-Paul?"

"I hadn't thought of her as a refugee, but I suppose she is. When we were looking for a concierge who would be able to handle Isabelle when she was off her meds, or when her meds weren't working, I thought, who better than a trained commando who can make a magnificent pot of *porrusalda*."

"Is that the soup we ate last night?"

"It is."

"I would hire her for that alone."

"*Bien sûr.* And so I did. She had no practical work experience, and after she came out of prison, what was she to do?"

"Prison?"

"Her separatist unit chose an unfortunate target," he said with a little Gallic shrug. "She did her time, the separatist issue has been resolved. Now Madame Gonsalves makes her soup and guards the gate, and there you have it."

"Another symbiotic relationship, sir?"

He laughed as he put me into the car. "We do whatever works best for all, yes?"

"Yes, my peacemaker."

We followed the ambulance to the hospital and waited in a hallway while Madame Gonsalves was put through a series of tests, and then we waited beside her bed for the doctor to come in with the results. Though she smiled and tried to show a brave face, I could see her quaking under the thin sheet draped over her body. Three different times, she told us hospitals were where people went to die. Fighting off street thugs scared her less. While we waited, a nurse came in and tucked a heated blanket tightly around her body. Pulling an arm free, our concierge joked that it was too soon for them to fit her for a shroud.

"Don't worry," Jean-Paul said, patting her shoulder. "When the time comes, we'll wind you in something nicer than a hospital blanket."

She giggled and the tension in the room disappeared.

An impossibly young doctor came in with a sheaf of diagnostic printouts. He rested a comforting hand on her leg and said, with a smile, "There is no skull fracture, no brain swelling, no symptoms of concussion. Any scalp injury that breaks the skin just bleeds like a son-of-a-bitch: there's a big blood supply up there and not much cushioning. We turned off the spigot and sewed the scalp back together, so except for some tenderness, Madame, consider yourself repaired. I am more worried about damage to the knees right now; you took a bad fall. X rays showed us some arthritis. After you're released, if the knees start to bother you more than usual, you'll need to see your regular physician for follow-up treatment."

"So I can go home?" she said, throwing back the blanket.

"Not so fast," he said, taking a corner of the blanket and covering her again. "I'm a bit concerned about the swelling on your right knee. I want to watch it overnight, just to be sure."

Madame Gonsalves turned to us, and, batting her eyes, said, "This handsome boy likes my knees. He wants to spend the night with them."

"Of course I do, Madame," the young doctor said with a chuckle. "But after seeing what you did to your attacker, I will keep a respectable distance."

"You saw him? He's here?" I said, getting to my feet. "Where?"

"Don't worry," the doctor said, smile suddenly gone. "He's under guard."

"Lucky for him," I said. Jean-Paul had his phone out of his pocket and was punching numbers. "Where is the bastard?"

The doc, nonplussed, faltered over a few starts before he managed to say, "Patient privacy forbids— I've said too much already. My apology."

I was trying to hear Jean-Paul's end of his telephone conversation, but the doctor was between us, and Jean-Paul had turned his back. The call was brief. Jean-Paul gave me a little nod as he slipped the phone back into his pocket. Then he turned his attention back to Madame Gonsalves. With a reassuring hand on her shoulder, he asked the doctor when he thought she would be released.

"If all goes well, and I expect it will," the doctor said, regaining his cheerful bedside manner, "Madame will probably go home some time tomorrow."

Madame argued that she wanted to go home, now. She grumbled a bit about being in the same building as her attacker, failed to negotiate a suspended overnight sentence for herself, and in the end, picked up the television control, asked what was for dinner, and bid us a good night.

I slipped my hand around Jean-Paul's elbow as we followed the doctor out of the room. In the hall, the men shook hands, the doctor promised to call if Madame needed anything or if there were complications during the night, we thanked him, wished him good night, and watched him walk down the hall toward the nurse's station. We went in the opposite direction, toward the elevator.

"Who did you call?" I asked as Jean-Paul punched the DOWN button. The door opened right away.

"A friend," he said, waiting for me enter the car before him. That nebulous answer, yet again, was the wrong thing for him to say just then. I stuck my hand out to hold the elevator's automatic doors open, balking, I suppose, until I got a little actual information from him. One look at my face and he understood he'd damn well better expand on his answer a bit; we'd had that conversation before. He put his head near mine, and quietly told me, "Sabri Qosja is downstairs, under guard, in a treatment bay. My friend with the city police has granted us permission to speak with the swine before he is formally booked."

"A good friend to have," I said, releasing the door and stepping inside the elevator. "Does he have a name?"

"Berg. David Berg."

I had to hold my breath to keep from choking: David Berg was the Préfet of Police of Paris. The capital's top cop. A man whose face had been on the news recently, addressing the public after a coordinated series of suicide bombings at a holiday concert created yet another round of public terror. By all accounts, he was well respected, a competent, calming figure.

As Jean-Paul pushed the button for the second floor, I asked, "Old friend from school?" because, of course, all his "friends" seemed to be old school friends.

With a smile, he leaned over and kissed me. "*Bien sûr.*"

7

"YOUR IDENTIFICATION, SIR." The officer guarding the door outside the immediate treatment suite crossed her arms and stood wide as she studied us. When Jean-Paul handed her his mangled passport, she grew still more wary. "Is that blood, sir?"

"It is," he said. "Whether it's mine or my colleague's, I can't say."

"Have you law enforcement or justice department credentials?"

"I have a national health card and a membership card for an American store called COSTCO," he said. "Which I would be happy to lend you if you should want to buy a new television or a gross of frozen buffalo wings. Beyond that, what I have is official permission. You were told by your superior that I was to be granted an audience with your esteemed prisoner, were you not?"

Her chin rose two degrees in grudging acknowledgment as she reached behind her to push the electric door opener. Jean-Paul took my arm and we started past, but she put up her hand to stop me. Jean-Paul looked her in the eye as he pulled out his phone and began tapping numbers. She sighed to show her displeasure, but stepped aside and let us both go through. Her parting words were, "This is highly irregular. Highly."

I leaned close to him as we walked past her into the hallway beyond, and said, "COSTCO?"

"Interesting place. On my first visit, I was able to acquire enough toilet paper to supply the Los Angeles consulate for the remainder of my tenure, buy my son a lifetime supply of athletic socks, and verify that the company had not ripped off a single French product."

"Did you ever go back?" I asked.

"Yes," he said. "I was curious to find out what a buffalo wing might be."

A second officer stood outside the third treatment room along the corridor. When the guard watching from the outer door gave him a nod, he pushed the door opener and, with a little bow, ushered us through.

Our first glimpse of Sabri Qosja made it clear that he had lost the fight. Enthroned in a big chair that looked like it was borrowed from a dentist, his arms bound to the chair arms, chest strapped to the back, his legs shackled, not by chains but by a solid metal bar and locked to the foot rest so he couldn't kick, and flanked by armed officers, he was the poster boy for abject defeat. Or maybe the captured racoon king. Both eyes were so black and swollen that I could not tell whether he could see until he spoke.

"You," was all he said.

"Us," Jean-Paul answered. He turned to the doctor who followed us in, and asked. "How is he?"

"There's nothing we can do here to cure his foul disposition, but for the rest? He isn't as badly off as he looks," the doctor said, gently palpating the purple mass in the middle of Qosja's face that, until a few hours ago, was a nose. "We'll need to build him a new sniffer, probably with a bone graft from his hip. But until the swelling subsides and we can get after it, he'll be breathing through his mouth."

"Take these fucking restraints off," Qosja demanded. "My feet have gone to sleep."

"Good," the doctor said, patting his shoulder. "Let them sleep. When they wake up, we'll see if you still want to kick people."

During that little back-and-forth, I pulled out my camera and snapped a couple of pictures of Qosja for Madame Gonsalves's scrapbook. Qosja turned his head, trying to avoid the camera, but he was locked down so thoroughly that all he could do was give me a good profile shot. When I had my shot, I flipped to the image I captured at the department store in Venice and offered the camera to the doctor. "Would you like to see him before he tried to mug the wrong woman?"

"Yes, indeed." The doctor walked around his patient, comparing the photo, a semi-profile, to the ruin in the chair. When he handed the camera back to me, he addressed Qosja. "Monsieur, we will do our best, but...?" And there he left it before walking out of the room again.

Slowly, Jean-Paul took off his coat and handed it to one of the blue-uniformed police guards, a gesture meant to establish his superior rank in the room, I thought. When he finally got around to speaking with the prisoner, he stood just a bit to the side, making Qosja work to see him.

"So, we meet again, Monsieur Qosja," he said, at last. "And once again I find you in shackles."

"If my hands were free, I would break your neck." Qosja's voice was surprisingly high-pitched for a tough guy. And nasal, but that was Madame Gonsalves's doing. "And hers, too."

"I have no doubt of that. And yet, your scattershot efforts over the last week to do some approximation of that have come to nothing, except that here you are, in custody again, and here am I, once again asking you questions."

"Go to hell."

"Perhaps I will. But in the meantime, let's chat, shall we?" Jean-Paul took a step closer, forcing Qosja to look up at him. "We know that you are being paid through an entity called ProtX4, and we know, of course, that ProtX4 is also paying a hacker to track our movements and report them to you. But what, exactly, are you being paid to do?"

"I don't have to talk to you."

"You do, you know. You are in France, sir, not Argentina. A

little under-the-table *mordida* or *baksheesh* will not buy your freedom here; don't expect your employer to sweep in and save your ass. Trust me, the charges will be serious, and you will be a guest of the miserable French prison system for a very long time. Because your activities amount to international terrorism enhanced by the attempted assassination of two Eurozone officials and the cold-blooded murder of a young nurse, not to mention the attempted bombing of a ship in harbor, you can expect to be brought before the same international court you faced after the Kosovar War. Except this time your father will not be around to take the fall for you."

"You bastard," Qosja spat. "You fucking bastard. You killed my father, and I will kill you."

Jean-Paul turned to the policeman holding his coat. "You heard what he said. Please include his threat on my life in your report."

"Of course, sir," the policeman said, but I could see a bit of a tooth-sucking grin behind his starchy façade.

"And, just so we are clear, Monsieur Qosja, your father, may he rest in peace, took his own life. That was, what, sixteen or seventeen years ago? A long time. But, if memory serves, before he hanged himself in his cell, your father confessed to the very crimes you stood accused of committing. Rape and murder of women and children, correct?"

"Not correct, pig. Anything he and I did were legitimate acts of war. Payback for what was done to my mother and sisters."

"Even in war, sir, there are rules. You broke those rules, and your father paid the ultimate price. So, tell me, Monsieur, is that what all this stalking crap has been about? Payback?"

"No. But why waste an opportunity?" Qosja leaned his head back and gulped air. Maybe he had accepted the reality of his situation, or maybe he was just saving energy for whatever was to come next. Whatever the reason, he seemed calmer. After another deep, gulping breath, he turned his swollen eyes to me. "I don't know why you're here. You are that idiot Bord's job, not mine."

"Job?" I repeated. "Job to do what, exactly?"

"Same as me," he said. "We were hired to keep you both out of Paris."

"Why?"

"No one told me why, and I did not ask. It isn't my place to ask questions."

"How were you to keep us away?" I asked.

"No one told me that, either. I'm a professional; I know what to do. Bord thought he was some kind of chick magnet: you know what that is?" When I nodded, he said, "He thought he could get you to go out for drinks with him, slip you some roofies, park you somewhere until the job is over."

"When will that be?"

"When they tell us it is over."

"*They* are ProtX4?"

"Yes, but I don't know who their client is."

"The client is a company or consortium called InterCentro."

"If you say so."

I said, "You weren't hired to kill Monsieur Bernard, just to keep him out of Paris?"

"Correct."

"But you did try to kill him."

"Sure," he said, a cocky bastard once again. "No one said not to. If it had been anyone else, I would have just kidnapped him, maybe drugged him for a while, like Bord planned for you. But when I realized who the job was—"

"You wanted revenge," Jean-Paul said.

"Call it what you want."

"*Un grand faux-pas?*" I offered. "You failed."

Jean-Paul laughed. "Remind me, *chérie*, to help with your vocabulary of French obscenities."

"I will. I have been at such a disadvantage."

Qosja chimed in. "Just because you have me, you think it's over?"

"Bord is out of commission, too," I said.

"So what? Men like us, we're a dime a dozen. Now ProtX4 just goes to the next guy on the list, and the game continues."

"It isn't a game," I said.

Qosja laughed, an ugly, guttural burst. He strained forward and sneered at me. "You're about to find out how wrong you are."

One of his guards kicked the bottom of his foot and he winced. The guard grinned at his partner. "Looks like the foot isn't asleep after all."

"The irony here, Mr. Qosja," I said, keeping my distance, "is that if you hadn't dropped a bomb on Monsieur Bernard, indeed if you had simply left him alone, he would have returned to Paris only long enough to meet me and take me away again. You have wasted a great deal of time, energy, and someone else's money. And for what?"

"For what?" he shrugged. "I told you. I don't ask."

Jean-Paul collected his coat from the policeman and stepped over to take my arm. He turned and studied Qosja long enough to make the prisoner shrink into himself to get away from the scrutiny.

"Monsieur Qosja," he said, "I recommend that you use your time in prison wisely. Learn a good trade, because, sir, if you ever gain your freedom again, you will need a new line of work. Clearly, you are an abject failure in your current field."

With that, we turned and left the room.

"Do you believe him?" I asked as we walked out of the hospital.

"About being hired to keep us out of Paris?"

"No, about the client sending someone else after us?"

He toggled his head, a yes-or-no answer. "Except, we are here, in Paris, yes? So what would be the assignment now?"

"I do not want to find that out."

"We may," he said, leading me down the ramp into the underground parking garage. "Qosja is a great liar. But, in spite of himself, he did give us some useful information. First, as these things go, from the beginning the effort to stop us has been a low-budget, private operation. Whoever is behind this went for cheap, hired mediocrity. Remember, Qosja also failed his last assignment and had to be rescued out of Argentina. Bottom of the barrel; if either he or Bord was good at what he does, we'd be dead or drugged and tossed into a dark hole by now."

"They misjudged their target," I said, pulling up the collar of my coat against the cold.

He laughed softly. "Yes, one should always send in the A Team against a filmmaker and a bureaucrat."

"Ninja filmmaker and bureaucrat who has the phone number of every official in the Eurozone," I said. "A tough pair."

"Tell yourself that, but don't forget to watch your back."

"Jean-Paul," I said as we approached his car. "If this is as you say, a low-budget operation, then whoever is behind it will run out of funds at some point. I'm sure that by now he's weighed the value of whatever he's after against the cost of obtaining it. Maybe it's over."

"Maybe." He pulled out his car keys and punched the automatic unlock. "You have an idea what he's after?"

"So do you. In Paris, what links us?"

"Other than a shared bed?"

"Other than that."

"Number seven, rue Jacob."

"And the treasure in the basement."

As we pulled out of the garage, a white Citroën with a blue stripe down the side emblazed with the word POLICE in red, fell in behind us.

"We have an escort," I said. "Courtesy of your friend David Berg?"

"Probably. Do you object?"

"Not at all. But what did you tell him?"

"Not much. David's a good cop. I'm sure he made a few phone calls of his own."

It was already dark by the time we drove through the big gates at number seven, rue Jacob. The police car that followed us from the hospital was still parked across the driveway when the gates closed behind us. Jean-Paul and I carried in his bags and the groceries we bought at the shops in Vaucresson that afternoon. Though the food had sat in the trunk for several hours, the car was at least as cold as a refrigerator, so I wasn't concerned about anything spoiling. Except for maybe some produce that might have frozen.

In the kitchen, I put the heat under the remains of the soup Madame Gonsalves had brought the day before, and stowed the new purchases.

"Is there enough soup for tonight?" Jean-Paul asked.

"It's soup," I said. "If there isn't enough, I'll just add some water."

"Water?" He sounded dubious. I confess, I am no cook, but why not water? He left the kitchen before I could ask, headed toward the bedroom with his bags. I followed him as far as Isabelle's office. Dinner could wait until I'd had a look at the library, I decided as I fished the keys out of her desk drawer.

When I went back out into the salon, I could hear men talking somewhere outside the apartment. In the courtyard? In the entry hall downstairs? I wasn't familiar with the sounds of the building, of neighbors coming and going or regular service people doing their jobs, so I stopped to listen, not to eavesdrop, but to try to figure out where the voices came from. There were muffled good-byes, and a door closed. Barry Griffith's door downstairs? The keys were in my hand when someone knocked on my door. I froze for a moment to listen again before I went over to the wall panel and flipped on the monitor to see who was there. Philippe, the elder of Freddy's two sons, stood there holding a turquoise bag from a Patrick Roger chocolate shop—a very expensive chocolate shop—by its little handle.

"Company, Jean-Paul," I called out as I opened the door. Poor Philippe, clearly nervous, turned bright red the instant he saw me. The chocolates he bore were doubtless a peace offering.

"Aunt Maggie," he managed to say.

"What a nice surprise," I said. We exchanged *les bises* and I drew him inside. "Come in. It's freezing out there."

"This is for you." Standing in the vestibule, he held out the bright little bag on both hands like the offering of a penitent. "I came to tell you I am sorry for all the trouble my friends and I caused you. I hope I can forgive me."

"How kind of you, Philippe," I said, accepting the offering. "Thank you. Certainly, I forgive you, though I would love to hear exactly why you think you need forgiveness. Monsieur Griffith downstairs might be tougher to convince than I am, however."

"I just left him. We're okay. Except I had to promise him I would go shopping with him during the school holiday to buy a new computer and set it up for him."

"Is that terrible?"

"No. He's very nice really. He was a good friend of Mamie Izzy."

"Mamie Izzy. Is that what you called her: Granny?"

He smiled, finally. "She would not let us call her Grand-mère. Besides, it would be too confusing to have two Grand-mères, yes?"

"I suppose it would." We had progressed as far as the salon when Jean-Paul walked into the room. Poor Philippe blushed all over again.

"Philippe, good to see you again, man," Jean-Paul said, offering his hand and leaning in for *les bises*. I forget sometimes that Jean-Paul's family and mine had been friends long before they conspired for us to meet. "How is school?"

"Oh, you know, sir. School is school. Very difficult this term. How is Dom?"

"I think he would give the same answer," Jean-Paul said, showing Philippe to a comfortable chair. We sat opposite him, on Isabelle's down-stuffed sofa. "What brings you all the way across the Channel to Paris?"

The poor boy colored yet again.

"Would you like some water?" I asked. "Or a cider?"

"Have any cyanide?"

"Oh, Philippe." I went over to him, sat on the arm of his chair and wrapped an arm around his shoulders, which he tolerated. "It can't be that bad. Tell us what happened."

He took a breath, sighed, stalling while he steeled himself. "Did Papa tell you my friends and I stayed here over the New Year?"

"He did."

"We had permission to stay one night, New Year's Eve, to see the celebration. But—"

We waited.

"But—*Je suis un imbécile.*" He dropped his face into his hands. We waited some more. Finally, he straightened up, looked from Jean-Paul's face to mine, and began again. "It started when my friends said they were disappointed we couldn't stay to see the fireworks. In Paris, it's really big, you know? Papa agreed we could, if we promised not to get drunk and be stupid, and to get on the Chunnel train back to school in the morning. So, after Papa and Robert left, we hung out with a guy I know in the Marais for a while before going over to the Champs Elysées for the show. There were concerts, and— We stayed out pretty late. After, when we got home, I thought, it's New Year's, we should have some Champagne. So, we went down to Mamie Izzy's wine cellar to get some."

"Isabelle had a wine cellar?" Apparently, from his reaction, this was news to Jean-Paul. "Where?"

"Uh, in the cellar, sir." Philippe pointed toward the floor.

"Why not? There's plenty of space down there," Jean-Paul said with a little shrug. "Wish I'd thought to put one in. Sorry to interrupt. Go on."

"So, we went down to get the wine. And that's when things got crazy."

"Crazy how?" I asked.

"It's my fault. My friends, Val and Cho, had never seen basements like that. Cho called it Hogwarts. He thought it would be so great to play this sort of laser tag we play at school with our phones sometimes. It was really late; I should have said no."

"What happened?" I asked.

"So, we were running around, shooting at each other. Cho got the keys from me and he started opening doors down there to find hiding places and make barricades. Monsieur Griffith came down and told us to shut up. I grabbed Cho and told him we had to quit. But we couldn't find Val. We looked all over. By then it was about noon, and we were supposed to go to the train, but I couldn't leave without Val, could I?"

He looked at us, expecting maybe affirmation. I said, "Did you try calling his mobile phone?"

He grimaced. "Yes, finally, when I got a little sober."

"Champagne?" Jean-Paul asked.

He shook his head. "Uncle Antoine's *eau de vie*."

Eau de vie is a wicked, aged apple brandy my cousin, Antoine—actually, he's Philippe's cousin, as well, but the appropriate age to be an uncle—distilled from cider produced on the family's estate in Normandy. A short snifter as an after-dinner *digestif* was all that I could manage of the potent, but delicious, stuff. If those kids had been swilling it all night long, I'm surprised that only one of them got misplaced.

"But there's no phone signal in the basement," Philippe said.

"You did find him, though?"

"Yes." He blushed yet again. "Finally, I looked in the library. I showed it to them earlier, when we got the brandy, but I warned them that it was forbidden to go in there without me, totally off limits. But Val went in anyway, alone. I think he slept in there."

"Tell me Val's whole name," I said.

"Vasily Barkoff. But he hates it. He gets mad if you call him Vasily."

I looked at Jean-Paul. "Son of Boris?"

"Val has a temper?"

Philippe raised his palms in a "maybe" gesture. "He's full of himself. Brags a lot. His father has a lot of money, so he thinks that makes him an *übermensch*."

"*Übermensch*?" So, the kids were reading Nietzsche.

Phillipe said, "You know, some kind of special guy. Super man."

"What was this *übermensch* doing when you found him in the library?" Jean-Paul asked.

"Looking at books. His father is some kind of expert on old Russian books; he brags about that, too. Val found the Russian stuff and started piling it up on a table. He said he was just looking at it, but I know he was planning to steal some of it."

"Why do you think that?" I asked.

"Because he hid one under his sweater. I found it later."

"Excuse me for just a sec." I got up and went into Isabelle's office to fetch the little volume of Psalms. I held it up for Philippe to see. "This one?"

"Yes. I think maybe he forgot it was there. When he stripped to go to bed, it fell out."

"What was he going to do with it?"

"He said he just wanted to send a picture of it to his father, but he couldn't get a signal downstairs, so he brought it up. I told him I didn't believe him."

"And?"

"And then Cho threw up and we all went to sleep. When we got up, it was too late to get the train. It was a holiday, so there wasn't much to do. We just hung around, ate takeout, watched movies, went back to bed."

Jean-Paul leaned forward and spoke softly. "Everyone had an *eau de vie* hangover, yes?"

The kid's guilty grin was answer enough.

"How long did you stay?" I asked.

"Till the day after that. We didn't have to be back at school until the fourth, so we decided we'd hang out in Paris until the third. But the next morning Cho and Val wanted to play tag again. They got really mad that I wouldn't let them have the keys for the basement, but they got down there somehow. Maybe they followed someone who was going down. Anyway, they chased each other around until Monsieur Griffith threatened to call Papa. I told Cho and Val to grab their stuff and leave, like now."

"What happened with the cleaners?" I asked.

"That was bad," he said, sniffing the air, distracted for a moment, I thought, by the aroma of soup, and I wondered when he had eaten last. "The cleaners are nice ladies, but they're really strict Muslims. We weren't supposed to still be in the apartment when they came. The younger one, Saida, she's really nice and really pretty. Val tried to mess with her, pulled off her head scarf, touched her. She got blindly upset, and they left."

"And wouldn't come back." I said.

"I tried to apologize, but, yeah. So, when Papa called last week to schedule them to come in, they said they wouldn't, and if he had questions, he should ask me." He took a deep breath. "Anyway, I am sorry Mamie Izzy's place was a mess when you got here. I was going to come and clean during the Easter holiday, but—"

"But I showed up."

He nodded.

"Val came by looking for his coat," I said. "Will you take it to him when you go back to school?"

He shook his head. "He left. I came back from a tutorial one day and he was gone. Just gone. Cho didn't know where he went either."

I looked at Jean-Paul, and said, "Suddenly Val's gone. Just gone."

"Aunt Maggie?"

"Yes, Philippe."

"Do I smell Madame Gigi's soup?"

"If Madame Gigi is the concierge, you do."

He sniffed the air again.

"You'll stay for dinner, of course." Jean-Paul rose to his feet. "But first, let's go have a look at the library."

I pulled the keys out of my pocket and started for the front door with Jean-Paul close behind.

"Not that way." Philippe gestured for us to follow him to the kitchen. "This way is shorter."

There was a narrow door at the back of the kitchen between the washer and dryer and a small table. If I had paid attention to it, and I had not, I would assume it led to a broom closet or pantry. Phillipe asked me for the keys, unlocked a deadbolt, opened the door, and flipped a wall switch that turned on a row of recessed ceiling lights above a steep, narrow stone stairway that seemed to end in a dense, black abyss. At the bottom, he flipped another switch, illuminating a chamber that was no more than five feet square. There were bolted doors on the right and the left, and a solid wall straight ahead. Not a happy place for anyone with claustrophobia issues.

"Wine," Phillipe said, opening the door on the right and turning on the light. Indeed, there was a well-stocked cellar, rows of racked bottles extending into the gloom beyond the reach of the fanciful chandelier—rescued from a château?—hanging above my head.

"*Merde,*" was all I could think to say, calling upon that lovely universal French obscenity once again. I stood just inside the doorway, washed over, or rather bowled over, by the heady perfume of wine-soaked wood and old cork, trying to figure out what the hell I had tumbled into by the accident of the union between my beloved late father and this enigma, Isabelle, the ultimate *inconnue,* the unknown, and now unknowable woman who had given birth to me. Jean-Paul walked straight inside with a happy grin on his face and started pulling out random bottles. He'd study a label and put the bottle back, except for four, which he handed Phillipe to set on the stairs to take up with us later.

"Isabelle was a connoisseur," he said, smiling at me. "If it's all right with you, I've selected something very nice to have with soup tonight, and something to take to my sister's lunch tomorrow."

I held up my palms. "*Bien sûr, pourquoi pas?*" Sure, why not? My wine is your wine. My wine? I needed to step out to catch my breath.

Jean-Paul turned off the lights and Philippe locked up after him. The door on the opposite side of the stairway had a recessed pull instead of a knob of some sort. Phillipe inserted a key in a bolt and slid the door into a wall pocket, releasing a burst of chilly air into the warmer passage. He hit a switch and, after a pause, rows of filtered museum lights flickered on. Again, I hesitated before venturing inside. When I first heard about the convent's library and scriptorium, I imagined something lifted out of a medieval castle, or a movie about a medieval castle: stone walls and carved paneling and heavy tapestries. What I saw could have been a newly appointed reading room in the rare books section of any university library. I confess that I was a bit disappointed by the industrial-looking glass-front shelving, the spare utilitarian tables and chairs. Everything in the room was perfectly tidy, except for twin towers of volumes stacked at the far end of one of the tables.

When the door was closed behind us, it disappeared, becoming just another part of the solid wall between two bookcases, a puzzling contrast to the heavy, electronically secured door on the far side of the room. Next to that door, there were two computers on small desks, above which were posted instructions for library visitors to log in and for accessing the online card catalogue.

"Once again," Jean-Paul said, venturing further inside, "Isabelle has surprised me. I knew nothing about this second entrance. She and I, and the curator from the Louvre, have electronic fob keys for the other door. Just so you know, for security, each key has a different signature that is recorded every time it is used. But I think that Isabelle wanted to come and go without anyone knowing. Philippe, do you have any idea when she installed the door?"

The question merited a slight lift of one shoulder, which I read to mean that the answer was obvious. "It was always here. I mean, for as long as I can remember."

"You're eighteen, Philippe?" Jean-Paul asked, and was answered with an affirmative lift of the chin. "The same as my Dom. We started the restoration when you two were just babies. So, you're right, the door probably has been here for most of your life. I simply don't know."

I looked around at the shelved volumes—old, leather-bound works—and at the long drawers for texts that needed to be stored flat. It was a cold, uncomfortable room, the temperature and humidity regulated by a machine affixed to the far wall. Not a pleasant place, at all, to hang out. Curious, I asked Phillippe, "Did your grandmother come down here often?"

"Oh, yes. Mamie Izzy would bring her work down sometimes. It's very quiet. The books were good company, she said. Sometimes, when I visited her, I would bring my school work, and we'd sit here and she would do her work and I would do mine."

"Her work?" I repeated; Isabelle, like my father, was a nuclear physicist. "She was working on a church-related project?"

He laughed at that. "Mamie Izzy was an atheist. She thought that these books were pretty, but she said that between the fancy covers, everything on the pages was superstitious bullshit. Excuse me, but that is her word."

"And I thought she was so genteel," I said.

Jean-Paul's snort had a sardonic edge. "But then, you never knew her."

"Except," Philippe said, "for the things she called the refugees. She did like looking through those sometimes."

"What are the refugees?" I asked.

"Papers that were brought here for safekeeping during the Revolution," he said.

I turned to Jean-Paul. "You told me about that."

He nodded. "The convent gave sanctuary to precious children and precious documents, both. For a price, I suspect."

"You think the nuns rented out space?"

"In a sense," Jean-Paul answered. "I'm sure that if the nuns weren't given cash they were given special favors of some sort for the risk they took. Words can be dangerous, yes?"

"Mightier than the sword."

He chuckled. "When the men whose words they safeguarded—kings and nobles and priests—were losing their heads, I'm certain the nuns knew the danger they faced. From the look of the place when we found it, no one spent a minute longer down here with the contraband than it took to open the door, shove it inside. And lock the door behind. It's difficult to imagine now, but when the workmen found the old library, this room was a filthy mess. There were stacks of crates and chests pushed against the walls. Some had collapsed from the burdens of time and weight, and spilled. I confess I felt overwhelmed. We knew that what was here was important, but what to do with it?"

"That's when you called the university?" I asked.

"Your mother did. As soon as Isabelle saw the royal crest on some crates, she called the Sorbonne, and they in turn brought in the Louvre. It was a great relief to have the experts take over sorting and organizing. Too bad they went public about the discovery."

"Because that brought in the Vatican and the local diocese."

"What a headache." He looked around, and sighed. "Or maybe nightmare. Sometimes I wish the workmen had never opened that door to begin with."

I put my hand along his cheek, beside the fresh scars. "Roger that. I'm new to all this, but already I wish it would go away."

"You've no idea." He took my hand and kissed it. "From the beginning, my role at rue Jacob has been managing financial and legal issues. Bankers, lawyers and lawsuits. So, as you have figured out by now, I did not pay very close attention to what was happening in here. Other than to check on the security system when it was periodically upgraded, I did not visit the library. For her own reasons, Isabelle neglected to mention she had put in a second door. One that is not connected to the alarm system."

"She could be sneaky," Phillipe said with a grin. "But when I said she liked the refugees, I wasn't talking about refugees from the French Revolution. It was the other ones."

"Sorry," Jean-Paul said. "Which other ones?"

"From the Russian Revolution." He pointed to the stacks of books on the far table. "Those are the books Val was interested in, too."

For just a moment, the only sound in the room was the soft beeping of the humidity monitor. Jean-Paul was the first to speak. He turned to me. "The Russians. Another headache that won't go away."

"When did they arrive?" I asked. "And who brought them?"

Both Jean-Paul and Phillipe shrugged. Phillipe said, "Sometime after 1917 when the revolution began."

"A lot of Russian nobility, and probably clergy, fled to Paris around then," Jean-Paul added. "We assumed that someone rescued, or looted, church artifacts and texts when the Bolsheviks shut down the churches and outlawed the priesthood, and somehow parked what they could save here. By then, the library was probably already in a shambles."

I looked around the room. "Philippe, from Isabelle's back stairs, is there a way to get into the rest of the basement other than going through the main library door over there?"

"No. You have to go back up, out the apartment's front door, and down the main stairs. Do you want me to show you?"

"Later maybe. Did you bring Cho and Val in here through the pocket door, or the main door?"

"The slider," he said, indicating the door we had come through. "I know I shouldn't have brought them in at all, but Val is always bragging about his father and his precious Russian book collection and how it's worth millions. It gets very boring. When we came down for the brandy, I pointed to the library door and told Val that there were very old Russian books in here, worth a ton. He didn't believe me, so I said he could pull up the museum site and see for himself. He tried, but he couldn't get a phone signal down here, so I took him in, but just to show him the catalogue on the computer."

"And he saw the list of Russian holdings," I said.

"Not exactly. He only saw that there were things from Russia. I'll show you." He booted one of the computers near the main door and pulled up the library catalogue. Besides the location on the shelves, the catalogue included a brief description, and sometimes a photograph, of the original holdings of the St. Jérôme Émilian convent library. Anyone interested in the refugees, as Philippe called the material brought into the convent for safekeeping during dangerous times, was to contact the curator of rare books at the Louvre for a catalogue of the holdings or to apply for permission to see them. Those materials were listed only as *Collections: Saint-Germain-de-Prés, Paris; Saint-Germain l'Auxerrois, Paris; Saint-Sulpice, Paris.* And *Vladimirsky Cathedral, St. Petersburg.*

"Why aren't the contents of the refugee collections in the accessible catalogue?" I asked.

When Philippe, having no answer, raised his palms, Jean-Paul stepped in. "It has to do with lawsuits, as well as issues of provenance, and degree of pain-in-the-ass."

"I don't see any of the royal papers in the catalogue," I said, scrolling through the menu.

"That's because they aren't here," Jean-Paul said. "The Vatican has no claim on them, so they were shipped out to the Louvre right away. Interesting though, some of the documents were actually produced right here, in the scriptorium of the Little Sisters of Saint Jérôme Émilian."

"I understand how the Vatican can claim the books, texts, whatever, that were in the convent library. But can't we pack up everything that belonged to the three local churches on the list, drop it on their doorsteps, ring the bell, and run like hell?"

Philippe laughed. "Mamie Izzy said almost the same thing."

"I'm game," Jean-Paul said. "I'm damn tired of dealing with it all. The museum lawyers and the diocese lawyers agree with you, but the Vatican doesn't and they are happy to pay their lawyers until Judgment Day. That still leaves us with the Russians, and right now I would really like for the Russian material to be somewhere else."

"I don't see how either the Vatican or the local diocese can claim any of that," I said. "So why don't we just truck it over to the Louvre?"

"Because they won't touch it with a fork," Jean-Paul said.

"Why not?"

"First, the Louvre won't accept anything that may have been improperly acquired. We have no idea who left the stuff here, or how the nuns came to possess it. Next, the museum already has enough problems getting Russia to return pieces of their collection that the Nazis stole during the war, and that the Soviets in turn stole from the Nazis. Fine French works that belong to the Louvre still hang in Russian museums."

"Maybe we could arrange a swap," I said. "A lovely stolen Book of Psalms for a stolen Monet."

"Please don't do that," Phillipe said, with surprising heat. "Please. Mamie Izzy studied who should have the Russian books. But they can't go to Russia. She said someone went to a lot of trouble to rescue them from destruction, and she couldn't bear to see them sent back into what she called a cesspool of corruption. There was nowhere to send them: not the church, not the museums. She said the reactionary Patriarch of Moscow—he's the head of the church—is in the pocket of the reprehensible

Russian government and she would do nothing that would seem
to support his sexist, racist, xenophobic agenda. And that anything
sent to a museum or university would probably end up in the
hands of some oligarch who would only sell it for cash to pay his
whores."

"Your grandmother said that?" I asked. I didn't necessarily
disagree with her, but is that the way Isabelle spoke with her grandchild? Lordy, she was an ever-deepening puzzle to me.

I looked up to see Jean-Paul watching me. The bob of his head
told me that, yes, that was something Isabelle might say.

Philippe was looking at the stack of books that his friend Val
took off the shelves, when he said, "Mamie Izzy thought the best
thing was to keep it all here, where it was clean, quiet, and safe,
until she could figure things out. But, she died, and, well, that was
it."

"Philippe, son," Jean-Paul said, putting a reassuring hand on
the boy's shoulder. "Thank you for sharing your grandmother's
thinking. Isabelle was right. Until a solution can be figured out, it
would be best to keep the Russian collection here, safe. And quiet.
But I'm not sure, in light of recent events, how possible that will
be."

"I'm an idiot for saying anything to Val, aren't I?"

"No, you're not. We should be free to talk to our friends without worrying that they might steal from us. Or worse."

"Gentlemen," I said. "It's cold down here. Let's go upstairs and
see if I've managed to burn the soup."

"What should we do with those books?" Philippe asked, eyes
again on Val's pile.

"Leave them for now," Jean-Paul said. "We'll want to take a
closer look at what he found so interesting. But right now, let's
have something to eat, yes? I would not want to have to report
to Madame Gonsalves that we ruined her soup through neglect."

We turned out the lights and locked the door behind us. About
halfway up the stairs, Jean-Paul's phone got a signal again and
began to ding with messages that had come in while we were in the
basement. As he passed through the kitchen, he excused himself,

set the wine on the counter and continued on into the salon. I could hear him talking to someone, but not what he was talking about.

Though the soup hadn't burned, it had become thick enough to stand a spoon in. I filled a cup from the tap to thin it, but before I could dump water into the pot, Philippe stopped me.

"Madame Gigi adds chicken broth when she needs to thin the soup." He opened a cupboard, pulled out a liter box of chicken broth, and set to work.

"You like to cook?" I asked as I pulled out the mortadella we lugged all the way from Bologna, and the cheese and bread we acquired in Vaucresson that afternoon. Leftover soup, a little salad, cold meat and cheese sounded like a perfect Saturday night meal to me.

"I'd rather cook than study physics," he said. "But I'd rather jump out a window than study physics."

"I think the physics gene skipped both of us," I said. "What do you want to study?"

"I don't know. Nothing, really."

"When is your spring break? Sounds like you're ready for it."

"Not for two more weeks."

"Think you can last?"

He shrugged as he stirred the soup, but he smiled. We were talking about school and plans for the summer when Jean-Paul came into the kitchen. As he searched drawers looking for a corkscrew, he announced, "I hope it's all right; David Berg is going to drop by."

"When?" I asked.

"I just opened the gate for him."

"How lovely. Shall I open the wine?"

"Do you mind?"

What was there to say when the man was already driving through the gate? I reached for the corkscrew. "Of course not."

"Is there enough soup for one more?"

I glanced at Philippe, he nodded, and I answered, "Certainly."

When Jean-Paul left to go downstairs to let in his friend, I appealed to my co-chef. "Guess we're having a dinner guest. How thin can we make the soup?"

"No worry." He pulled a box of stewed roma tomatoes out of the cupboard, dumped them into the pot, added some tarragon and thyme, and the rest of the box of broth. Next, he cut a wedge off the mortadella, slivered it, dropped that into the pot, and chased it with a healthy shot of apple brandy he found somewhere.

"I'm glad you're here, Philippe," I said. For my part, I took the roasted chicken we'd bought from the butcher's smoochy wife out of the refrigerator. I thought I would slice it and we could eat it cold after the soup, but with what on the side? The edges of the salad greens had turned brown while they sat in the frigid car all afternoon, though the hothouse green beans looked just fine. I washed them, and holding the dripping colander over the sink, asked, "Any ideas about what to do with these?"

"Sure, sure." Philippe pulled out a sauté pan, olive oil and a head of garlic. I left him to it, picked up the wine and went out to greet our guest. Except, there were two men in dark suits taking off snow-flecked coats in the vestibule, not one.

"Maggie," Jean-Paul said, reaching for me. "This is my old friend, David Berg."

"Enchanté," the older of the two said, an elegant man of about fifty, the same age as Jean-Paul. He offered his hand and leaned in for *les bises.* "I am so very happy to meet you at last."

"Monsieur le Préfet." I sneaked a peek at myself in the mirror on the wall behind him. He looked as if he'd just stepped out of a showroom. I looked like I'd had a long day. "How nice to meet a friend of Jean-Paul."

Still holding my hand, he leaned in a bit again to say, in a low voice, "I beg you, call me David, or Davey, or anything else except Monsieur le Préfet."

"Shall I tell her what we called you at school?" Jean-Paul asked.

"Please don't." Berg found a hook on the hall tree for his coat. "Maggie, I want you to meet Thierry Dusaud, my assistant."

I offered my hand to Dusaud. He took it and bowed over it,

a more formal greeting than kissing the air around my cheeks. I said, "Welcome."

"I hope we aren't a burden," Dusaud said as he released my hand. "My wife would kill me if I dragged in dinner guests without advance warning."

I liked him right away. "Dinner, I'm afraid, will be potluck."

Berg unwrapped a cashmere muffler from around his neck and draped it on a hook beside his coat. "Something smells wonderful."

"I take no credit."

Philippe came out to the salon long enough to be introduced and to collect a short pour of wine, as is French custom, when Jean-Paul was serving the adults. He raised his glass with us, and then excused himself and, wineglass in hand, went back to the kitchen. He insisted, quite assertively, that he would set the table and serve dinner. He owed me, he said. And though I protested, I thought he was happy for the opportunity to be useful. It was probably better that he was busy elsewhere, out of earshot, while Jean-Paul answered his friend's question, "What the hell is going on?" in some detail, beginning with the drone attack in Greece a week ago.

A week ago? Could it be only a week ago? The last three days alone felt like months.

"Maggie?" Berg sat forward in his chair, opposite my seat next to Jean-Paul on the sofa. He seemed earnest. "You arrived in Paris Thursday?"

"Yes. In the morning."

"The last leg of your trip was from Abu Dhabi, yes?"

"You checked up on me?"

"I didn't," Berg said. "But a one-hundred-and-ten-pound, fifteen-year-old hacker in Taiwan did. You were tracked from Vientiane, Laos, to the airport in Bangkok, on to Abu Dhabi, and finally to Paris."

"How did he track me?" I asked. "Through flight manifests or customs records?"

"You tell me how." He pulled a little notebook out of his pants pocket, and with a smile, reported: "Tuesday, at the airport in

Vientiane, you bought something to read and something to drink. In Bangkok, it looks like you had both lunch and a late dinner in the airport, and then you went to a hotel. Your flight was delayed?"

"Damn credit cards," I said, knowing now the source of his information. "It's such a bother when you're in transit through a country to exchange currency just to buy a cup of coffee, a newspaper, and a sandwich. And yes, a delayed flight out of Bangkok. The first of several."

"A long trip, yes?"

"Longer than it needed to be. If I'd known every purchase was being tracked, I would have stuck with airline peanuts and water."

"I have only one question," Berg said, referring to his notes. "And that concerns what you were doing last Saturday afternoon."

"Saturday afternoon in what time zone?"

He laughed. "Around the time our dear boy was being blasted by a toy drone."

"What time was that?"

"After lunch," Jean-Paul said. "Around two o'clock, maybe."

I had to think for a moment, but in the end, I gave up. "I don't know. I think the time difference between here and Laos is five hours. Is Greece an hour ahead of us?"

"I think so," Jean-Paul said. "My watch changes automatically, so I don't have to think about time zones anymore when I travel."

"Watch, past tense," I said.

"Ah, yes. Gone the way of my telephone."

Berg raised an eyebrow. "Blown up?"

"No. It was still running when I traded it to some Greek fishermen for passage to Italy."

I looked across at Berg. "So, around six o'clock on Saturday, I was with my film crew in a tiny Lao village near the Thai border. Probably having dinner, or using a bucket to take a shower. Why?"

"Thierry?" Berg turned to his assistant. "You're primary on this, what do you know?"

His assistant scooted a few inches forward on his seat and leaned toward me. "You disappeared from the hacker's surveillance from Saturday morning until Monday evening. Something interesting must have happened during that time, because your bar tab in Vientiane when you reappeared on Monday was impressive."

"Believe me, I wasn't in Greece launching a drone," I said, though I knew that he was only looking for information and not accusing me of anything nefarious, except maybe having a drinking problem. "There are places in the world, my friend, where credit cards are useless. We could only use cash, Lao *kip*, in the village where we filmed that weekend, though the innkeeper was okay with U.S. dollars. We finished filming Monday afternoon, packed our gear, and headed for Vientiane. That night, I hosted a wrap party for the crew, as is our tradition when we finish final filming. They can drink impressive quantities of hooch. Tuesday morning, we all flew out. Or tried to fly out."

"I only asked because when we got hold of the hacker's log this afternoon, we saw that you disappeared offline at about the same time as Monsieur Bernard—"

"Jean Paul," Jean Paul said.

"Thank you," Dusaud said, with a little nod. "We had some concern that something, let's just say dire, was happening to you during the same time that Jean-Paul was under attack in Greece."

"Happily, no," I said. "The more I think about how vulnerable we are to anyone who wants to, as you say, do something dire to us, the more I like that Laotian village. Even though we had to be vaccinated against several deadly diseases, walk gingerly around areas with live ordnance, and truck in our own water, I felt safer there than I do right now, here in very civilized Paris. So, what happens next?"

"Davey?" Dusaud deferred to his superior.

"Wish we knew. If we'd had this information sooner, I might have a better answer for you." Berg set aside his wineglass and nailed Jean-Paul with the sort of look angry mothers aim at naughty children. "My dear old friend didn't see fit to tell me a damn thing about what was going on for one long week. So, we've hardly had time to figure it all out. This afternoon, I did as you suggested, Jeep, and I called Luca Ponti for information. You might like to know that, based on the information you gave him yesterday, police in Taiwan took *la petite merde* who hacked your accounts into custody."

It seemed to me that Berg was truly hurt that Jean-Paul hadn't come to him immediately. Why, I wondered, hadn't he? I turned to Jean-Paul. When I saw his discomfort, I asked, "In this case, does the feminine article, *la*, refer to the gender of the person who is a little shit, or is shit a feminine noun?"

"The noun is feminine," Jean-Paul said. "But the hacker: Davey? Thierry?"

Berg answered, unable to hide a little smile. "Your little shit is a boy."

I asked, "So why is *merde* a feminine noun?"

Jean-Paul said, "If it makes you feel better, fart— *pet*—is masculine in French."

"It does, a little bit. And I'm happy that our *petite merde* will be separated from his computer for a while. But how does that help us? Won't ProtX4 just go to the next hacker on their list in the same way that, if Qosja's threat is correct, they'll hire the next thug in line to come after us?"

Berg sat up taller. "He said that to you?"

"He did."

Dusaud moved the conversation back on topic. "We haven't had time to learn much about either ProtX4 or InterCentro. After his arrest, the kid in Taiwan handed over every bit of information he had collected. But all he knows about whoever hired him are a bank routing number for the money that was deposited on his credit card and the access code for an anonymous message drop box. About ProtX4, we know only what anyone can find out by pulling up their web page. They seem to function entirely online. We left a couple of messages on their contact link, but they haven't responded."

"Anything on InterCentro?" Jean-Paul asked.

"Not yet," Dusaud said. "Other than that they claim to be a center for the study of traditional Russian culture."

Philippe had been in and out of the salon, carrying dishes and eating implements as he set the table. Occasionally something that was being said would catch his attention and he would pause, but he generally went about the tasks he had taken on himself without paying much attention to the conversation on the far side of the room. The table was ready, a second bottle of wine was open and breathing on the sideboard, when he came in carrying a soup tureen. He set the soup near bowls stacked at one end of the table and announced, *"À table."*

"Gentlemen. Dinner is served." I rose, and they followed. Jean-Paul still had the use of only one arm, so I asked Philippe if he would serve the soup, but his eyes grew wide with horror at taking over for the host, and instead he pulled out the chair in front of the tureen for me, putting me at the head of the table, instead of him. The soup was good. The stewed tomatoes and herbs Philippe added brightened Madame Gonsalves's rather heavy, but delicious, potato-leek *porrusalda*. Conversation during dinner, like conversation during our lunch with Luca, went everywhere except anywhere near the real topic for the evening. We discussed children and parents and school, making films for television, hating or loving physics, fighting international terrorism. Philippe did his best to participate, and the men were gracious about finding subjects that included him. The soup was cleared and he brought out a platter with a heap of sautéed green beans in the center of a necklace of cold sliced chicken drizzled with a sort of sriracha aioli that he improvised, he told us, by adding a few drops of vinegar, olive oil, and hot sauce to the *crème fraîche* he found in the refrigerator. It was delicious.

"Young man," Berg said after savoring a bite. "Did your mother teach you to cook?"

Philippe blushed furiously: if there were a tabu topic, especially in my presence, it would be anything having to do with his mother. After taking a sip of water, he said, quietly, "No, my grand-mère is a famous cook."

I knew he did not mean Isabelle, but her mother.

Jean-Paul raised his wineglass. "Here's to the cook. Who the hell needs physics when he can throw together a meal like this from nothing?"

The last course was cheese, fig jam, coffee, and brandy. As we lingered with the brandy, the conversation finally moved to the library in the basement, and to Val Barkoff's interest in the Russian texts.

"I remember when you found the old library," Berg said, breaking off a chunk of aged Roquefort and daubing it with fig jam. "That time, you came to me because you needed my advice about what should be done with it."

"You were a great help," Jean-Paul said. "I'm asking for your help again."

"Other than trying to keep you two alive just a little longer, what is it, exactly, that you want me to do, my dear Jeep?"

"I have a question for Philippe first." Making eye contact with Philippe, Jean-Paul asked, "Have you met your friend Val's father?"

"Yes, a few times. He came for sports days and parent meetings."

"Do you know his Christian name?"

Philippe covered his mouth to hide a giggle. When he caught his breath, he said, "It's Boris."

"Is that funny?" I asked him.

"Well, yes, because he is short and fat, and his wife is tall and thin, and her name is Natasha. He's Russian, and he always has these security men around him. So, Boris Badenov and Natasha Fatale. Get it?"

"You watch American cartoons?" I asked.

"Sure. Rocky and Bullwinkle, moose and squirrel."

Jean-Paul said, "Maggie, I'll teach you how to swear in French if you'll help me with the American idiom. I have no idea what you two are talking about."

"I'll explain later. But, yes, Boris Barkov, expert on antique Russian texts, board member of InterCentro, apparently is Val's father. It's pronounced the same, isn't it, even though he spells his name differently. A difference in conversion from the Cyrillic to the Latinate alphabet, I suppose."

Jean-Paul nodded acknowledgment and turned back to Berg. "I would like to know what Monsieur Barkov's interest is in the library. But more importantly, what is his interest in Maggie and me? Someone has gone to great lengths to keep the two of us away from this apartment. At first, there were little forays made to get access, but they failed, and then escalated the closer we came to the time when Maggie was to arrive."

"Maggie." Dusaud set down his brandy snifter when he turned to me. "Who knew about your plans to stay in Paris?"

I had to think for a moment. "My friends, our families, my co-workers."

"And everyone who sees the entertainment news," Philippe said. That got everyone's attention. The poor kid blushed yet again, but he continued. "There were stories that said you worked on a film in Normandy all summer, Aunt Maggie, and that you were talking about moving to Paris to work with French television once you finished the project about bombs."

"Jean-Paul," I said, covering his hand. "Right now I need something juicer than just *merde*. And remind me to call Uncle Max."

"When was this?" Berg asked.

Philippe shrugged. "After the holidays. It was when Aunt Maggie was filming battlefields in Flanders. When Grand-mère saw the report, she was so happy to think you are staying in France forever."

"Did your friend Val see the report?" Jean-Paul asked.

"Oh, yes. I got into a panic about cleaning the apartment before Aunt Maggie came. But we had exams, and I couldn't get away."

"Until now," I said.

He sighed. "I'm not supposed to be here. Papa will kill me if he finds out. But I had to come and explain."

"How did you know I had arrived?" I asked.

"Madame Gigi. She scolded me so hard."

"When did you talk to her?"

"Yesterday. She said I could stay over at her apartment tonight if I came today to apologize. She isn't answering her phone, but her hearing isn't very good."

"If you stay anywhere tonight," I said, "you'll stay right here with us. Philippe, Madame Gonsalves had a little accident this afternoon. She's in hospital."

"Oh, no." He started to rise from his chair, but Jean-Paul put a hand on his arm and he settled back down.

"She'll be fine," Jean-Paul said, giving him a pat. "Just a little bump on the head. You'll come with us to check on her in the morning, then you'll come to lunch with us at Karine and Émile's. Their girls will be very happy to see you. After lunch, we'll put you on the train back to school. *D'accord?*"

"Yes." Philippe glanced at me to make sure it was all right. When I nodded, he repeated, "Yes. Thank you. Yes."

Berg folded his napkin beside his plate, signaling that the meal was over for him. "Philippe, unless you're too tired after your kitchen labors, I would like you to take us down to the library so that we can have a look at the books that your friend found so interesting."

My nephew turned to me, expecting permission, I suppose. I said, "Go ahead. You made dinner, I'll clear away. I expect that Jean-Paul wants to go down with you."

For the second time that day, lights went on over the back stairs, and Philippe led a party of inquiry down into the basement. I did dishes.

8

EXCEPT FOR A BREAK at Christmas, when I went back to Los Angeles to be with my mom, my daughter, Uncle Max, and Jean-Paul for the holidays, since October I had been living out of a suitcase, wearing the same week's-worth of clothes over and over and over. Everything in that case was basic, washable, functional. Boring. I had grown to hate the sight of it all. So, the big issue for me upon rising on Sunday morning was which shirt and which sweater would I pull on yet again. First thing, we were going to check on Madame Gonsalves in the hospital. After that, off to Karine and Émile's for a family lunch. Jean-Paul's mother would be there. From our first meeting, Victoria Bernard had been very gracious to me, very welcoming, because, she told me, her son had been so very sad after his wife died that she was afraid he would never be happy again. But I made him laugh. As kind as she was, she was also rather formal. A bit too perfect. And always beautifully dressed.

Feeling less than chipper that morning, I lifted my sad little wardrobe out of the suitcase on the floor intending to put it into the tall armoire that served as the room's closet, to get it out from underfoot. Though Freddy's two boys had left quite a few things in the room they shared during the year and a half the three of them had stayed at Isabelle's apartment after her death—dragging their feet, or maybe angry, over having to move out—Freddy had completely cleared away all evidence of himself. So, I expected the armoire to be empty. I was surprised, then, to find it full of clothes. A woman's clothes. Isabelle's, of course.

Before we went to bed, I had put the black slacks I wore all day Friday into the washer, and popped them into the dryer before breakfast that morning. When I got out of the shower, I put them on, still warm, yet again. Isabelle and I, I had been told often enough, were built very much alike. It took one more look at the well-worn stack of shirts in my hand to get over any qualms about rifling through that late stranger's things for something different to wear. I chose a silk blouse that was about the same shade as very old pearls, and a soft blue cashmere V-neck sweater. For good measure, I looped my long string of pearls around my neck a couple of times and declared myself ready for whatever the day ahead held.

As I walked into the salon looking for Jean-Paul, Philippe came in through the front door, leaving a wet trail.

"You were out?" I asked.

"For a minute." He hung up his coat and slipped off his soggy shoes. "I wanted to get something to take to Madame Gigi. Flowers or sweets or something. But it's Sunday morning and the shops are all closed."

"Why don't we take her the chocolates you brought yesterday?"

"But I gave them to you."

"You did, and I treasure the gesture. But, as you said, it's Sunday morning, nothing's open, Madame Gonsalves is in hospital, and you're right, we can't go to her empty-handed. So, could we declare the chocolates a gift from us all?"

He thought for a moment before saying, "Madame Gigi does like sweets."

"Good. Then agreed?"

"Agreed."

Something occurred to me as he headed off toward his room. "Philippe?"

"Yes?" He turned.

"How do you come and go?"

He shrugged, not sure what I was asking.

"Do you have keys?"

He pulled a set out of his pocket, two latch keys and an electronic gate clicker. "I still have Papa's keys from when we stayed at New Year's. Is that wrong?"

"No," I said. "Of course, you would have keys. I hadn't thought until just now to ask who all has sets. Do you have any idea?"

"You know that sometimes Mamie Izzy had—" He just couldn't find the right words to explain about Isabelle's issues. "Sometimes things would get so bad with her that Madame Gigi would call Papa or Grand-mère or Uncle Gérard to come. They had door keys in case she wasn't letting anyone in. And Madame Gigi has keys, of course."

"Makes sense. Thanks." I started toward the kitchen, still looking for Jean-Paul. We were going to have to change the locks. As soon as possible.

"Do you want me to leave them here?" He dangled the keys between two fingers.

"Oh." Yes, I did want him to leave the keys. I also didn't want to make him think I didn't trust him, or that he wasn't welcome. He was welcome, when we were there to greet him. "All things considered, it's probably a better idea to leave them here than to have to bother with them at school."

"Sure." He set them, very quietly, on the table behind the sofa and continued on toward his room.

I found Jean-Paul coming up the back stairs from the basement. I said, "Looking for reading material?"

"No." He held up a squat, brown bottle. "Liquid refreshment. I decided that brandy would be better to take to Karine's than wine. Émile will have been very careful about choosing the wine for lunch, and I wouldn't want him to think I question his taste."

"Dandy," I said. I told him about discovering that there were multiple sets of keys. "We need to change the locks."

"If you say so."

"I have a meeting in the morning with French TV. Will you be able to take care of it?"

"*Bien sûr.* When does Guido come?"

"Tonight. His plane arrives at six. I asked him to take a cab."

"I'll get on the locks first thing."

Philippe re-emerged from his room wearing a turtleneck and a sweater he found among the clothes he, or maybe his brother, Robert, had left behind. Jean-Paul stowed the brandy in a muslin shopping bag. We all pulled on coats and scarves, and tucked gloves into pockets. It was wet out. Val Barkoff's coat hung over a bucket of umbrellas. As I moved it aside to get one, I thought about the boy who had left it behind. The coat was too big for Jean-Paul, who was just about six feet tall and well built. The Barkoff boy, then, was a large kid. Tall like his mother, Natasha, round like his father, Boris? Not that it mattered.

Last thing, I went to the panel beside the front door, and switched to the street-view camera to make sure that the police car was still parked there. It was. When we drove out, the little white-and-blue Citroën fell in behind us. Along the way, we passed several bakeries that were open. All of them had displays of beautiful sweets in the window. I glanced back at Philippe and the little bag of chocolates on the seat beside him, and wondered, again, why he had gone out earlier that morning if it wasn't to buy something to take to his Madame Gigi. His eyes were locked on the phone in his hands. His face told me nothing.

Madame Gonsalves was enjoying her hospital stay. She exclaimed over the chocolates, the perfect gift, she said, all the better because it was Philippe who chose them. Her head was fine, but there was water on her knee from the fall. She was to stay over another night so that it could be watched. If necessary, an orthopedist would come in that afternoon and tap it. He was, she said, very handsome. And she was very comfortable. And we were not to worry.

Philippe kissed Madame Gonsalves's cheeks and clung to her hand until it was time for us to leave, but he said very little. To anyone. The generally exuberant youth remained quiet during the short drive into the western suburbs, checking from time to time to make sure that the police car was always behind us. Clearly, something weighed heavily on him that cold gray morning. The police escort? The prospect of lunch with Jean-Paul's family? Had I offended him when I asked about the keys? Or was it that his once golden life had devolved into a giant, endless cockup?

Karine and Émile lived in a large, traditional, and unpretentious house on a large lot in a newish development of similar houses. When Jean-Paul turned into the driveway, our escort found a space out front, and parked. Jean-Paul drove around to the back where there was a wide, graveled parking area in front of the garages. Others had arrived, and parked, before us.

I recognized the green Jaguar at the same time as Philippe. He muttered, "*Merde*. Papa is here."

"If I had to guess, Philippe," Jean-Paul said as he pulled in next to a Volvo sedan, "your father drove your grandmother in from Normandy. You know what that means, don't you, Maggie?"

"I'm afraid to ask."

"The family has gathered to talk about a wedding."

"We should have eloped," I said.

"It's not too late," Philippe chimed in. "We could just back right out and go off and get you two married."

"Sorry, but it is too late," Jean-Paul said, releasing his seat belt. "We've been spotted."

Émile appeared at the back door. We followed him into a stone-floored mudroom where we exchanged *les bises* and shed our wraps and commiserated about the miserable weather. Émile exclaimed about what a lovely surprise it was that we had brought Philippe. Before we could go through into the rest of the house, Émile pulled Jean-Paul aside.

"To soften the blow before she saw you, I told your mother you had been in a little accident. I'm glad I did, because she had a total meltdown. Her poor little boy, and, well, you know the rest."

"Her little boy is fifty years old," Jean-Paul said with a chuckle. "Somehow, I have managed to make my way for a full half century, but— Ah well. Shall I pull a bag over my head to spare her the sight?"

"No. But I am going to take the brace off your shoulder so she won't see you with an empty sleeve. That would be too much for her. The bone is healing nicely, but let's not test it, promise? No push-ups, no gymnastics. Philippe, go on in. Your dad, your brother, and your grandmother will be so happy to see you."

"Thank you, no. I want to wait and go in behind Jean-Paul. If everyone is freaking out about his scars, maybe they'll forget to be angry I'm here."

"Who would be angry?" Émile asked, but in the question, he found the answer. "AWOL from school?"

The sheepish look on the boy's face told him all he needed to know.

We helped Jean-Paul out of his shirt and sweater and unbuckled the brace. Émile examined the collarbone and the progress of the flesh wound before he let Jean-Paul put his clothes back on. As Émile folded the brace and set it on the washer, Jean-Paul raised his arm and moved it in a slow, experimental circle. "What a relief."

Émile watched him closely. "I'll pop out some of those sutures before you go home. But take it easy, huh?"

"Two arms again," Jean-Paul said to me with a gleam in his eye. "Think of the possibilities."

"Congratulations," I said, taking his arm on the delicate side, hoping to protect it from the oncoming crush of family affection.

We made an entrance. Between Jean-Paul's mother's anguish over her boy's injuries and Philippe's father's over his son's surprise appearance, there was a fair amount of exclaiming and explaining going on.

"What happened, my angel?" Jean-Paul's mother, Victoria, wanted to know as she clung to his side, fingers gingerly tracing the scars on his face.

"Slipped on the ice, Maman."

"I don't believe you. Tell me the truth."

"The truth: A drone appeared out of nowhere and dropped a bomb on me."

"It did not. Don't tease."

"I was in a car wreck."

"Now, did that need to be so difficult?" she said, crisply. "I wish you had simply told me the truth when you called last week to say that you had lost your wallet and needed a favor. Maggie, dear, you need to watch this one closely. He's a terrible tease."

"So I've discovered," I said.

Poor Philippe was head to head with his father, explaining mightily with hand gestures and a variety of explanations of his own. When Freddy looked over his son's head and caught my eye, I ventured into the fray. Without mentioning all that had gone before, I told him that there had been attempts made to get into the library, and that Philippe had been very helpful by giving us information. Freddy seemed skeptical. His eyes elided toward Jean-Paul for confirmation as I spoke, and I knew I needed a better story because Jean-Paul, of course, would know at least as much about the library as Philippe. I was saved from miring myself further in their family issues by the appearance of my grandmother. After the drive in from Normandy that morning, she had gone upstairs for a little lie-down. As soon as she heard our voices, and there were a lot of voices, she brushed her hair and joined us.

My grand-mère, Élodie Martin, age ninety-three, wore the mantle of elegant grande dame deceptively well. I say deceptively, because she actually was an earthy, gutsy survivor. The efficiency with which she dispatched a unit of Nazi soldiers during the Occupation of France had become the stuff of local legend. From the first time I met her, I knew that, given the right provocation, Grand-mère could do something similar all over again.

"My dear, dear Maggie," she said after a prolonged exchange of kisses. "I was so hoping you would be able to come for a visit when you were filming in Flanders; it's not so terribly far from us. We missed you at Christmas. It would have been our first together since you were a tiny little one. But this year, you will be there, I insist. Now, when are you coming for a nice long stay with your Grand-mère?"

"That will depend on what comes out of a meeting I'm having

tomorrow. If that conversation goes nowhere, I'll come and see you before I head back to Los Angeles to look for my next job. But if it goes as I hope it will, then after I get the current film finished in L.A., I'll be around here for a while."

"I'll have my fingers crossed for you tomorrow, my darling." Then she smiled and said, "And fingers crossed for myself."

Fortunately, nowhere in that conversation did she remind me how ancient she was and how tenuous life is. She merely patted my face and went over to check on Philippe, who, though Karine and Émile's fifteen- and sixteen-year-old daughters, Vic and Suze— Victoria, for her grandmother, and Suzanne—and his younger brother, Robert, were doing their best to cheer him up, still looked uncomfortable and sad. The two boys had been through a great family trauma the year before, and I thought they both had a lot of grief, still, to overcome. When they were with strangers, maybe they could shunt their feelings aside. But with family, the situation around their mother was always the greatest presence in the room. Doubly so when I, who had been the target of their mother's crime, was there with them.

At last, lunch was served. Conversation was noisy and wide-ranging, from politics to the tiresome weather, the cost of an American education, the state of French national health, and the best way to prune roses. At the end, Karine brought out an apple cake with the cheese, and right away the women, except me, zeroed in on the real topic *du jour*: wedding plans for me and Jean-Paul. I might as well have been in the kitchen doing dishes for most of it. After I said that I agreed with Jean-Paul that a civil ceremony was sufficient, and that a religious ceremony afterward was unnecessary, I wasn't consulted further. They could survive without a church blessing, but they were not to be deprived of a big party. My daughter's participation was assumed, but no one mentioned a role for my mom, the woman who raised me after Isabelle gave me up. When Jean-Paul caught my eye, and nodded toward the kitchen door, I followed his lead, folded my napkin under the edge of my plate and quietly slipped into the next room with him. No one seemed to notice.

"Did you invite me in here to make out?" I asked when he took me into his arms. Both arms.

"Perfect idea." He showed me how perfect. Until someone behind us cleared his throat. Startled, I turned to find Philippe standing just inside the kitchen door leading to the mudroom.

"Excuse me, please. I'm sorry, but—" He looked as if he were on the verge of tears.

Jean-Paul reached for him to come closer. "What is it, son?"

"Papa wants to take me to the train later, so I don't know if I'll have a chance to talk to you again. You know, without everyone hanging around."

"Has anyone noticed we abandoned them?" I asked.

"Suze peeked in and told them you were just kissing, and that made everyone happy. I went around the house and came in through the back. I'm sorry to interrupt."

"We're parents, we're used to it," I said. "Tell us what's on your mind."

"It's just..." He struggled for air. I patted his back for a moment and he managed to breathe enough to say, "Aunt Maggie, I've seen most of your films, so I know you've met some really hardcore criminals. Do you think some people are born to be criminals?"

"Is there a bad seed?" When he nodded, I said, "I believe there are some people who are simply evil from the beginning. But, no, I think circumstances created them, not their genes."

"But if they're raised by a criminal, does that like, predispose them?"

"Maybe. But only by exposure to the parent."

When his only response was to nod, I asked, "Does this concern have something to do with your mother?"

"What she did was really terrible," he said, looking at the floor. "It's bad that she stole money, but worse that she stole from you and Mamie Izzy because you're family."

"Have you done something, Philippe?" Jean-Paul asked in a very soft voice, watching Philippe's reaction to the question as closely as he listened to the answer he gave.

"Maybe."

"Go on," I prodded.

"When we were goofing around in the library, me and Cho and Val, I told you that I bragged about how valuable the books were. So, we took pictures of some of them and put them up on the Net on a couple of auction sites, just to see if anyone would bid. We weren't going to sell them, I promise you. It was just a dumb thing we did."

"Was this before, during, or after the brandy?" Jean-Paul asked.

"During. But early. I mean, we'd had some, but Cho wasn't throwing up yet, so we hadn't had a whole lot."

"Does Cho throw up a lot?" I asked.

He nodded. "He says it's genetic. He can't metabolize alcohol very well, so he turns bright red and throws up before everyone else. Usually, when he gets to that point, I know it's time to stop."

"But that night you didn't stop," Jean-Paul said.

"No. I was kind of mad." He gave me a very direct look. "I liked living in Paris. I grew up here. My friends are here. It was hard when all that stuff happened around Maman and we had to move out of our house in the Marais and into Mamie Izzy's apartment, but it was still Paris. I hated it when we had to go live on Grand-mère's estate in Normandy. There's nothing to do out there."

"Except make cheese and grow carrots?" I asked. Finally, he smiled. I asked, "Are you mad that Isabelle left the apartment to me?"

He let out a long breath and looked away.

"That's perfectly understandable," I said. "I would be pissed if I thought I owned something like that, and then found out at the worst moment in my life that I didn't."

"Can you ever forgive me?"

"There's nothing to forgive. Hell, Philippe, I just learned a few days ago that your dad was shut out of rue Jacob. It was cruel of Isabelle."

"Sometimes she did things," he said.

"So I understand."

"Did anyone bid on the books?" Jean-Paul asked.

The poor kid, I thought he might faint. When Jean-Paul gripped his upper arm, he steeled himself. "They did. They bid a lot."

"How much is a lot?" I asked.

"One book was going for about seven hundred fifty."

"Seven hundred fifty dollars, euros, pounds?"

"Seven hundred and fifty *thousand* Swiss francs."

"What's the exchange rate?" I asked Jean-Paul.

"About the same as a dollar, one for one."

"Does *merde* suit this situation?"

Philippe let out a bark that could have been a laugh.

"What did you do?" I asked.

"I took them down, off the site, and posted they weren't for sale."

"Them?" I said.

"We put up four books."

"Were all of them Russian?"

He nodded. "Val said if we put up those books, he'd be able to find out how good the offers were."

"Did your friends understand that you were just goofing around?" I asked.

He nodded vigorously. "But when they saw how much money we could get, they wanted to go through with it."

"What did you do?"

"We argued. It got bad. That's when Monsieur Griffith came down and told us to shut up. And that's when I kicked them out."

"But Val tried to steal one of the books, anyway, right? The little book of Psalms."

"Yeah."

"Was that the book someone was ready to pay three-quarters of a million for?"

"Yeah."

"Are you afraid your friends still want to sell the books?" I asked. "If they can get their hands on them."

"I know they are. I checked. The posts are back up."

Jean-Paul had been quietly listening, but I could see that his mind was far from quiet. He said, "I'd like you to tell all this to David Berg or Thierry Dusaud. Will you?"

"Papa is making me go back to school tonight."

"Papa is thinking hard about that."

We all turned around at the new voice. Freddy had been listening in from the mudroom, leaning against the washer with his arms folded. He straightened up and came into the kitchen. With barely a glance at either me or Jean-Paul, he went to his son and wrapped an arm around his shoulders. They were nearly the same height now, but Philippe seemed to shrink, a child nestled in the safety of his parent's embrace.

"I have only the vaguest idea what you've been talking about in here," Freddy said. "But I can see that whatever it is has caused you great pain, Philippe. I hope you're ready to talk to me." Freddy kissed the top of his son's head. "We've been through hell this last year and a half, haven't we?"

When Philippe bobbed his head, acknowledging an understatement, his father smiled. "I keep thinking the worst is over, so you, Robert, and I can relax and try to figure out what normal is. But shit just keeps piling up, doesn't it?"

Freddy turned to me. "And, yes, I was really pissed when I found out that Maman shut me out of rue Jacob. My dear wife's legal defense ruined us financially, and worse, much worse. I could only get to sleep at night by reminding myself that I still had a big cushion to fall on, a prime property on the Left Bank of Paris. And then the cushion disappeared."

"Ah, Freddy, I'm sorry. I didn't know."

His shoulder rose a bit. "You have nothing to be sorry about. Maman did what she did. You didn't even know she existed."

There was no rancor in his voice, only sad resignation. He got the raw end. But he was used to that; he grew up with the woman.

"Maggie," he said, "in America, I understand that some kids take a break the year before starting university. They use the time to grow up and figure things out."

"Some do."

"I think Philippe may have earned a break. I thought that a preparatory year in England would be a breather for him. A new environment, new friends, a new start. But I can see I was wrong. He carried all the same distractions that prevented him from sitting for the *baccalauréat* exams last spring across the Channel with him." He looked at his son. "So, Philippe, if you agree, we'll find something that will make you useful and keep you worn out, keep you out of trouble, and give you some time to think. Do you agree?"

"I don't want to make cheese."

"I understand that completely, because neither do I. Any idea what you might want to do?"

"Learn to cook."

"*Oh-là-là.*" Freddy rolled his eyes, and smiled. "Why the hell not?"

Karine came in carrying a stack of dishes. "Here you all are. What are you up to?"

"We're talking about a wedding feast," Jean-Paul said. "Philippe has some good ideas."

"Lovely lunch, Karine," I said. "Just lovely."

She set the dishes on the counter. "You two better go back in there before things get completely out of control. Élodie and Maman Victoria are already comparing guest lists. Suze and Vic are talking about dresses, and Émile is looking up venues big enough for a crowd."

As we turned to troop out, Jean-Paul caught up with Freddy. "After you have a conversation with Philippe about what happened at the apartment over the New Year, I encourage you to take him to speak with a friend of mine. His name is David Berg."

Freddy froze, alarmed. "I know who David Berg is."

"Most likely, he'll want you to speak with his assistant, Thierry Dusaud. Please don't worry, and please don't put it off. And while you're still in the city, Maggie and I would like to sit down with you for an important conversation as well."

"Has Philippe hurt anyone?"

"No. But he wandered into something that may have gotten out of hand. We need to help him get out before it's too late to save himself. But that isn't all that we need to talk about."

"I'm putting Robert on the train to Normandy this afternoon because he has school tomorrow. But I was planning to stay in town tonight with Grand-mère. Traveling one way between here and Normandy is about all she can manage in a single day; we'll drive back tomorrow. I'll hang onto Philippe overnight, too. Maybe we can speak with Berg's assistant in the morning. Do you have a number for him?"

"Yes. Better if you call him today."

"Call the assistant to the Directeur Général of the police on Sunday?"

"Yes. Trust me, he'll be happy to hear from you." The two men took out their phones so that Freddy could copy the number from Jean-Paul's contacts into his own.

On the way back out to the wedding planners in the salon, Freddy caught my arm. "Maggie, where was Jean-Paul when he was hurt?"

Funny question. "On a Greek island."

"Were you with him?"

"No. I was still in Laos when it happened. Why?"

"Just brotherly concern," he said, giving my shoulder a pat as we went through the door and into the fray. "There's an orthopedic brace on the washer that wasn't there when we arrived. I was worried that you had been injured, too."

"Thanks for the concern, but I'm fine."

Karine was right, the conversation between Grand-mère and Victoria about a wedding party had gotten completely out of hand. I thought it best to stay out of it and went looking for my other nephew, Robert, who wasn't with the others. Usually the more social of Freddy's boys, Robert was by himself in a quiet corner of the sunroom off the main salon, fiddling with his phone. While Philippe looked very much like his father, all angles and bones, Robert was more like Grand-mère and Isabelle, with rounder, softer features. I went over and stood in front of him.

"How are you, Robert?"

He looked up, surprised, I think, that I had spoken to him, or that I was there at all. "Aunt Maggie."

"May I sit here?" I asked.

"Of course." He scooted over on the sofa to make room for me. Stiffly, he asked, "Have you been well?"

"Yes, thank you. And you?"

He thought for a moment before he nodded. "Very well, thank you."

"Robert," I said, "I've had some interesting conversations with your brother about his love for cheese making."

There was a delay before Robert laughed. "And about how fun it is to press apples into cider?"

"And grow carrots."

"Uncle Antoine calls me and Philippe city slickers. I had to look that up on the Net. It's true, though. I am a city slicker."

"Philippe likes to cook. What about you?"

"I want to be a mad scientist, like Mamie Izzy. I don't mean an actually crazy person, just one who's mad for science."

"You probably love physics."

"Oh, yes! Do you?"

"Afraid not," I said. "Robert, about Isabelle's apartment."

He dropped his head and let out a long breath, clearly not happy with the topic. "I'm sorry. Very sorry."

"Sorry about what?"

"Papa told me and Philippe to get all of our junk out of there before you moved in. That's one reason we went to Paris after the Christmas ski trip, to finish packing our stuff. But we fooled around instead. So, Papa let Philippe and his friends stay one more night to see the New Year fireworks if they promised that they would finish packing up before they left. But I guess they didn't."

"Robert, if you and Philippe want to leave some things there, it's fine with me. I hope that you know you're welcome to visit."

He gave me a puckish smile. "With or without friends?"

"Preferably without. If you bring friends, I won't be able to spend much time with you."

He furrowed his brow. "Why would you want to?"

"To get to know you. We're family."

He studied me for long moment. "Do you think that's as weird as we do?"

"Maybe weirder. You at least knew that I existed."

"If it makes you feel better, you can give us Mamie Izzy's apartment back."

Chagrined, I had no comeback. I looked into his face, at a loss, and he began to cry. Quiet tears became soft, desperate gasps for air. I wrapped an arm around him and he buried his face against me. He wiped his nose on the back of his hand and managed to say, "I'm sorry, Aunt Maggie. I didn't mean to say that."

"Maybe not. But, obviously, that's what you're thinking. Robert, I didn't evict you; you could have stayed. You moved to Normandy because your father is working on a project there."

"Yes. But not forever. Where do we go when he's finished?"

"There's plenty of time to figure that out." He was not mollified. "Damn, Robert, we've had quite a year, haven't we?"

I felt his head nod, and offered him my sleeve. Isabelle's cashmere sleeve. He laughed and used his own to wipe his nose. I said, *"Merde."* And he laughed again. After a few deep breaths, he was composed enough to sit up straight.

He asked, "Is Philippe in big trouble?"

"Not from me."

"I hate his friends."

"Cho and Val?"

He nodded. "I don't like Philippe when he's around them."

"Why?"

"They're so full of themselves. *Crétins arrogants.*"

"Can you translate that into English for me?"

"Arrogant pricks," he said. "Both of them."

"A lot of empty talk?"

"I hope it's empty talk."

"About what, for example?"

"They were always talking about how rich they were," he said. "Papa got tired of hearing it. He said, if your parents are rich, all you are is a dependent. And that it was foolish to wait around expecting to inherit, because you might get nothing. Like us, I suppose. So, then all they could talk about was how they were going to get rich themselves. It was just stupid."

"Sounds boring."

"Very."

Freddy came into the room just then, looking for Robert. "Ready to go, son?"

Robert smiled at me, shrugged, and got up.

"Have a safe trip home," I said to him as we followed Freddy out.

After a beat, he asked, "Can I really visit you sometime in Paris?"

"Of course. I'd love it."

He seemed to file that bit of information.

There was a general movement of guests toward the exit. Good-byes took a while. Promises to call, to get together soon, to stay well, to be careful on the roads; the sun was low, the roads might ice up. Finally in our cars, there were last waves as first Freddy's Jag drove out, and then Victoria's Volvo. We were the last in the queue. I knew that Jean-Paul had let the others go ahead because he did not want them to see the police car pull out right behind us.

"Why do people always talk about the weather?" I asked, watching our tail fall into place behind us.

"Probably because it's the one thing we all have in common," he said. "Speaking of weather, this winter has been unusually cold and miserable. But you do know that gray and damp is normal for Paris from fall till spring. Do you think you could adjust to living here?"

"I could say that you are sunshine enough for me, but I honestly don't know. As a Californian, I've visited winter as a tourist many times, always knowing that when I get home again I can fold away the long johns and go outside for a dose of vitamin D. I suppose I could learn to remember to put on a coat when I go out."

"Then you're willing to give it a try?"

"I believe we decided that a long time ago, my dear." Icicle flags were forming around the side-view mirror out my window. "New topic: I want to talk with you about Freddy and the *résidence*."

"Yes?"

"What Isabelle did was cruel. At the very least, she should have told him a long time ago not to have expectations about rue Jacob."

"What are you thinking?"

"There needs to be an adjustment of some sort."

"You want to give him a share in the property?"

"I need to consult my partner before I do anything."

"Your partner doesn't object in concept. We have to be careful, though, that we don't give Freddy a gift he can't afford to maintain. If you think taxes are high in America, taxes in France will take your breath away. So, my concern is that if he found himself short of cash, Freddy might encumber his share with a loan that he could have trouble keeping up with. If he defaulted, we'd all be in financial jeopardy. My dear, I have too much invested in rue Jacob to put it at risk because we wanted to make a *beau geste*. I hope that doesn't sound cold."

"It doesn't. But there must be something I can do."

"We'll give the idea some hard thought. I have found you a very good, English-speaking *notaire* with strong financial credentials. Unless you object, I'll go with you when you speak with him. I hope he can sort out the terms of Isabelle's will for you. And maybe he can give us some guidance about what we can do for Freddy while we're there."

We were quiet after that. So many things to think about. We managed to get back to Isabelle's apartment without skidding on ice, losing our police tail, or being chased by the next creep on ProtX4's list of hired goons. Considering recent events, arriving unscathed felt like progress.

"Do you think they're finished with us?" I asked Jean-Paul as I put the key in the front door.

"No more than you do."

"Philippe's friend, Val, came very close to walking out the door with three-quarters of a million francs in his pocket. That would be a massive temptation to turn away from." I hung up my coat and helped Jean-Paul off with his; his shoulder was still stiff after being immobilized for a week. "From all accounts, he's a braggart. How many people have he and the other boy, Cho, told about their near-miss with wealth?"

"You think those kids set all this up?"

"Set it in motion, anyway. We have no idea who they might have inspired. I do know I'll sleep better when the locks have been changed."

"Right now, I think I could sleep through just about anything." He looked drawn. All that family chitchat and drama had worn him out. Though he tried very hard to cover it, he was still on the mend from his ordeal. I reminded him it was time to take his antibiotic, and suggested that he have a nap. He agreed that a brief lie-down would be nice, and within a few minutes, he was snoring softly.

According to AnoNino, no one was tracking our personal mobile phones or computers at the moment, though that was small comfort. As we had learned, there are other ways to stalk people. After making sure the deadbolt was set on the front door, and that the back door was locked, I retrieved my phone from the suitcase I had stuffed into the armoire in the second bedroom, the one Freddy's boys used, and went into Isabelle's office to make some calls. In Los Angeles, it was nine o'clock Sunday morning. I turned the phone back on and called my mom, just to reassure her that all was well. I also called my daughter and asked her to do the same service for me, that is, to reassure me that everything in her world was under control. Roddy Combes had called a couple of times, checking on our well-being. I called him to reassure him that we were still above the sod and to thank him again for taking care of us. He was still in Munich, hoping to sleep off a three-day *Fasching* drunk before he had to get onto a train to cover the Great Spitalfields Pancake Race in London on Tuesday. We made the usual promises to get together soon and said good-bye.

Last, I called Uncle Max, told him where I was, made sure all was well in his realm, and asked him not to send out any more press releases until he'd cleared them with me first. When he protested, I explained, in brief, what had been happening since we spoke last. He was horrified, but also excited that there might be material in our ordeal for a film project. Uncle Max, who loves me dearly, was always looking out for my interests. For a few minutes, we discussed strategies for the meeting in the morning. He reminded me that he needed to see any contract or memo of understanding before Guido and I signed anything.

I booted Isabelle's computer on the desk in front of me. First,

I snooped through the Internet search history and lucked upon several searches from early January, when the boys were in the apartment goofing around, as Philippe said. I found the four books he told us they had posted on auction sites, copied the images and printed them. The books had been posted, taken down, reposted and taken down again. They were currently listed as not for sale, but the bidding history was still up on one site, as was the seller's contact information. I set up an anonymous email address and used it to send an inquiry to the contact: "At what price could the books be made available to an interested buyer?"

In Isabelle's computer files, I found a database for the library holdings. The convent's collection was formally catalogued, but the Russian books were not. Instead, there was a simple list of titles, in Cyrillic, a shelf location, and nothing more. I found a translation site that converted Cyrillic letters to their Latinate equivalent, printed it, took the basement keys out of the desk, and headed down the back stairs.

I've seen too many horror movies where the stupid innocent heads down into a dark basement, alone, to find the boogeyman. And, of course, the boogeyman finds her first. As a precaution, on my way through the kitchen I grabbed a wicked-looking boning knife, thinking that if I ran into Johann Bord down there, he'd take one look at the knife and run like hell to save himself. Or, if, by some weird circumstance, Qosja or anyone else popped up, I'd rely on instinct again to simply do what needed to be done while screaming like bloody hell. In a deep, dark basement where no one could hear me.

The stairs were clear and no one lurked in the library. But just in case someone came to my party late, after I closed the pocket door I pushed a heavy table in front of it to slow an intruder. Feeling a bit foolish, and vowing never again to watch a movie where basements figured in the mayhem, I tucked the knife next to the pile of books Val Barkoff left on a table, and pulled out my list. With a pencil, I began checking books against the list. Some of the volumes had plain, homely leather bindings, while other leather covers were ornately embossed and brightly colored. The true treasures were encased in copper, or maybe silver, and decorated with intricate cloisonné designs or gemstone inlay. They ranged in size from massive tomes with large lettering that I thought were probably lectionaries to be read aloud during church services, to quite small, personal books like the little volume of Psalms upstairs, a book that would easily slip into a pocket or under a thief's waistband. What all of them had in common was age.

There were two hundred and fourteen Russian books on the list, but only two hundred and three were in the room, plus the book upstairs. I underlined the titles of the ten missing volumes, and using one of the computers in the room, searched for any mention of them online.

A book of Gospels that had been in the private collection of Sofia Alekseyevna, who, according to an auction catalogue, had served as regent for her younger brothers, tsars Peter I and Ivan V, was sold through the London branch of a Moscow auction house for an enormous amount of money a little over a year ago. A diary of private prayer was sold by the same auction firm last spring. I couldn't find the other eight. But what I did learn was that the two volumes that had been sold had not been saved, or looted, from the Vladimirsky Cathedral of St. Petersburg during the Russian Revolution, but had once been in the private collection of a Russian aristocrat who fled St. Petersberg in 1917.

I looked at my watch. Guido's plane should be on the ground already. I turned off the computer, tucked the list into my pocket, moved the table back where it belonged, turned out the lights, locked the door, and went back upstairs.

"There you are," Jean-Paul said when I walked into the kitchen. He had the cork out of a bottle of wine and had pulled three glasses out of a cupboard. "Wondered where you'd wandered off to."

"I was snooping in the library." I tipped the glass he gave me against his and took a sip. Rarely had I tasted a wine as large, and pure, and as delicious. "What am I drinking?"

He turned the bottle so I could see the label. The date was the only part that meant anything to me; it was ten years old. Putting the bottle back on the counter, he said, "Isabelle knew wine."

"I only know what I like," I said. "This, I like."

"I thought you would. It's a Bordeaux, good vintage year, from a very small family winery," he said.

"Expensive?"

"*Bien sûr.*" Of course it was.

"I've been wondering about something." I pulled the Russian list out of my pocket and smoothed it open on the kitchen counter. "The convent property cost an enormous amount of money to acquire and restore, right?"

"Yes, of course. Both cash and bank financing."

"May I ask how you came up with your share of cash?"

He shrugged, scratched at his itchy scars as he thought. "Marian's father left her quite a nice inheritance, as did mine. We had been looking for a good place to invest it, something that was significant and would have long-range earnings potential. For those reasons, this property was interesting to us."

"How much did it cost to buy the property and complete the restoration?"

The figure he gave me was both staggering and somewhere in the neighborhood of what I expected.

"How much of that had to be cash?"

Another soul-jarring number.

"I've seen how my Uncle Gérard works," I said. "He probably came in with cash that he borrowed from a couple of silent investors. As you said, he also brought building expertise, and let's just call it 'involuntarily shared materials and crews from a different project,' right?"

He laughed softly. "Don't forget charm. He always brings charm."

"Isabelle was a civil servant. A high-level civil servant, I grant you, but that still wouldn't make her wealthy. She had income from the tontine, as did my father. For my parents, the royalty payments that fed the tontine were a boon, but they were rarely more than supplemental income to Dad's public university salary. If my ballpark guess is correct, if Isabelle squirreled away all her royalty payments for a couple of decades, I can see how she could accumulate sufficient cash to buy in as a one-third partner for the purchase of the property. But, it would have stripped her resources before she contributed to the restoration."

"It was a stretch for all of us. I had to borrow from both Karine and my mother. When we were finally able to lease the apartments and generate a regular income stream, it took a while to pay them back. For maybe five years we ate a lot of soup."

"You make wonderful soup."

"Thank you for that. Now, tell me what is stirring inside that lovely head."

"Did Isabelle move into this apartment right away?"

"No. Originally, she rented the apartment downstairs, where Griffith is now. A smaller unit."

"At some point, though, she bought this one," I said. "How did that come about?"

"It was during the second part of making dust," he said. "After the initial work of finishing the apartments was complete, we ran out of money, so we left some of the basement areas for later. All that time, we were negotiating with the Louvre and being sued by the Vatican. In the meantime, the library sat very much as it was discovered. The museum came up with money to at least protect the resource until everything was settled. Walls had to be opened for the new ducting. Isabelle and I agreed that it would be a good time to go ahead with the work to finish the basement, but it would be costly, and I would be out of the country most of that time because I sat on a panel, as I told you, that investigated Kosovar War crimes."

"That's where you ran into Sabri Qosja."

"Unfortunately, yes," he said. "I wanted to put off the basement work until I could be on hand, but Isabelle made the ultimate bargain with me: she assured me that she would be fine supervising the contractors alone, and to pay for the work, she offered to buy her apartment. For cash."

"She paid cash?"

"She did." He leaned back against the counter and crossed his arms. "We negotiated a fair price, and she deposited a check for the full amount into the rue Jacob account. Remember, she was also buying the apartment from herself."

"It would make sense that Isabelle had the back stairs and the wine cellar put in, and her secret library door installed at the same time the rest of the work was being done."

"It would."

"You were still eating a lot of soup?"

He chuckled. "Yes. And taking on extra work, like the war panel."

"While she was stocking a wine cellar and paying cash for an apartment."

"So it appears."

"Where did she get all that money?"

"Where?" He shrugged. "I didn't ask. If I thought about it at all, I'm sure I assumed it was income from the tontine."

"Trust me, the tontine was never that flush," I said, leaning beside him. "You told me that Gérard had pilfered fixtures from the original building. And some books."

"Aha. I see where you're going. Like brother, like sister?"

I handed him my list. "The books with check marks are down-stairs on the shelves or stacked on a table. One more is up here in Isabelle's desk."

"And those without check marks are not?"

"Exactly. I found that two of them were sold at auction last year, after Isabelle died. But there are eight more that I can't account for, or anything that may have disappeared before anyone got around to recording titles. If I had better information about the Russian books, information I would find on a standard library catalogue listing, I might be able to track them down. But I have next to nothing."

"Is this number you wrote in the margin next to the two that sold, the amount they sold for?"

"It is," I said. "When did Freddy learn that he was not inherit-ing a share of rue Jacob?"

He put his finger next to the first of the two books sold. "About here. Roughly the same time Gérard would not let him encumber your grandmother's Paris townhouse."

"We all know that Freddy's wife destroyed him financially. But somehow, he was able to come up with funds to get his building project in Normandy underway last summer."

"Did he and his mother both pick the pocket of the library?"

"I have a lot of questions for the *notaire*," I said. "When do we talk to him?"

"Tomorrow afternoon."

"Perfect," I said. "Because I'm wondering whose pocket was picked. I understand the Vatican staking a claim to texts that belonged to a once-sanctified church property. And the French state museum claiming documents that are historic state documents. But ownership of books from a private collection that may have been in the basement of a legally acquired house for about a century is, it seems to me, a very different matter."

"You think the book sales were legitimate?" he asked, looking at me over the top of his glass before he took another sip.

"Not entirely. No more than it was legitimate for Gérard to sell off fixtures to the property without bothering to speak with his partners, you and Isabelle. If what I'm thinking is correct, then Isabelle stole from you to buy this apartment, and to stock the wine cellar. So, drink up. Enjoy."

He laughed as he took me in his arms. Both of them.

The gate buzzer interrupted a very pleasant moment.

"Guido is here," I said, and went to let him in.

Poor Guido had deep, dark circles under his eyes. After eating something in Laos that he knew he should have stayed away from, he was thinner than ever.

"Rough flight?" I asked, taking his bag from him and leading him up the stairs.

"Is there any other kind? And damn, it's freaking cold here."

"No colder than Ukraine. Hope you packed long johns."

"I never had a chance to unpack them." He was out of breath climbing the single flight of stairs. "My cousin Luigi told me to tell you that when you're ready to dump Jean-Paul, you should call him first."

"That isn't going to happen, but thank Luigi for me. Poor guy didn't know what he was getting into when he picked us up in Ravenna."

"He still doesn't know, but he had a great time. Felt like James Bond or Mad Max out there on the road. Did you really take out a motorcycle with a bottle of Prosecco?"

"Jean-Paul did." I opened the apartment door. "Thanks for helping us, my dear friend."

Jean-Paul greeted him with *les bises* and a glass of wine. "*Ça va*, Guido?"

"I'm okay. You?" He got his first real look at Jean-Paul after his first gulp of that exquisite wine. "Holy shit, man. What happened to you?"

"A drone dropped a bomb on me," Jean-Paul said.

"Uh-huh. Slip on some ice?"

"The other is a better story, but sure."

Guido left his shoes by the front door, found a comfortable chair, and plopped down. "Do I ever have to get up again?"

"If you want dinner you do," I said. "We're going out. But later, when you're ready. Your choice, Chinese or Mexican."

"Is the cook at the Mexican a Mexican?"

"She is," Jean-Paul answered.

"I've had MexMex, TexMex, NewMexMex, and CaliMex. So I need to try FrenchMex to see what it's all about. This wine's good, by the way. Now, tell me what we're doing tomorrow."

We talked about the meeting with the French television people in the morning. The big question for Guido was, would he be interested in working in Paris? For one project, for several years? For the rest of his career? We knew that anything more than a brief absence from American television could be risky if he ever wanted to nose himself back into his old slot. Staying out of sight by working abroad could either be a disaster, or a huge career boost if our work received some recognition. The entire proposition was, like many things in life, akin to standing on the edge of a precipice not knowing whether, when we took the leap, we'd soar or plummet. In our twenties, and maybe into our thirties, we could risk landing on our faces once or twice. But in our forties, we don't bounce very well anymore. Not in the world of television. So, I asked him, "Are you ready to make a commitment to work here?"

He said, "Can I answer that tomorrow when we see what's on offer? If anything. And you?"

"Same answer."

"Max said to remind you that he's ready to fly in if they hand us anything to sign."

And there we left it.

Last fall, when we returned to Los Angeles after filming the farm and harvest seasons at Grand-mère's Normandy estate, we had put together a short video as a pitch for our producer to show her bosses at network, to keep them interested in the project. I thought it was very good, even though it failed to beguile our producer's immediate superior. During the short time between his return from Laos and taking off again for Paris, Guido had tweaked the video, made it a little longer and more tailored for a French audience. The three of us huddled around his laptop and watched it through twice. When the last image faded to black the second time, I refilled his glass and raised mine to him.

"It's beautiful," I said. "Know what would make it better?"

"I'm holding my breath."

"Some footage of Grand-mère's farm now, in the dead of winter, when everything is quiet."

"Did the airlines lose the camera equipment you were lugging?"

"No. It's here. You can rent anything else you need."

"Okay. Yeah. You coming with me?"

"I have some things to take care of first. If you want to go in the next day or two and you need a cable puller and a sound man, my nephews, Robert and Philippe, are there, looking for something interesting to fill their time."

Later, at dinner, we agreed that French Mexican food had lost something on its way across the Atlantic. It was good, but it was about as Mexican as deep dish pizza is Italian. During the meal, we regaled Guido with our adventures of the last few days, and what we thought it had all been about, namely, getting access to some very valuable books. He and I agreed that if the French television people wanted to discuss a follow-up project, we would pitch them a story about the convent, the restoration, the books. By the time the *crème brûlée* pretending to be flan was presented, my two dates were both ready to go home to bed, but I felt wired.

That night, I tossed, I turned, finally managed to fall asleep only to jolt awake out of a nightmare about being chased. Not wanting to wake Jean-Paul, I gave up and went out to the salon in search of something to read as a distraction. I poured a finger of apple brandy into a snifter and curled up with an old copy of *National Geographic*. The feature article was about the Mayans, an appropriate topic, I thought, to accompany the Mexican dinner that seemed to have fused into a hard knot that was lodged behind my breastbone and breathing fire. Maybe brandy wasn't the best treatment, but it felt good going down.

The house was quiet. Once, I heard the little dog upstairs yap at the wind, but only once, and nothing more. Eventually, I fell asleep, curled on the sofa around the magazine. Jean-Paul came and wakened me enough to lead me back to bed, where I slept wrapped in the safety of his arms. I can't say that morning dawned. At some point, the sky outside the bedroom windows became a little less gray, and the denizens of the building, and Isabelle's apartment, began to stir. I could hear water running through pipes in the walls, occasional doors close followed by footsteps on the stairs. Guido made the usual gassy morning toots as he padded down the hall toward the bathroom. Jean-Paul nuzzled my neck with his scratchy chin and asked what time it was. It was time to get up.

The locksmith arrived before we were dressed and set to work. I put out toasted two-day-old brioche and yogurt with fruit and Guido, Jean-Paul and I somehow managed to get showered in bathroom shifts. As I pulled on jeans over my long johns, I asked Jean-Paul, "What would it take to add a second bathroom to the apartment?"

He shrugged as he thought about it. "Permission of the owners, of course. And they're tough, I hear. A city permit. And maybe the sale of a little Russian book to pay for it."

"How many bathrooms are there at your house?"

"Three," he said. "Plus the one in the guest house where Ari lives. It would be easier to add several to the house, if you think you need more, than to put another one in this apartment. Where would you squeeze it in?"

"I hadn't thought that far."

Thierry Dusaud called to let us know that Berg could no longer justify keeping a policeman on watch at our gate. There seemed to be no reason to continue to do so. The two men who actively stalked us were in custody. Little crouchingdragon had been shut down, and ProtX4 had been contacted and warned to back off. No one at InterCentro answered or returned calls over the weekend, but now it was Monday morning and police in England would make a visit to the London office listed on the web site. We were officially free to go about the world again. After Jean-Paul put away his phone and recounted the conversation, he said, "But watch six anyway."

The three of us went over the schedule for the day. Guido and I had the meeting in Issy-les-Moulineaux with our French television counterparts, and Jean-Paul needed to go into his office in La Défense to check on things and write his report about the status quo at the refugee camp he and Eduardo visited in Greece, where this strange odyssey began. The two districts, though not far apart, and both west of the city center, were on different banks of the Seine because of a meander in the river. We made a tentative plan to meet for lunch somewhere in between if the timing could be worked out, after which Jean-Paul and I would go speak with the *notaire*. Guido promised to stop by the locksmith's shop on his way home to pick up the new keys. I showed him where to find my camera bag in case he felt motivated to go down and shoot the library. Or to raid the wine cellar.

~

IT IS always difficult to know how well a meeting has gone until you get a call back later. Sometimes much later. Guido and I gave our pitch, in English for Guido's benefit, explained our division of labor and our history of working together and apart. We showed the six people in the small conference room our Normandy video, and talked about the direction we wanted to take the film as we finished it. Originally, for American television, we had focused on my discovery of Isabelle's family in France and getting acquainted with them; a personal piece. But for French television, we pitched the film as an exploration of the bucolic charms of traditional French country life amid the challenges of the globalization of agriculture, using the seasons on Grand-mère's farm estate as an archetype to represent issues in common with other family-run farms. Our French counterparts loved the existential elements, or said they did. When they asked about possible follow-up projects, we pitched the transformation of the convent of the Little Sisters of St. Jérôme Émilian from orphanage to modern residence, with a valuable library caught in limbo beneath. Changing social mores stirred a good discussion, so did the recalcitrance of the Vatican. But the energy of the meeting truly picked up when a very hip-looking young woman, a vision in tones of black from her hair to her boots, asked if it was true that Freddy's wife had tried—in her words—to rub me out to cover her embezzlement. Grudgingly, I admitted that she had, and I think that sealed the deal. We moved right from there to questions about when we would be available, and what our salary expectations were. Availability we could answer, the salary question we deflected to Uncle Max.

The meeting adjourned to a restaurant overlooking the river for lunch. I called Jean-Paul and asked him to join us, but he told me that Madame Gonsalves was being released from hospital and, if I would excuse him, he wanted to pick her up and make sure she was settled in her apartment before he met me at the office of the *notaire* later that afternoon.

By the time coffee was served at the end of the meal, my head was abuzz from four hours of lively conversation about film and life and the relative reality of the two. Guido had a familiar light in his eyes, and I knew he was hooked. These were people he wanted to work with. And so did I. Uncle Max still had to hammer out the ugly details around money and terms, but I was ready to get started. First, however, Guido and I had to finish the unexploded bomb project, and figure out how to make our exits from California.

Before the meeting, I had turned off my telephone's ringer and set it to vibrate. After several days without a phone, I got used to the quiet. So, every time an incoming message buzzed in my pocket, I startled, and then had to fight back the urge to pull the thing out to check the message. It was disconcerting. After the last good-byes with our hosts, and after we reassured our companions that we could walk across the bridge to the far side of the Seine unescorted to catch a Métro, both Guido and I were antsy to see who had called during the meeting with such insistent regularity.

Max had texted both of us several times. We found a bench in a protected alcove about halfway across the bridge, sat on the cold stone, and called him to report on the meeting. Before our meeting even began, someone from their legal department had contacted Max about setting up a time to talk terms. When he asked us what we wanted, we told him we wanted the usual, lots of freedom and lots of money, and trusted him to get the best possible deal for us.

The next message in my mailbox came from the auction site where I had left a message the night before. Using a dummy email I set up for the purpose, I'd asked whether the Russian books that had been taken off offer could be made available for the right price. The site did not respond, but another potential buyer did. He asked to be contacted if the books were, indeed available, so that he would have the opportunity to counter any offer made. He left an email address. I sent a response: "Dear BBIC (his email moniker), Are you still interested in the Russian psalter? Contact me." And signed it, RJ, for rue Jacob.

When I put my phone away, Guido was on his feet, leaning against the bridge rail, looking at the high-rise buildings on both sides of the river. I rubbed my cold bottom as I walked over to him. I asked, "What do you think?"

"I think it's really ugly here." Guido took my arm and we continued across the bridge toward the train station. "We could be in the middle of downtown Chicago or, except for the river, the Silicon Valley. Did you get a load of the parking lots behind the buildings? Could be L.A., too. Same companies, same architecture, same damn cars."

"Are you disappointed?"

"Yeah, a little. It isn't a deal breaker. Hell, we'll either be out shooting or locked in an editing bay, so what does it matter? But Paris, you know? If we're going to work here, I wish it looked more like Paris."

"Close your eyes," I said. I turned him until he was facing roughly northeast. "Now, open."

It took him a moment before he spotted it. With a silly grin, he said, "There's only one, right?"

"One Eiffel Tower is enough."

"How far away is it?"

"I don't know. A mile and a half? Two? Look on your phone."

He did. "It's walkable. If you're okay getting yourself back to the apartment—"

"Just don't forget to pick up the keys, or we'll all be locked out." With a wave, he went striding off toward the Eiffel Tower.

I had about three hours to kill before meeting the *notaire*, enough time to take care of a few things. At the Issy–Val de Seine station, I found the next scheduled train to Vaucresson, Jean-Paul's neighborhood, and bought a ticket. The experimental trip out to the suburbs took less than twenty not unpleasant minutes, including two stops on the way. In a car, it would take longer than that at rush hour just to exit one of the massive parking lots Guido mentioned. I looked around the Vaucresson station for a few minutes before buying a return ticket. Back in Paris, I got off at Montparnasse and walked to the Louvre.

With no idea how to get to the people I wanted to talk to, I pulled out one of my business cards with the flashy network logo and went to an information kiosk in the plaza outside the Louvre's pyramid-shaped entrance. Dredging up the name of the museum contact that I had seen on the directions posted above the computers in the basement library, I stood in line, and when it was my turn, flashed a sappy American smile, hoping that I looked as clueless as I felt. Handing my card to the uniformed attendant, I said, "I have an appointment to see Madame Celine Pirenne, director of rare books collections, but I have no idea where to go."

The attendant smiled benevolently as she took my card, asked me to wait a moment, and placed a call. After a brief conversation, she hung up and told me to wait right there, and someone would come and get me. Who knew it was that easy?

Standing on the leeward side of the booth, out of the wind, I pulled my scarf over my ears and watched the crowd, huddled in coats, waiting in the long queue to go inside, or taking pictures of each other, or themselves, with the iconic structure as backdrop. While I stood there, BBIC responded to my email, saying he would like very much to speak with me. He left a phone number with a forty-four prefix, the country dialing code for England. I still had a burner phone in my coat pocket. I pulled it out and dialed the number.

"InterCentro, London office. Boris Barkov here."

"Mister Barkov, you left a message about your interest in some books that were posted for sale on an auction site."

"And taken off offer, yes. Do you know something about those books?"

"I do." A tall thin man wearing a beautiful coat over wool slacks, hands deep inside his pockets, necktie flapping in the wind, strode with purpose across the plaza, eyes searching the area around the kiosk until he spotted me. I took a step forward and waved at him. "I would like to meet with you. Tomorrow? Your office?"

"Of course. I am most interested. Most. Could we say eleven o'clock?"

"We will be there."

Barkov was asking for my name when I cut off the call. The man with the windblown tie was only three strides away.

"Madame MacGowen?" He extended his hand toward me. "Guillaume Fouquet. Everyone calls me Billy. Come with me."

I fell into step beside him, trying my best to keep up. Looking at me askance, he said, "Madame Pirenne is afraid that she neglected to make a note of your meeting. She is not available to see you this afternoon, but she knows that Marie Volz, the curator of the religious texts collection, has been eager to speak with you."

"Has she?"

"Yes." He smiled an upside-down smile that was full of irony or something else I couldn't read. "We have all been curious. Madame Volz was trying to get up the courage to call you."

"Explain to me why she would need courage to call me?"

"I'll let her explain."

I had to show identification to the armed guard at the side entrance Billy led me to, and sign in as a guest of Marie Volz escorted by Billy Fouquet, send my bag through a scanner, and stand still long enough to have a snapshot taken for my visitor badge. Once credentialed, I walked—quick-marched—with Billy along back passageways, down several floors in a freight elevator, and finally out into a vast room lined with glass-fronted cases filled with books that could be cousins to the much smaller collection under my inherited apartment building. Billy made the introduction to Marie Volz, curator of rare religious texts.

She was a Central Casting rare-books curator. Sixtyish, thin, graying hair pulled back into a bun at the back of her neck, a below-the-knee woolen A-line skirt and matching gray twinset. Sturdy black shoes. And a delightful twinkle in her eye.

"My superior asked me to sit in for her," she said after introductions. "She does apologize for failing to make note of your meeting."

"Madame Volz," I said, "I have no appointment. I was eager to speak with someone here who might know about the library in the basement at number seven, rue Jacob."

"Have a seat, please," she said, ushering me into her frigid little office. "Tea?"

"If it's convenient, yes, please."

"You may not be used to our cold weather." She signaled to Billy, who was lurking nearby, before she came all the way into the room to sit behind her desk. She shoved a stack of files aside, opening a canyon she could look through to speak to me. "I am delighted to meet you, at last, Madame. Tell me, what are your concerns about the Little Sisters of Saint Jérôme Émilian collection?"

"Actually, I'm more interested in the books from Vladimirsky Cathedral in St. Petersburg."

"Ah, the Russians. I can't tell you very much about them."

"I'm curious to know how it was determined that they came from the Vladimirsky?"

Her eyebrows rose, surprised, I thought, by the question. "The information came from your mother."

"Before we go further: You seem to be rather familiar with who I am, and that surprises me."

"Does it?" She smiled. "Your mother was very proud of you. She spoke of you often."

I was happy that Billy brought the tea at that moment, because I did not know how to hide how very creepy that made me feel. Isabelle Martin was a stranger to me. She was not part of my life. And yet, I was very much a part of hers. I did not know how to handle the growing shadow of her that hung over my life.

Billy handed us tea in heavy china mugs. It was hot, and lovely. I clutched the mug with both of my red, cold hands.

"Madame MacGowen was asking about the Russians in her basement," Madame Volz said, peering at Billy over the top of her steaming mug.

"You were saying that Isabelle told you about the origins of the Russians," I said.

"That was before you arrived, Billy," Madame Volz said. "But we have talked about it. Yes, Madame, your mother told us that she had a letter; I don't remember who she said it was from—this was maybe fifteen or more years ago—demanding that the Russian texts be handed over to the Metropolitan of the Eastern Orthodox Church, or the Patriarch of Moscow, or maybe someone else. I was never convinced, however, that there was such a letter or that all of the books were part of a church library."

"Why?"

"Many of them were, let us just say, too personal. A book of hours—" She extended a hand toward me. "You know what that is? A book of prayers, a diary of sorts, the sort of thing a person might read at certain times during the day, over the seasons." When I nodded, she continued. "There is an exquisite book of hours, and several psalters, some meditations on sermons, and so on. There

is a lectionary of the sort a priest might read from to his congrega-
tion, or, perhaps, a father or master of a household might read to
his dependents. Several of those books belong in a museum, and
not on the shelf of a damp church somewhere, so I was happy they
were in a controlled environment."

"Did you ever try to acquire the Russians for the museum?"

"I let Isabelle know we would be happy to have them, if they
came without complications. Our resources were already stretched
by the war between us, the Vatican, and the local diocese. When
she told us that the Eastern Orthodox Church wanted those books,
we abandoned all interest in acquiring them; a second legal-war
front would be too much. In the interest of scholarship, we offered
to catalogue them, but Isabelle declined."

"I would think she would be happy to have that done for her."

She started to say something, but hesitated. It was Billy who
answered. "We think she didn't want to make it easy to trace books
that disappeared."

"You're saying books did disappear?" I asked.

"Now and then, yes."

"Where do you think they went?"

The two of them exchanged a glance before Billy said, "To the
highest bidder."

"Did you ever challenge her?"

"We had no right to do so," Volz said. "What you need to
remember is, your mother and the property's co-owner, a very
influential man, had already donated two collections to us. We
were delighted they had, but our lawyers reminded us that they
were a gift. The owners of rue Jacob could as easily have sold them
on the open market or tossed them into a trash bin, or disposed
of them any way they chose, despite what the Vatican believes."

"Did you ever mention the disappearing Russians to this very
influential man you referred to?"

"No. I'm sure that Jean-Paul Bernard had other things on his
mind. He was sitting on an international war tribunal during much
of the negotiation period." She leaned forward and spoke in a soft,
conspiratorial voice. "Do you know who he is?"

"Jean-Paul Bernard? I've heard the name, yes."

"I have met him, of course. A very charming man, but a very busy man. He made it clear early on that he would handle issues with the Pope, and Madame Martin would handle the curators of the Louvre. He is not the sort of man one interrupts to chat about unsupported concerns over something that was not our business. Besides, he may have agreed with her completely."

"But you doubt that he did."

A little shrug told me she did doubt.

I asked, "Is it possible for scholars who use the library to walk out with a volume?"

"Anything is possible," she said. "But I am certain that has never happened. No one is ever in the reading room alone. Scholars are always proctored by one of very few approved people when they are working with the texts. Every entry into the library is electronically registered, so we know who comes and goes. And the door is alarmed should someone try to break in. If anything did go missing, we would know exactly who to ask about it."

"Unless someone entered through the back door."

"There is no back door."

"I'll be happy to show it to you. Just give me a call when you're available."

"I had no idea. Billy, did you?"

He shook his head. "I would have seen another door."

"A secret panel," I said, "to a buried treasure."

"Marie," he said, "do we need to do an inventory?"

They both looked at me, but I held up my hands. "I only learned about the library a few days ago. I can't help you."

Her polite smile told me she agreed that I knew nothing. She asked, "Have I answered your concerns?"

"In part, yes. Thank you. One more question: Do you know, or have you heard of a man named Boris Barkov?"

"I have not," she said. "But Billy is nodding, so he may have a different answer."

"A man with that name contacted us several times," he said. "He wanted to know about getting permission to use the library. I

sent him to the site on our web page where application for access is
explained. Sometime later, he called again. The application on the
web asks scholars to list the texts they wish to study by catalogue
number. But, he was interested in the Russians, and they are not
catalogued. When I told him that those books are not part of the
museum's holdings and I had no authority to grant him access, he
was not happy."

"How not happy?" I asked.

"He got quite huffy. Wanted to go over my head, so I gave him
the director's number, and Celine transferred the call right back to
me. He said something that sounded very spitty, probably in Russian, and slammed down the phone."

"When was that?"

He shrugged and held up his hands. "A month ago? Six weeks?"

"But you remember him?"

"I was curious, so I Googled him. I didn't learn very much.
Except that he is Russian and he gives talks on old texts."

"That's all I found out, too." I looked at my watch. "Thank
you for your time. Please excuse me, but I need to run. I have an
appointment."

I did not mean that I literally had to run, but Billy walked so
fast that's what it felt like. I came out of the dim, gray back halls of
the Louvre into the dim gray of the Paris afternoon. The *notaire*'s
office was five blocks away, above a very expensive children's clothing shop, and I needed to maintain the pace Billy had set to get
there on time. Jean-Paul was already chatting with the *notaire*, Levi
Gosselin, when I arrived. I could hear their laughter as soon as I
opened the door from the outside hall. A male clerk took my coat
and ushered me into Gosselin's private office. The two men stood
when I walked in. Jean-Paul came to me, and under the pretext of
sharing *les bises*, he asked, "All go well?"

"Good meeting," I whispered as my lips touched his ear. He
seemed very happy to hear that.

Introductions were taken care of, demitasses of coffee offered
and accepted. Jean-Paul and I were taken into a small conference
room where stacks of legal files were laid out, ready to be explained,

and it was time to settle in for the big talk. There was a fresh
pad of paper and several pens on the table in front of the seat I
was shown to. Jean-Paul was on my left, Monsieur Gosselin on
my right.

"Madame MacGowen," Gosselin said, looking at me over the
top of his reading glasses. "Ordinarily I would be reluctant to take
on a client, such as you, who is being advised by a fully competent
colleague. However, after speaking with your original *notaire*, it
became clear to the two of us that issues concerning language had
created some unfortunate confusions, and that you would be better served by someone with greater fluency with English. So, I am
delighted to be of service to you."

"Thank you," I said.

"And now, we start from the beginning." He opened a file folder
and took a breath. Flashing an impish grin, he said, "I promise
you that most of this conversation will be very dull no matter
what language we use, full of legal and financial terms. However,
in the end, I know that you will have found our discussion to be
most interesting. If, at any time, I have failed to explain something
adequately, please tell me so. When you walk out of here this afternoon, my greatest hope is that you will have a clear understanding
of the terms of your late mother's will, as well as the terms of the
partnership between you and Monsieur Bernard in the property
at number seven, rue Jacob."

He was correct: the passage through the legal papers was excru-
ciatingly boring at times, but at others I found myself fascinated.
As if I needed confirmation, Isabelle was an odd cookie. She could
also be petty and vindictive, and Freddy seemed to be her favorite
target. He had every right to be angry about the uneven distri-
bution of her assets, but I wished he, and his wife, had focused
their anger on the source, Isabelle, and not on me, her designated
primary heir. Some of the arcane French property laws, however,
protected his inheritance rights to several very valuable assets.

I was surprised that my grandmother's will was among the
files that Gosselin explained to me. In France, real estate follows
blood. When Grand-mère married my grandfather, she received

the right to live on and derive her support from the Normandy estate for the rest of her life, if she never remarried. Because she was not of her husband's blood, actual ownership of the property would pass to their children when she died. When Isabelle died before Grand-mère, her claim to half the estate passed equally to me and Freddy. Gérard, of course, would inherit the other half. If my daughter gave formal permission, I could assign my share to either my uncle or my brother. Or, the three immediate heirs could decide together to sell. The message I took from that was, things could get very messy if anyone disagreed with the other heirs. I dog-eared the page of notes I took about the Normandy estate, and turned to a clean sheet.

Grand-mère, the only surviving child of her parents, had inherited from her father the Paris townhouse in the Marais he had purchased before the war. Grand-mère, then, owned the house outright, and could do whatever she wanted with it during her lifetime. But, if she didn't dispose of it before she died, then it came half to me and Freddy, and half to Uncle Gérard. I dog-eared that page, too.

Rue Jacob was complex. The most interesting part of the contract of sale between the Vatican; the diocese; and Isabelle, Jean-Paul, and Gérard, was the language that gave the purchaser full ownership of the land, its improvements, furnishings, fixtures, and residual movable property.

"Would movable property include rare books found in the basement of the property?" I asked.

"It should, yes," he said.

"Let's say the seller forgot about the books and left them behind when he sold. After he signed the sale contract, could he say, Oops, and reclaim them?"

"In my opinion, he could not."

"Could he make a claim if his grandparents left the books and he didn't know they were there until later?"

"If the grandparents acquired the books legally, then no. If the grandparents stole them, then the heirs of the legal owner could probably make a case."

"If the books had been in the basement for a hundred years, and no living person knew how they got there, who would own them?"

"I suspect that you're referring to a specific situation. Would you care to explain it to me?"

We did. Jean-Paul gave Gosselin a wonderfully succinct summary of how there came to be a library in the basement at number seven, rue Jacob. Gosselin folded his hands over the open file on the table in front of him, and listened. Twice, he raised a finger to signal that he had a question, and then continued to listen until Jean-Paul finished. I added the nuggets of information I had learned from Marie Volz and Billy Fouquet, and then it was his turn.

"Madame, Monsieur, if you found an old table, even a very fine antique table, in the basement, or a basket of scanties left behind by the nuns, would there be questions of ownership once the sale was final?"

Jean-Paul turned to me for my answer. "No. The table I might dust off and use, or sell. The scanties I would probably laugh over before throwing out."

"But you would not question your right to whatever you chose to do with them, yes?"

"Yes."

"Bernard, you agree?"

He nodded.

"I believe that the curator at the Louvre was correct. If you had chosen to sell the books when you first found them, or even to throw them out, you would have been within your rights. Instead, you donated them. Or, at least, most of them. And because no good deed goes unpunished, complications ensued. But that does not change your rights of ownership. Does that answer your question?"

"It does," I said. "So it was legal for Isabelle to sell any of the books that had not been donated, *if* her co-owner agreed, correct?"

"Yes. If anyone has recourse against her, it is Jean-Paul, though it is a bit late to pursue anything now, I believe."

I put my hand over Jean-Paul's and looked him in the eye. "I think it's time for us to tell the Vatican to go to hell, and for us to tell the Louvre to come and get their books. What do you think?"

"I agree. I wanted to do that a long time ago, but Isabelle had other ideas."

Gosselin cleared his throat. "Other questions?"

"Not at the moment," I said. "But may I call you if I do?"

"Bien sûr," he said.

We collected our coats and walked back out into the gathering dusk, though in the shadows of the buildings around us, it was difficult to know whether the sun was already gone from the sky or not. Arm in arm, we walked toward the Seine with no particular destination in mind.

"Who calls the Louvre?" he said. "You or me?"

"You do. Marie Volz is so thoroughly intimidated by your exalted status that when you tell her to come and get the books, she just might back the truck in herself."

"Exalted status?" He laughed. "I know she didn't say that."

"No. She said, 'very influential' in reverential tones."

"All right, I'll speak with her. And you call the Vatican."

"After what I've heard today, I am persuaded that the Holy Father has no standing. I only hope the Louvre doesn't put out another press release to alert him."

"Are you in a hurry to get the collection out of the house for some reason?"

"I am. For the moment, let's just look beyond the probability that someone damn near killed us trying to get at the books, and think about something else. To begin, yes, the meeting went well. Guido and I both like these people very much. That may change after we've worked them for a while, but I don't think so. They want the Normandy project, and asked us what was next. Their legal department is already talking to Uncle Max about terms."

"What does Guido think?"

"He's working things through. When I last saw him, he was walking toward the Eiffel Tower with a goofy look on his face, so I think he's aboard. The next big issues are, housing and work space. In Paris."

"I'm guessing you've given the issues some thought."

"You are free to veto any of this, but, if the convent collection goes home to the mother ship, the Louvre, where it belongs, the space the library takes up now would make an excellent work-room for me and Guido. It's climate-controlled, and secure. Next, I cannot figure out where to put a second bathroom in Isabelle's apartment, so the only alternative is for us, the you-and-me us, to move our feast to your house in Vaucresson."

"Let me guess: and Guido moves into the rue Jacob apartment."

"What do you think?"

"I like that better than having him as a permanent house guest. Anything more?"

"Just one thing. We have an appointment to speak with Boris Barkov tomorrow at eleven. In London."

9

THE LONDON OFFICE of InterCentro was a single cavernous room off the lobby of a two-star hotel in Chelsea, in a space that had once been a barbershop. The glass front was draped in heavy brocade that I can only describe as faded imperial red. It was 10:30 when Jean-Paul opened the door and preceded me in.

Two big men, body builders from the look of them, stopped us from getting more than a few feet inside. Except that one was black and one was Asian, they could have been twins in their matching black polo shirts with PX4 embroidered on identical places on their similarly exaggerated pecs. We gave them our business cards and didn't argue when they asked us to hang our coats on a rack. Very politely, they asked me to open my bag so they could peek inside, and for Jean-Paul to open his suitcoat and raise his sweater so they could see that he wasn't hiding a gat under his waistband. They smiled during the entire process. When they were finished, the black man turned and walked across what looked like half an acre of red carpet to the back of the room and handed our cards to a man who was seated behind a desk in the far corner. After they exchanged a few words, we were signaled to come.

The man behind the desk rose and walked to meet us. He was

as Philippe described him, short and round. Wearing a beautifully tailored Harris tweed suit, he presented a fair imitation of a
traditional Englishman, until he spoke. Looking from our cards to
us, he said, "Miss MacGowen, Mr. Bernard, how can I help you?"

"We're a little early," I said. "We have an appointment at
eleven."

"Ah." Flicking the edges of the cards with his pinkie, he studied
us for a moment, clearly unsure about trusting us. "We share an
interest in fine books?"

"I think we share an interest in some very particular books,
Mister Barkov."

His eyebrows rose when I said his name. "Please, have a seat,
and let's talk about these books."

I checked on the guards at the door as we followed Barkov to
an arrangement of chairs and a low table opposite the desk; one
guard watched us, the other the door.

The room was sparsely yet comfortably furnished to accommodate one man and two guards. I got the impression that Barkov
did not have many visitors. We were offered tea from an electric
kettle, served Russian-style in tall glasses.

"Now, then," he said when we had settled in. "You first. What
brings you?"

I opened my bag and took out the little book of Psalms, freeing
it from its protective wrapper: a square cut from an old white cotton T-shirt I found in Philippe and Robert's room. When Barkov
saw the book displayed across my palms, beads of sweat appeared
on his upper lip.

"One moment," he said, rising. He opened a cupboard at the
back and took a pair of white cotton gloves out of a box. He pulled
on the gloves before he asked to examine the book. Reverentially,
he caressed the cover, turned it over, examined the back and the
spine. And then, after a hesitation, he lifted the cover and carefully turned the pages, sometimes taking longer to examine a page
before turning to the next. When he reached the end, he closed the
book and looked up at us. "I can't believe I have this in my hands.
I can't believe it exists."

"What do you know about it?" Jean-Paul asked.

He opened the cover again and turned to the elaborately illustrated title page, and held it for us to see. "We know that *Tsarevna* Sofia Alekseyevna commissioned a Polish calligrapher named Petrus to produce a set of books for her personal use. She was unusually well educated for a woman of her time and her place: seventeenth-century Russia. But, then, she was altogether a remarkable woman."

"How can you be sure that this book was hers?" Jean-Paul asked.

"There is an inscription to her worked into the design of this capital. Do you see?" His fingers hovered over the outlines of a charming rabbit and lamb intertwined with ivy that artfully formed a series of Cyrillic letters. "There is no mistaking that this is the work of Petrus, or the name of the original owner. I had the privilege of seeing two of the other books from the *tsarevna's* collection. One was on exhibit at the Beinecke Library at Yale University. And the other was on offer at a Paris auction house about a year ago. A Book of Gospels. It fetched an amazing price, but for a book so rare and so beautiful, I wasn't surprised."

"Did you bid on the book?" I asked.

He smiled sadly as he shook his head. "I am not a collector, Miss MacGowen."

"Your message to me suggested otherwise," I said.

"Forgive me for misleading you. But it did have the desired effect: You're here. And I now know for a fact that this beautiful volume exists." He closed the book, wrapped it back into the scrap of fabric, and handed it to me. "You see, I found it highly unlikely that an item of this caliber, of this significance, would be listed on Internet sites along with used cars and vintage clothing. I was curious. I suspected that the seller was perpetrating a fraud."

"We could play cat-and-mouse for a bit longer about how you happened to notice this treasure among the old car listings," I said. "But let's get to the purpose for our visit, Mr. Barkov. We know that your son, Val, had something to do with posting four very valuable books for sale, even though he and his friends did not have the books in their possession and did not have permission to sell them. Someone has gone to great lengths to keep me and Mister Bernard away from our property in Paris, where the books are under lock and key. We have very good reason to believe that was done to give the person, or persons, who posted the books an opportunity to break in and steal them in order to deliver them to a buyer. I need you to tell us what role you had in that plan."

Barkov turned bright red and half rose from his chair. "I know of no such plan. I am not a thief."

"What, exactly, are you?" Jean-Paul asked quietly, deflating the rising tone of the meeting.

Barkov needed a moment to settle back down. He wiped a hand over his brow, sweeping back some wispy strands of hair that had dislodged from the arrangement across his nearly bald pate by his sudden movement. After a breath or two, he said, "I am an advisor to collectors. The collection of rare books is quite new in Russia. Very few tsarist-era volumes survived the Soviet purges. With very little material to work with, there are also very few of us who are considered experts on Russian rarities. When I find a book, or other object, I alert clients who might be interested. If they wish to acquire the object, I broker the sale for a commission."

Jean-Claude cocked his head a few degrees as questions formed. "Might these be clients who, for whatever reason, preferred not to bid themselves in order to keep the purchase anonymous?"

"On occasion, yes. There are very good and legitimate reasons to do so. At other times, clients bring me objects that they wish to divest, and for similar reasons don't want it known that they are selling."

"Private sales," Jean-Paul said.

"Sometimes, yes."

"Of objects without certified provenance or permission of previous owner?"

"I do not deal in stolen objects, if that's what you are asking."

I held up the little psalter. "This book was not offered with permission from the owner."

"Nor did I attempt to buy it," he said. He got as far as saying, "My son..." before he could get no further.

"Your son and my nephew, Philippe, attend the same school," I said. "Or did until recently. Your son first saw this book during a visit to my apartment in Paris. What do you know about that?"

He needed a few moments to compose his answer. "Yes, my son visited Paris with his friend Philippe over the New Year. While he was there, he sent me photos of several books and asked me if I knew what they were and how much they might be worth. After he assured me that he and his friends were merely curious, I gave him an answer. I was hopeful that Val, at last, had found something that interested him. But—"

We waited for him to finish the sentence. Instead, he looked from me to Jean-Paul and asked, "Do you have children?"

"We both do, yes," I said. "Around the same age as Val."

"We all try to do the best we can for them, but sometimes they don't agree about what is, in fact, the best thing." Again, he paused before continuing. "My son is susceptible in some ways to the influence of his friends. And sometimes he gets carried away with someone else's idea and doesn't know when to stop. Twice now, my wife and I have moved him to new schools to get him away from situations created by more assertive friends."

"I was told that you took him out of school around the time he asked you about the books."

"Not long after, yes."

I made sure the bodyguards were still at the far end of the room before I said, "I noticed the logo on your guards' shirts. It's ProtX4, isn't it?"

He hesitated too long before agreeing that it was.

"Two men hired through ProtX4 by your company's London office—that is, I believe, you alone—aggressively stalked Mr. Bernard and me until they were arrested. You can't tell us you didn't know about it."

When he sat stone-faced and mute, Jean-Paul said, "Sir?"

"This is very difficult for me. I assure you that, if you were harassed in some way, I had no hand in it. I don't know what it is you want from me."

"Some truth," I said. "Did you hire men to come after us?"

"No," he said sadly.

"But you know something about it."

"Kids and their pranks." He shook his head. "What can we do? Last week an invoice came from ProtX4 for additional services I did not order. When I inquired, they gave me a telephone number for the contact listed on the order form. I called the number and Val answered. I challenged him. He told me that he was being bullied at school. Knowing the way people react when I show up with Marc and Troy, he hoped to stop the bullying by having some muscle shadow him."

"Surely he needed your help to hire the men," I said.

He shook his head. "It is all done online. When I need additional services, I fill out a form on their web page telling them what I want, they deliver the personnel and bill my account. We never speak."

"Did you believe Val?" I asked.

"I knew he was lying." He waved a hand toward the guards. "I need protection because I frequently courier items that have great value. Their presence deters anyone from trying to relieve me of those items. When I learned that Val had hired bodyguards, I immediately thought of those books he asked about and went online to search for them."

"You did more than that," I said. "You went to Paris and inquired about the books in the library at number seven, rue Jacob. How did you know to look there?"

"Because I know my business," he said. "Think of me as a detective in a very narrow corner of the book market. When a very beautiful volume from the collection of Sofia Alekseyevna showed up on the market last year, coming out of Paris, I went to work, looking for its mates."

He tapped the psalter in my hands. "Let me give you a little history. I told you that Sofia Alekseyevna ordered a set of books. Religious books, because anything else would be inappropriate.

The collection passed through the Romanov family, generation after generation. The last known owner was a cousin of the last tsar, a Prince Oleg. In 1917, when the tsar and his family were arrested, later to be executed, Oleg filled his personal railroad car with possessions, and fled Russia. Records show that he made it as far as Paris, where he had been educated. In 1918 he fell victim to influenza during the pandemic, and died. And there the record ends.

"There has been speculation and rumor in the book world about what happened to the collection, but there was no solid information. Then, about twenty years ago, one of the *tsarevna*'s books resurfaced mysteriously and was sold at auction, in Paris. The Beinecke acquired it. Then, over the years, three or four others appeared. Always in Paris. Always an anonymous seller, though one who could adequately provide provenance to the auction house.

"And then Val showed me a photo of a book, and I knew right away what it was. He was in Paris, staying at a friend's family apartment. I had the address; Philippe's father had given it to me when he asked if Val could stay over New Year's. So, I did some research and discovered that a library of rare books was housed at that address. And that it included a collection of Russian texts. There was a catalogue, but it excluded the Russian collection. I tried to find out what was there. Were these the lost books of the *tsarevna*? The curator at the Louvre was no help, so I went to the Sorbonne, was shunted from office to office, and also found no help. In all, a dead end."

"Where is Val now?" I asked.

"At home, working with a private tutor under the watchful eye of my wife and a very expensive Harley Street shrink."

Jean-Paul had been listening with quiet intensity. "Hiring a psychiatrist for your son was a smart move, Mister Barkov. It will help establish a history. Finding him an excellent barrister would be another. Because of what he set in motion when he hired thugs from ProtX4, a young woman is dead, an old woman was assaulted, and you can see by looking at the fresh scars on my face that we are not talking about child's play."

Barkov stood and gestured to his guards. "Our conversation is over."

Marc and Troy took two paces toward us and stood, arms crossed over the bulwarks that were their chests, and waited for us to leave. I put the book back into my bag and rose with Jean-Paul. Looming over Barkov, he said, "Interpol has been in touch with the London police. You'll be hearing from them."

We gathered our things and headed for the door. He stopped us before the guards parted to let us pass.

"Miss MacGowen, Mister Bernard." We turned. "What price would make Sofia's psalter available?"

I took Jean-Paul's arm and we walked out the door.

We crossed the street and headed for the nearest Tube station. When we turned, I pulled out my phone, reversed the camera lens, and shot the street behind me, making sure no one followed. Jean-Paul, smiling, nudged me. "Anyone there?"

"I can't see anyone. Maybe the hired help slipped locators into our coats again."

"I hope they did," he said. "It would make them easier to spot."

We ran into the early lunch-hour crowd when we headed underground to catch a train. I felt more comfortable with masses of people around me than I had out in the open. Standing on the platform, waiting, I looked up at Jean-Paul.

"When you said that a young woman was dead," I said, "he didn't ask questions, challenge you, or defend his son. Do you think he already knew?"

"I don't. We can't know for sure, of course. But if he knew there was a murder involved, I can't believe he would have spoken with us at all. I suspect he thought his son was involved in nothing more than a big prank or a bit of larceny and needs some counseling."

"What do you think will happen to the kid?"

"Depends on where he's tried." He took my arm. "Now what?"

I looked at my watch. It was just past noon. "Our train is at two. Shall we check with Roddy Combes and see if the Great Spitalfields Pancake Race is on? Could be fun."

He smiled and bobbed his head, meaning, I thought, Why not?

I texted Roddy, told him we were in London, and got an immediate return answer. "Runners are warming up. Half an hour until first heat. Tube is jammed, forget parking. Chopper best way in. Meet for dinner after? Married yet?"

Staying for dinner would mean either a very late return to Paris, or getting a hotel for the night in London. We asked for a rain check. And answered the last question with, Not yet. France had a forty-day residency requirement to get a marriage license. That left two choices: wait until after I was back in France after finishing the unexploded bomb film in L.A., or marry in California. We had a nice lunch in Mayfair, and caught the two o'clock Eurostar to Paris.

We checked on Madame Gonsalves when we got home. She had hobbled around her kitchen to get a pot of chicken soup simmering on the stove, and seemed happy enough to just sit in her big chair with her sore knee propped on an ottoman to watch her television programs.

Guido had carried every lamp in Isabelle's apartment down into the library to use as spots and filler lights so he could film the room. He was in the process of hauling lights back up the stairs when we came in.

"Yo," he said, handing me the two bedside lamps he had taken from the master bedroom. "I think you have mice."

"In the library? That can't be good."

"No. In the wine cellar. You might want to arm yourself with a broom or something next time you go in there."

"Did you look?" I asked.

"Hell no. I hate mice."

"We'll talk to Madame Gonsalves about an exterminator." I followed him down the stairs for the next load. "Other than the vermin, how do you like the apartment?"

"It's cool here. This is real Paris, you know? I went out for a walk and must have shot frames of a hundred great doorways. I love the doors."

"Do you think you could live here?"

"In Paris? Definitely."

"Yes. But could you live in this apartment?"

"If we sign on to work here, Maggie, I'll have to." He handed me a reel of heavy cable. "While I was out, I picked up some rental listings. We'll have to get paid a hell of a lot more than I think we'll be offered to afford both a work space and another apartment. So, though I know it isn't ideal for you lovebirds, looks like we'll be roomies for the duration."

"Do you think you could manage here alone? With or without mice."

"Where would you go?"

"Jean-Paul's house."

"I hadn't thought of that."

"If we persuade the museum to come and claim their books, we could use this space. And if they don't, Jean-Paul tells me there's still plenty of room in the basement to set up a work room."

"Wow." He looked around the library with new eyes. "Yes. Absolutely, yes. You want to grab that gaffer's tape?"

The tape was on a table near the stack of Russian books that had been left out. As I reached for it, I noticed something, and stopped. "Guido, did you move some of these books? Put them away, maybe?"

"I shifted their angle to get a better shot. I didn't put anything away, though. Don't know where they go."

"I left a knife here."

"Mag, what's up?"

"Was anyone in here with you?"

"No. You're scaring me."

"Let's lock the door and go up. We can finish this later."

"Maggie, for chrissake. What?"

"There should be three more books on the table," I said, nudging him toward the door. "A very particular three books. And I don't think we have mice. Let's go."

I hefted the roll of cable over my shoulder, grabbed the gaffer's tape, and headed for the door with Guido close behind carrying Isabelle's desk lamp and a collapsed tripod. In the passageway outside, he had to set down the tripod to lock the door. That's when I heard his mice. Only, it wasn't mice.

"What the hell?" he said and pushed the new key into the lock on the wine cellar door.

"Don't!" I said as the door flew open, thrusting him against the wall as a streak all in black shot out with the boning knife in his upraised hand. I threw the roll of gaffer's tape at him, but he deflected it with his forearm and came for me. I dropped, dumped the cable, grabbed the tripod, and swung it at the knife in his hand. Guido clipped him from behind with the desk lamp, sending him sprawling flat onto his face. Guido is small, but wiry. And he's a pro with cable. He grabbed an end and started wrapping the thick wire around the guy's legs, hobbling him as he struggled.

"Dammit, kid," I spat, pressing the end of the tripod against his head. "You might as well hold still. It's over. All over."

I still hadn't seen his face, but I had a fair idea who he was from the reek of vomit that followed him out the door. When Guido put his knee between the kid's shoulder blades and pulled back his elbows, the kid lay still and started to whimper. I yelled up the stairs, "Jean-Paul, call the cops."

He appeared at the top, looked down, saw what was happening, and pulled out his phone.

I kicked the knife out of our captive's hand, sending it spinning into the darkness beyond the open wine cellar door. The passageway was small and the black-garbed bulk on the floor took up most of it. I had to step over him to hit the light switch inside. The chandelier over the door still swayed from the rush of air made by the kid's fast exit past, shooting arrows of light into the gloom beyond. Jean-Paul was down the stairs by then. He and Guido rolled our captive over and sat him up.

"Hello, Cho," I said. He hung his head, defeated, chagrined. "Tell me those very valuable books aren't as soaked in wine as you are."

He shook his head.

"How did you get in?" Jean-Paul asked.

"A key."

I started to challenge him, because we had changed the locks the day before. But then I got a look at him in the light. He was dirty, he reeked of wine and vomit. I asked, "How long have you been down here?"

"Since Sunday night."

"You got locked in?"

He nodded. "I don't get it. The key worked before."

"Before the locksmith came," I said. "You must be hungry."

The mention of food made him retch.

Jean-Paul stifled a laugh. "How much did you drink, man?"

"Too much. I thought I'd die locked in down here, so why not?"

"You're not going to die, but you might wish you had. Police are on the way."

I asked a question I was afraid I knew the answer to, but wished I didn't. "Where did you get the keys?"

"A guy I know."

"Philippe?"

"Hey look, don't blame Philippe. None of this was our idea." He let out a breath as if he was deflating.

"And yet," I said, "here you are, caught with the goods. Want to explain how that came about?"

"No, not really."

Jean-Paul said, "It's better if we hear your version now, before you have to tell it to the police. If you help us understand how you got into the mess you're in, we may be able to soften the consequences. Or we can throw you to the wolves and let them feast on you. Your choice."

Cho thought that over, and then launched his defense. "Over New Year's, we were just goofing around."

"And drinking," Jean-Paul said.

He acknowledged that by retching again.

"And?" I said.

"Philippe got fed up with this other friend of ours—"

"Val," I said.

"Yeah. Val has a big mouth. Kept bragging about his father and his father's books, and all his money. Philippe just wanted to shut him up, so he told him that his grandmother had books that were more valuable than anything Val's dad had. We didn't believe

him. So, he brought us down here and showed us this one bunch
of books he said no one knew about except his grandmother, and
she's dead. Then he said that when his dad needed money, he just
took one and sold it, and no one noticed. We didn't believe him,
so we posted some of the books on the Net, and fuck me, man.
It was incredible. All the money people would pay for one stupid
little book."

"And so you decided that you would go ahead and sell them,"
I said.

"No. Not exactly. Philippe took them down off the site. But,
later, he found out that Val put them up again."

"What happened then?"

"They had a big fight, and Philippe kicked us out."

"And?" I prodded.

He shrugged. "And nothing. We just went back to school."

"Something must have happened, because here you are trussed
up like a Christmas goose and some of the books are missing,"
Jean-Paul said. "I figure you have maybe three, four more minutes
before the concierge escorts the police through our front door."

"Okay, okay. Val came in one day at school and said that he
had sold the books and we had to go get them, like now. He said
that if we didn't these really hard-asses were going to come after us.
Philippe told him to screw himself. And maybe two days later, Val's
parents came and took him out of school. He told me that they
were putting him in protective custody because of those guys that
wanted the books, and that the guys were after us and our families
unless we got the books. But a friend of ours saw him in London,
just hanging out, so we knew he was lying."

"When was that?" I asked.

"Maybe two weeks ago. Val kept calling, so Philippe blocked
his number. Wouldn't talk to him."

"Two weeks ago?" I said, fitting what he said into what I already
knew about the timeline of events. "Why did you break in Sunday?"

"Philippe called me on, like, Saturday night." He looked up at
each of us, checking our reactions, I thought, before continuing.
"He told me that he heard his aunt and her boyfriend talking to

the police. Someone had hurt the boyfriend really bad; broke his bones, cut him up. And the same guys were chasing his aunt, this American movie star he talks about a lot. He was really scared. So he called Val, and Val told him that, yeah, the same guys had beaten up his father and that they'd go after Philippe's dad and mine next. Unless we got the books to him. Philippe called me and said I had to come and help him."

"And that's why you're here," I said.

"Yeah."

"How did you get into the apartment?" Jean-Paul asked.

"Philippe had keys."

I remembered the table in the salon where Philippe had put his keys when he came in Sunday morning. They weren't there any more. He must have pocketed them again before we left for lunch.

"What time did you get here?" I asked.

"Kinda late. Philippe said everyone went out, probably to dinner. You got back before we got out again."

"We?" I repeated.

His eyes elided toward the wine cellar. Jean-Paul caught it, too. Someone pulled the door shut from inside; the key still dangled from the lock. We heard banging on the front door. Jean-Paul handed the tripod to Guido, who had been quiet during all this, listening intently, and said, "Police. I'll let them in."

After a few minutes of explanation about what the kid was up to and who they should call—specifically, Thierry Dusaud, assistant to the Directeur Général—two of the four fit-looking officers who responded hauled Cho, still trussed like a goose, up the stairs. The two who stayed behind watched their colleagues get through the kitchen door before addressing Jean-Paul.

"You think there's another one inside?" the more senior of the two asked, nodding toward the wine cellar door.

"Be careful," I said. "I think it's my nephew. He's scared and he may have a very sharp knife."

They shooed us up the stairs, out of their way. We found Cho seated on the stone floor of the vestibule with plastic restraints on his hands as the officers unwound Guido's film cable from his legs.

Jean-Paul watched from the salon while he talked with Dusaud on the phone.

I went into the kitchen to watch the activity below. I heard the wine cellar door open, I heard the officers shout, and the scratchy sound of a radio response, some swearing, and then feet pounding up the stairs. I backed up against the counter, out of their path as they laid Philippe, trailing dark red blood from his slashed wrists, onto the floor.

One officer grabbed kitchen towels off the counter and used them to make tourniquets on my nephew's wrists. Philippe was deathly pale.

"Forgive me, Aunt," he whispered as I dropped to the floor beside his head. I caressed his cheek and put my lips against his ear.

"Shh," I said. "Don't talk."

"But—"

"Philippe, don't talk. Don't talk in the ambulance, don't talk to the doctors, don't talk to anyone. Do you understand?"

Clearly, he did not.

"The next person you talk to will be your lawyer. Your *avocat.* Promise me."

Tears rolled down his cheeks. "You're in danger."

"Not anymore. It's over. I promise you. All of it. Finished."

"The books."

"Fuck the books, Philippe." I smoothed his hair and kissed his cheek, tasting salt tears. "Val lied. No one is coming to hurt us."

10

FREDDY WALKED INTO Monsieur Gosselin's office looking as if he were facing the executioner.

"How is Philippe this morning?" I asked, taking his hand to guide him to the chair next to mine after introducing him to the *notaire*. He looked as if he hadn't slept at all since that dreadful Tuesday two weeks ago when yet another corner of his world collapsed.

"Better." He nodded at Jean-Paul, and took his hand when it was offered. "The wounds are healing, the spirit will take longer."

"And you?"

"Numb. Grieved."

"I hope," I said, "that after our conversation today, a few parts of your world will feel more secure."

"Secure?" He gave me a sardonic smile. "Secure as in locked behind bars?"

"No," Jean-Paul said. "No one is going behind bars, except maybe the kid, Val Barkoff. I have a feeling that's where he belongs. The question is, whose jail wants him more?"

He chuckled at that, a joyless chuckle, but a chuckle nonetheless. "So, why are we here?"

"Freddy," I said, "Jean-Paul and I agree that some adjustments need to be made in the terms of Isabelle's will. She screwed you, my brother. It's natural that you resent her, and that you, and your boys, have resented me because of that. So, this is what we have in mind. If you think it's still unfair, now is the time to speak up."

He eyed us both cautiously, still wary. The poor man was still in shock, granted, over his son's desperate suicide attempt, and was ready to hear yet another shoe drop. All he said was, "Okay."

"Freddy, for reasons we don't need to go into here, I am keeping number seven, rue Jacob. However, my daughter and I, and Uncle Gérard, are in the process of legally relinquishing all inheritance claims to Grand-mère's Paris townhouse. One day, it will be yours alone. In the meantime, Grand-mère would be delighted for you and your boys to live there when you finish your building project in Normandy."

Finally, he smiled, a little. "I suspect Grand-mère comes with the house in the meantime."

"Probably. That's between the two of you. Now, about the damn books in the basement."

He paled when the *notaire* pushed a printed list into the space in front of him.

"The Louvre has agreed to find a new home for the convent library because it has become too dangerous for us to have them underfoot. With the publicity around what's happened, we have been barraged by inquiries from book collectors, dealers, museums, and libraries. So, adios convent. That leaves the very valuable books from the collection of *Tsarevna* Sofia Alekseyevna."

"There's something I have to tell you about that," Freddy said.

"No, I think you don't. We know you sold at least two of those books to get your project underway. We have also learned that, from time to time, our mother sold off a few books without consulting the co-owner, Jean-Paul."

Freddy looked over at Jean-Paul. "You co-own the books?"

There was a pause. A fairly long one, while we parsed that

question. It was Jean-Paul who answered, but with another question. "Freddy, my friend, until you learned otherwise, what did you assume you had inherited at rue Jacob?"

"Maman's apartment."

Jean-Paul and I exchanged knowing looks. Where Isabelle was concerned, as I well knew by then, nothing was easy or straightforward. I said, "Freddy, Isabelle and Jean-Paul owned the whole building."

"Where would she get the money for something like that? I understand that she used money from the tontine to buy an apartment, and that's why I had no claim. But I never thought the tontine is so rich she could own the entire building."

"It isn't," I said. "She had partners. And when she ran a little short of cash, she tapped the building's assets she only co-owned."

Freddy's a bright guy. He figured it out, and finally he laughed. "The books. The damn books."

"Yes. So, in front of you is the best list we could come up with of the books that have been sold out of the Russian collection. When we add up what they fetched, someone owes Jean-Paul a great deal of money."

Freddy's smile faded again. "I'm sorry, I can't come up with cash right now."

"Don't worry about it," Jean-Paul said. "My partner, Maggie, and I have worked it all out between us. As our part in squaring things with you, we have agreed that your mother also stiffed your sons. We have put a beautiful little psalter in the hands of a reputable auction house. The proceeds from the sale will set up a nice trust income for Philippe and Robert. It will more than cover university costs if they choose to attend somewhere other than France. A second volume, a diary of prayer, is also on offer to cover Philippe's legal defense and any expenses related to his recovery."

"That is more than generous," Freddy said.

"Not by half," I answered. "The rest of the Russians are going into a vault, far away from rue Jacob, as a hedge against future rainy days, for any of us. All except these."

I pulled two volumes wrapped in a scrap of T-shirt out of my bag and handed them to him. "These are for you. Do whatever you want with them."

He looked at the bundle in front of him as if it were radioactive before opening it. "You're giving us four books. The four books that started all this?"

"Yes, Freddy. I am your sister. Your half sister, I grant you. But family just the same. I want to be able to come to you when I need a brother to lean on. Can you do the same favor for me?"

Freddy wrapped his arms around me and wept.

Jean-Paul joined the embrace. "I love a happy ending."

fin

ABOUT THE AUTHOR

Edgar Award–winner Wendy Hornsby is the author of twelve previous mysteries, ten of them featuring documentary film-maker Maggie MacGowen. Professor of History Emerita, she lives in Northern California. She welcomes visitors and e-mail at www.wendyhornsby.com

K.K. Beck
Tipping the Valet
ISBN 978-1-56474-563-7

Albert A. Bell, Jr.
PLINY THE YOUNGER SERIES
Death in the Ashes
ISBN 978-1-56474-532-3

The Eyes of Aurora
ISBN 978-1-56474-549-1

Fortune's Fool
ISBN 978-1-56474-587-3

The Gods Help Those (forthcoming)
ISBN 978-1-56474-600-9

Taffy Cannon
ROXANNE PRESCOTT SERIES
Guns and Roses
Agatha and Macavity awards nominee, Best Novel
ISBN 978-1-880284-34-6

Blood Matters
ISBN 978-1-880284-86-5

Open Season on Lawyers
ISBN 978-1-880284-51-3

Paradise Lost
ISBN 978 1 880284-80-3

Laura Crum
GAIL MCCARTHY SERIES
Moonblind
ISBN 978-1-880284-90-2

Chasing Cans
ISBN 978-1-880284-94-0

Going, Gone
ISBN 978-1-880284-98-8

Barnstorming
ISBN 978-1-56474-508-8

Jeanne M. Dams
HILDA JOHANSSON SERIES
Crimson Snow
ISBN 978-1-880284-79-7

Indigo Christmas
ISBN 978-1-880284-95-7

Murder in Burnt Orange
ISBN 978-1-56474-503-3

Janet Dawson
JERI HOWARD SERIES
Bit Player
Golden Nugget Award nominee
ISBN 978-1-56474-494-4

Cold Trail
ISBN 978-1-56474-555-2

Water Signs
ISBN 978-1-56474-586-6

What You Wish For
ISBN 978-1-56474-518-7

TRAIN SERIES
Death Rides the Zephyr
ISBN 978-1-56474-530-9

Death Deals a Hand
ISBN 978-1-56474-569-9

The Ghost in Roomette Four
ISBN 978-1-56474-598-9

Kathy Lynn Emerson
LADY APPLETON SERIES
Face Down Below the Banqueting House
ISBN 978-1-880284-71-1

Face Down Beside St. Anne's Well
ISBN 978 1 880204-02-7

Face Down O'er the Border
ISBN 978-1-880284-91-9

Sara Hoskinson Frommer
JOAN SPENCER SERIES
Her Brother's Keeper
ISBN 978-1-56474-525-5

Margaret Grace
MINIATURE SERIES
Mix-up in Miniature
ISBN 978-1-56474-510-1

Madness in Miniature
ISBN 978-1-56474-543-9

Manhattan in Miniature
ISBN 978-1-56474-502-0

Matrimony in Miniature
ISBN 978-1-56474-575-0

Tony Hays
Shakespeare No More
ISBN 978-1-56474-566-8